SKAVENTIDE

Other great stories from Warhammer Age of Sigmar

SKAVENTIDE

GARY KLOSTER

BLACK LIBRARY

A BLACK LIBRARY PUBLICATION

First published in 2024.
This edition published in Great Britain in 2024 by
Black Library, Games Workshop Ltd., Willow Road,
Nottingham, NG7 2WS, UK.

Represented by: Games Workshop Limited – Irish branch,
Unit 3, Lower Liffey Street, Dublin 1,
D01 K199, Ireland.

10 9 8 7 6 5 4 3 2 1

Produced by Games Workshop in Nottingham.
Cover illustration by Catherine O'Connor.

A CIP record for this book is available from the British Library.

ISBN 13: 978-1-80407-693-4

See Black Library on the internet at

blacklibrary.com

Find out more about Games Workshop
and the worlds of Warhammer at

warhammer.com

Printed and bound in the UK.

_____

To Brin – For now, for the future, for never giving up.

The Mortal Realms have been despoiled. Ravaged by the followers of the Chaos Gods, they stand on the brink of utter destruction.

The fortress-cities of Sigmar are islands of light in a sea of darkness. Constantly besieged, their walls are assailed by maniacal hordes and monstrous beasts. The bones of good men are littered thick outside the gates. These bulwarks of Order are embattled within as well as without, for the lure of Chaos beguiles the citizens with promises of power.

Still the champions of Order fight on. At the break of dawn, the Crusader's Bell rings and a new expedition departs. Storm-forged knights march shoulder to shoulder with resolute militia, stoic duardin and slender aelves. Bedecked in the splendour of war, the Dawnbringer Crusades venture out to found civilisations anew. These grim pioneers take with them the fires of hope. Yet they go forth into a hellish wasteland.

Out in the wilds, hardy trailblazers restore order to a crumbling world. Haunted eyes scan the horizon for tyrannical reavers as they build upon the bones of ancient empires, eking out a meagre existence from cursed soil and ice-cold seas. By their valour, the fate of the Mortal Realms will be decided.

The ravening terrors that prey upon these settlers take a thousand forms. Cannibal barbarians and deranged murderers crawl from hidden lairs. Martial hosts clad in black steel march from skull-strewn castles. The savage hordes of Destruction batter the frontier towns until no stone stands atop another. In the dead of night come howling throngs of the undead, hungry to feast upon the living.

Against such foes, courage is the truest defence and the most effective weapon. It is something that Sigmar's chosen do not lack. But they are not always strong enough to prevail, and even in victory, each new battle saps their souls a little more.

This is the time of turmoil. This is the era of war.

This is the Age of Sigmar.

CHAPTER ONE

THE HALT, AQSHY

Sometime past midnight, the Heart of the Halt pulsed once, and the heat of it woke Brevin Fortis from dreams of shadows and smoke.

He sat up and stared across his workshop. He'd moved his pallet in here years ago, when he'd first come to this place on the edge of everything, to be closer to his work. The night was quiet and cool, but his skin was slick with sweat and he could feel a heat gathering in his chest where the Halt had marked him ten years before. He stood, thin sheets sliding off, pressed one hand against the raw basalt of the room's wall, and murmured.

'Where?'

Beneath his hand the cold stone warmed and then began to glow red like approaching dawn, like blood flowing. The glow bloomed around his hand in a perfect circle, then moved upwards, like a brush stroked through ink, away from the Heart, towards the top of the Halt. As he watched, it dimmed to nothing but a lingering heat.

Brevin frowned and took his hand away. Then, he stepped to the rack next to his bed where his armour hung, the silver sigmarite gleaming in the gloom, and began to dress.

It was three hundred steps to the top of the Halt from Brevin's workshop, but he took them three at a time, well acquainted with the shallowness of each stone tread. This fortress had been built long ago by mortals, and its rooms were scaled for them, despite the enormity of the place.

The Halt was a wall, four hundred feet tall and almost three times as long, a bastion of basalt that stretched between the sheer cliffs of Warrun Vale. The vale itself cut through the Adamantine Chain, the gigantic mountain range that separated the dry, hot plains of Aqshy's Great Parch from its lonelier lands bordering the Ocean of Tears. In some distant age, a forgotten empire had built a line of fortresses into these mountains, an attempt to block every route in and out, denying passage to an enemy now unknown. Warrun Vale, located almost in the centre of the Chain, was the widest of those routes, and so the Halt was the greatest of the ancient fortresses.

And deep within that giant pile of basalt, those mortals had set the Heart, the relic that had been Brevin's blessing and curse for ten long years.

Brevin reached the top of the steps, breathing easy despite the climb and the altitude. The Warrun Vale might lie far below the snow-capped peaks of the Adamantine Chain, but it was still high above the Great Parch. The air here was cold and thin, but Brevin's body had been crafted by the gods. The guard at the top of the stairs was mortal though, and when the woman stepped out to challenge him, Brevin could hear the chatter of her teeth, the panting draw of her breath.

'Who–' she started, but her voice fell to a stammer as she saw him in the lantern light. 'Lord-Ordinator!'

'Golden Lion,' he answered, keeping his voice low. It was deep in the night, and most of the Halt's defenders were asleep. Or should have been. He'd heard mutters as he mounted the steps, the sounds of restless sleep broken by dreams. Or nightmares. 'How goes it?'

'Quiet, Lord-Ordinator.' The woman finally remembered herself and moved back, giving him space to pass. Beneath her cloak she was wrapped in a breastplate, its steel enamelled crimson and emblazoned with the golden head of a lion snarling over two crossed swords. Brevin didn't recognise her, but Brevin didn't recognise most of the mortals guarding the Halt. The 27th Regiment of the Golden Lions had marched here four years ago, the latest regiment sent by the distant free city of Hammerhal Aqsha to guard this lonely bastion. Eight hundred men and women with polished armour and determined faces, the first line of defence for the vast open lands that surrounded Hammerhal Aqsha and the other free cities of Sigmar.

Another set of children wrapped in costume armour, waving toy swords.

That was unfair, Brevin thought. The Adamantine Chain was far from any place that could be called safe. In the years they'd been here, these mortals had faced feral orruks, screaming grots riding malformed troggoths, bands of blood-mad Khorne worshippers from gods-cursed Hel Crown, and even a pair of towering gargants. They were soldiers, brave and true, even if they were half his size.

Besides, he'd been mortal once himself. How he would have bristled then to be thought of as a child when he'd fought for his people. But it was hard to remember that the Astral Grandhammer he carried now was over twice as tall as he once was. Before Sigmar had taken his soul and poured it into a body remade for war.

'My lord Stormcast Eternal,' the guard said as he passed. 'Are you looking for General Kant?'

'I was not,' he answered honestly. 'But I am now, if she is here.'

'Yes.' The soldier pointed towards the centre of the wall. A figure stood there, a shadow against the dim glow rising from the face of the wall below. 'She said she couldn't sleep.'

'I know the problem,' he said. Nodding his thanks, he walked towards the Golden Lions' leader.

General Delia Kant was in her mid fifties, a lean woman with grey hair and weathered brown skin marked with scars. Despite the hour, she wore the Golden Lions dress uniform with its crimson cap and jerkin. The only time Brevin had seen her out of that uniform was when she wore her armour. Armour which was just as well kept as her uniform, but ruthlessly utilitarian. Kant was a practical woman, organised and meticulous, patient but demanding with her soldiers. Brevin had got along with her well since she arrived, though they seldom spoke. The general was private, disciplined. Contained. But when he stepped up to the low rampart that ran atop the Halt's face, she looked grateful for his company.

'Brevin Fortis, honoured Lord-Ordinator of the Hallowed Knights. Good evening. Or should I say good morning?'

'Morning would be more accurate,' he said. It didn't feel accurate though. The sky was black, the stars bright. Dawn did not touch any part of the horizon, and the only light came from the stars, the three moons that spun over the realm of Aqshy, and the steady glow of the face of the Halt. The wall was made of basalt, dense volcanic rock without seam or joint. But the face of it was covered with a sheet of quartz a foot thick, gleaming crystal covering the dark stone. Threads of crimson ran beneath the quartz, a web of glowing red veins. Emberstone. Aqshy was the Realm of Fire, and emberstone was its magic in crystalline form, fire made solid. Volatile and valuable, small pieces of emberstone could fuel vast conflagrations of magic. The amount of it contained in the face of the Halt was anything but small, and Brevin had only heard of one place that used more emberstone in its construction. That was the Whitefire Court, the home of the Collegiate Arcane in the city of Hallowheart, and the mages that lived there were constantly fighting to keep that power contained.

In the Halt, the emberstone's power was chained to its Heart, and Brevin could feel the heat of that ancient artefact in his chest as he stared at the glowing veins of power in the wall below.

'The Heart woke me from dark dreams,' he said. 'It told me to come here.'

'Dark dreams,' Kant said, frowning out at the darkness.

Warrun Vale was kept clear for the distance of a bowshot, but beyond that the pass was overrun with pines, massive old trees filling it from cliff to cliff except for the thin track that disappeared into the forest. The Golden Lions ran patrols out into the wilds on the other side of the Adamantine Chain, and occasionally traders would try their luck in those distant lands, though they seldom found anything there but death. The Warrun Vale was a lonely place, and beyond the mountains, foothills gave way to flat plains that ran down to the Ocean of Tears. During the day, you could see what felt like forever from here, across a haze of green to the distant sea, but there was nothing civilised out there. And now there was nothing but night.

'I dreamt of darkness too,' Kant said. 'Darkness that flowed and choked. Dreams are strange lately. My sergeants tell me my soldiers don't sleep, and when my dreams woke me tonight their cries kept me awake.' She looked up at him. 'Did the Heart speak to you of dreams when it woke you?'

'The Heart spoke to me of nothing,' Brevin said. 'It just wanted me awake.'

Over a decade ago, Brevin Fortis had come to the Halt to study it. Lord-Ordinators were the engineers of the Stormcast Eternals, those mortals to whom the great god Sigmar in his wisdom had granted immortality so that they could battle anyone or any-thing that fought to despoil the Mortal Realms. Brevin had been a builder in his first life, before he was reborn a Hallowed Knight, and his ability to shape stone was valued just as much by his god as his ability to hew flesh. After his soul was Reforged, he was taught to raise edifices that would protect and inspire Sigmar's faithful. But there was always more to learn, and when Brevin heard of a massive wall in the mountains which stood uncorrupted and unchanging through countless years and attacks, he set out to understand it. With ten other Hallowed Knights he'd come to the Halt, and found the Heart buried deep within it. He had touched that artefact, and was touched by it, and now this was his home.

He was part of the Halt now. Tied to it with chains of fire that wrapped around his heart. But did he understand it, after all those years of study? Not really.

Kant shook her head. 'I've campaigned over thirty years. Came here to put in my last years before I retired somewhere to count my scars in peace. I liked it here, because it was predictable. Run-ning patrols and breaking up fights between bored soldiers, with the occasional chance to throw rocks down on orruk heads from safe atop this wall. It seemed like a good plan. But these last few nights...'

The general frowned at the sky, as if looking for portents. 'Some-thing's coming. I don't know what, but I can feel it. So can my soldiers. They have trouble sleeping when they should, then fall asleep when they shouldn't, and they talk of dreams they cannot remember.' She breathed deep. 'It's affecting me too. Like tonight. Like every night for the last week. Dreams of choking dark, dreams of... I don't know. Something's wrong, something's coming, but I don't know what it is.'

'Nothing is happening, but nothing feels right,' Brevin said, and she nodded.

'Maybe this doesn't happen to you any more, Stormcast,' she said, 'but maybe you remember it. That feeling when you're struck and you know it's going to hurt. But the pain hasn't hit yet, and you're just waiting for the hurt to come. That's what it feels like.'

'I remember,' Brevin said. 'You have caught the feeling well.'

'Lord-Ordinators…' Kant hesitated for a moment, then pushed on. 'I've heard that you're trained to read the stars. To see the paths of the future in their dance. Could that be why you were brought up here?'

'By the Heart?' Brevin laughed, a rueful chuckle. 'My ability to read the heavens was always limited. But when I touched the Heart, what little skill I had was wiped away. My perceptions are tied to the Halt now, and this wall is more concerned about stone than sky. But it woke me tonight for some reason, and I can feel something here.' He tapped the armour over his heart, gauntlets ringing faintly against the polished metal. 'Something is wrong, something is coming, as you said. But I cannot say what, or when. I wish I could read it in the heavens. Or anywhere.'

He raised his eyes, and then, across the vast gulf of darkness he did see something.

A flicker of red like flame. A shifting flow of sparks, like crimson lightning flowing across the distant horizon. Was it a storm? No. These flashing lights were red as blood, red as the veins of ember-stone running beneath the quartz face of the Halt. This was not lightning, this was something else, and in his chest Brevin felt heat and a low pulse of pain. This was something wrong.

Up and down the Halt, the soldiers on guard duty were calling out, pointing to the distant light.

'What is that?' Kant asked, straining her mortal eyes. 'Wild-fire? An eruption?'

'No,' Brevin said. The pain and heat in his chest were increasing, and with the pain came knowledge. 'It's emberstone.'

'Emberstone?' Kant said. 'What? How?'

'I don't know,' Brevin said, watching as the crimson light stretched across the sky, like some false dawn. 'That much. That much!' The words hissed between his teeth as the pain in his chest grew. It was as if a thorn of fire had been driven through him. The power out there, being released… That much light, that far away, must mean whole veins of emberstone were being torn from the roots of the realm. Aqshy itself was being ripped apart, out in the distance, falling into fire and death and destruction, but as he watched, it became worse.

Amid the burning redness came flashes of green, a poisonous emerald just as bright as the crimson. That colour dug into his eyes, and in his chest the burning pain twisted and he felt suddenly sick, like the nausea he dimly remembered from being mortal. The green intensified, ripping into the red, and up and down the wall, guards were turning away, some vomiting, others falling to their knees.

And then the horrible light was gone.

Red and green, the bright fires were swallowed up by a darkness that swept across the sky and blotted out the stars.

'What is it?' Kant asked, staring at the rising dark.

'Smoke,' Brevin answered. A tidal wave of smoke, rising from whatever apocalypse was occurring on the horizon, rushing towards the mountains. Towards them. 'It's coming. Sound your warnings, here and all through the Chain.'

General Kant began to shout orders to her soldiers on watch, telling them to take messages to the candelarium and to sound the bells. The soldiers scrambled away, and soon the bells were ringing, rousing the whole of the 27th.

'Lord-Ordinator!'

The deep voice cut across the sound of the bells, and Brevin saw Therus striding across the wall towards him. The Hallowed Knight was fully armoured in his silver sigmarite, the heavy pauldrons on his shoulders enamelled in shining blue and gold. Behind him were the other Stormcasts in Brevin's command, their size serving to clear space around them as mortal soldiers poured out onto the top of the wall.

'What orders?'

Brevin opened his mouth to speak, but stopped when a sound rippled through the air. It sounded like rocks breaking, and beneath his feet the whole Halt shifted, as if the ground itself had rippled like a wave. The pain in his chest sharpened, then loosened, and the Lord-Ordinator stared out one more time at the horizon. It was a wall of black threaded with jagged lines of crimson and emerald, and it was rushing towards them like a charging beast.

'Stand ready,' he told Therus. 'Line up along the Halt, and show the mortals that whatever happens, Sigmar is with them.'

Therus nodded, and the Hallowed Knights began to fan out, moving carefully through the crowd. Brevin looked back to the smoke. The terrible curtain was rushing forward, eating up everything beyond the Vale. It moved like a tidal wave, and it broke when it hit the edge of the mountains. It smashed into that great line of stone and recoiled, but then rushed forward again, pouring up Warrun Vale. A river of darkness seamed with terrible light, it crashed into the high sides of the valley and poured forward.

The Golden Lions were shouting and cursing as they gaped at the onrushing darkness. Some started to turn, trying to escape the top of the wall, trying to hide behind it before that terrible gloom reached them. But they were barred by the press of soldiers still ascending the stairs. Beside him, Kant turned, half-stunned, but she saw what was happening and her trained mind snapped into action.

'Golden Lions, stand! Stand, damn you! Stand!'

Her shout rang out, and near her the crowd began to still, but the Halt was too huge; the soldiers farthest away couldn't hear their general and Brevin was sure that panic would take them soon.

Raising his massive hammer into the air over his head, Brevin bellowed, 'Lions! Golden Lions! Hear your general and halt!'

Sudden silence fell over the soldiers, and Brevin caught Kant up with his free hand, helping her atop the Halt's parapet, holding her steady as she stood over the crowd.

'My Lions!' she shouted, and this time their eyes turned to her. 'Form ranks and stand firm!'

The order rippled down the wall, General Kant's words taken up by the sergeants who'd found their way up, and soon the 27th was standing in rigid lines, formed up for parade even though many of them were still pulling on armour. Every eye stared down the Vale, and General Kant nodded her thanks to Brevin as they both turned to stare out too.

The smoke still rolled towards them, though its rushing advance had slowed as it moved up Warrun Vale. But it rolled through the trees and crossed the clearing before the Halt. Brevin glanced at the mortals standing in their formation. They were still, but their eyes were wide and watching. What would happen if that smoke crept up the Halt and touched them, ran across their skin and up to their faces? Would it fill their lungs like fire? Would it choke them, kill them? Brevin didn't know, couldn't tell what this dark cloud would do to them any more than he could say what it would do to himself or the other Hallowed Knights who stood like silver statues along the wall. Whatever happened to them now, they were in the hands of Sigmar, and they would face this doom unblinking.

So he stood with General Kant, his heart burning, and watched the smoke come until it finally reached the Halt.

Flickering with flashes of red and green, the dark cloud ran into the glowing face of the wall and a ripple of light went through the quartz, like water struck by a stone. In his chest, Brevin felt the pain increase again, a deep, aching throb. The smoke poured forward and it rose up the wall to the height of a Stormcast, higher, a flood of stinking dark. Its stench was acrid and greasy, like gangrenous bodies burning. The pain and the stench made even Brevin want to stagger, but he held himself still, ignoring the sweat that slicked his face and hands. He kept his pose as the smoke finally, slowly, ceased its rise. It had made it maybe twenty feet up the wall. Now it drifted there like mist, contained but constantly moving. Shifting in response to the vibrations that ran through the ground, smaller now but still present, as if the realm itself was twitching in pain.

Raising his eyes, Brevin could see the tops of the trees at the clearing's edge, could see the cliffs rising out of the dark, but most of Warrun Vale and the land beyond was gone, swallowed by smoke. Looking down from the Halt was like looking into a void, and the pain in his chest was like being eaten alive. But he kept his voice steady as he spoke to Kant.

'Tell them.'

'Tell them what?' Her hard voice had an edge to it, of emotions barely held in check.

'Tell them they have to fight.' Brevin was struggling not to raise his hand to his chest. The pain was worse than dying. Worse than being reborn. But he made himself speak. 'Tell them.'

General Kant turned her back on the apocalypse and faced her Golden Lions, drawing her sword and raising it high. 'Something comes!' she shouted, and her voice echoed in the silence that filled the Vale. 'I can't tell you what it is. But I can tell you why.' She pointed with her sword away from the smoke, down the other side of the Vale towards Hammerhal Aqsha and all the rest of the Great Parch. 'It comes because out there lies civilisation. Order. Justice. Joy. But more than that, out there lie our homes.

Our families. Everyone and everything we love and want to live.'
She slashed her sword down, pointing it back at the smoke. 'I don't
know what that is. What made it, and for what purpose. I don't
have to! All I have to know is that it and its creators will not pass
this point. This is the Halt, and the Halt holds!'

Up and down the wall, a shout rang out.

'The Halt Holds!'

'Good work, general,' Brevin said, helping the woman down.
The pain in him had lessened a little, but she seemed to sense
something in his movements and looked at him.

'Lord-Ordinator–'

'Have no concern for me,' he said. 'Worry about your troops,
because our waiting is done. The pain, though – I think the pain
has barely even begun.'

She nodded, face grim, and went to speak to her sergeants.
Brevin watched her go, leaning on his grandhammer. In his chest,
the pain was slowly ebbing but still terribly strong. And in his
mind he saw the veil of smoke pulling itself across the sky again,
but in his memory there was something else. Something he'd seen
before the stars were consumed by that dark. Something Kant and
the other mortals had missed.

Something that might have been eyes. Baleful, green, inhuman
eyes, blazing across the sky.

CHAPTER TWO

HALLOWHEART

'Touch blades!'

The Cave of Knives was small and crowded, stinking with smoke from the torches and sweat from the jostling bodies that filled it. But there was a space around Sevora, wide enough for a fight, and she reached out to rest the edge of her father's knife against Rigs' heavier blade.

She didn't remember who started the argument, and it didn't matter. Merry insults had turned sour, and in the end they'd called each other cheats and that had been that. Through the Warrens to the Cave of Knives they went, escorted by a cheerful crowd of drunks. And Yevin, her brother.

'He's twice your weight,' Yevin whispered, worried.

'He's half my speed,' she whispered back, her eyes never leaving her opponent. Rigs was slow, but strong. If his blade caught her, it would hurt. Bad.

'He's going to take your hand off.'

Sevora started to sneer, but it turned into a frown. 'Did you *see* that?' she hissed.

'No,' he said with a sigh, clearly wanting to lie, and Sevora nodded, her confidence returning.

'Then watch my back and place my bets.'

Yevin moved into place, putting his back to hers as he watched the crowd to make sure no one interfered.

'Ten!' shouted the woman who stood as judge, and the crowd shouted the number back as the oddsmen set the stakes.

'Nine! Eight! Seven!' The crowd roared out the numbers, and Sevora went still, focused, ignoring the noise. Until the crowd shouted one, and she pulled her knife from Rigs' and whipped it around, catching him across the knuckles as his blade flew over her wrist.

It was a good hit – blood bloomed, instantly covering the exposed knuckle bones, and Rigs cursed. There were cheers and boos, and the judge looked at Rigs.

'Again!' he shouted, and Sevora placed her blade to his.

Another countdown, another strike, and Sevora pulled blood from Rigs' hand again, but he was far from done. 'Again!' he called, and Sevora set her blade to his. But as one was called, her brother bumped into her back, shoved by someone in the crowd. The bump threw off her strike, while Rigs' blade cut into the back of her thumb.

'Watch my back, Yevin!' she snarled. 'Again!' she told the judge, and raised her blade.

Rigs was grinning at her, vicious, and she knew another shove was coming. Knew too that her brother couldn't stop it. But she still touched her knife to Rigs' and focused. Focused so hard she didn't feel the breeze that twisted around her, stirring her hair. All she cared about was the count as it went down to one. And when it reached it, she felt her brother lurch into her again, shoved by one of Rigs' lackeys.

It should have let him get another cut in. But as the man twisted his knife through the air, a tiny orange spark riding that breeze blew straight into his eye. Rigs flinched back from the pain, giving Sevora enough time to regain her balance and stab the point of her blade deep into the back of Rigs' hand, making him scream.

'Told you he was slow.' Sevora tossed the little pouch of trade gems she'd won up into the air, then grabbed it neatly, despite the ragged bandage tied around her thumb.

'I saw what you did,' Yevin said. He was walking close, shadowing her like always. Yevin was thin and his face was pretty for a man, especially his deep brown eyes. None of this was an advantage in the Warrens, where being small meant someone was always trying to bully you, and being pretty meant someone was always trying to exploit you. Yevin's way of coping had always been to hide, to go unnoticed.

Sevora had mostly chosen the opposite of her twin.

She was of average height, lean, and pretty too, though in a different way to Yevin. Her skin was the same light brown as his, but smoother, and her features were not as delicate, but sharp and well defined. Her brown eyes weren't dark pools but bright, striking. And while he walked in the shadow, she had always chosen to be in the light, challenging. Not a bully, but someone the bullies let walk by, in the same way red bears didn't bother cats. Sevora was far from the most dangerous person in the Warrens, but she was dangerous enough to make most decide she wasn't worth it.

'What did I do?' she demanded. They were walking down a narrow stone corridor, dimly lit by patches of glowing lichen. It was enough light for her to see him raise his eyebrow, when she glanced back at him. 'The spark? The breeze?' She shrugged. 'That's not cheating. I can't control that, it just happens. Rigs was the cheater, having his gang shove you into me.'

'They weren't his gang,' Yevin said. 'Just someone trying to win their bet.'

Sevora shrugged again. She didn't care either way. She swung the bag, feeling its weight. A nice bit of trade, more than she'd had in a long time. 'We should do something special with this.'

'How about eat?' Yevin asked.

'Good idea!' Sevora said. 'But not down here. Let's go up the spire, and get good food. *Real* food.'

'Sevora, no,' Yevin said. 'I'm not going out there.'

She whirled to face him, stopping in the middle of the tunnel. 'Why not!' It was an old argument, and she was sick of it. 'We live in a hole like rats, eating rats from holes. The Warrens are for the low, Yevin. The lowest of the low. We can't spend our lives down here in the dark, in the dregs, so we have to go up. Why can't you see that?'

'Because I can see!' he snapped, sick of the argument too, apparently. So much so he reached out and grabbed her hand and did something he hadn't done to her in years. He made her *see* too.

They were running through the dark, a stolen handful of trade gems clutched in their fists. Enough for bread for days. Enough for meat! But behind them...

'Run, Yevin!' Sevora looked back, eyes flashing between the long strands of her dark hair. 'They're right behind!' She stopped, but when he tried to stop too, she pushed him past her. 'Go, I'll slow them down!'

And he went, hearing the sound of their boots.

The tunnel turned, and there was light up ahead. Light was dangerous, it meant eyes and attention, but behind him he heard a clatter, and Sevora shouting again, 'Run!'

Desperate, he did, and suddenly the walls opened around him. Opened into a cavern so great the sides were lost in a distant, shimmering dark. But there was light pouring down around him, more light than he'd ever seen before, and he looked up. The stone behind him ran high into the air, a spire carved with stairs and windows and doors and buildings. The buildings highest above shone silver and gold, flashing with light. And above them... Above them was nothing. Only an infinite blue that went on forever, a bottomless pit except it was above him. Something floated in it, something so bright it hurt his eyes, but he could still see. He saw light dropping down from the sky around him, and the light was chains. Chains of gleaming gold, and they fell down down down from that bottomless blue, and their links piled in heaps around him.

Then Sevora came, running from the narrow hole he'd emerged from, stumbling, blinded by the light. She touched one of those chains and it wrapped around her, wrapped her so tight she couldn't move, and it started to pull her up.

He screamed something, but he couldn't move. He could only stare up that chain, up and up and up, and somewhere in the infinity above he saw that chain and thousands more being gathered in a great, shining fist...

'Damn it!' Sevora slapped Yevin's hand away, blinking, the light of his vision still in her eyes. 'I told you, never do that.'

She lurched to the side of the tunnel, dizzy. How long had it been since he'd done that? Years? She'd told him the last time that she was going to thrash him if he ever did it again, and she was tempted to do it. But when she cleared her head enough to look at him, he was staring back, determined.

'I'm not going out there. Never again,' he said. 'Neither should you.'

'Because you saw something when you were little that scared you,' she said, sneering even though her knees were still weak from the memory he'd forced into her. 'I'd rather risk the light than die in this stinking dark.' He only stared back at her, silent, until she gave up and started walking again. 'Let's go home.'

* * *

Their place in the Warrens was a crack in the wall of a bigger cavern, chipped at and widened over countless years until it was a bigger crack in the wall. But there was space enough to sleep and a door with a lock that kept people out.

One wall had been whitewashed long ago, who knows why, but when her great-grandmother Aika had claimed this place almost a century ago she had written their family name across it in ashes. *Cinis.* Under the name she had left the print of her hand, grey and smudged.

There was a sad collection of prints below that, the cursed children of this cursed family, who had grown up in this narrow space, buried in darkness. Each one leaving their smudged handprint behind. Sevora could see hers, and she hated that. Hated that she'd added it one night while drunk, when she'd vowed that she never would, and her eyes went from it to the top of the wall, to the name written just over Cinis.

Corus.

It was barely legible. Someone had thrown a bottle of wine at it before Sevora was born, and mostly washed it away.

'Those gems won't last,' Yevin said. He was sitting on the floor, paring mould off the cheese they had stolen weeks ago, setting the good pieces aside. 'But I know how to make more. Mava needs hands.'

'Picking through miners' leftovers isn't worth it,' Sevora said. She was polishing her knife, cleaning it of blood.

'She's not picking over tailings,' Yevin said. 'She's going to hit a working mine.'

Sevora shook her head. 'Working mines have guards, and miners who'll kill you just as dead if they catch you dipping your hands in their haul. That kind of work's too dangerous for Mava. She's gonna get herself killed, and everyone with her.'

'You're always saying I'm too cautious.' Yevin gave up on the last of the cheese and threw it with the rest of the mouldy bits. 'Now you're the one worried.'

'Risk is one thing. Stupidity is another.' Sevora examined the knife carefully. It was getting dull again. The metal was bad, and didn't hold an edge well. She'd have to hone it again, carefully, or she'd wear it away to nothing. 'And I have a better idea.'

He stared at her, frowning, big brown eyes waiting for what she'd say. Knowing he'd hate it, whatever it was. She wanted to rub his face in the mouldy cheese, but instead she sheathed the knife and looked at him, really looked at him.

'We can't stay here. It's killing you, and it's turning me into our mother, which is worse. We have to get out of this pit.'

'This pit is your home.'

Sevora's hand flew to the knife she'd just sheathed as her head snapped around to face the door, but she knew already who had spoken. 'Stay out of this, Siki. It doesn't concern you.'

The older woman slid the door shut as silently as she'd opened it and climbed past them, heading for the farthest alcove. Dark spittle ran down her chin, and she was chewing, over and over. Dunroot, a kind of fungus found in the sewers below the Warrens. It numbed pain and gave energy, at the cost of sleep and hallucinations.

'My child mocking the home I gave her concerns me.'

What have you ever given me? Sevora almost snapped. But she reined in the words. Siki wanted an argument. She always wanted an argument. The bitter woman liked to while away the time by fighting with her children. It was the only use she had for them, besides stealing their things. So Sevora stayed silent until Siki had settled into her hole. Maybe she'd fall asleep there.

Maybe she'd die.

'We can't live like that,' she muttered to her twin. 'We can't become that. We have to get out, and the Whitefire Court is searching for apprentices.'

'The Whitefire Court?' Yevin looked at her, his eyes getting even wider. 'Are you insane? They are *mages*, Sevora. And with our history, why in all the hells would they want us?'

'Because we're mages too,' she hissed. 'I can summon the wind. You have visions. We're already connected to the realm's power, they could teach us how to use it!' *And we could control the city, and live in the light, in a white tower on the top of the spire.* But she didn't say that. She just looked at him, willing him to see it like he saw his visions.

But Yevin was shaking his head. 'You channel wind and sparks that you can't control, and I have fits and see nightmares. We're not mages. If we go up there, all we'll do is draw the eye of…'

'Of what?' Sevora asked. 'You saw the sky once, and ever since you've been too scared to look up again. What is it that scares you so much out there?'

'I showed you!' he snapped. 'I showed you and you almost hit me for it!'

'Gold chains and giant hands?' She did want to hit him. 'What does it even mean?'

'I don't know,' he said. 'But I don't want to find out.' Yevin stood. 'I'm going to go find Mava. She might be reaching, but she's not reaching for the very top of the spire!'

The narrow niche was quiet after he left, so quiet Sevora almost forgot Siki was there. Until her mother spat a line of brown dunroot juice out of her alcove, aiming it at the whitewashed wall and its handprints but falling short.

'He's right,' she said. 'You're witchy little brats. Knew that from when you were babes. Thought we should let you die, but your father thought we might be able to use it. But them up there… they don't want us. Don't matter what gifts you have – and yours ain't worth spit.' She hacked another brown wad at the wall, getting a little closer.

'Did I ask you, Siki?' Sevora said, but her mother went on.

'You think too much of yourself. Reach too far. Gonna get you killed, girl.' She chewed loudly, disgustingly, in her alcove. 'The boy is only a little better. Mava is stupid. Too stupid to hit a mine, and too stupid to know the danger. There's things out in the Shimmering Abyss now. Terrible things that bite, and rot.'

Sevora couldn't stand it any more. 'I don't know what to do, Yevin doesn't know what to do, only you do? Live in the dark and chew dunroot until our teeth are gone and we starve?'

'I know my place, girl, and it's here.' She spat at the wall again. 'With my cursed family.'

Sevora pulled out her blade and pointed it at the shadowed alcove, at the eyes glittering within. Eyes that might have looked like hers once, before they went hazy and mean. 'I should cut your throat, Siki, and put you out of your misery. But I don't want to deal with the stench.'

She went for the door, and as she stepped out into the cavern that lay beyond she could hear Siki shout, 'That was never even his knife!'

Sevora stalked through one of the Warrens' markets, her expression silencing the hawkers who sat beside their piles of refuse and scrap. They let her pass, a young woman with flashing eyes and a hand on her knife, and cursed the sudden wind and the sparks it carried that came from nowhere and tumbled the things they'd gleaned out of the rubbish heaps and sewer lines of the city above.

'Think too much of myself.' Sevora ducked into a low opening chiselled in the side of the wide tunnel of the market, moving with practised caution through the near-total darkness on the other side until her feet found the worn steps of a rough staircase. 'Insane.' She spat in the dark, and a fresh flash of rage coursed through her. She wasn't her mother. Wasn't some dunroot chewer.

Spitting and bitter, muttering to herself in the dark. Even if that was exactly what she was doing, minus the root.

The anger made her climb faster, and the dark faded to a dull grey of almost light. In that murk she found the cramped passage she wanted and walked down it to a tiny door. Light bled through cracks in the half-rotten wood, and she shouldered open the door and stepped outside. Out onto the flanks of the spire, out into the Shimmering Abyss.

The Abyss was a cavern, far vaster than anything the Warrens could contain. Its walls were a distant horizon from where Sevora stood, faintly gleaming with reflected light. The Shimmering Abyss took its name from the vast array of crystals that covered it, a gleaming tapestry that reached across stone floors, walls, and what was left of the arching cavern roof.

Part of that roof had collapsed millennia before, exposing the Shimmering Abyss to the sky so far above. It was dark now, and that distant firmament could almost be an extension of the Abyss, the stars gleaming crystals, but Sevora knew better. She'd seen the sky during the day, that blue that never ended, and all that light… For a moment, her brother's vision ran through her head, the infinite blue cut by golden chains, but she forced it away. The sky wasn't terrifying, it was intoxicating. It was freedom.

The spire rose from the Shimmering Abyss' floor beneath that opening. It was a huge spike of stone, its top almost reaching the place where the cavern roof had once been. Long ago, when the Abyss had been discovered and claimed for its crystalline wealth, a city had been founded on top of the spire. Now that city ran down its sides and claimed much of the great stone column. Hallowheart, city of crystal and magic, city of light in the dark. Hallowheart, city of stairs, Sevora thought, moving out of the narrow crack of the door and onto one of the broad stairs that switchbacked up the side of the spire.

She stopped when she reached the steps and looked up again. It was night, but Hallowheart was bright. This far down the spire there were only a few lights, mostly the dull glowing crystals which had been enchanted to illuminate the stairs. The Warrens didn't advertise its presence. Best the city forget the nest of beggars and thieves lurking below it. But further up the spire, the stone was carved with the facades of the factories, tenements, shops and warehouses that housed the heart of the city's industry and most of its citizens. Windows glowed there, yellow with lamplight, red with forges, and with the hundred bright colours of gems that had been enchanted to give light. Those lights grew brighter, clearer, as they got closer to the top of the spire. There, on the wide plateau at the spire's pinnacle, the towers of Hallowheart's palaces and cathedrals glowed in the night, gold and silver, white and blue. Beautiful and brilliant, they dimmed the stars above them.

But it was a long climb to reach those bright heights. Still holding her knife, and her anger, Sevora started up.

Sitting on a bench in the square that stretched before the tower of the Whitefire Court, Sevora smoothed her stolen skirts and tried to look like she belonged.

Despite the late hour, there were people abroad in the city. Hallowheart never slept, and the constant chattering crowds and jewel lights hanging everywhere made it impossible for Sevora to slip unnoticed through the shadows. She hated sneaking anyway, so she'd found a merchant selling cast-off clothes, picked out a suitable dress, and waited until the man was distracted enough for her to snag it and slip away unnoticed. She'd found a place to stash her old things and put the dress on, but the sky above was beginning to glow with coming day by the time she reached the square.

The delays kept her anger stoked, along with the stares she still got. The dress was fine once, but worn now. She had washed her face and hands, but she had none of the sparkling paints made of crushed crystals that everyone else up here did. And she had to be careful to keep her bare feet hidden beneath her skirts. It was a shabby disguise, and she got by mostly by being young and good looking, which was its own irritation because more than one gentleman had tried to chat with her. She'd dissuaded them all so far with dark looks and indifference, but it had been a fight not to stab them with her father's knife, hidden inside her skirt.

But she had a spot now to watch her quarry. The tower of the Whitefire Court, the tallest building at the top of the spire, was a leaping flame of white stone that shimmered with reds and blues and yellows and oranges. The whole edifice was eerie – look away from it and look back and it would change, its shape and height subtly adjusted. Never while you watched, but every time you blinked, it was different. But it was always the tallest tower, higher than the Celestrine Cathedral of the Cult Unberogen, those cowards, and higher than the Shining Citadel, Stormkeep of the Hallowed Knights. Yevin hadn't been wrong; the mages of the Whitefire Court were the true power in Hallowheart, their grasp tighter even than the cult or the Stormcast Eternals, and their strange high tower made this clear.

Sevora took a deep breath, concentrating. Trying to make the early morning air around her stir, to become a spark-touched wind blowing at that white tower. To prove that she was a mage, that she belonged in that place, in the light. But the air stayed still around her, whatever magic she had hidden, untouchable.

Hope is a lie.

The familiar words ran through her head before she could stop them. She pushed them away, rubbing her head to ease the headache her attempt at sorcery had given her. When she put her hand down, she saw something on the other side of the square. A man and a woman, giants, half again as tall as anyone else in the city.

The man wore silver armour marked with blue and gold, while the woman's was darker, like old silver gone black with patina. They were Hallowed Knights, Stormcast Eternals. The chosen warriors of the god Sigmar, heroes resurrected to serve his will in the Mortal Realms. Sevora snapped her eyes away from them and looked at the ground. They made her uneasy. Humans reborn as demigods. It probably made them right bastards.

But at least they didn't try to talk to her, though she felt the woman's gaze on her as they walked by. When they were gone, she looked at the tower again, and there it was. Her opportunity. The great gilded front door was swinging open.

Sevora didn't hesitate. She was up, striding across the square, unfamiliar skirts swishing irritatingly around her. When she reached the door there was a woman there, middle-aged, plain, but wearing a shimmering white robe and jewellery that would have bought everything in all the markets of the Warrens.

'You're taking apprentices,' Sevora said, making it more of a demand than a question.

'Tomorrow,' the woman said. 'There will be trials in this square. Dangerous ones.' The mage stepped out of the huge door, looking at Sevora with rude directness. Then she reached out and took Sevora's hand. The mage's touch was soft as she held Sevora, staring at the scars that marked the back of her hand. 'But danger won't mean much to you, will it, Warren brat?'

Sevora bristled and took her hand back. 'What's where I come from matter? I have skill. I can be a mage.'

'You have skill,' the mage said. 'I can see that. Powerful, but uncontrolled. You're flux-touched.'

'I'm what?' Sevora asked, her hand itching to go to her knife. Whatever that meant, it had sounded like an insult.

'Never mind,' the woman said. 'I'll explain it if you survive the trials. Here, tomorrow. Miss them, and you'll have to wait another year.'

'Trials?' Sevora asked, but the woman was turning away, walking back into the tower, and Sevora was left with two impassive guards who looked as if they itched to throw her off the edge of the spire.

Tomorrow. It was just past dawn. One day and a night. Plenty of time to go back. Plenty of time to argue with Yevin one more time.

She turned, and walked through the light, heading back into the dark for what she vowed would be the last time.

Sevora sat in the rough hole that was her bed, spinning her father's knife in her hands, waiting for Yevin to return. And trying not to kill her mother.

'Probably dead,' Siki said, peeling another dunroot and popping it into her mouth. 'Run off with Mava and got a pick through his skull. Or eaten by beasts.'

'Shut up.' Sevora thought of leaving for the thousandth time, but if she went to the cavern outside she'd end up in another knife fight with someone. Waiting for Yevin was winding her irritation to the breaking point. He was only supposed to be talking with Mava, not going off with her, but when Sevora had gone looking for him, all she could find was a grubby Warren brat who said he'd seen Yevin climbing down into the Shimmering Abyss. Why did her twin have to decide that *now* was the time to stop being her shadow and try something on his own?

She spun the knife and almost dropped it, its badly balanced weight making it wobble. It was impossible to tell how much time had passed in the Warrens, but she'd paid the same brat to listen for the pre-dawn bells drifting down the spire from the Celestrine Cathedral. If the brat actually did his job, if Yevin didn't argue too long, they would have time to make it to the top. To the tower of the Whitefire Court.

'He's dead, and you'll be dead soon. Them mages have it in for us. You'll see.'

Sevora kept silent this time. Siki had spent her whole life telling her and Yevin about how everyone was against them.

'You'll be gone, like your father, and I'll be all alone, 'cept these handprints.'

'Feel bad for the handprints,' Sevora muttered. And then, finally, the door to their place rattled. She rushed to it, knife ready just in case, and opened it up.

Yevin lay on the floor before the door, his face pale and coated in sweat, his shirt covered in blood.

'Somethin' bit 'im!' The shout came from across the cavern, and she could see Mava standing there. 'I brought him back! Wasn't my fault!' Then she was gone, running away.

Sevora swore and gathered Yevin up, pulling him inside.

'Dead. Told ya,' Siki said, sounding satisfied. Sevora ignored her, hastily lighting every candle stub they had until the narrow space glowed with light. Then she bent over Yevin.

Mava had put a cloth over the wound to staunch the bleeding, and Sevora had to carefully peel it away. The stench was incredible, the smell of blood mixed with the sickly-sweet smell of rot. Rot. He hadn't been gone that long, but the smell of gangrene was unmistakable. Gagging, Sevora pulled the cloth all the way off, and she could finally see the wound.

It was a savage V of tooth marks slashing down from Yevin's neck and onto his chest. The wound was deepest there, and each puncture brimmed with foul fluids. Her brother's skin was a dull greenish yellow around the wound, with bright lines of blood poisoning marking his flesh like hieroglyphics. Sevora could feel the fever boiling off him.

'Dead and rotting,' Siki said, suddenly close. She'd left her alcove to crouch over Yevin's head. 'Told ya. Things down in the abyss now that bite and rot.'

Sevora's hand flashed out and grabbed her mother's hair,

yanking on it as she dragged the woman's face close. It was so like hers. Siki looked more like her than Yevin did, but it was an ugly, broken resemblance. Siki might have been pretty once, but her years and her addictions had been hard, and her eyes were sunken and dull, her skin battered and hanging loose from the fine bones beneath.

'Shut. Up.'

'Or what?' Siki said, grinning. 'You gonna put me out of my misery, like ya keep promising?' Her smile was an awful twist of lips that revealed a crop of brown, rotting teeth. Sevora shoved her mother away, back against the whitewashed wall with its hand-prints, and leaned over her twin.

'Yevin. I'm here.'

'Sevora.' His voice was thin, a cracked, terrible thing. But when he opened his eyes, they were still sharp, despite the pain. 'Had to tell you. Had to live. To warn you.' Then he groaned, thrashing on the floor, blood and noxious yellow fluid leaking from his wound. She tried to hold him still, but his thin body convulsed, hands trying to claw at his belly. Sevora grabbed his wrists, pin-ning them down, and his eyes found hers again.

'They're coming for you,' he grated out. 'The ravens, the black wings, the yellow teeth…' His hands jerked in her grip, fighting her. 'Yellow teeth,' he groaned. 'The shadows came alive, and their teeth were yellow, like their missing eyes.'

Then, a surge of energy pulsed through her, and Yevin was gone, Siki was gone, everything was gone, there was nothing but black wings beating, and then darkness: darkness broken by the gleam of long yellow teeth as something opened its mouth to bite–

Then the vision fell apart, and she was leaning over Yevin, his wound weeping blood and thick yellow liquid like pus, foaming like the spittle on his lips. Beneath the rags of his shirt his belly was twitching, a convulsion trapped beneath his skin.

'Dead,' Siki said, crouched still against the wall. 'Rotting. Dead. Told you.'

'Get out!' snapped Sevora. Yevin was fighting her, trying to claw at himself with his hands, and all she could do was pin his wrists down. 'Go and fetch a healer!'

'No healer in the Warrens can handle this,' Siki said, pulling herself up. 'None of them would want to. We're cursed, girl, I've told you, cursed and abandoned by court and cult alike. All you have for help is family, and all your family left now is me.'

'Then do something, you root-addled hag,' Sevora snapped. It was the closest she'd ever come to asking Siki for anything, other than silence.

'You want help?' Siki asked. She stepped forward, hand striking like a snake.

Sevora didn't see the blade until it was flashing towards her brother's throat. The steel sank into her twin's fevered flesh, and Sevora tried to slap her mother's hands away but she was all tangled up with Yevin. In the seconds it took her to free herself, Siki had sliced a line from one corner of her brother's jaw to the other, a yawning wound that exploded into crimson. Hot blood sprayed across Sevora, Siki, Yevin, and the rock walls.

'There,' Siki said, her voice full of satisfaction. 'I help–' The rest was lost in a grunt as Sevora slammed her father's blade into her and knocked her breath away.

Sevora had meant it for her mother's heart, but Yevin had given one final convulsion beneath her and his flailing hands clawed across her wrist, throwing off her thrust. The knife hit Siki's arm instead, sinking into the woman's stringy bicep. Sevora pulled back, the blade red, ready to thrust again. But below her Yevin grasped at her, his brown eyes so huge.

'Coming.' The word was barely recognisable, Yevin's last breath foaming bubbles in the blood still rushing from the cut across his neck. 'Yellow teeth... black wings... Sevora...' And then his hands let go, the blood no longer pulsing from his throat, and those huge brown eyes went blank, her brother gone from behind them.

Dead. He was dead, and the rage in Sevora fell apart and she staggered back to lean against the rough wall. 'Yevin. No.' She looked up at her mother. 'Damn you, what did you do?'

'Damn me!' Siki laughed again, a terrible sound, her hand pressed against the wound her daughter had made. 'Damn you.' She looked down at Yevin, finally still. 'Look at him. I saved him.' Her hand touched his once pretty face, marked in death with pain, fear, blood, and the yellow foam that spilled through his clenched teeth and almost hid the wide cut across his throat.

Teeth. His now yellow teeth.

'Saved him pain,' Siki said. 'He was dying ugly, holding on like that. All so he could speak gibberish to you.'

'It wasn't gibberish!'

'What was it then?' Siki said, and Sevora shook her head.

'It was—' Sevora gave up. She wanted to vomit, she wanted to sob, she wanted to scream. She was covered in her brother's blood, spilled by her mother's knife; his dead body was lying between them, and Siki wanted to argue. 'Stop talking! Stop...'

Words ran out, there was nothing to say, and she stood there gasping until Yevin burst.

The contortions that racked her twin earlier were suddenly back, his belly twitching and moving, and then his body ripped apart. Bones shattered, flesh tore, and blood and tissue splattered across them and the walls. Sevora flinched back, pulling away from the thing that moved in the remnants of her brother, the thing that heaved and shrieked as it snapped at her face.

There was no thinking. There never was. The air spun around Sevora, a gust like a sudden hurricane, and slammed down the bloody, obscene thing that had been birthed from her brother's death. The wind pinned it to the cot, where it screamed again, orange sparks flashing against its claws and teeth, then both Sevora and Siki were on it. Their knives plunged into the thing again and again, and when the wind flagged and the sparks faded the thing lay dead between them.

A rat, a monstrous misshapen rat the size of a child, dripping with blood and yellow fluid like bile.

They stood over it, breathing, knives dripping in their hands. They both twitched when someone thumped the door behind them, and a child's voice rang through.

'Is the bells, lady, like ya asked. You coming? You said you'd gimme something more!'

Siki looked at Sevora, her eyes bright with madness in their mask of blood. 'Don't. I told you. Cursed, our whole line, to this darkness, this hole. He couldn't get out, and neither can you.' She waved a hand at the gory walls that surrounded them. 'This is home.'

Sevora stared at the cracked, wasted version of her face, splattered with blood. 'I hate this place,' she said, her voice strangely calm, strangely clear. 'And I hate you, and I'm never coming back.'

She kicked open the door, and when the child on the other side saw her he ran screaming. She ignored the sound, the way she ignored the jeering laughter of her mother as she walked away, the last remnants of the wind she'd made swirling around her and drying the tears that were cutting tracks through the blood that covered her face.

CHAPTER THREE

THE AQSHIAN WILDS

There was a storm brewing over the Polychromatic Sea. A tower of black clouds rose over the iridescent waters, and waves were already beginning to smash into the shore below the dead village. In the bell tower of its abandoned church, Amon Solus stared through his spyglass, searching for his prey.

He found it as the day turned to night, and the storm swept in. The ship looked half-wrecked, its sails stained, its rails splintered, its ugly flag in tatters. But it moved with purpose, guided by the lithe figures that scrambled through its rigging and scurried across its deck. The ship was heading straight for this lonely shore, just as the smugglers had said.

When he'd questioned them, they hadn't wanted to talk about the ship that flew a flag marked with a golden rat skull, biting crossed swords. Amon understood that. The Stormcast Eternal hated talking too. So instead he had started burning their boats, one after another, until they told him of this abandoned town, and the cursed ship that claimed it. One of the smugglers had even offered to bring him here, for a price, but Amon had walked away, the burning boats crackling merrily in the harbour behind him.

He could have paid the man, and saved himself the walk. But he hunted best alone.

The ship anchored offshore, and a longboat dropped over the side, a black shadow breaking through the multicoloured waves.

Amon watched it patiently, the heavy rain soaking his long black hair and running in little streams down the deep-violet plates of his sigmarite armour. The black cloak he wore could do little to stop the water; it was coming down fast and hard, blown by the storm's gusts. But Amon didn't notice it. He was focused on the longboat as it ground onto the shore far below and spilled shadows onto the beach.

They could have been mistaken for men, in the dark and the storm, but with the spyglass and his supernaturally acute eyes, Amon could easily spot the differences. The shadows were shaped wrong beneath their cloaks, their eyes too big, their heads too long, and in the flash of lightning he caught the twisting shape of tails behind them. Skaven. Ratmen. At least a dozen, and none the one he wanted.

But one thing he'd learnt about skaven: there were always more.

Three more shapes unfolded themselves from the dark longboat, two of them massive. They stood over twice the height of the others, and when the lightning flashed again, Amon caught sight of massive tusks jutting from their long muzzles. Long scything claws tipped their fingers, and rusted spikes ran down their spines. Rat ogors. The other skaven stayed out of their reach, except for the one who had come out of the longboat with them.

He was tall, if not nearly as tall as the rat ogors, and wore a long coat made from gold cloth over leather armour. The bright threads gleamed in the flickering storm light, though the coat was stained and worn. The captain. In his tower Amon smiled. Finally, after long months, this hunt might be over. But he kept hidden, waiting, as the captain snarled and shouted, his words unidentifiable in the distance and the rain, and the other skaven all piled back into the longboat and pulled back out to sea. Leaving their captain, the rat ogors, and one wet skaven holding a shovel. When the boat was gone, they began to walk away from the water, up the hill into the ruins of the town. Heading straight for the church Amon hid in, and the Knight-Questor whispered a prayer of thanks and watched his quarry approach.

Sigmar was in a generous mood that night.

The skaven captain led his little group to the graveyard beside the church, and then spent a while staring at a half-burned book he hauled out of his coat. He then picked a grave, cuffed the one member of his crew that he brought with him, and pointed at the ground.

The skaven started to dig, and from his perch high above Amon watched the mud fly. They were right below him. He itched to draw his weapons and drop, but that was not his hunt. So he waited, until the skaven crew member tossed his shovel out of the hole he made, then brought up a small, iron-bound chest that he settled at the captain's feet. Amon looked out one more time at the black boat, still bobbing in the water, its longboat at its side. The crew wouldn't have time to interfere.

Amon stood, shutting his spyglass and slipping it away. Then he grabbed the thick rope of the temple's bell and jumped. He fell down the centre of the tower, rope hissing through his gauntleted hand. His boots cracked the flagstones when he hit the floor, and above him the bell rang, a deep-throated toll that filled the air as he rushed out into the storm.

Where the captain and his minions were waiting.

The captain had jumped to the top of a tomb at the sound of the bell, his long yellow teeth bared at the Knight-Questor. He had a curved sword in one hand, and the other was raised, claw pointing at Amon. The rat ogors were already moving, smashing gravestones as they rushed towards Amon, tusks shining in the lightning.

Amon shrugged back his cloak and drew his weapons. In his right hand swung his broadsword, a heavy blade whose edge emitted a low growl like thunder as it cut through the air. In his left Amon bore a long-handled mace, the head an ornately wrought cage of spiked metal bands shaped like a chalice of sigmarite. Floating in its middle was a spark, a glowing yellow mote. Amon waited as the monstrous skaven closed the distance, and that yellow spark gleamed in his eyes. The rat ogors were almost on him, and he could smell the stench of their wet fur, the carrion reek of their breath.

'Fire and thunder,' Amon said, and slammed the flat of his sword against the haft of his mace.

The rat ogors were rearing up before him with mouths agape when sword and mace came together, and they took the brunt of what happened straight in their teeth. The little spark burst out like a bonfire, a wash of flames that swirled around Amon. With the light and heat came thunder, a roaring wave of pressure that rolled away from the Stormcast Eternal. The monsters in front of him were bathed in fire and then the thunder rolled through them, shaking their bones. They stood before Amon, stunned and burned and blind, and couldn't see him spread his arms, swinging up his sword and the now blazing mace, its head a great spiked torch. Couldn't hear him as he shouted, 'For Sigmar!' and charged.

But they could feel his blows.

Amon ran between the rat ogors, catching the first in the belly with his broadsword. The blade snarled as it cut through hide and muscle and the skaven bellowed, whipping its tusks towards him. Amon twisted and brought his mace down on the beast's muzzle, spiked metal smashing into heavy bone, cracking it and breaking the thing's tusks. Fire spilled out, a wash of red searing the rat ogor's mouth, charring its tongue and blistering its gums. The beast fell back, spitting blood and boiling foam.

Then claws slammed into his back.

Their deadly edges clacked off his armour, but the force of the blow pitched Amon forward. He rolled, holding his weapons instinctively out of the way, and was back on his feet in an instant. The sigmarite armour he wore was heavy, but it didn't slow him. The precious metal moved fluidly with him as he rose and kicked back, his boot catching the second rat ogor in the chest as it lunged after him. It staggered, then roared and came forward again, claws sweeping. But Amon ducked and swung his sword in a vicious uppercut, catching the monster in its chest. The blade split the skaven's hide and blood poured out. Amon stepped forward and kicked again, knocking the rat ogor back, pitching it into its burned counterpart. They fell over each other, snarling and snapping, mad with pain and battle lust. Amon left them to it, turning with weapons raised before him.

He charged the tomb where the captain crouched, eyes and golden coat gleaming in the torchlight of Amon's mace. The Stormcast leapt to the marble top and swung his mace low at the skaven's legs. The captain jumped, barely clearing the flames, and twisted in the air, landing back on the tomb and swinging his blade. Amon raised his sword, just catching the curved blade of the skaven leader before it slashed him across his eyes.

'Come to die die, storm slave?' the captain spat, then swung his sword again, a flurry of blows that rang off Amon's weapons. Thunder growled when the blade struck the Knight-Questor's sword, and sparks flew when it hit the mace. The skaven captain was fast, a blur in the rain, and Amon was forced back. Meanwhile, in the mud below, the skaven crewman stared up at the battle, ears flattened back in fear. Then he turned and skittered into the night, pausing only long enough to pick up the chest to take with him.

Cursing silently, Amon swept both blade and mace up, catching the captain's sword between them, then shoved the skaven back. The captain's claws scraped across the stone of the tomb, but he kept his balance, sword raised. Amon didn't follow through, though. Instead, he swept his mace down and broke the tomb open, driving the flaming end of his weapon onto the wooden coffins inside, setting them ablaze. Flames roared up and the captain leapt back, landing on the top of a weather-beaten obelisk.

It gave Amon the space he wanted, and the Knight-Questor charged into the dark, chasing after the skaven with the chest.

He couldn't see him, but Amon could hear the rattling thump of the things locked in the chest. Amon followed the noise, long legs eating up the distance between him and his prey, leaving the captain and rat ogors behind. He finally caught sight of the smaller skaven trying to scramble up the stone wall that surrounded the graveyard, but the chest was slowing the ratman, and he was scrabbling to the top when Amon caught him.

The Stormcast charged forward, one boot hitting the wall, sending him up in the air so that he could swing his mace around. Sigmarite-caged fire slammed into the little chest, smashing iron and crushing the weathered wood. The blow knocked the skaven off the wall and back into the graveyard, splashing down on his back in the mud.

Amon landed beside him, and with a flick of his sword he took the skaven's head, his blade growling as it cut. Then he raised his mace and shone it over the ruined chest. There were jewels and jewellery, an ornate mask, a foul-looking bronze idol. They glittered in the light, but none of them were what he was looking for. He turned, eyes hunting through the rain, searching...

There. It lay near the wall, a heavy iron knife with a curved, claw-like blade. It was crudely made, the blade chipped and spotted with rust, the handle worn and scarred, but in its pommel a huge opal had been set. The gem shone like a star in that rough and rusty metal, but there was a shadow in its bright centre, like a stain in the stone. In the light of the fire from Amon's weapon, that stain seemed to shift and move.

Like a rat, twisting its head away from the light.

Amon picked the knife up and set it atop a granite gravestone. He could hear a snarling roar and the crack of claws as the rat ogors ran towards him, crashing through the grave markers, but he ignored them. Amon raised his mace, and the shadow imprisoned in the opal writhed and twisted. Then he brought the weapon down and shattered the jewel between sigmarite and stone, the shards of opal flashing with flame as they spun away.

A shriek cut through the air, like a rat caught in the talons of a hawk. It rose higher and higher, driving through Amon's head like a stiletto. Then it was gone, not fading away but rising so high his ears could no longer perceive it. But he could hear the deep bass squeals coming from behind him. Smoothly turning from the broken jewel, Amon slid into a ready stance, sword and mace raised. The rat ogors were there, paws covering their tattered, bleeding ears. Behind them, also clutching his head, was the captain. But that skaven's eye was on Amon, still focused on him despite the pain of the inaudible squeal. Amon met those mad eyes and nodded.

'My hunt is done,' the Knight-Questor said, satisfied. 'But I have time to take some trophies, ratman.'

The captain snarled as he straightened, the blood from his ears running down to stain his golden coat, and Amon smiled at him. Then he charged, the fire of his mace streaming as he swung it through the air.

* * *

The storm broke as Amon walked away from the dead village, the wind softening, the rain ending, and the puddles before the rusty graveyard gates were rippled only by the blood dripping from the line of skaven heads he had hung from them.

Skaven. Amon walked along the shore as the night began to give way to day, leaving behind the shattered opal, the finished hunt. Moving down the sand, letting the coloured tide eat his prints as that ugly name ran through his head. His last three hunts had involved the filthy children of the Horned Rat.

Amon didn't question what his god asked of him. He was given as much detail as was deemed fit. Sigmar left the how to him, and the why didn't matter. But he'd never had a string of hunts like this, all of them focused on one of the many enemies of mankind. It troubled him. It made him think that something was breaking, something was coming. And when he saw the raven waiting for him, he wasn't surprised at all.

The black bird was perched on a rock jutting out from the beach. Its feathers blended in with the dark stone, but that didn't hide the raven from the gulls that swarmed around it, screeching their displeasure at the dark interloper. It ignored their cries, sitting unmoving, a feathered gargoyle until Amon walked close. Then it stretched its wings and shook out its feathers, whipping the gulls into a frenzy – until it blinked, and its deep brown eyes suddenly went blue as the sky arcing above.

At that change the gulls exploded away, shrieking with ecstatic terror, and the raven turned its head from them. Those shining blue eyes fell on Amon and he crashed to his knees in the sand, brought down by its ancient gaze. A voice filled his head. It could have been the sound of his own thoughts, but for the strange sense that accompanied them, of a temporary but absolute stillness, as if part of him were caught suddenly in some unseen, perennial realm, while beneath him, his palms pressed firmly into solid

46

ground. The wind and waves and the distant gulls faded into the background of his mind, drowned by thoughts that now flowed into him, rapidly and overlapping, yet as clear as pristine waters.

Amon Solus. Knight-Questor of the Astral Templars.

'Here I am,' Amon spoke aloud, his head bowed as if lost in one of his prayers. 'My blessed Lord Sigmar.'

Your hunt here has ended, but now another lies before you. Greater and more challenging than anything you have ever faced. The burden will be strong, and you will not hunt alone. Others must join you, for without them you will fail, as they will without you.

Amon raised a knuckle and tapped it to the sigmarite band that held back his hair, frowning. Others? But when he spoke, he said only, 'I understand.'

The one you seek is of the Hallowed Knights. His name is Lord-Ordinator Brevin Fortis. Go to him.

'And when I do?' A Lord-Ordinator? Of the Hallowed Knights? What was this? Amon wondered. All of his hunts ended in blood.

Bring him home. Great black wings suddenly spread, and the bird took to the air, circling over Amon, who dug his fists into the sand as his vision blurred.

Brevin Fortis. The words seemed to distort as, almost at once, the sea crashed around him, even louder than usual, and the bird croaked rough and harsh as it wheeled over him. *Fear!* it shrieked. *Fear the shadow of what you trust. Trust the shadow of what you fear.*

A raven's cry, inhuman and strange, but the black bird's eyes still glowed a blue as brilliant as all the sky. Then it spun away, the blue in its eyes fading, the voice becoming a cry that echoed out over the empty sand and endless waves. Until it was gone, and Amon was alone again.

Alone for now.

Ignoring the gulls circling back in, Amon started down the beach, and whatever misgivings he felt about the idea of others faded away the faster he walked. He was on the hunt again, and unlike Lord-Ordinator Brevin Fortis, it seemed, that meant he was exactly where he should be.

CHAPTER FOUR

THE HALT

Brevin Fortis faced the darkness, and it seethed.

Shadows coiled and moved, making knots of night, filling his eyes with nothing. Then the pain came. It ripped through his chest, a knife of acid eating through flesh and bone, dissolving his lungs, ripping into his heart, burning a hole to his very core. And then there was light. A poisonous green light that shone from the hole in his chest, a sickly glow that rolled the darkness back like a curtain.

Beyond the darkness was a hill. Rocky and barren, the trees on it bone white and dead. At the crest of the hill was a heap of broken basalt that had been a tower once. From that ruin came an echo of the green light, pulsing like a dying heart.

Your pain has a source. Find it. End it. The voice filled Brevin's head, deep as an ocean. It was the voice of an answer. It was the voice of amelioration. It was the voice of a god. It was the sound of everything, and it shook the darkness and broke it and Brevin woke, blinking at the shadows, his chest aching.

And from the cracks around the door came the scent, faint but unmistakable, of that poison smoke.

The Halt was a wall, but it was a fortress and barracks too. The great length of stone that stretched across Warrun Vale was honeycombed with halls and rooms. When Brevin left his workshop, he stepped outside to one of the ledges that ran along the back of the Halt, a wide walkway linked by the stairs to the other ledges that crossed the smooth basalt. There was a soldier waiting there, pacing nervously back and forth. When Brevin emerged, the mortal spun to face him, his hand going to his sword, and Brevin shifted his weight, readying himself for an attack. But the man shook his head and dropped his hand.

'Lord-Ordinator. I'm sorry, I... I haven't had enough sleep.'

Sleep. No one had enough any more. Not since the smoke had come. The dark cloud had drifted outside the Halt for weeks now, always moving but never changing. It just waited there, dark and stagnant, hiding the Vale and everything beyond. A mystery of poison, its presence made the nights stretch long and taut with nightmares.

'It's all right,' he told the man, pressing down his own irritation. His chest hurt – not as badly as that first night, but there was a deep ache there now. Ever since he'd been Reforged, pain had been a fleeting thing, his divinely wrought body shrugging off injury and healing quickly. But this low pulse of agony wouldn't leave him. It was the Heart, feeding its pain into him, and he couldn't stop it.

Find it. End it.

The words from his dream ran through his head, and he barely noticed that the mortal was talking until after the man had trailed off, staring up at him.

'Say it again,' he said, waving a hand wearily.

'General Kant wishes to speak to you, Lord-Ordinator. She is in the candelarium.'

'Tell her I'll be there. But I have something I must take care of first.'

The man hesitated, probably ordered to fetch Brevin personally. But then he saluted and left, disappearing through one of the doors leading into the Halt. Brevin watched him go, then started down the stairs.

He wound back and forth, ignoring the mortal soldiers watching as he passed. Usually the back side of the wall was a busy place as the Golden Lions performed the myriad chores necessary to keep their regiment going. But since the smoke arrived, a sullen silence had crept in, and the soldiers moving across the wall were as likely to hide their faces and duck away from him as they were to salute. The Halt felt like a city under siege, and it was – by vapour and fear.

Brevin stepped off the stairs onto the lowest platform, a ledge of stone that stood fifty feet above the ground. Below him, the town of Halt's Shadow sprawled, a collection of dwellings, inns, and farms built into the ruins that lay behind the wall, the shattered remnants of an ancient city. It was a strange town, standing amidst the foundations of old palaces, but it was the only pocket of civilisation for hundreds of miles and it existed to support the soldiers based at the wall. Normally the raucous noise of rural industry could be heard from the town, but like the wall, an ominous silence now lay flat over Halt's Shadow.

The Halt had stopped the smoke, but it hadn't blocked its fear.

There was a stab of pain in Brevin's chest, as if fresh acid had been poured into him. He forced it down, and went to the single door that opened off this ledge, a heavy stone portal without latch or keyhole. It was a plain block of basalt, set in an arched doorway carved with sigils that flowed through each other, their curves overlapping so much it was impossible to delineate any discrete mark. But when Brevin approached, the block of stone shifted aside, as if sliding into a socket in the wall. Except there was no socket there. The stone simply moved and was gone, seemingly absorbed by the wall beside it.

Brevin had spent years studying that door, its arcane sigils and the magic behind it. It operated according to the same principle as the magics behind the one great gate that ran through the Halt, and he desperately wanted to understand it. But right now he barely noticed the stone's strange workings. He stepped through the doorway and into the corridor behind it, an arched passage that ran deep into the stone. Behind him, the door flowed back into place, cutting off the daylight, and for a moment there was nothing but darkness.

Darkness that seemed to seethe like smoke.

Then a ruddy glow filled the tall, narrow corridor as a light appeared in its roof, a line of red glowing in the stone, leading Brevin deeper, towards the Heart of the Halt.

The builders of the Halt had loved straight lines and perfect curves. The hall that led to the Heart was like every other hall running through the wall, a tall corridor with a smoothly arched ceiling. Its walls were unpolished basalt, unmarked with joint or crack, giving no indication of how this place was made. Sorcery was the only answer, and it was arcane sorcery beyond Brevin's ability to understand, no matter how he tried.

The key to that magic lay at the end of the corridor he walked, where a great spherical chamber opened up. The entrance to that round room opened onto a platform that bisected the chamber into upper and lower halves, making a floor across its centre of wrought-iron bars that were intricately woven together to form shapes and symbols of some strange, unknown alchemy. The bars were thick enough in some places to walk across easily, but in others they spread apart like metal lace, open to the emptiness below. It was a floor that demanded attention, but as always Brevin was drawn to the centre of the sphere, where the bars of the floor bent into a swirling shape like a whirlpool around a circular opening. Floating in that circle was a stone, glowing like a flame, filling the chamber with deep crimson light. This was the centre of the Halt, the source of the wall's power: a piece of emberstone the size of Brevin's torso, perfectly carved to look like an enormous heart. It looked so real, in fact, Brevin expected to see it beat. But the stone was still, as unmoving as the mountains that surrounded it, despite the fact that it drifted unsupported in the air.

It had taken Brevin two years to get past the door that led here. Then he had spent another year staring at the Heart, trying to gauge its secrets, haunted by visions that he should touch it, let its heat flow like blood through him. He had resisted that call for a long time, but in the end it was too much. His curiosity was too much. Brevin had reached up, and laid his hand on the Heart.

His teachers, mortal and immortal, had always said he was impetuous.

It had burned him, of course. Fire had seared through him, and he had thought he would flare to ash, to dissolve into death, lost until Sigmar chose to Reforge him once more. But the fire had run through him and left its mark inside, in the heat that he could feel in his own heart, and since then he'd been linked to this place, to this thing.

And damn little good that had done to help him understand it.

Brevin was bonded to the Halt. He could feel its strength, and he could feel its pain. When the gargants had attacked years ago, they slammed their clubs into the Halt, trying to smash their way through. Brevin had felt their blows, like punches to his chest, but those blows had felt weak, the pain from them dull. The low ache vanished when the Heart's magic ran out to repair the damage, knitting together quartz, basalt, and emberstone veins, leaving the Halt unmarked by the gargants' blows.

The enigma of the Heart had kept the Halt standing, unbroken, for thousands of years. But now, in the pain gathered in his heart, Brevin could feel it breaking. Whatever had happened out beyond the mountains, whatever had torn open the land and raised up that cloud of smoke, it had injured the Halt. The jolt through the earth had been a hammer blow a thousand times worse than the gargants' attack. The wall had healed itself from that, but then the cloud had come, with its caustic touch. That dark vapour was eating at the wall, scouring the quartz that covered it. It would have shattered and fallen away long ago, but the Heart kept repairing it. But it was costly. Brevin could feel its power being drained.

Brevin reached his arm out and laid his hand on the emberstone. Its light flared at his touch, and he felt the pain in his chest spike as if he'd been stabbed. But he kept his hand on the stone, feeling its heat in his palm, just on the edge of burning.

'You are attacked,' he said, his low voice filling the chamber. 'We are attacked. I want to stop it. I want to stop our pain. I dream of an answer, but I don't know where these visions come from. And the place I dream of I can't reach. The smoke…' Brevin thought of the goat that General Kant had taken from Halt's Shadow. She'd ordered her soldiers to lower the poor animal into the smoke on the other side of the wall. When it had stopped screaming, the thing they'd hauled back out hadn't lived long. 'The smoke is poison. It will take me apart faster than it destroys you.'

For a long time there was nothing. Just heat and light and the pain in his chest. Then the floor shifted beneath his feet. The iron bars moved, curling around on themselves, growing thinner, more intricate, until they formed an iron disc, marked with symbols. Its centre was empty, hollow, but as Brevin watched, a gleaming circle of quartz half the size of his palm rolled across the floor along one iron bar and stopped at the edge of the iron disc. The circle of quartz was sized to fit perfectly in the disc's empty centre, and the Lord-Ordinator could see the spark that lay in the crystal, one tiny grain of emberstone embedded in the quartz.

'I understand,' he said, memorising the symbols marked on the iron disc and their placement. When he was done, more circles of crystal rolled to him, five, then ten. Now he had eleven quartz circles, one for each Hallowed Knight at the Halt. 'Thank you,' he said, taking his hands from the Heart and bending to pick up the circular slivers of quartz. But as he did, one more rolled up. One more than he needed. Twelve… Twelve was sacred to Sigmar, so he picked it up and added it to the stack. They were warm and bright in his hands, and for the first time in days Brevin thought he might know what to do.

Tucking the emberstone talismans into a pouch on his belt, he walked away from the Heart as the iron bars of the floor twisted themselves back into place.

The candelarium was three-quarters of the way up the wall, amidst the chambers claimed by the officers of the 27th Regiment. It was a circular room, wide as the Heart's chamber, but the floor was smooth basalt and its ceiling a shallow dome that glowed with a faint, rosy light. The curved wall was carved with dozens of niches, arched doorways opening into shallow chambers that each held a short basalt plinth, rising to a mortal's waist height. Floating serenely over each pillar was a circle of quartz, similar to the ones that Brevin had taken from the chamber of the Heart. But these had no speck of emberstone embedded in them. Instead, their glassy surface bore the reflection of a candle flame, despite there being no candle near them.

The only candle in the room stood atop a basalt pillar in the centre of the cavernous space. Its golden flame burned before the quartz circle floating in the air beside it. Unlike the other stones in the room, this piece of quartz was dark as night. It seemed to be drawing the light away from the flame, and its surface bore no reflection.

Mortals known as candelers moved around the chamber, each carrying a wax tablet, a stylus and a cushion, and they paused before each niche, carefully examining the flame reflection on the floating quartz disc before moving on. They were careful to avoid any of their number who stopped to kneel on their cushions before a particular niche. In these, the candle flames were flickering, their light vanishing and then reappearing in a strange, staccato rhythm. The candelers watched and carved symbols in their tablets as the flames appeared and disappeared.

General Kant stood with one of her sergeants next to the single candle in the centre of the room. They watched as a candeler stared at a sheet of parchment clipped to a stand in front of him, then began to wave a wooden paddle between the glowing candle and the hovering dark crystal with precise twitches of his wrist.

When the Halt and the other fortresses along the Adamantine Chain had been claimed by Hammerhal Aqsha, the first explorers found rooms like this in each of them, their purpose inscrutable. But with experimentation, members of the Collegiate Arcane had determined their purpose – or at least *a* purpose. Place a flame before the dark central quartz, and that flame would be reflected in the quartz floating in the niches of every other fortress. A cute trick, a way to know that there was someone in the fortress maintaining that candle at least, but its value grew immensely when the soldiers inhabiting the fortresses found they could send each other simple messages by blocking and unblocking the light of the flame. It wasn't long before a complex code was established, and now every fort along the Adamantine Chain contained a small group of candelers, scholars that were skilled at passing messages back and forth along the mountain range.

Another magical puzzle, but one Brevin had no time to study. There were too many mysteries out here in this fortress on the edge of the realm and not enough time. Especially now, when it felt like all their time was running out.

'Lord-Ordinator.' General Kant's voice was a little above a whisper. 'Thank you for finally coming.'

There was resentment in that *finally*, unexpected from Kant. The general could be brusque, but she had always been deferential to Brevin and the other Hallowed Knights. But even in the low light he could see the dark circles under her eyes, the stress gathered in the way she carried her shoulders beneath the armour that she always wore now. Her sleep seemed to be no better than that of her soldiers.

'I came when I could.' He kept his voice low too, out of deference for the candelers scribing and sending messages. It was free of anger, but unapologetic. They were all doing what they needed to do now, and General Kant nodded to him in silent acknowledgement.

'You need to see this,' she said, leading him around the edge of the candelarium, past the niches. Neatly painted along the wall beside each one was the name of the fort it belonged to.

'Have you heard something from one of the other forts on the Chain?' Brevin asked, reading the names as they passed.

'I've heard too many things, all the same,' she said. 'This smoke spreads along the entire mountain range, from the Magmar Fjords down to the Jagged Isles. All our forward positions have gone dark, their candles snuffed out. All the higher fortresses are staring out into a sea of black, as we are. No one knows what happened. No one knows what we face. And no one can send help. We are all pinned down, waiting to see what might come.' She frowned. 'I sent messages that first night to Hammerhal Aqsha, by raven and horse and portal. They've only now messaged back, days later than they normally would. Hammerhal Aqsha speaks of trouble across the Great Parch, and tells me to hold since we're not under attack. Not under attack!' Those words came out like a curse. 'I've sent two groups of scouts out, both moving along the ridgelines above the smoke. Neither of them has returned. My best mountaineers. They didn't fall, something took them. And last night, one of my guards disappeared from the top of the Halt. Gone without a trace, except a few drops of blood. Something's out there, Lord-Ordinator, using that smoke as cover. I don't know what it is, and we've no help coming.'

'The Halt will hold,' Brevin said, ignoring the pain in his heart.

'The Halt will hold,' General Kant answered. 'I just wish I knew against what.' They passed an alcove that was unattended, its flame burning steadily. Lettered on the stone beside the niche was the name *Rookenval*. 'They are the only ones that never answered,' Kant said. 'But then they never do.'

'The Hallowed Knights who gather at Rookenval do so for a certain purpose,' Brevin said. 'They will answer only in the utmost extremity, and only to another Stormcast Eternal.'

'Like you?' she asked, her voice careful.

'The situation, as bad as it is, is not sufficient for me to ask for help from the Ruination Chamber,' he answered. 'Thanks be to Sigmar.'

'No sacrilege intended, but my thanks feel thin lately.' The general stopped in front of a niche. A candeler knelt in front of it, but her wax tablet was unmarked. 'You asked about Gallogast, the ruin at the start of Warrun Vale.'

A jolt of pain went through Brevin's chest. The ruin on the hill, the one from his dreams. 'You said it was lost the night the smoke came. That its candle had been extinguished.'

'It had,' she said. 'It's come back. But wrong.' She nodded towards the disc of quartz floating over the basalt pillar. In its gleaming circle there was a glow, steady and unwavering, but unlike all the others it was not golden. Its light was vivid emerald, the same colour from Brevin's dreams. The same colour that sometimes flickered through the smoke gathered outside.

'The soldiers I left at Gallogast never returned,' Kant said. 'There has been nothing from there since the smoke came. I assumed them dead. Now… I don't know.' She looked from the green light to him. 'Why did you ask me about that place? Did you know this would happen?'

'This? No. But something,' Brevin said. 'There is something out there. I have seen it in my sleep. Every night for the last week I've dreamed of that ruin, of Gallogast.'

'Something.' General Kant sounded almost hopeful. 'I want something, something to fight. This' – she waved a hand towards the Vale – 'this smoke and shadow… This isn't what my regiment was made to battle. We're meant to bleed a little, and make our enemies bleed a lot. Not sit and stare into the dark, unable to sleep, unable to fight, waiting and wondering about what lies behind that black curtain.'

General Kant shook her head, as if trying to dislodge something from her thoughts. 'All my dreams of late have been nothing but nightmares. But if yours can find us an enemy, praise be to Sigmar. We need to face something that isn't smoke.'

Brevin stared at the green flame in front of him, its colour as poisonous as a viper, and his hand touched the pouch on his waist where the quartz circles rested. 'Have no fear, General Kant. I will find your enemy for you, drive them out, and then…'

And then no more sleeplessness, no more mystery, no more smoke and shadows.

'Then the bleeding can begin.'

'Hallowed Knights. Are you ready?'

Brevin stood before them atop the Halt, ten heroes harvested from all the ages of the Mortal Realms. Men and women who'd proven themselves when they were mortals, giving their strength, their commitment, their lives to the service of Sigmar and his vision of order and peace. Ten proven souls, given bodies forged for war by the gods. They stood before the Lord-Ordinator, their silver armour glimmering in the starlight, their helms in their hands, their faces set, determined.

'Lord-Ordinator.' Therus, standing before the others, answered him. 'By Sigmar, we are ready!'

'By Sigmar!' the others shouted, their voices one, then donned their helms in one smooth motion, covering faces pink and brown and black with stern visages of silver.

Fixed to each helm was a charm, a disc of wrought iron scribed with symbols around a circle of quartz, softly glowing from the speck of emberstone set within. Brevin had spent the last day working the iron and fitting the quartz the Heart had given him inside. When he'd finished the first talisman he stood with it over the fire of his forge, breathing deeply. He hadn't even smelled the smoke, and the heat hadn't touched him. It wasn't a guarantee that the charm was proof against the poison gathered at the base of the wall, but it was enough to make him ready to try.

'Tonight we face the enemy that hides its face. Tonight, we go out to drag whatever evil lurks in that darkness into the light!'

'Tonight! The light!' The Hallowed Knights raised their fists as one, and behind them a cheer went up from the soldiers assembled on the wall. It seemed like most of the Golden Lions had gathered to watch, lined up along the top of the Halt in their arms and armour, waiting to see what happened when the Stormcast Eternals dropped down into the dark. Watching them with eyes desperate for hope.

'May the light and the storm walk with you.' General Kant stood at the edge of the wall, looking stern. She faced Brevin, but her eyes were moving, flicking up and down the Halt. While Brevin had laboured last night, three more guards had disappeared. No one had seen anything, and the only sign left behind once again was blood, crimson drops on the dark stone. Much of the 27th was watching them, but there were many soldiers on guard duty, their attention fixed on the darkness gathered before the wall. Soldiers waiting to see if they would be the ones to disappear tonight, snatched away by shadows.

'May your faith be a shield and a hammer,' Brevin said back to Kant. One hand held his grandhammer, and the massive weapon glowed in the night. Leaving in the dark seemed dangerous, but it had felt right to Brevin. The dark was when the dreams and the danger came, and he intended to run a sweep along the face of the Halt before leading the rest of the Hallowed Knights to Gallo-gast, to see if they could flush out whatever had been taking the Golden Lions. 'We will light a new candle in the ruins, and blot out the one that glows emerald.'

'You wi–' Kant was cut off by a sudden scream. It rang off the cliffs bordering the wall. Brevin raised his hammer in an instant, and Kant was moving, the golden plumes on her helm bending as she raced towards the sound. Her hands moved as she ran, signal-ling her sergeants to hold her soldiers steady, and Brevin gave the same sign to Therus and the other Hallowed Knights as he followed.

They moved down the Halt to a knot of soldiers gathered at the edge of the wall.

'What happened?' Kant snapped at a bushy-bearded sergeant who had drawn himself up and saluted as they approached.

'We lost a watcher, general. He fell off the wall.'

'He didn't fall!' A soldier, a young man whose fearful eyes were underlined with dark marks of exhaustion, stood beside the sergeant. The bearded man raised his hand to cuff him for his interruption, but Kant frowned and the sergeant hastily lowered it.

'What did you see?' she asked the soldier.

The man – boy, really – looked ready to cry. 'I was partnered with Teros, watching the cliffs. He thought he saw something, stepped forward and the smoke took him.'

'The smoke?' Brevin asked.

'Yes, my lord,' the boy said. 'A piece of black grabbed his neck and pulled him over! Took him, like it's going to take us all!'

The boy's panic filled his words, and every soldier in earshot stared at him. Fear had been the companion of every watch since the smoke had come, and it was only getting worse. Kant twitched her head to one side and the sergeant nodded and grabbed the boy's wrist tight enough to interrupt the hysterical flow of his words. The sergeant growled in the soldier's ear, and when he was done the boy walked away, heading towards one of the pools of lantern light on the inside edge of the wall.

'He hasn't slept in days,' the sergeant said, loud enough to carry. 'He's seeing things.'

'More than likely,' Kant agreed. 'Take me to where this Teros was standing.'

The spot was on the outer edge of the Halt, just a few yards from where the wall met the sheer cliffs. A lantern hung from a bracket hammered into the cliffs, and in the golden pool of its light Brevin could see a crimson slash across the dark stone. Kant crouched, staring at it for a long time, but there were no answers in that thin line of blood and Brevin looked away, searching the cliff. Nothing moved along the stones, from their sharp tops down to the darkness pooling below.

A flash of green went through the smoke, and Brevin traced the rippling spread of that noxious light. There was no sign of the man named Teros except that bit of blood. The rest of him presumably lay somewhere below, being eaten away by the corrosive poison. Would there be anything left when the smoke finally retreated? If the smoke ever retreated?

It was an ugly thought, and Brevin started to look away when something dark flicked out from the cliff.

Brevin didn't know what it was, but it was headed straight for the woman who'd just stood up before him. Years of war had honed his reflexes, and he jerked General Kant back with one hand, flinging her down and out of the way. Something whipped through the space where she'd been, dark and silent as a coil of smoke but fast as a serpent's strike. It slashed through the empty air, and found the sergeant. The black line whipped around his neck and vanished into his beard. Brevin surged forward, reaching out to snag that dark line, and he could see now that it was a chain, links of steel covered with barbed hooks. Blood bloomed through the sergeant's beard as the hooks bit in, and the expression on the mortal's face changed from confusion to pain. Then the black chain jerked, and the sergeant was pulled from the wall, vanishing over its edge.

Brevin cursed. His fingers had come within inches of the chain before it had been snatched away, but being close hadn't saved the man. He'd no time for regret, though. His eyes were searching – not down over the wall; he didn't need to see the sergeant's fall, his terrible fate was all too certain. Brevin was looking towards the cliff, where that chain had come from. There he saw a piece of shadow the size of a mortal detach itself from the cliff face and drop. The shadow skimmed down the stone and vanished into the smoke below, gone an instant after he'd seen it.

'Did you see it?' General Kant had pulled herself back up, and was looking down at the smoke where the dark shape had disappeared.

'The shadow? Yes,' Brevin said. 'And I saw the chain it cast at you.'

'A chain,' she said. 'A weapon.'

'A weapon means a wielder,' Brevin Fortis said. 'A clever one. It looks like you were targeted tonight, General Kant. You must be wary. The Halt must be protected.'

'And it will be,' she said. Then, louder, 'The Twenty-Seventh will not fail! The Halt will hold!'

'The Halt will hold!' The shout rippled along the wall, but it was ragged compared to the earlier cheer for the Hallowed Knights. The brief resurgence of the Golden Lions' spirit had flagged with the almost silent deaths of their compatriots.

'The Halt will hold,' Brevin repeated – not a shout but loud and deep enough to spread through the night. Then he looked to Therus and nodded.

Therus took up the massive coil of rope that lay at the edge of the wall. The thick coil must have weighed hundreds of pounds, but the Stormcast picked it up as if it were nothing and tossed it over the edge, letting it uncoil as it fell down the face of the wall, eventually vanishing into the smoke below. Brevin bent and took the rope in his hand.

'The Halt is weakening, General Kant.' He pitched his voice low, for her alone. 'This smoke tears at it. I can feel it in my chest, flowing like acid through my connection to the Heart. I must find the source of this darkness, and destroy it. But while I am gone, you must hold. The Halt must be defended, by its magic and by the strength of your arms and your faith. If you fall, it falls, and that smoke will pour down the Vale and into the Great Parch. You must hold.'

She looked up at him and nodded, her exhausted eyes hard with determination. 'You are warriors of the heavens. You will not fail us.' Kant spoke her words loud, loud enough for her Golden Lions to hear. 'You will destroy the source of this disaster!'

'We will serve Sigmar, and the heavens will triumph!' Brevin raised his hammer, and it flashed in the night. 'Evil may assail us, but it will not go unpunished. We will find it, and destroy it!'

One more cheer, weak at first, but then the Hallowed Knights raised their weapons to join Brevin. The sight of those heroes, holding aloft shining hammers and blades, emboldened the Golden Lions and made them roar.

With that, Brevin threw himself back off the Halt. He flew through the air, plunging down until the rope caught him and swung him back. His boots hit the glowing quartz that covered the face of the Halt and light rippled out across the wall.

Brevin ran down the wall, hammer in one hand, rope in the other, charging the smoke. It seemed to reach for him, dark tendrils spreading wide like a gripping hand, and then he was in it.

In the dark, in the dim, in the foul ink of it. In his chest the pain sharpened again. It grew a little every time he took a breath. But he *could* breathe. The air held a taint of acid, a reek like dead flesh and charcoal, but he could breathe. He hoisted himself up, far enough to clear the smoke and see the top of the Halt far above. He raised his hammer, and at the top of the wall Therus raised his blade in return, then swung over the wall and began to descend.

Brevin dropped to the ground, stepping away from the rope into the murk. The talismans let them breathe, but they would barely be able to see. A mortal would be blind. But the dim light coming from the Halt's face let him make out the quartz. The smooth crystal was pitted, its surface eaten away inches deep in some places. He ran his hand over one of the pits and felt the pain in his chest sharpen again, but when his hand pulled away the quartz had regrown, the damage almost gone.

Beside him the others landed, their armour gleaming in the murk. When the last was down, they tugged the rope and it was pulled up. They were in it now, caught on the other side of the Halt.

'Lord Sigmar.' Brevin's voice was low, but certain. 'We stand in the shadow of evil, in the despair of darkness. But with your strength, we shall bring your light.'

The others echoed him, 'We shall bring your light,' and he raised his head, the pain in his heart forgotten.

GARY KLOSTER

'Stay together. We sweep the wall.'

They moved along the face of the Halt, searching the dark. Brevin waited for the shadow of a chain to flash towards them, but there was nothing but stillness and silence. Back and forth once, and that was enough. Brevin could feel the acid in his heart, eating into him, an echo of what was happening to the Halt. Whatever lurked here was a distraction. The true threat lay deeper in the dark.

'Hallowed Knights,' he said. 'To Gallogast.'

CHAPTER FIVE

HALLOWHEART

The day was close to ending by the time Sevora reached the high tower of the Whitefire Court, and her shadow stretched behind her, dark as she felt. When she reached the golden doors they were shut, but she raised a fist and beat it against the gilt.

It made a tiny little sound, a dim thump that was answered by silence.

Hope is a lie.

'I know,' she whispered to herself. 'But I'm not going back.' She raised her hand and hit the door again, as hard as she could, making that same little noise. It mocked her, the insignificance of it. She wanted thunder, wanted these doors to fall beneath her fist, beneath the anger that filled her. But there was only that weak thump, and her hair stirring in the fitful breeze of her rage.

She pulled her father's knife and hit the doors with its handle. The noise was barely any louder, but as she went to strike again a long black line split the golden panel before her. The door silently opened.

'I've come for the trials,' Sevora said, dropping the hand that held the knife, though she didn't bother tucking it away.

The guard standing in the door nodded and turned, walking away but leaving the door open behind him. Not knowing what else to do, Sevora followed him inside.

'My name is Lysiri.' The mage Sevora had met the day before was dressed much the same, her robe that same perfect white. She wore none of the crystal powder paint, but her skin was clean and she smelled of something faintly sweet. She swept across the room where the guard had led Sevora, a parlour with shimmering white walls, furnished with heavily upholstered chairs. A servant followed her and silently laid out tea between them, cups and pot and little bits of food, the smell reminding Sevora that she hadn't eaten all day.

But when she thought of food, she remembered blood, and her stomach twisted.

She'd cleaned the blood off. That had been the first thing, the most important thing. There were baths in the Warrens which were cheap and didn't care about things like blood. She'd done her first cleaning there, in cold water with a harsh bar of communal soap, then bought a set of shabby clothes, keeping only her pouch of trade gems and her father's knife.

Then she'd started climbing. Up the stairs, heading for the top of the spire, every step like climbing a cliff, like lifting a load of iron. She'd almost been at the top when she ran her fingers through her hair and found a gummy, sticky spot of blood near the roots.

The baths close to Hallowheart's heights were much more expensive. But the water was hot and the soap was hers alone. She sat in her tub a long time, drinking the wine that the attendants brought her and staring into nothing. Trying not to think about the sound of her mother's knife, cutting Yevin's throat. Or the smell of her twin's body, that blood and rot smell, when that thing had ripped its way out of him.

Eventually she left that bath, bought another set of much more expensive clothes, her little pouch of trade gems now empty, and staggered up the rest of the stairs.

She wasn't drunk. She wished she was. She was nauseous, and wished she wasn't.

'My name–' she started, but Lysiri waved her off and handed her a cup of tea.

'You're Sevora Cinis.' The mage settled into the seat opposite her, picking up her steaming cup. She finally noted Sevora's stare. 'Inquiries were made about you,' Lysiri said. 'After your visit yesterday.'

'Inquiries?' Sevora shook her head. She'd been surprised to be met by one of the mages of the Whitefire Court again, much less the same woman, and now this. It should have made her wary, but she was all rage and grief, held back by bitter determination. She had nothing left for mysteries.

'Did you come here because of some impulse for revenge?' Lysiri asked. She took a sip of tea, and when Sevora only stared at her she continued. 'I looked at your family's history. Apparently there were accusations.'

'No,' Sevora said. 'That was–' Stories her mother told. She shook her head again, and wind skittered around her, fluttering her hair. 'Sorry. I don't understand what we're doing here. I came for the trials.'

'You came late then,' Lysiri said. 'They're done. Over two hundred tested, six accepted, and fourteen dead. A quiet year. There won't be another until next year.'

'*Next year?*' Sevora said. She thought of darkness, and blood. Of not going back. 'But you said I was powerful. Flux-touched.'

'I did.' The mage set down her cup, staring at Sevora for a long moment. 'I can see it in you. I can feel it too, when you make the air move. You have a powerful natural affinity for sorcery. Too powerful, perhaps.' Lysiri sighed. 'It is a curse and a blessing common to this place. The Shimmering Abyss surrounds Hallow-heart, and its crystal formations gather magic, concentrate it. That power affects everything that lives in this cavern, including us. Especially us. Sometimes children are born with affinities like yours deep in their blood. Those children have the potential to become powerful mages, but they also have the potential to flare out in an uncontrolled burst of power that kills them and everyone around them. They're called flux-touched, and it's a matter of debate in the Court whether we should train them, kill them on sight, or by Sigmar's grace leave them be.'

'And what do you think?' Sevora asked, her wind suddenly swirling around her, orange sparks spinning in it. The little tempest knocked over the tea pot and whipped her hair and Lysiri's around their faces.

Lysiri shrugged, and made a small gesture. Suddenly the wind was gone, the sparks extinguished, and a jolt of pain went through Sevora's head. Across from her, the mage moved her foot to avoid dripping tea and patted her hair back into place.

'I think it's a question I don't have to deal with in this particular case,' Lysiri said. There was a hard knock at the door, and she smiled. 'You and your magic will be someone else's problem. Come in!'

The door swung open and a figure in armour came through, ducking her head to fit. It was an immortal, a Stormcast Eternal. The woman Sevora had seen on the square the day before, and her eyes were on Sevora now as she stepped into the room.

'Sevora Cinis?' the Stormcast Eternal asked. Her voice was a husky alto, and it filled the room.

She filled the room. The Stormcast towered over Sevora, taller than the tallest mortal, and her shoulders were broad, made broader by the armour she wore. It was heavy and ornate, but its silver had been allowed to patina, to dull to black. The cape hanging from her shoulders was black too, with tiny runes stitched along its edges in silver thread. The Stormcast wore a massive sword, and in one hand she held something that resembled a staff, a long shaft of ebony bound with dark metal that was as tall as the Stormcast herself. At its top was a cage of metal, with a single spark floating in its centre. That spark was small, but so bright it was hard to look at.

Sevora stared at the demigod, numb. 'I am,' she said, no emotion in her voice.

The woman nodded. Her hair was shaved bare, and her skin was as dark as her armour. Her face was broad, and had a calmness to it. The smile she flashed Sevora was encouraging, even kind. But her eyes… Her brown eyes were hard, penetrating, carefully measuring everything she saw.

The Stormcast walked over to her, and Sevora could feel the vibrations of each step through the floor. But when she moved, something else caught Sevora's attention, something that made her jerk to her feet, her hand going to the blade she'd hidden in her dress. A huge animal was pacing behind the Stormcast. Its body was like an enormous fox, lean and graceful, its paws silent on the floor despite the thing's size, but its head was shaped like a bird's, with a sharp beak, bright brown eyes, and black feathers that shimmered with muted colours. The thing stood waist high to the Hallowed Knight, which meant its eyes were almost level with Sevora's. She watched it pace over, and it regarded her in turn, its gaze as penetrating as that of the immortal it walked behind.

'My name is Morgen Light,' the Stormcast said. 'I am a Lord-Veritant of the Hallowed Knights Ruination Chamber.'

'The Ruination Chamber…' Sevora repeated. She had never heard the name.

'That's right. I have come here to see you.'

Morgen Light let go of the strange staff, and it stayed upright, solid as a pillar despite the metal spike at its tip. The Hallowed Knight paid no attention to it as she pulled something up from her neck, a black scarf that had been knotted neatly around her throat. 'This will take just a moment,' she said. Then she slipped the scarf over her eyes and tightened it again, blinding herself. Taking the dark staff back in hand, she tapped it once on the floor.

The bright spark blossomed into flame, brilliant tongues of fire that leapt through the spiked metal cage. There was no trace of smoke, no smell of burning, but Sevora could feel the heat on her skin, could see the shadows in the room dance to the bright rhythm of the flames.

She had to look away, the torch too bright, and her eyes went to Lysiri. Maybe this was some part of the Whitefire Court's trials? But the mage had been silent since the Hallowed Knight had walked in, watching the Stormcast with a cool impassivity, utterly ignoring Sevora. Sevora was on her own, standing in front of the blindfolded Stormcast and her beast. There was a smell to them both, a scent of fresh rain, but it did nothing to calm her. Her head throbbed, and a breeze stirred again, ruffling the feathers of the beast, and she forced herself to stare up at the empty ceiling, trying desperately to rein in the wind of her magic.

Maybe she did, or maybe it was distraction enough that the armoured woman reached up and slid down her blindfold. Her eyes flashed for a moment, as if their brown had momentarily been turned to silver, but then the flames of the torch winked out, became that tiny spark again, and in its gleam Morgen Light's brown eyes settled on Sevora.

'Yes,' Morgen said, deeply satisfied. 'You are the one I seek. Thank Sigmar for guiding you to the square outside yesterday. Sevora Cinis, I lay my claim upon you, for you are required by the Stormcast Eternals to fulfil your duty, and realise your destiny.'

'Required?' This day was still spinning out of control. The Stormcasts were heroes dedicated to destroying monsters and daemons, blessed by the god of storms. Sevora had nothing in common with them. 'This is a mistake.'

'There is no mistake,' Morgen said. 'Fate's mark is upon you. I have seen it, and so has Peace.' The beast by her side tilted its head, setting an eye on Sevora.

'Fate,' Peace croaked, in a deep, unsettling voice.

Sevora turned away from the Stormcast and the thing she named Peace and looked at Lysiri. 'I came here for the trials.' To escape the Warrens, the dark, the shattered, cursed remnants of her family. Not… whatever this was.

Hope is a lie.

'And you missed them,' Lysiri said, rising from her seat and bowing gracefully to the Stormcast Eternal. 'She is yours, Lord-Veritant, and good luck to you. I don't know what you can see with that divine spark, but I feel obliged to tell you of her hazard. She is flux-touched.'

'Sigmar has given me eyes to see the soul,' Morgen said. 'I know what she is. She is, as I said, needed.'

'Then take her,' Lysiri said. 'For she is not needed here.' Then the mage turned away and left the room, leaving her to the silver-armoured immortal and her beast.

The Shining Citadel sat on the edge of the spire, a massive fortress-cathedral whose highest tower was crowned with a silver hammer. Sevora had never been this close to it, had never seen the intricate reliefs of a Stormcast battling daemons that were carved into its walls.

'Lord Gardus,' Morgen said as they came close. 'He was a healer, in his mortal life. As was I.'

Sevora didn't answer. She hadn't said anything to Morgen since the Stormcast had led her out of Whitefire Court's tower. She had nothing to say. Her life had shattered, all in one day, and the pieces were dancing around her like a whirlwind.

The gates into the Stormkeep, as Morgen called it, were open, and the Lord-Veritant led her into a massive marshalling yard. The fortress was ornate, beautiful, but meant to hold out against armies. In that way it matched its inhabitants. The Hallowed Knights were elegant in their polished silver armour, embellished with midnight blue and gold. But there was no mistaking what they were – weapons, designed for war.

Most of the people in the yard were mortals, dressed in uniforms of silver and white. Servants hard at work at the mundane tasks that kept the Stormkeep running. But the Hallowed Knights dominated the space. Their size, their armour, the predatory way they walked, they drew the eye. Numb as she was, they made Sevora uneasy. She had grown up leery of authority, and the Stormcasts were authority forged in flesh and sigmarite.

'Fear not,' Morgen said. 'You will get used to it.'

Used to what? Used to this place? Or used to the overwhelming presence of the Hallowed Knights? Neither of those had any appeal. Sevora had been desperate to escape the misery and the dark of the Warrens. This place… there was light here, but with a sudden chill certainty she was sure it was the light her brother had feared, the light from his vision. Light like golden chains.

But she had little time to think of that. Peace had fallen back from where he'd been pacing beside Morgen and flanked Sevora. 'Fear,' he croaked. Sevora shuddered and caught back up with Morgen. A gryph-crow, Morgen had called Peace as they walked through the city. Whatever he was, he made Sevora nervous, with his sharp beak, staring eyes and strange mimicry.

They passed out of the yard and into the citadel. The great hall was vast, brightly lit even though Sevora could see no windows.

Instead there were huge silver mirrors hanging from the ceiling that glowed as if daylight had been captured within them. Morgen cut through the space, leading her through a tangle of passages to a small room empty of anything but a few chairs and another door. Morgen tapped the one mortal-sized chair in the room.

'Sit,' Morgen said, and took her own seat in the chair across from it. She set her great torch to one side, and Peace sat down on his haunches on the other.

'I don't want to sit,' Sevora said. 'I don't want to be here. I only came because–'

Because Morgen Light would have compelled her to if she hadn't. She hadn't tried to run because she was sure Peace would have chased her down. As polite as the woman was being, Sevora knew she was trapped.

'I want to know why I'm here.' Her numbness was threatening to break, and if it did she would fly apart.

'Of course you do,' Morgen said. 'Do you require refreshment?'

'No.'

'Let us begin then.' The Hallowed Knight folded her hands on her lap, a delicate gesture that looked out of place on a warrior armed and armoured. 'What can you tell me about your family, Sevora Cinis?'

'Nothing.'

Morgen tilted her head, considering. 'I have asked one question. What *can* you tell me. You have answered a different question. What *will* you tell me. And I fear that will be the trend of this conversation if I continue to ask questions. So instead, I will tell you what I know about you, and your family. Your great-grandfather was Corus Cinis. A minister of Sigmar. A minister who cost his congregation their lives.'

Sevora stared at the woman, silent. She knew this story of her family. Along with another story.

'Corus was young and promising,' Morgen said. 'Until he led his following to the Oasis of Tears, and tried to found a settlement there without the permission of the Grand Conclave. The beginnings of a new city, a great undertaking he claimed was dedicated to Sigmar – but was really all about his own glory.'

'Glory,' Peace croaked, and Sevora glared at the gryph-crow. But he stared back with his deep brown eyes, and they dug deep into her, and she had to look away.

'In the end, there was no glory of course,' Morgen said, acting as if she hadn't seen the exchange. 'A band of murderers found the settlement and slaughtered every child of Sigmar they found. They desecrated the church your great-grandfather had built with a pile of bloody skulls, and the one on top belonged to Corus, who watched every one of his followers get put to the axe. Except for Aika, his pregnant wife. Somehow she slipped away, and made it back to Hallowheart. To the Cult Unberogen, to beg for solace and shelter, but she found neither. Aika had aided her husband's mad plan, a plan that resulted in the deaths of many faithful. She had supported Corus' pride, pride that cost the cult far too many lives, and so she was granted nothing but rejection, cast out from the cult and left to die.

'But she didn't.' Morgen looked at Sevora. 'She crawled into the Warrens below the city and bore her daughter. Corus' daughter. And that woman survived to birth your mother, Siki. And so we come to you, one of the last of the line of Cinis.'

'The last,' she said hollowly. 'My brother Yevin is dead.'

The Hallowed Knight cocked her head, and for a moment she looked so much like the gryph-crow sitting beside her. 'Ah. All the sorrow in you, the torment. Your family... Did you know that the name Cinis is a word for ashes?'

Was she being sympathetic? Or trying to provoke her? Sevora didn't know, but she wanted it to be provocation. Sevora wanted to be angry, not hurting. But she could feel her hair shifting, stirred by a forge-hot breath of wind that came from nowhere. That came from her. She had to say something, or her magic was going to break loose into a gale, and so she spoke, low and harsh.

'Siki told me that story. She told me it was a lie.'

Morgen looked at her, her eyes level with Sevora's despite the fact that she was sitting, and nodded. 'It is.' She leaned back, and the heavy chair creaked. 'There are threads of truth to it. Your great-grandfather was a minister of the cult. He was part of an ill-fated settlement attempt on the Flamescar Plateau. But that attempt was not his idea, and its terrible fate was not his fault. That story is a lie, fabricated by the man who did cause the disaster. A mage of the Whitefire Court, who manipulated Corus and many others to attempt that settlement in an effort to claim a set of ancient ruins of the fallen Agloraxi Empire. Ruins the mage believed contained a lost library of hidden knowledge. As it happened, there was no library, and the only result of his attempt was the slaughter of over a thousand people, including your great-grandfather. A man who fought to save his following despite having little training as a warrior, a man who honoured the lives of his wife and unborn child before his own, who martyred himself, enduring days of torture while never, ever, turning on his faith. The mage was able to hide his hand in the disaster by shifting the blame to Corus, aided by the uncaring incompetence of cult officials. So your family was left to die by the cult they had served for so long because of a lie.'

The smell of rain was strong in the room, drifting over from the Stormcast and the beast that sat beside her. A calming smell, but Sevora wasn't calm. Morgen's words ripped through her, tearing her anger into confusion. Her mother had muttered this exact story when Sevora and Yevin had shared stolen bread with her. Sevora had grown up both believing in its bitter truth, and simultaneously doubting it. Because Siki lied, and she lied best when her story made her a victim of a world cruelly set against her and her family.

Hearing this same story from a Stormcast cut a deeper, saltier wound into Sevora's heart.

'Is that why you set yourself to join the Whitefire Court?' Morgen asked. 'Were you seeking vengeance?'

'No,' Sevora said. She was still stunned, standing in this quiet room, the horrible pieces of her family history rising to join the storm that was already spinning around her. 'They asked me that too. I wasn't. Not exactly. They owed me. They owed my family. I was going to prove myself, and I–' *I was going to live in the light.* 'How do you know these things? How do you know the truth, when the Cult Unberogen does not?' Or says it does not.

'Because I know someone who was there,' Morgen said. She rose from her chair, took up her torch and walked to the door on the other side of the room. 'Come. I know your day has been long, but I have something more for you.'

The room beyond was small, plain, empty except for a shrine of Sigmar built into the far wall and the man who knelt before it. He wore armour darkly patinated like Morgen's, and his cape was also black. When the door opened he rose and turned, and he was huge, taller and broader than the Lord-Veritant, but all Sevora could see was his face.

It was strangely familiar, and she paused, until she saw the Hallowed Knight's eyes. They were wide and brown, pretty eyes. Yevin's eyes, except for the sparks that danced in their pupils, like flickers of lightning in the black.

'Sevora Cinis,' Morgen said. 'Allow me to present Corus Stormshield, Reclusian of the Ruination Chamber and your great-grandfather, Reforged by our god Sigmar to help save the realms from the forces of evil.'

* * *

The wagon lurched, sending Sevora into the wooden edge of her bench again. She hissed as it banged against her ribs, hitting the bruise that was spreading down her side. On the heavy warhorse that paced beside the wagon, Corus looked at her, his lightning-haunted eyes concerned, but he said nothing.

Sevora sensed he'd quickly learned not to say anything to her.

But Morgen Light had not. 'You could put a bag of beans there, honoured Memorian.'

She could. Maybe she would have. Except Morgen had called her Memorian, and Sevora hated that title with a passion. So she ignored the Lord-Veritant, despite how hard that was with the woman sitting right beside her, the worn reins of the wagon's horse team held loosely in her hands.

Sevora had been doing a lot of ignoring lately. It was her only defence. The world had crashed down on her three days ago, and she'd lost everything, and if she didn't shut them out, didn't hold onto what she could, she would lose herself too.

To this Ruination Chamber.

'We are mortals, granted immortality,' Morgen had told her, days ago. 'But there is a cost. When we die, when we are Reforged, sometimes a portion of ourselves goes into the flame and we become less.'

They had been standing in the marshalling yard, the Shining Citadel towering behind them. Corus was with a ring of other Hallowed Knights, their bright armour a contrast to his dark. One of them stepped forward and bowed, and Corus had bowed back, smiling. Sevora had been forced to look away. His size should have been difference enough, that armour wrapped around him should have been difference enough, that damn smile should have been difference enough, but none of it was. With those eyes, even marked with lightning, he looked too much like Yevin. When she'd looked back, Corus' helm was on and the other Hallowed Knight was charging him, sparring weapon raised. Corus had slipped out of his way with fluid grace, slammed his shield into the other Stormcast's back, and smashed him down. Then set the wooden blade of his sparring axe against the other man's throat.

'He doesn't seem less,' Sevora had said.

'I'm not talking about his skill at arms,' Morgen had replied. 'I'm talking about his soul.'

His soul. Her great-grandfather's immortal soul had been taken by a god and replanted in a body forged in the heavens. He'd been reborn a Stormcast Eternal, and for decades he battled Sigmar's enemies across the realms. Fighting, dying, and rising again, until that cost Morgen had mentioned finally caught up with him.

'The beans aren't a bad idea,' Corus said, abandoning his silence. 'Aika. Sevora.'

His correction was almost instantaneous, but the misspeak was there.

'I'm not your wife,' Sevora said flatly. 'She's dead, and her daughter's dead, and *her* daughter Siki is a murderous monster, and I don't want to be anywhere near you.'

Corus made a noise, a sigh, a growl, and tapped his heel to his horse. The beast trotted ahead, happy to leave the slow wagon behind. Sevora watched him go, until she heard the voice from behind her, low and inhuman.

'Monster.'

Sevora didn't turn. Peace had been present in the back of the wagon ever since they had got in it, the lithe gryph-crow lying on top of the pile of supplies like a giant fox, the feathers of his head blending with the feathers of his tail as he curled in a black circle. She frowned, glaring straight ahead at the dry grass of the hills that rose around them and the mountains beyond.

The day after meeting Corus, Morgen told her they were leaving the Shining Citadel. Dressed in the robes she'd been given – black and deep grey wool, more finely made than any she'd ever worn before – Sevora had followed the Lord-Veritant to the caravan of wagons and horses that had been assembled in the marshalling yard. The people of the caravan were almost all mortal servants, except for Morgen and Corus and one other Stormcast, a brooding man in more dark armour. Dreskir was another Reclusian, and beside him had been a fussy, middle-aged mortal dressed in robes identical to Sevora's. Avil Tawn, his Memorian. Morgen had introduced them, and had told her where they were going, but the name had meant nothing.

Rookenval.

Sevora could have asked where it was, but she didn't want to know anything more. Too much had happened to want to know anything more.

When the caravan left Hallowheart, they'd crossed one of the dizzying ramps that arced down to a wall of the Shimmering Abyss. There, among the crystals and the raw wounds of the mine entrances, had been a cave entrance barely wider than their wagons, low enough that Corus had to dismount and lead his horse. They'd walked into its darkness and emerged suddenly, shockingly, into light and heat. The cave had concealed the entrance to a realmgate, a portal that connected vast distances. Sevora realised that in a moment, but it was still shocking. As shocking as the sky stretching wide over her head, an infinite reach of blue, interrupted only by the great range of white-capped mountains that reared up ahead of them.

It was stunning, and beautiful, and sudden, and she'd stared up at the vault of heavens and cursed at the sight.

Corus had watched her, worried, and she'd cursed his eyes when she noticed.

'How much longer?' she asked.

'We'll reach Rookenval before the light goes.' Morgen looked ahead, over the heads of the huge draught horses. She should have seemed foolish, a holy warrior driving a wagon full of sundries, but there was something to the Lord-Veritant, something more than her size and her armour and her weapons. She could make herself humble, could refuse a warhorse and drive a wagon instead, but she would never lose that razor-sharp perception in her eyes. Some of that perception cut into Sevora as the Stormcast looked at her now.

'Hurting him won't heal yourself,' Morgen said.

'Heal? I barely had time to feel the wound, when you came for me and snatched me up.' Morgen had asked her once if she had wanted to talk about Yevin, and Sevora had stalked away. 'My life was shattered, and you kicked the pieces around, all because you want me to be nice to some resurrected relative I never met before so they will keep killing for Sigmar. What do you want me to do, pretend I am Aika?' The thought was horrifying. It was bizarre to find out that she apparently resembled her great-grandmother the way Corus resembled her brother.

'Absolutely not,' Morgen said. 'You must remind Corus of who you really are. Of what happened to his wife. He must know who he is now, and understand the truth of his situation.'

'I don't care about his situation!' The fragile wall of numbness she'd tried to keep wrapped around herself was crumbling, and Sevora fought to be angry. It was better than grief. 'I don't care about anything!'

'If you didn't care about anything, you would be no use to us. I would have left you under Hallowheart, hiding in the dark, fighting for survival. Like your mother. Like a rat.'

'Don't talk to me about my mother! Don't talk to me about rats!' In her head, Sevora was in that tiny room again, covered in her brother's blood, screaming at her mother while that *thing* tore its way out of her brother's chest. 'Don't talk to me about anything!

I don't care what you know about my family or how you know it, you don't know anything about me!'

'But I do,' the Hallowed Knight said. 'I know you better than anyone, Sevora Cinis.' The woman never let go of the reins, but she turned her face to Sevora, and that facade of kindliness was finally stripped away from her eyes. 'I am a Lord-Veritant of the Ruination Chamber. I bear a fragment of the light that flows from the Lord of the Storm, and with it I can kindle a flame that lets me see into the souls of mortal and Stormcast alike. I have seen your soul, Sevora, its strengths and its weaknesses. I've seen the scars your life has left on it, and the terrible new wounds that have not yet closed. I know you, Sevora Cinis, like no one ever has. Neither the mother you perceive as monstrous, nor your lost brother, nor yourself.'

The great torch Morgen carried stood behind her, rising out of the wagon like a bizarrely ornate lantern. In between the metal bars at its top, the spark drifted, a light too bright for Sevora's eyes to meet.

'That first day,' Sevora said. 'With your torch, and your blindfold. You were looking at me. I thought… I thought you were seeing if I was me. If I was Corus' great-granddaughter.'

'That, and more,' Morgen said. 'I was judging whether or not you would make a good Memorian. And I saw that you would, in spite of everything. Once you get through all that has happened to you, all the pain and the anger and the grief, once you accept what your fate is.'

A good Memorian. Memorian was the name given to the mortals chosen to be companions for the Stormcasts of the Ruination Chamber. Stormcasts like Corus and Dreskir. Relatives almost always, mortals tied by blood to the Stormcast and expected to help them with their fractured souls. Somehow.

'Once I get through. Once I accept it.' Sevora glared at the mountains ahead. 'Didn't your torch tell you saying that would make me fight you harder?'

Morgen laughed. She'd pulled her kindly facade back over her face. 'There is nothing I can say that will make you fight less hard, Sevora. There is nothing I want to say that will do that. You are part of the Ruination Chamber now, and nothing is easy about our path. But walking it will make you stronger. So I will tell you the truth, and let you pick your way.'

'The truth,' Sevora said. 'You say you will give me that, when you've given me nothing. You introduced me to a dead man, and told me I must help him, but didn't tell me how. What is the Ruination Chamber? What–' The questions piled up and stuck in her throat, but before she could clear them a scout returned to the caravan from the hills along their route.

'Rookenval!' he shouted, then turned and cantered away again.

'What is Rookenval?' Sevora said, watching the rider disappear over the hill's crest.

'A complicated place,' Morgen said. 'A ruin, a fortress, a cathedral. A place where life can be drawn out, or cut off. But the simplest, truest answer for you, and me, and Corus, is that Rookenval is home.'

'Home?' Sevora asked, and in her head she heard her mother's voice. *This is home.* The memory made her shudder. 'That is not a good word for me.'

They rode in silence after that, until the wagon finally crested the hill. A valley stretched before them, its bottom seamed with the twisting curves of a river. At its far end, below cliffs that reared up into the mountains, was the river's source. It was a wide lake of dark water, fed by dozens of waterfalls that tumbled down those jagged cliffs. In the middle of the lake was an island forested with pines, its peak crowned with a tower built of the same dark stone as the cliffs. The wind gusting off that lake and down the valley was sharp with cold and the scent of water and stone. It tousled Sevora's hair, and she had to brush it back to stare at the distant tower. It was massive, rising high above the black water and towering trees, so high it challenged the cliffs behind it. But its top was broken, the smooth walls ending in rough blades of broken stone, shattered by time or disaster.

A shape swung through the air around that broken tower, a thing with wings the colour of storm clouds.

'Rookenval,' Sevora said. 'Home.' And then she laughed. The bitter sound was blown away by the cold wind that swept down the valley from the lake, but in the line ahead Corus turned his head to face her. In the failing light, his expression was unreadable beneath his lightning-marked eyes.

CHAPTER SIX

THE GREAT PARCH

Amon Solus reached the top of the hill and there was the Adamantine Chain, the high wall of the Great Parch, the white fangs of the Realm of Aqshy. He looked at them in the morning light, breathing deeply. He'd been running for hours – crossing the Parch was easier at night, when the heat was less intense. As long as you were ready to face what hunted in the dark.

It had taken him a while to find word of Brevin Fortis. The Lord-Ordinator of the Hallowed Knights had left most of his brothers behind a decade ago, taking just a small guard with him to one of Hammerhal's most distant outposts, a place called the Halt. Which lay somewhere in this chain of peaks.

The Knight-Questor pulled out his spyglass, lifted it to his eye, and the mountains leapt forward. Amon patiently ran the glass along their rocky slopes, stopping occasionally to trace a line of broken stone that could be the remnants of a wall or tumbled tower. The Adamantine Chain was full of ruins, from empires human and duardin and other, more terrible things, but from all he had heard the Halt should be easy to recognise. So he searched, until his eye fell on something in the far distance. Not a wall but a broken-topped tower, rising from a dark lake. Not what he was looking for, but his eye was drawn to it by a hint of motion. Wings. Birds and something else, something larger, and the memory of battlefields passed through his head. Of winged warriors swooping over the carnage, javelins blazing like lightning in their hands. Prosecutors, the heralds of Sigmar, his winged retribution. But the Prosecutors in Amon's memory had wings of brilliant white, not grey-blue like a darkening sky, and he suddenly knew what he must be looking at.

Rookenval. The Ruination Chamber for the Hallowed Knights.

Amon shut his spyglass. Rookenval was not the Halt, but he knew where he was now. He started out again, swinging into a distance-eating lope, unencumbered by his armour or weapons. Moving through the growing light, leaving behind the tower and the cold feeling of foreboding that had come from spying those stormcloud wings circling its broken top.

Miles passed beneath his thunderous tread. Hundreds, maybe a thousand. Amon did not count, too roused by the thrill of the sprint. The raw desert wind burned his cheeks as he ran. When he finally reached the Halt, he cut a swift path through layers of harried-looking guardsmen, a few of whom directed him with dutiful courtesy deeper inside the fortress, through slender passages and gloom-shrouded chambers, and then out onto a wide battlement, where he was introduced to a woman named General Kant. She was standing with her back to him, at the far edge of the wall, looking down. But the Knight-Questor barely noticed her, or the wall beyond, or the soldiers spread out upon it. Or his guide, who had repeated his introduction to the general, who didn't seem to have registered their presence. Amon's gaze fixed upon the dark smoke that filled the Vale beyond the wall, a curdled black tide of vapour that stretched off between the mountains and filled the realm beyond to the horizon.

'By Sigmar, what is that?' he asked, staring out at the roiling dark.

'We don't know,' the general said, turning to face him. She moved slowly, as if reluctant to take her eyes off the smoke. 'I was hoping you might.' Kant looked tired, her eyes ringed with shadows as if she hadn't slept in days, and her voice was husky with fatigue. Or maybe that was the smoke too.

Amon had picked up the scent halfway into the Warrun Vale. He had spotted the pass first, a narrow cut through the line of mountains, and then the shadow of the massive wall as he moved further through the valley. Acrid and harsh, he had frowned at its ugly, poisonous smell then.

It had grown worse with every step, and now it filled his head, a stink of ashes and rot.

'General Kant.' Amon nodded, uncertain of what salutation these mortals used, and not particularly caring. 'I am Amon Solus, Knight-Questor of the Astral Templars. I have travelled far, and learned many things, but I cannot help you answer that. It doesn't look like any smoke I have ever seen.' And it didn't. It was too dark, and clung to the ground instead of rising, coiling around itself like a nest of centipedes. As he watched, an emerald flash of light flickered through it, like a flame but not at all. 'Have you reported this?'

She barked something like a laugh. 'Weeks ago, when it flooded in from the lands beyond the Chain. Every fortress along this mountain range knows about it, because it roils at their gates too. Unless they were one of the unlucky ones that were choked by it.'

'Weeks?' Amon asked. All along the Chain, thousands of miles? What was happening out here, on the edge of the realm? What disaster was brewing behind that curtain of dark? 'And no one has come?'

'Hammerhal Aqsha told me that they are facing a thousand disasters. Their armies march in every direction. They have no forces to spare for smoke and shadows.' She shook her head. 'Smoke and shadows. I've lost soldiers to this poisonous smoke, and more to the shadows moving through it. I've lost almost as many to it now as I did to our battle with gargants. And I've never, ever lost Stormcast Eternals here. Not one. But now they're all gone.'

The silent, menacing presence of the smoke went out of Amon's head, and he suddenly regained his hunter's focus. 'Gone? What of the Lord-Ordinator Brevin Fortis?'

'It was Lord-Ordinator Fortis' idea,' General Kant said. 'He had dreams.' She paused, her haggard features twisting into a frown. 'We've all had dreams. None of them good. But the Lord-Ordinator said his dreams were leading him to Gallogast, the ruined outpost that lies at the mouth of Warrun Vale. He took his Stormcasts there three days ago.'

'Three days.' Amon tapped his knuckle to the band around his head, frustrated. So close. 'How long is it to Gallogast?'

'For my troops? Half a day. Before the smoke.'

Half a day for mortals. Amon cursed to himself. Of course it couldn't be so easy as running across the Great Parch to search for one Stormcast Eternal. Lord-Ordinator Fortis was lost somewhere out there, in that poisonous dark.

'How do I follow?' he asked.

General Kant looked him up and down. 'Knight-Questor. I've met one of your kind before, though he was a Hallowed Knight, not an Astral Templar. You are the roaming eyes and hands of Sigmar, or so it is said. Is the Lord-Ordinator your quest?'

Amon stayed silent. This mortal was an ally, but she didn't need to know any more about his work for Sigmar than anyone else did. But Kant took his silence as an affirmation.

'You want to go after him, I can't stop you. But I'll counsel you this. Wait. The day is dying, and the night will come, and with it the killing shadows and the nightmares. See what I'm talking about. See a fraction of what I think you might face out there. And then at sunrise you can make whatever decision you want. To go ahead alone, as you want to do now, or to make your own attempt to send for help.'

'Wait or not, I am going to go. Alone,' Amon said. 'That is the method of the Knight-Questor. We are always alone in our quests, even when we are joined briefly to an ally.' It was Amon's method, at least. And if Sigmar wished him to work with allies this time, he would send them.

'Go then,' General Kant said. 'But go in the light, when that smoke is weakest. Go then, and I will give you a trinket that Lord-Ordinator Fortis left behind. A talisman that he thought would protect its bearer against the smoke.'

'He didn't take it along?'

'He took along others, Knight-Questor. But he had one extra, for some reason.'

'I will claim it then,' Amon Solus said. 'And be gone at daybreak.'

Amon Solus was no mage. He could see the glowing fleck of ember-stone embedded in the talisman, could trace its runes, but he had no idea if the thing actually *did* anything. But a Lord-Ordinator had made it, and then disappeared off into that sea of black.

And not come back.

The night had passed quietly, though the smoke seethed below them. Kant had explained the attacks that had been taking her soldiers, that had almost taken her. The shadows in the dark, plucking guards from the wall. But nothing had happened last night. The stars slid overhead and vanished in the dawn, but no shadows shifted, no soldiers were lost. It had been quiet – except for the faint screams from the barracks below, where the off-duty soldiers were trying to sleep. Trying to sleep through the nightmares that apparently came, over and over again.

Kant had told him about those, too. Dreams of darkness and smoke, of things that lurked behind the curtain of black. She had spoken of them as if the dreams were something only happening to her soldiers, but it was easy to see that they were happening to her too. No wonder her eyes were hollow and exhausted. Kant had told him that the smoke was weakening the wall, draining its magic, slowly destroying it. It was easy for Amon to see that it was doing the same to its defenders.

The 27th Regiment of the Golden Lions was falling apart, piece by piece, slowly losing to an enemy that it hadn't even seen yet. And General Kant knew it.

'The Lord-Ordinator claimed the talismans worked. I don't think it was the smoke that took him and those with him.' Kant stood atop the Halt, the first light of the new day gleaming on her perfect armour. Her back was straight, her expression stern, but Amon's keen eyes could see the exhaustion she was fighting so hard to hide. 'I don't know what did. That's what's killing me here, what's killing us all. The not knowing. I know you have your mission, Knight-Questor, and I want you to find Brevin Fortis and bring him back. The Halt is tied to him. He knows the heart of it, and is connected to it. This wall, and everything that lies beyond it, needs him. But I need to know what's out there too. So I ask you, Astral Templar. Can you look into the dark for us, and tell us what lies there?'

Amon fixed the talisman to the band that held back his hair. This delay may have been worth it, if the thing worked. The delay may have been worth it simply for the food and rest he'd snatched while here. But this interaction was wearing. Promises, ties to others, made him uneasy. He served Sigmar. That should be enough. But every time he interacted with others, mortal or Stormcast, they had always wanted something more.

'I have never failed a hunt, General Kant. I will serve Sigmar that way, as I was reborn to do. But if I can help you too, I will. That is all I can promise.' He went to the coil of rope beside the edge of the Halt, took it and checked how it was tied off. Satisfied, he threw the line over, letting it fall to the edge of the smoke, where both the wall and the rope vanished as suddenly as if they had disappeared beneath the ground.

Taking the rope in one hand, Amon jumped from the top of the Halt.

He fell fast, fast enough that he barely heard the gasps and shouts of the Golden Lions. There was just the sound of wind rushing past his ears and the sizzle of the rope through his sigmarite gauntlet, and the black cloud rushing towards him like night. Then he closed his hand. Amon gripped the rope, jerking himself to a stop, and his checked momentum swung him into the wall. His boots slammed into the quartz, and a ripple went through the clear crystal, brilliant rings of light scattering beneath his feet. He hung there for a moment, like bait on a line, but nothing came for him. Whatever hid itself down there refused to be drawn into the light, so Amon eased up on his grip, and slowly let himself down into darkness, into poison, into death.

Below the smoke, the light nearly disappeared. It went dark as night, the bright daylight filtered down to a dull, ruddy glow. In the dim, Amon could now see the ground, the grass pale and twisted as if it had been covered too long by a stone. It was just below him, and he let go, landing on his feet.

The smoke was deep enough to cover his head. Looking up he

could see the wall fading out above him, but he couldn't see its top. The cloud was like a dark fog, shrouding the world. He could see maybe five yards in front of him, but then it faded to empty black.

Amon could feel it against his skin, and in his eyes. It burned like normal smoke, but there was a greasiness to it, a kind of nasty thickness. It felt like moving through rancid oil. Amon had to blink, and his eyes filled with tears, blurring his vision but doing little to stop the burning touch.

He hadn't dared to take a breath.

Amon could smell the smoke in his nose; he could taste it in his mouth, acrid and bitter and spoiled, like a cairn of corpses burning, but he hadn't even opened his mouth. He kept his breath held and touched the talisman he'd attached to his helm. It went warm against his skin and the awful smell faded, along with the stinging in his eyes. Amon blinked, clearing them, and then he took one slow, careful breath. The smoky, greasy air filled his lungs, and he felt a touch of nausea, a tickle that made him fight a cough, but that was it. He could breathe, and he could see, and that would do.

Amon drew his sword and his mace, tapped them together and made the spark in the head of his mace flare into flames. He raised the weapon like a torch, and the smoke curdled back from it as if frightened. The smell and sting of the poison vapour dropped to almost nothing. Was it the light, or was it because the flames grew from a spark of the divine? It didn't matter. This would more than do.

His light flashed off the quartz face of the Halt, revealing the pits that marred the crystalline sheet. Some were small as pinpricks, while others were as large as the Astral Templar's palm, and they covered every bit of the wall the smoke touched. None of them were deep, not yet, and the thin red veins of emberstone that threaded beneath the quartz were untouched. What would happen when the smoke reached those bright red lines though?

That was a question for the Lord-Ordinator, and it was time to find him.

Amon tugged on the rope, signalling he was done with it, and started forward. He walked with a loose, predatory stalk that made him quiet despite his size and armour. Moving away from the Halt, he crossed the dying grass until he reached the woods. The trees were dying too, the needles on the tall pines gone pale and starting to curl, like flesh shrivelling on a corpse. Amon's eyes were everywhere, searching the decaying forest. Even so, he barely saw the thing before it was on him.

It came from behind one of the trees, dead needles flying up under its clawed feet, its teeth flashing in the light of the flames rising from his mace. With jaws spread it hurled itself at him, and Amon barely had time to raise his sword, but he smashed its edge into the monster's jaw as it tried to snap Amon's face off his skull.

His broadsword growled like thunder, and jagged teeth shattered beneath the heavy blade, falling from the beast's mouth like broken glass. Dark blood and yellow foam splashed down Amon's arm, thick and hot, but the thing didn't seem to care about the damage. It slammed its mouth shut, scraping its broken teeth across his armour. He moved with it, letting the momentum of the monster's strike pull him to the side as he brought his mace around and smashed it into the beast's shoulder. Fire wrapped around and the thing coughed out a howl of pain, hitting the ground and rolling away. It came up, shaking itself, sparks still dancing in its matted fur.

It was a ridge wolf, or it had been, before the smoke had corrupted it. The beast had gone pale like the grass and the trees, the dark grey of its fur fading to a dingy white, its dark brown eyes now light as sand. But its shift in colour was nowhere near as bad as the twisting of its body. Its teeth had grown, the ones that Amon hadn't broken pushing out of its jaw at awkward angles, and its tail was longer, the fur on it ragged and half-gone, revealing scabrous skin that wept yellow pus. Worst of all was its belly, which hung heavy beneath it as if the thing were hugely pregnant. It had lost most of its fur there too, and the skin was marked with fissures, places where it had stretched so far and fast it had torn. More pus leaked from those rents when the wolf's belly writhed and moved, as if hideous things were grappling beneath its broken skin.

The corrupted wolf growled, a clotted, sputtering sound that sprayed out a gout of yellow foam. Then it charged again, leaping forward on its malformed claws. But with this much warning it was easy for Amon to raise his blade and drive the point into the wolf's chest. It sank in too easily, the skin too loose, the bone and muscles beneath too soft, and the ridge wolf drove itself halfway down his sword. Death didn't come easily though. The beast still snapped at him, claws flailing as its blood poured down his blade. Amon swung his arm, sliding the thing off his sword and slamming it into the ground. It twisted, trying to rise, but his other arm crashed his burning mace into the wolf's head. The spiked sigmarite broke through bone and hide, and the brain that spattered out flashed to sizzling steam in the flame. The beast gave one last twitch, its whole body arcing as if it were going to bend itself backwards, then it went still.

Still except for the motion in its distended belly. The thrashing there grew, and the rents in the skin tore wider. There were things on the other side, things with claws and teeth, and they were trying to get out.

'Sigmar,' Amon said, as much curse as prayer, and he smashed his mace down on the thing's belly, over and over until it was a steaming puddle of slime and tattered flesh. A few things still twitched in it, convulsing with their deaths as they slid out of the wolf's ruptured belly. They were not wolf pups. This was no pregnancy, this was an infection.

The things spilling out looked something like rats, but rats with thin, atrophied limbs and long, furless bodies. Rats like scaleless serpents with mouths like lampreys, rings of hooked teeth pulsing and twitching around a nest of sharp, writhing tongues. Would all the beasts trapped out here beneath the smoke be like this? Amon wondered. And what of the mortals?

'Sigmar's wrath,' he whispered, and behind him came a sound, low and sibilant.

Shhhhh.

Amon spun, dead pine needles flying up from beneath his boots, but there was nothing but the trees and the smoke. Nothing. Until something flew over his shoulder and wrapped around his neck.

It was a steel chain with barbs worked into its links, barbs that scraped across his armour and dug into his skin like thorns. It was a whip of steel instead of leather, but it was silent, silent as owl feathers as it went taut. Amon felt the barbs digging in as the chain whip pulled at him, but it didn't jerk him over. Whatever was at the other end wasn't strong enough to bring him down.

But when Amon spun, sword smashing up to clang off the chain whip, he could see nothing. The weapon vanished into the darkness between the trees, as if it were wielded by shadows. There was a weight on its other end, though, and that meant there were hands holding it. Amon took a step forward, circling the chain with his sword so that it wrapped around his armoured arm, and pulled. The sharp prongs around his neck eased their digging into his flesh as he tightened the weapon around his arm. He could breathe again, and he heaved on the chain. There was a moment of resistance, and then it was gone, the chain whip suddenly slack. Amon could see the handle, dropped amongst the needles, abandoned.

'Coward,' he growled, and reached up to pull the thing from his neck.

From the trees and the shadows and the smoke came the sound

again, harsh and low. *Shhh.* And then the next chain whip lashed out of the dark. It came silent and low, wrapping around his left shin, its barbs scraping against his armour and boots. The Knight-Questor shifted his weight to pull his leg back, but as he did, another chain wrapped around his right wrist. The blade at its end flicked by his face, missing by a hair's breadth, and he felt the pull of both chains on arm and leg. He spun, moving fast, trying to pull the weapons out of the wielders' hands, but another chain whip snapped around his right leg, catching his ankle, and he was jerked to the ground, pine needles crunching beneath him.

The chains holding his limbs went taut, though he still couldn't see what held their ends. He was caught, like vermin in a snare, and he snarled as he pulled on the chains that held him, ignoring the pain of the barbs that had slipped past his armour to dig into the skin beneath.

Shhh, came the hiss again, from all around him, and another chain whip shot out, the sharpened blade on its tip flying at his face. The Astral Templar twisted and the blade flashed by, opening a cut on his cheek. Then it was yanked back, only to come flying out again.

The blade was darting at him, a constant flickering movement like a striking snake, and Amon was forced to twist and shift as much as he could to keep its edge from finding his face, his throat. His blood was hot on his skin, flowing from the cuts made by the strikes he couldn't avoid. The other chains were pulling harder and harder, stretching him out and slowing him down. Through the blood and the smoke he finally saw something – a clot of shadow pulling out of the trees, that hateful chain whip spinning around it, lashing out to strike at his face again and again. But it didn't matter what was hiding within that darkness. It was death, what-ever it was, and the failure of his hunt. But one of his arms was still free, and Amon raised his mace with a roar.

Shhh, came the sound again, and the chain whip was falling like a storm, its blade splashing up blood from his skin and sparks from his armour.

'Shush this,' he said, and twisted, slamming his mace down. The motion opened him up, let the blade of the chain whip land on the side of his face, ripping open the skin, shattering his cheekbone beneath, but it didn't matter. He had pulled in his right arm just enough for the mace to hit his sword. When it did, the ringing crash of it exploded, a thunderous boom that shook half the needles from the trees around them. Almost lost within its reverberations were screams, so high and piercing they were almost as painful as the thundercrack of the weapons coming together.

A wave of flames from the head of the mace spun out in a circle that spread through the trees and pushed back the black smoke. The fire struck the clot of darkness that had been slowly closing on Amon, and the shadows shattered, flying away from the creature they concealed like a flock of startled birds.

It was a rat, a rat the size of a man, its fur as dark as the cloak that flared around it like the wings of a raven, a rat whose eyelids were stitched shut with yellow thread over hollow sockets. A skaven, but a skaven that moved with horrifying speed and precision as it snapped its chain whip back to itself, the weapon whipping around its body like a lightning strike.

Amon barely had time to take the thing in. The chain whips holding him had slackened at the crash of thunder, and he jerked his limbs in, rolling on the ground and pulling himself free. He came to his feet, and he could see the bladed tips of the chains that had been wrapped around him vanish, whipping back into the dark, gone like shadows into shadow.

The skaven before him shook its eyeless head, hissing. When Amon took a slow step towards it, it tilted its head, lips pulling back to bare its teeth. In its claws, the chain whip shifted, its metal links completely silent as the skaven spun it in a slow circle. Amon stopped his advance, blinking away the blood that was flowing into his eyes. Eyes that were beginning to burn.

He blinked, and on the needles at his feet he saw the talisman that had been attached to his sigmarite circlet. The quartz crystal was shattered, and the grain of emberstone that had been caught within it was charring its way into the dirt at his feet. That last strike from the chain whip must have caught it and smashed it, and now the smoke was creeping in, its foul, acrid smell growing, its stinging touch beginning to burn his eyes and skin.

How long before it blinded him? The poison smoke filled his nose and throat, ran like vines of thorns through his lungs and he coughed, trying to breathe, starting to choke. He raised his mace, praying the flames would force the fumes back, but he knew they wouldn't be enough. As if sensing his weakness, the skaven began to spin its chain whip faster, building velocity for another strike. The others he couldn't see would be doing the same, getting ready to attack, and Amon needed to move.

His sword whipped down, caught the tiny fleck of emberstone and flipped it up into the air before him. It hung like a spark, shining in the dark, and then he swung his mace at it. Sigmarite and flames hit the tiny glowing speck, and for a moment the fire at the end of his mace roared up, flames spiralling, fuelled by the emberstone. Then they died back as the spark arced away, towards the skaven.

Amon hadn't been sure what it would do. He'd hoped the fleck of emberstone would hit the skaven and burn it, give him an opening to charge. But when the tiny piece of raw magic hit the smoke, the woods all around the Knight-Questor suddenly lit up as a sheet of fire cracked through it, spreading out from where that spark of emberstone had been. It ripped through the air, brilliant as lightning, red rippled with flashes of green, searing what it touched. Bark flared to charcoal and branches burst, needles falling as flaming rain. The fire slashed through the trees, swallowed up eventually by the dark, but it left an afterglow, a gleaming echo of light.

The Astral Templar stood, unharmed by the flame. It had flashed around him, following the curve of the hollow that his weapon's light had carved in the smoke. He'd felt the heat, but it hadn't been enough to burn. But of the skaven that had stood before him, there was nothing but a pile of ash, charred bone, and the softly glowing links of its chain whip, a dim red glow in the growing dark.

'Sigmar,' Amon whispered, and from the shadows somewhere he heard an echo, softer than his whisper.

Shhh.

Then he turned and, blinking streaming eyes, he ran back to the Halt.

Amon waited until he was alone with General Kant, shuttered in a dark, narrow guardroom just below the top of the Halt, before he let himself cough. A long, hacking fit that bent him over and made his aching eyes stream with tears. The general watched and waited, and when he was done she handed him a cloth to mop his face and a cup of water sized for a Stormcast.

He drank it fast, trying to wash away the awful taste of that choking poison. It didn't, but it helped, and his breathing eased. When had he last needed to cough? It was such a strange thing sometimes, being Reforged to a new body. So many of the things that had plagued him as a mortal were gone now, things like illness and all the symptoms that came with it. But that smoke had made him cough. It had almost killed him.

'Knight-Questor,' General Kant said as she refilled his cup from a pitcher. 'What happened?'

He drained half the cup. The acrid taste was still in his mouth, but lessened. With the rest of the water he wet the cloth and wiped his aching eyes. The smoke had burned like acid, and the world was blurry around Amon as they healed. Then he wiped the cloth across his face again, cleaning off the cuts left by the chain whips.

'Skaven,' he said finally, the bloody water pattering down on the stone around him.

'Skaven.' Kant frowned, but her shoulders straightened, as if a burden she carried had been shifted. 'Ratmen. I've never faced them before, but I've heard of them. Dangerous in numbers. But... Skaven. You've given a face to our enemy, Astral Templar. Finally. I thank you for that.'

'I've given you little,' Amon said. He decided to set the cup aside before he threw it. 'I've fought skaven before. I fought them not long before I came here, on the shores of the Polychromatic Sea, and more times before that. Every time I've fought them, the battle has been different. The ratmen are true children of Chaos, and every clan is distinct.' He thought of the black-furred figure in its black cloak, with its sewn-shut eyes and silent movements. 'I battled skaven in that smoke, but not like any I have ever faced before. And four of them almost killed me.' Would have killed him, if not for the fire that had ripped out from the emberstone, and that was something else he didn't understand.

'It is still a name I can put in my messages back to Hammerhal Aqsha,' the general said. 'Something that might make them listen, something more than smoke and darkness.'

Messages. Amon swiped at his face one last time, stripping away dried blood and soot, feeling the jolt of pain as he touched the cheekbone that was knitting together. He might like to hunt alone, but he wasn't stupid. That talisman had been the only thing that let him venture out into the smoke, and it was gone now. If he was going to reach the Lord-Ordinator, he was going to need help.

Sigmar had told him.

'How long for a message to reach Hammerhal Aqsha?' he asked.

'A few weeks,' Kant answered. 'We send messenger-birds to the nearest portal, and they relay the messages back.'

'There is nothing else? Nothing faster?' Weeks was too long.

'We have a way to communicate through the other forts in the Adamantine Chain almost instantly. I will use it to tell them what you found, the enemy we all face, because the smoke gathers before their gates too. But they can spare no one.'

'No one,' Amon growled. 'There is no member of the Collegiate Arcane in any of those places? No other Stormcast Eternal?'

'We are on the frontier, Knight-Questor. There's nothing but us mortals,' she said. Then paused. 'No. There is one other. A fort on the other side of the mountains that the Hallowed Knights claimed.'

A fort on the other side of the mountains. 'A place called Rookenval?'

'You know it?'

Know it. That broken tower standing over a lake, with those wings swinging around it. He had told himself that his glimpse of the Ruination Chamber was just chance, not an omen, but here it was again.

'I know I will send no messages there. But I will send word to Hammerhal Aqsha.' And search for any way to advance his quest while waiting for a reply.

'Your word will be appreciated, Knight-Questor,' General Kant said. 'I–'

A knock at the door interrupted her. She opened it, letting in the last light of day. A soldier stood waiting, her dark face twisted with exhaustion and fear.

'General. There's something out there. In the smoke.'

Kant looked back at him, and Amon picked up the pitcher, drained it of its last swallow of water.

'Show us,' the general said, and they followed the soldier to the top of the Halt.

It was easy to see the thing they'd been called for. In the roiling smoke below, there was a flash of colour. It was the same ugly green Amon had seen before, but this was no lightning. It was a rough circle, the bright sign of something glowing beneath the smoke, moving slowly but steadily towards the wall.

'What is it?' Kant asked. Soldiers with shields had surrounded her when she had stepped out on the top of the Halt, a prudent precaution against assassination, but she could barely see.

The green light was a hundred yards from the wall now, its glow getting brighter as it began to move faster. It accelerated as it closed on the wall, flashing through the smoke, its poisonous emerald growing blindingly bright. Then it slammed into the wall.

The Halt trembled underfoot, as if a ram had crashed into it. Soldiers stumbled around Amon, and there was a scream from further down the wall as a guard plummeted over the edge. The Knight-Questor stood by the edge too, but he kept his balance easily, his eyes fixed on the base of the Halt. The smoke swirled, and for just a moment it parted, letting that green glow shine through.

There was a figure standing there, tall and broad. A Stormcast, a shadow Stormcast wrought from the cursed smoke, with something on its chest that glowed with that ominous green light. Amon's grip tightened on his weapons, staring at the terrible thing, and there was a ripple of sound from the mortal soldiers – groans and gasps and ragged, whispered prayers. The thing stood before the Halt, a huge hammer of darkness in its hands, staring at the rings of fractured quartz that now marked the face of the wall. The glow of the broken quartz was fitful there, flickering, like a candle about to stutter out.

The shadow shape raised its hammer, pulling it back to strike at the wall again, but Amon slammed the bottom of his mace against the basalt stone at his feet, and the spark within its cage flared to life, blooming into flames. The sudden wash of light was dimmed by the distance to the ground, but it still made the thing stop its swing and stare upwards. One black eye found Amon's, and he stared into that terrible, empty darkness. Then it was gone, the smoke rushing in burying the figure, hiding it and the damaged wall.

For a moment, the green glow still pulsed through the smoke, like one of Aqshy's moons gleaming through a cloud. Then that was gone too, and there was nothing but darkness below.

'That was him,' General Kant said, her voice harsh in the silence. 'Gods, it couldn't be. He wouldn't. But that was his face.'

'The Lord-Ordinator's,' Amon said, knowing the answer before the general nodded. He flicked his wrist, and the fire in the mace guttered out, its light fading, as in his head pieces fell heavily into place.

Fear the shadow of what you trust. Trust the shadow of what you fear.

'Sigmar, why?' he whispered to himself, knuckle tapping against the sigmarite band binding his hair back. Then he turned to Kant. 'I will still pen a message to Hammerhal Aqsha. But show me your way of reaching the other forts along the Chain. I would also speak to Rookenval.'

CHAPTER SEVEN

GALLOGAST

Brevin Fortis, Lord-Ordinator of the Hallowed Knights, lay in the dark and screamed.

The sound of it echoed through the tiny cell he was in, bouncing from wall to wall. When he stopped, it still seemed to go on and on, filling the cell, filling his head, filling the hollow where his heart should be, but that had been torn out, ripped from his chest by yellow teeth and broken claws.

'Killed me,' he whispered, his voice threading through the never-ending echoes of his scream. 'Should have. Should be...' Should be dead and born again. He should have felt the heat of the lightning taking him apart, that awful pain of death and rebirth as he flashed into the heavens to be remade. But he hadn't. They'd taken his heart, but he still lived.

That's what happened. What had happened?

He was sitting on stone, stone behind him, and iron bound him around his wrists and neck. He was alive, he was captured, he was chained, and he couldn't run a hand over his chest to feel for the wound that must be there – the great hole through muscle and ribs, the gory hollow where his heart should be. He was caught. He wasn't dead.

What had happened?

Slowly, painfully, he made himself remember.

Brevin and the Hallowed Knights moved through the smoke, weapons in their hands, their armour glinting dully in the dark. It was hard to see, but their eyes were keen and they had a path, faint as it was. Brevin had found the track that disappeared into the woods of Warrun Vale, and he led the other Stormcast Eternals down it, navigating as much by the feel of the ruts beneath his feet as he did by his limited sight. He moved slowly, wary of ambush. The dark here could be cover for anything.

'There's something out there,' Therus said, his deep voice a whisper in the gloom. 'I can't see them. Can't hear them. But I can smell them. Old blood and steel, and something else.'

'What?' Brevin asked him, just as quietly, eyes searching for something, anything, in the unnatural dark. The smoke was a sea of poison and silent menace, and every one of his Stormcasts was on edge, waiting for the inevitable ambush that just never came.

'Madness. Hate. Fear. Can such things have a smell?' Therus said. 'If they can, they ride the wind tonight.'

Brevin frowned. Therus was usually a man of brutal, straightforward thoughts. All of the Hallowed Knights who marched with him were like that. As disciplined and focused in their thinking as they were in their fighting. He chose them for that, to help keep him grounded, focused. But the silent menace of what might lie in the darkness was gnawing at them all, trying to shake them the way it had unnerved the soldiers on the Halt.

It wouldn't work. They could not be undone like mortals. But as they moved through the forest, Brevin could feel the tension tightening, tightening, like a noose around his neck, and when the first chain came whipping out of the smoke it was actually a relief.

The weapon lashed around one of the Hallowed Knights' ankles, its barbs glancing harmlessly off the sigmarite of the woman's greaves, but she stumbled as the weapon jerked her leg. Another chain whip caught a second Stormcast around the throat, then another one wrapped around Therus' wrist. Its barbs drove into the joints of the Hallowed Knight's gauntlet, and he grunted as his hand was wrenched open and he dropped his sword. Then the chain whips flicked up, spiralling off the Knights they had caught around and flashing back into the dark. They moved in perfect silence, their barbs making no sound even as they scraped across the Stormcasts' armour.

'There!' Brevin pointed into the dark where the chain whips had vanished.

In answer, a sibilant hiss came from the dark. *Shhhh.*

'Shush?' Therus snarled, bending to pick up his blade. They were all moving, shifting to face the threat, but Therus started his charge the moment his bloody hand closed around the hilt of his sword. He'd barely taken two steps when a chain whip flicked out, its blade cracking against the talisman set on his helm. Therus barely seemed to notice it... And then an explosion of crimson flame ripped out from the Hallowed Knight. Therus dropped, his armour blackening, and a stroke of lightning split the smoke as the Stormcast Eternal dissolved into elemental electricity and returned to his god.

Brevin didn't have time to curse before the explosion hit him. He turned his head, protecting his eyes as the fire washed over him. He felt the heat, but it was less than the pain in his chest and he ignored it. What hurt worse was the crash of lightning through the smoke as another Hallowed Knight fell, caught by the flame.

They hadn't even seen the enemy, and Brevin had lost two

Stormcasts. 'Hallowed Knights,' he shouted. He had to bring them together, to keep whatever was out there from separating them in the dark. 'To–'

But then the dark came for him.

The smoke drifting around him suddenly coalesced, tightened around his arms and legs and head like ropes going taut. Where it touched his exposed skin it felt like rough silk, but it was as strong as steel. Brevin was caught, unable to move, unable to speak. Only his eyes were free, to watch as shapes writhed out of the black. They were bestial things the size of men but twisted, their heads drawn out into muzzles full of broken yellow teeth, their long fingers tipped with claws. Patches of matted fur pushed through the rags that wrapped around their bodies, and long tails with scales like scabs twitched behind them.

Skaven. Brevin had battled the ratmen before, but these were different. Their skulls were malformed, their bodies bulging and asymmetric, and they were horribly hybrid in a hundred different ways. Some had ears like bears or eyes like wolves; some had antlers like deer or were beaked like birds. There were scales and feathers, but worst of all were the little pieces of humanity that some bore – smooth stretches of skin, human eyes, or ears, or hands. Skaven, but skaven who had somehow stolen pieces from both beasts and men. And there were hundreds of them.

They boiled out of the smoke, eyes frenzied, mouths foaming. The remaining Hallowed Knights spun to face them, weapons flashing in their hands, and the first that reached them fell to blade and hammer blow. But the smell of blood encouraged the others, and they piled over the Stormcasts. Silver armour vanished beneath a tide of teeth and claws, and there was nothing but a heaving pile of bodies and blood. Until the lightning started.

The bolts split the dark, shattering bodies as they streaked up into the sky, carrying the souls of the slain Hallowed Knights away from this slaughter, back to their maker to be remade for vengeance. Brevin was left behind, caught in the dark, raging against the smoke that bound him.

'Listen.' The word was whispered in his ear, and when he heard it, the Lord-Ordinator stopped straining against his bonds. Hope flared through him. That voice. He knew it. It was the voice in his dreams, rich and resonant even when it was so quiet.

'Listen.' It came from his other side now, and something was moving past him. A figure wrapped in yellow, a robe that hid its wearer in thick folds and a deep hood as it walked around to stand in front of Brevin, staring at the heaving mass of skaven that still growled and snapped before them. 'Your pain has a source.'

The figure turned, its hood falling back as it did, and the hope in Brevin became horror and rage. A skaven stood before the Lord-Ordinator, his sleek fur the grey of ash. A Grey Seer, a skaven sorcerer. The skaven's eyes were closed, the lids sunken, stitched together by thread the same yellow colour as his robes.

'You have found it,' the Grey Seer said, his voice still deep, still beautiful, but it was changing as he leaned forward, one claw reaching out. He pulled the talisman from Brevin's helmet, and the curl of smoke that had bound the Hallowed Knight's mouth shut became nothing but vapour again. Brevin opened his mouth to shout his defiance, but the smoke poured in, rolling over his lips and tongue and filling his throat, his lungs. He choked, and barely heard the skaven when he spoke again. The dream voice was gone now, the deep smooth certainty of it replaced with a low, smug snarl of arrogance.

'Now it will end. End the pain, storm-cursed.'

The smoke filled him, and the pain in Brevin's chest grew and grew. There were shapes all around him, black figures with eyes stitched shut by yellow thread, holding chains made of a hundred silent knives. They whirled and blurred, and the night went to pieces, falling apart into suffocation and pain. His chest. His chest was being torn apart. The smoke was turning into hands, hands with a thousand clawed fingers, tearing into his flesh, ripping him open to expose his beating heart and tear it free.

'Breathe my blessing,' the Grey Seer hissed, the terrible whisper of his voice tearing through him like the knives of smoke. The skaven leaned forward, and hanging from his throat there was a pendant, a sphere of warpstone flawed with a streak of yellow, like a slitted pupil. That terrible eye seemed to stare into Brevin's soul as the skaven hissed, 'Breathe. Breathe and be free.'

He still had his heart, but he didn't want it.

Brevin hung from his chains, staring into the dark. His throat was still harsh from the coughing and the screaming that the caustic fumes and hallucinatory visions had drawn out of him. At least the air was clear here. There was no smoke in this place, even though he knew it lay under the smoke. He knew where he was, even though he had no memory of being brought here.

This was Gallogast, the place of his dreams. The place where his pain came from. The place where he'd been promised it would be ended. Promised by a child of the Great Horned Rat, a trickster piece of filth that had killed Therus and the other Hallowed Knights.

No. Brevin shook his head. *He* had killed Therus and the others. The Grey Seer's claws had woven those dreams, but he'd listened to them. Too impetuous, as his instructors had said. This was his fault, and they had died for it. So would he.

There was a sound at the door, a thin scrape of metal on metal, and it swung open. There was no light beyond it; the low squeal of the door's hinges and the brush of air across his skin were the only signal to Brevin that the door had moved. But that was enough. He hurled himself up and kicked out. His captors had taken his boots, his weapons, his holy armour, but he was still strong enough to shatter a skaven's bones.

His kick found nothing though, foot passing through empty air, and when he cursed all that came back to him was the sound of a hiss: *Shhh*. Then a chain whipped around his throat, cruel barbs biting into his skin and choking him silent.

They took him to Gallogast's candelarium.

As in the Halt, the room was circular, its curved wall lined with niches, the ceiling a shallow dome. But here the niches were empty, the plinths broken, the quartz circles gone, and the ceiling was cracked and dark. The only light in the room came from a rough chunk of green-black stone the size of a mortal's fist, fixed to the end of a rod of tarnished copper that had been wedged into the floor. Another piece of warpstone, it glowed with that same baleful green light that hurt to look at.

Brevin wished he could knock over the copper rod, or slap away the jagged piece of quartz that floated before the stone, catching its light and sending it out to the Halt and all the other forts that lined the Adamantine Chain. But the skaven had leashed him with chains and he could barely move.

The green-lit room was full of shadows, but it still seemed bright after all the darkness. There was no light now in Gallogast, not a torch or lantern, and that ugly green flame showed Brevin why. All the skaven that filled this place had hollow pits for eyes, covered with lids sewn tightly shut with yellow thread.

The eyeless skaven were silent and almost still, except for the twitching of whiskers, the slant of heads. Some pointed their heads towards Brevin when he was pulled into the room, but they swivelled back to face the Grey Seer, who stood in the centre of the room in his yellow robe, the flawed warpstone pendant around his neck. Another skaven crouched before him, his fur and clothes dark like the others, but this one still had his eyes, great black circles that gleamed green in the warpstone glow.

Brevin's guards jerked on his chains, trying to force him to drop to his knees beside the ruined candelarium's wall.

'No,' he said, and from all around the room came the hiss.

'Shhhh,' spilled from between the skaven's long teeth as Brevin's guards pulled his chains again. The links were silent as they pulled, but Brevin was not.

'No! I will not kneel for you,' he shouted, and his words echoed around the chamber. The dark-robed skaven bared their teeth at him, but the Grey Seer walked forward, his paws silent on the stone. He made a motion with his claws, and the guards stopped trying to pull Brevin down, though they kept hold of his chains.

'Quiet,' the Grey Seer said. 'Quiet, storm-cursed. Still your tongue, or feel it ripped out. Out with your tongue, then your eyes.'

Brevin glared at the yellow-robed skaven, considering a lunge, but the chance of killing the sorcerer was too uncertain. Brevin had no dream of escape except through death, but he wanted to take this grey one with him, so he checked his tongue and stayed still. The skaven waited, then finally turned and went back to his place before the skaven whose eyes remained. The crouching skaven hadn't even turned to look at Brevin. When the Grey Seer was back in front of him, the one with eyes spoke, his words a bare whisper.

'Skein, Grey Seer and master-master. I am Lisstis. I offer myself to the clan.'

'Offer silence. Receive darkness.' Skein folded his arms, hiding his claws in the sleeves of his yellow robe. 'Darkness and silence, or death.'

Lisstis rose, lifting a chain whip from the floor as he did. Its steel links made no noise as the skaven spun the weapon around himself, the long whip whirling and flicking in and out like a serpent striking. It was a swift, smooth dance that ended suddenly. Lisstis stood before Skein again, but he had wrapped his chain whip around his own throat. He gripped the steel links in both hands, holding the weapon taut so that the barbs dug through his dark fur and pressed against his skin. Lisstis stayed like that, still, until two of the eyeless ones stepped forward, each taking one end of the chain. They held it tight, and Lisstis waited, a trickle of blood running down his furry throat.

Skein pulled his paws out of the yellow sleeves of his robe. Metal glinted, shining hooked blades he had slipped over his thumbs. Skein pressed those blades below Lisstis' eyes, and the Grey Seer's empty sockets seemed to stare at the other skaven for a long, silent moment. Then he sank his knives in.

Skein cut around Lisstis' eyes, slicing through muscle, tendon and nerve, without cutting lid or eye. Lisstis' fur rippled, but he didn't pull back his head. He stayed still while the Grey Seer pulled his eyes like gory fruit from his sockets. Skein set them aside, then made a low hiss. The two skaven holding the chain whip jerked the maimed skaven's head up, and Skein struck Lisstis in the throat with his claws.

The two black-robed skaven let go and Lisstis fell to the ground, choking. He knelt there, spitting blood, more blood streaming down from his empty eye sockets. The two that had held the chain watched and waited until the Grey Seer made a clicking noise with his tongue. Then they pulled their chain whips and attacked.

Bladed chains shot out, heading straight for Lisstis. Still choking, he threw himself out of the way. He rolled as they struck again, picking up his own chain whip, swinging it towards them. There were sparks as the blades struck, and the chains lashed and spun, blocking, smashing together, still eerily silent as they collided until–

Until Skein raised a claw, and all three of them stopped, still as statues, their weapons hanging from their claws.

They were all bleeding now, cut from blade and barb, but they stood silently waiting until Skein nodded. Lisstis moved over to kneel before him, and Skein drew a needle and yellow thread from his robes to neatly stitch the skaven's lids shut over his still-bleeding eye sockets.

'Listen,' Skein whispered when done. 'Listen. The lie of light dies. Dies the light in silence, and a new brother in silence is born. Lisstis is born, so we grow. Grow, and become the death of all lies, all clans but one. One clan, our clan. Sisseris.'

'Sisseris.' The skaven's voices were a hiss that filled the chamber. 'Sisseris.'

'Sisseris,' Skein repeated. 'Darkness and silence. Silence and darkness. Death. Death. Death.'

The skaven left the candelarium like shadows, silent on their clawed feet, the yellow thread stitching their eyelids together glimmering in the green-tinted dim before the dark swallowed them. Only Brevin and his four guards remained, standing before Skein, and Lisstis, still weeping blood from his eye sockets and throat.

'Yes,' the Grey Seer said, the word a liquid hiss flowing out around his long teeth. 'Yes. Time now for this.'

'Past time,' Brevin said, then he swept his arms up, throwing them in a circle that caught two of the chains that ran to the collar wrapped around his neck. His wrists were manacled together, but this meant that both arms were slamming into the chains. The force of the blow ripped the chain from the hands of one of the skaven guards and sent the other one stumbling towards the Hallowed Knight. Brevin smashed him out of the way with his shoulder, barely feeling the guards behind him trying to haul him back. He was reaching for the Grey Seer's throat when Skein raised his arm and clenched his claw into a fist.

Pain ripped through Brevin's chest, acid filling him, dissolving his heart, his body, leaving his limbs untethered and uncontrolled, and he was on the floor, thrashing. He fought for control of his limbs, but there was nothing but agony in his body. Something struck his back, Lisstis landing on him, one hand knotting in Brevin's hair while the other pressed the bladed tip of his chain whip into the corner of the Lord-Ordinator's eye.

'Listen,' Skein hissed. 'Listen. I feel it. It is in you, the Heart. I feel its heat. Feel it.'

Brevin snarled and shouted, 'No!' and the pain in his chest was joined by another spike of agony as Lisstis dug out his eye with a quick flick of his razor-edged blade.

'You are the key.' Skein reached out a claw, and Lisstis handed over the eye he'd gouged out of Brevin. The Grey Seer raised it to his mouth and bit into it, ripping through the fibrous outer layer and spilling the clear liquid inside over his yellow teeth. 'Key to everything, storm-cursed. Clawlord Reekbite comes, with his Verminus army, and his path to the lands beyond the mountains will be cleared. Cleared by you.'

The eyeless grey skaven swallowed, then ran a tongue over his lips. 'Warpstone and emberstone will meet, Halt will fall, and the lie of light will be wiped out from your lands, storm-cursed. Cursed shall be your people, and the Horned Rat will gnaw the corpse of your god.'

Glaring defiance through his remaining eye, Brevin spat at Skein. 'I will do nothing for you! Nothing!'

'Shhhh,' hissed his guards, as they fixed his chains to hooks mounted on the walls. They stepped away and Brevin jerked at them, but the steel was too strong, the pain in his chest too much.

'Nothing,' Skein whispered. 'Nothing is all I need.' He clicked his tongue, and from the doorway another skaven appeared. He was smaller than the others, his fur a patchwork of brown and white and rust red, his only clothing a rough smock stained with soot and blood. Unlike all the others, he still had his eyes, and they twitched and rolled, staring everywhere but jerking away every time they fell on Skein. He carried a satchel with him, which he set carefully on the floor between Brevin and the glowing warpstone. Then he edged forward, staring at Brevin, eyes gleaming green as he studied the Lord-Ordinator.

'Yes.' The new skaven's voice was a harsh whisper, and for the first time Brevin noticed the scars on his throat, almost hidden beneath the short fur. 'Yes-yes.' The skaven moved back, and from the satchel he pulled out a copper triangle, the red metal tarnished green in large splotches. He held it up before the warpstone and slowly moved it back and forth, between Brevin and the stone. Long, silent minutes passed, the skaven's thin arms beginning to tremble beneath his patchwork fur as his movements grew more and more minute. Until he finally stopped, and with a slow hiss of breath let go.

The triangle floated in the air, its metal gleaming in the ugly green light. The spotted skaven finally forced himself to look at Skein then, his eyes blinking as if the Grey Seer were a light that shone too bright.

'Now?' Skein asked, moving to the triangle. 'Now, Varus Hish?'

'Yes,' Varus hissed, then shrank back as Skein reached out to touch one side of the triangle.

When Skein's claws brushed against the copper sides of the triangle, something bloomed inside it. It was like a thin sheet of water, hanging impossibly between its three sides, but it was tinged green. Like water gone bad, stagnant, contaminated.

'Yes,' Varus said again, and standing opposite Skein he reached out and took hold of the triangle's lowest point. He pulled on it and the copper flexed, growing larger, the green film inside stretching with it.

Brevin watched, concentrating on his pain, on denying it. Staring at the Grey Seer, trying to plot a new way to reach the ratman's neck before he could be stopped.

But as he stared at Skein, he could see the warpstone through that triangle. It was brighter, sharper, its colour more poisonous. It hurt his eye, and Brevin twisted his head, trying to watch Skein while not being blinded by that growing light. That's when he caught sight of his shadow.

It stretched black across the wall behind him, dark as the smoke gathered before the Halt, and like that smoke flashes of green rippled through it, the same terrible green as the warpstone. And it was moving.

Brevin looked back and forth, between shadow and skaven, watching as Varus pulled at the sides of the triangle, somehow stretching and shrinking the metal as his claws moved over it. Seemingly trying to focus in on some perfect size, and as the skaven moved the copper sides Brevin's shadow grew and shrank too, the green flashing through its darkness as it changed. Then it stopped.

Varus had found what he wanted, and the skaven stepped back, whispering 'Yes' in a low hiss. Skein let go of the copper too, folding his claws in his sleeves as he cocked his eyeless head.

'This, storm-cursed, this I needed. Needed to use you to block lie of light. To write truth in darkness. Darkness to serve, darkness to destroy, darkness to triumph. See it, *Lord-Ordinator*. See it.'

He did. Damn him, Brevin saw it. He saw his shadow start to move again, but this time it wasn't growing or shrinking. Its dark dimensions were fixed as it stepped away from the wall, leaving the shadows of the chains holding nothing. His shade moved until it stood beside Brevin, and the Hallowed Knight could see that it was a perfect image of him, every detail of his broad features and his armour carved out of the absence of light. It was close enough to him that he could feel it, not cold like he expected but hot like a fever. Like smoke. It stared back at him with one black eye, and then it touched him.

The shadow laid a hand on his chest, and the pain in Brevin roared, a storm of acid burning through him – and then it was gone. Suddenly there was nothing left of the pain, and Brevin stood in the chains, saying a prayer of thanks to Sigmar. Until he realised what else he'd lost with the pain. His feeling of the Halt was gone, his connection with the Heart missing. The pain had gone and left him hollow, empty.

'Listen.' Skein was speaking to the shade. 'Listen. Break the clear stone. Bare the red stone that burns, emberstone that kills.' The Grey Seer pulled the warpstone pendant from around his neck, then set the copper chain around the shadow's neck, where it stayed even though Skein's claws brushed through its darkness. The warpstone pendant with its yellow flaw hung from the shade, and a flush of green rippled from it through the shadow, tainting it with its noxious light. 'Bring down the wall. Bring down the humans. Bring down the light, and lies, and let darkness blot out these realms.'

The shadow nodded, then stepped back. Melded with the darkness that filled the door to the room, and all that could be seen was the glow of the flawed warpstone. Then with one last flicker of green it was gone.

'It won't work,' Brevin growled. His defiance felt as hollow as his voice, which he could barely raise above a whisper, but still Brevin forced it out.

'No,' Skein agreed. He padded back to pick up the eyes he had set aside from Lisstis. He popped them both into his mouth, biting down on them slowly, appreciatively, while Lisstis stood beside him, eyelids twitching against the yellow thread that bound them shut. 'No. Your shadow will fail, will return, and the wall will stand. So we will do it again.' Skein swallowed the eyes. 'Again and again. Until it does break. Then, storm-cursed, we drag you with us into our new realm.'

CHAPTER EIGHT

ROOKENVAL

The water in the lake looked dark to Sevora, but really it was clear as glass and the darkness came from the black sand and stone that made up its bottom. She could see that as the wagon rolled along the strange bridge, see the black stones mixed with the trunks of long-dead trees so far below. The water was clear, but the tower that rose above them was as opaque as a night wiped free of moons and stars.

'Who made this?' she asked, staring up at the massive, splintered tower. It crowned the top of the island, dark stone piled high into the heavens. Its base was square, a massive block of stone that was windowless and featureless except for a lone gate. The tower rose from that featureless block, a great column ringed with windows, dark holes that gaped like empty eye sockets.

'No one knows,' Morgen said, her hands careful on the reins. The bridge had no walls to either side, and deep, still water waited inches below its edge. It didn't have any supports either. It was not a real bridge, but a neat line of basalt that crossed the water from shore to island as if the stone could float. It had made Sevora nervous when they had first gone out on to it, but there had been no change in the wagon's jolting advance. However it worked, the road was solid, for as long as whatever magic that had wrought it kept working.

'This tower, and all the fortresses built throughout the Adamantine Chain, were put there long, long ago. Most say it was the Agloraxi Empire, but those dead wizards get credit for everything unexplained in the Great Parch. The truth is no one knows who built them, how they did it, or why. We just claim what is left, like Morrda's flock.'

'Morrda?'

'The exiled one, kith of Sigmar. Those are his birds.' Morgen nodded towards the tower, and the shapes moving through the air around it. The great stormcloud-coloured wings Sevora had seen when they first spotted Rookenval had vanished, but these darker ones remained. They were small at this distance, but they were birds, large black birds that looped in and out of the empty windows, or dove through the jagged, broken stones of the tower's truncated summit.

'Vultures?' she asked. Vultures seemed appropriate here. The peaks of the Adamantine Chain were high and stark, and their white tops blended in with the clouds. Everything here was black and white and grey, and the wind blowing across the lake was cold, making Sevora shiver in her robes. That same wind carried the sound of the waterfalls that fed the lake, a low, unceasing rumble like distant thunder, but that was the only sound beside the plod of hooves and the creaking wagon. It was an unsettling place, its stark, chill openness uncomfortably different to the Shimmering Abyss, and it made Sevora feel even more lost and unbalanced.

'No. They are more like ravens, though bigger,' Morgen said, and her words sent a chill through Sevora that had nothing to do with the wind.

Ravens. Black wings.

She whispered a curse to herself. The clasp on her collar and on Morgen's cloak was shaped like a stylised black bird. She had seen that, but been too numb to *see* it.

'What's wrong?' Morgen asked, sensing something, and Corus turned his head, his brown, flickering eyes focused on Sevora. The line of wagons and riders had tightened on this strange bridge, and her great-grandfather had fallen in beside their wagon. He rode near Morgen, the Lord-Veritant like a wall between them. But Sevora barely noticed Corus. She was pressing a fist against her lips, trying to keep her mouth from opening, but she failed and her laughter spilled out, the dark, bitter sound rolling across the lake and shattering into faint echoes against the distant cliffs.

'Yevin. He warned me before he died that something was coming for me. Yellow teeth and dark wings. Ravens…' She shook her head, the laughter threatening to pour out again, but she fought it. She didn't want it to turn to tears.

'Your brother had the sight,' Morgen said. 'But he didn't understand what he could see. Few can. We did come for you, Sevora. But we mean you no harm.'

'What people mean,' Sevora said, looking over at her great-grandfather, with his almost perfect reflection of Yevin's eyes, 'and what they do seldom align.' She sighed and pulled her robes closer, but she couldn't stop shivering. There was a rustle, and Morgen held something out to her, a great fall of black cloth. A cape, black except for the design in silver embroidery around its edges, hammers with twin lightning bolts. Its clasp was another raven. Sevora frowned at the cape, then reached out. She was cold, damn it. She wrapped the cloak around her, and it was thick and heavy, warm and smelling of…

A memory flickered through her, of huddling in the dark with Yevin and the other Warren brats with their stolen meat, the scent of it mixing with the smell of her brother's sweat. She looked at Morgen, and realised the Lord-Veritant still wore her cape. This one had come from Corus.

'Dark take me,' she whispered, but she pulled the cloth around her, like the wings of a great black bird, and stared up at the tower. She watched the ravens spin against the grey sky, and another memory came and she opened her mouth to softly sing.

'Alas my love has travelled on
And left me here to weeping.
For death has come and laid their claim
To the one I loved so deeply.'

She left the song there, but Corus lifted his head and finished it, his deep voice beautiful in the still air.

'Black Wings have taken them,
Black Wings have flown them on
Black Wings my heart they took, too,
For my love still held it, Black Wings.'

'That was my Aika's favourite song,' he said, looking up at the tower. 'I used to tease her about it. Who sings funeral hymns while making dinner?'

'It was my mother's only song,' Sevora said. 'The only one she ever sang to us. She learned it when she went to funerals, waiting for the mourners to leave so she could rob the tomb.'

'I'm sorry,' Corus said.

'Are you?' Sevora said, thinking of that whitewashed wall in that narrow crack that was their home. Of darkness and filth and wanting. Of the lie of hope. 'Then where were you?'

'I don't know,' Corus answered. 'I'm told I was fighting for the Mortal Realms. For Sigmar. But I don't remember, and I don't know why if I was doing all that fighting, I wasn't fighting for you. I'm sorry, but I don't remember.'

When they reached the island, the road continued through pines so green they looked almost as black as the basalt. Sevora had never been in a forest before, had only seen a few trees growing in Hallowheart, but these pines were nothing like those carefully domesticated park decorations. The way they loomed was strangely threatening. When the ravens came diving out of the branches she couldn't stop her hand from going to her knife.

Morgen saw, of course, but the Lord-Veritant said nothing to her. She called out instead, to the birds.

'Greetings, guardians of Rookenval!'

One of the mountain ravens landed on the edge of the wagon. It was much like the corvids Sevora had seen stealing scraps in Hallowheart, but larger. This one's beaked head would have almost reached her waist if she were standing. The bird was black except for a stripe of grey that ran down from its dark brown eyes, like a track of tears. It croaked at them, a deep, scolding sound, and Peace raised his head and echoed the sound. The corvid fluffed its feathers, seemingly offended, and took off again, black wings taking it back into the air.

'The bleak ravens are allowed their opinions, Peace,' Morgen said. 'They were here first.'

'Are they part of the Ruination Chamber?' Sevora asked, watching the huge bird fly away.

'Informally,' Morgen said. 'Nothing gets to this island without attracting their eye. And so we know when we have visitors.'

As if anyone in the tower couldn't have easily seen them working their way across that bridge. But before Sevora could mention that, other wings rose from out of the tower and she went silent.

The first set were the stormcloud wings she'd seen from the hills. They spread from the shoulders of a woman wrapped in the silvery, patinated armour of the Ruination Chamber. She bore a javelin in her hands, and its edge flashed as she soared up into the cloudy sky.

From the tower came a rider, his steed much larger than that of a city cavalier, and dark as the mountain corvids. It was a beast shaped something like Peace, part gryph and part raven, but with great black feathers on its long limbs. It cawed mournfully in the air, the sound oddly chilling. On its back was another Stormcast wrapped in that sombre armour.

'That is Prosecutor Jocanan and Lord-Vigilant Avarin Day,' Morgen said, staring up with her and Corus. 'His gryph-stalker mount is named Korfan.'

While the Prosecutor stayed high in the air, circling the tower, Korfan prowled low through the trees. Everyone in the column raised a hand in salute, everyone except Sevora. She just shaded her eyes against the setting sun and watched him pass.

'The Lord-Vigilant is the leader of Rookenval, and the Ruination Chamber of the Hallowed Knights of Aqshy. He is my commander and now yours, Corus Stormshield. And yours too, Memorian Sevora Cinis.'

Sevora watched gryph-stalker and rider move away, her head turning with Peace's. 'Ruination Chamber. Is it a point of pride for you to be so bleak?'

Morgen shook her head, but Corus smiled, while Peace turned his gaze away from where the Lord-Vigilant had vanished behind the trees. 'Bleak,' he croaked once, and then the road broke from the trees and they were before the tower, Rookenval's black walls stretching to the grey heavens above them.

Rookenval's gate was a featureless arch of dark wood bound with iron. Passing through it, the wagon entered a long tunnel of stone. The day was almost gone, and the dark in the tunnel seemed oppressive, too much like the Warrens. Sevora felt frustration mix with her unease. Outside was too wide, inside was too close, was there any place she could exist without fear? She didn't know, but as the wagon left the tunnel and rumbled out into the courtyard beyond, she knew that this place wasn't going to grant her any peace.

High walls surrounded them, formed of the same black stone. There were windows on this inner face, narrow arched openings that hinted at the presence of rooms and halls inside those thick walls, and iron-banded doors that led into them. The tower rose from the back, its curved wall pushing into the paved courtyard. The massive door that opened into the tower lay open, but Sevora could see little of the hall beyond.

The gryph-stalker Korfan sat before it, his eyes on the wagons as they ground to a halt in the courtyard. Lord-Vigilant Avarin Day stood beside his mount, his face hidden behind his helm, but Sevora could feel his eyes on them.

'Come,' Morgen said, jumping down from their wagon. Peace followed her, nimble and silent. Sevora jumped down too, not as gracefully, the giant cape wrapped around her trying to catch on everything. She thought about giving it up, as she was likely about to be presented to this Lord-Vigilant, but she decided she didn't care. The Ruination Chamber had plucked her unasked from Hallowheart to this freezing place. What did it matter if she was wrapped up in a cloak?

Morgen led them from the wagon, and both Corus and the other new Reclusian, Dreskir, fell in behind her, Dreskir's Memorian Avil Tawn walking beside him, his attempt to look pious ruined by his gaping at the gryph-stalker. The Lord-Veritant probably wanted her to walk like that, beside Corus, but she followed two steps behind instead, staring at his back, no longer covered by his cape.

There was a crowd of other Reclusians waiting for them, neat lines of armoured warriors facing each other across a wide gap, a walkway that led to the Lord-Vigilant. Smaller figures stood with them, one or two for each, men and women dressed in dark robes or leather armour. Memorians. Their mortal frailty emphasised the size and power of the Stormcasts. But something else caught Sevora's attention.

The Reclusians were stern, their faces set and hard, but their eyes – their eyes were haunted in a hundred different ways. Some were too intent, some lost, some bleeding tears, while others were hard as stone. Sevora slowed her step, sweeping her gaze over those implacable faces holding so many wounded eyes. Storm-cast Eternals were... Eternal. Figures larger than life, beyond petty human concerns like pain and uncertainty and... grief. The meaning of some of what Morgen had been telling her suddenly hit home. Hurt. Lessened. All of these demigods, they were like that too. Injured by their immortality somehow, the way her great-grandfather had been.

Was this what a Ruination Chamber was?

They moved down the gap between the armoured figures, heading towards the Lord Vigilant, and as they did so the gloom that filled the courtyard in the dying day was pushed back by new light. Spaced among the Reclusians were more Lord-Veritants, easily recognised by the blindfolds pulled over their eyes, the gryph-crows sitting beside them, and the huge torches they held. As Corus and Dreskir moved past, the spark in those torches blossomed into bright flame, flame that spread light through the darkening courtyard and made vast, shifting shadows on the walls.

In one of those shadows something glinted, catching Sevora's eye. There was another giant figure standing there, apart from the others, their darkened silver armour making them almost invisible. Their helm was a stylised mask of a vaguely human face sketched in hard lines. It could have been male or female, angry or sad, beautiful or hideous. This Stormcast held an axe larger than the one Corus carried, a two-handed weapon with a hooked blade on one side and stylised flames on the other. They were an eerie, formidable figure, especially set apart like that, watching over the procession like one of the ravens that perched in the tower windows far above. And then they turned their helm towards Sevora, as if they sensed her regard, and as they did the strange mask that covered their face seemed to twist, to become a reflection of Sevora's own features, like a sculpted mirror of dark metal.

Sevora shuddered and snatched her gaze away from the figure just in time to stop behind Corus. They'd reached the Lord-Vigilant. This close, Sevora was able to smell the feathers-and-fur scent of the gryph-stalker, could see the raven skulls worked into Avarin Day's armour. She could see, too, the small sparks that snapped and danced between the Lord-Vigilant's fingers as his hands shifted.

Morgen bowed her head and raised a hand to her eyes, covering them, while her other hand tapped the end of her torch against the dark stone beneath her feet. Fire blossomed in the torch, and Korfan snapped his beak, eyes glinting in the light.

'Lord-Vigilant, I am returned, and I bring two more to join our ranks, along with their Memorians. This is Dreskir Skyvault and Corus Stormshield.'

The Lord-Vigilant nodded to the Lord-Veritant, then reached up and removed his helm, sending more sparks dancing between his hands and the sigmarite armour. He was a bald, dark-skinned man with a thick scar that split the brow of his right eye then ran up over his head. His eyes were sharp, more present than most of the Reclusians, but there was a distance in them, as if Avarin Day was watching the world from a long way away.

'Our thanks to you, Lord-Veritant Morgen Light,' he said, his deep voice crisp. 'We welcome our new brothers to Rookenval.' The Lord-Vigilant looked from Corus to Dreskir, weighing them with his distant eyes. 'You have lost much, I know. Here, we all know. But whatever you have lost, you are still Stormcast Eternals. Still Hallowed Knights. You are the justice and vengeance of the Lord of the Heavens, and you will serve him now as

Reclusians of the Ruination Chamber. For we are the forces of last resort, the warriors of battles feared lost, and we carry the spark of light into the darkness.'

Through the courtyard, the Lord-Veritants slammed the butts of their torches into the ground, making a sound like thunder as firelight flared like lightning.

'We are the Ruination Chamber! Hope when hope is dying!'

'We are the Ruination Chamber!' Every Stormcast Eternal boomed out the words, and they filled the courtyard and echoed back from the distant cliffs, but Sevora was frowning.

Hope when hope was dying.

Hope is a lie.

She shook her head, but her eyes caught on Corus as she did, saw him mouthing the words but not say them, his brown, lightning-cursed eyes staring up at the broken tower with its black-winged attendants, uncertain. Lost.

As lost as Sevora felt.

'Why is it a prison?'

Sevora stood on the edge of one of the balconies that ringed the inside of Rookenval's tower, staring down at the only door that led into the broken building's hollow heart. When she'd been led inside the night before, she'd stared up at the cavernous space with awe. But that awe had quickly been washed away when she realised that the outer walls of the tower were made up of cells, rings of small rooms that ran around the outer wall circumference. There were floors and floors of them, rising from the ground to the top of the vast space. It wasn't open to the sky – the huge chamber ended in a vaulted ceiling halfway up the high tower, supported by a column that stood in the tower's centre. That made it a gloomy place, despite the high windows and the torches that the Lord-Veritants carried.

Morgen had called it the panopticon the night before, but that seemed a large word for a cage.

'A prison?' Morgen asked. She stood beside Sevora, her torch lit only by that small spark in its centre, her helm hanging from her belt. The Lord-Veritant had come for Sevora when dawn's light had finally spilled through the tower's windows, rousing the ravens. 'Do you see bars? Do you see locks? What prison is there here?'

'A prison of eyes.' Sevora nodded towards the inner column. It was made of the same dense basalt, but compared to the rest of the tower it was delicate as lace, every storey a series of open arches that looked out at the cells in the outer wall. Most of the other Lord-Veritants were there, moving past those arches with their flaming torches or looking out at the Reclusians who knelt silently in their cells, heads bowed, arms crossed over their chests.

'A prison of guards.'

The cells all lacked a fourth wall; they were open to the rest of the tower without even a curtain for privacy. Sevora had spent the night in the narrow cot given to her, watching the Lord-Veritants circling that centre tower, the shadows cast by the glowing beacons of their torches sliding across the walls. When she couldn't stand it any more she'd turned her back on them and stared out the window in the rear wall of the cell. The ravens huddled there had stared back at her with dark, knowing eyes.

'You don't need bars. You have yourselves and this damned tower in the middle of nowhere. This is a prison, even if the prisoners come here voluntarily. Corus and all the other Reclusians are trapped here, with their guards and...' She trailed off, staring down.

Far below, a figure was moving through the deeper gloom of the windowless lower floors. They were hard to see through the dim, but Sevora could pick out the huge axe balanced over one shoulder, the mask that covered their face.

'And their executioner.'

'Do not demean the Lord-Terminos with that name,' Morgen said, her voice hard. The rebuke should have made Sevora quail, coming from that terrifying woman, but she was still numb from everything that had happened. Or maybe she had simply given up.

'Demean them?' Sevora asked. 'By speaking the truth? The Lord-Vigilant made their job very clear to us last night. To slay any of the Ruination Chamber whose soul becomes so eroded by Reforging that they lose sight of what they are, or what the difference is between a weapon and the hand that wields it.'

'Executioners punish the guilty for their crimes.' Morgen looked down at the Lord-Terminos, disappearing through an arch crowned by a skull with an onyx raven perched atop it. 'The Lord-Terminos grants release. They may do so to those who lose all mercy, all humanity, but that is uncommon. When their blade finds the neck of a member of the Ruination Chamber, it is almost always because it has been asked for.'

'Suicide?' Sevora snapped, and a thin breeze wrapped around her, carrying a few wan sparks like dying stars. 'They kill those who would kill themselves? That is supposed to be better than an executioner?'

'They kill those who wish a final death.' The soothing smell of rain that usually surrounded Morgen was gone, as if pushed away by Sevora's wind. Or the Lord-Veritant's anger. 'Stormcasts are immortal. When we die, we are reborn to serve again. But for some, every Reforging is a guarantee that they will lose more of themselves. They have passed beyond the Storm's Eye, the place where most of us fight to hold ourselves, a grace that lets us keep our souls intact. But they no longer have that, and if they die, they lose more and more, and slip towards becoming something inhuman. Some amongst the Stormhosts seem to think such a change a blessing, that they are becoming a true champion of

Sigmar, untainted by the petty concerns of humanity. But they are fools, because they have not seen it, not felt it. It is a terrible, painful way to be undone. It is a flaying of the soul, Memorian, and the only way to end it is the true death that is found at the edge of the Lord-Terminos' axe.' She shook her head. 'It is a terrible choice. But it is the only one that may give them peace. By Sigmar and Morrda, the bleak raven of death, I hope it does. I pray it does. Because no one deserves to be torn apart the way the Reclusians are.'

'No one deserves to be torn apart,' Sevora said, thinking of her twin, of his blood hot on her face. 'And yet so many of us are, without anyone to give pretty speeches about how awful it is.' She turned and stalked away, heading for the stairs, not knowing where she was going but not wanting to listen any more.

Morgen's gentle voice followed her. 'Corus is downstairs. Practising in the courtyard.'

Sevora took the stairway up.

The stairs went back and forth, winding up a few more storeys until they reached the top level. The cells here were deserted, empty except for the ravens and their nests. The birds called to her, low caws that could have been greetings or warnings, but she ignored them, searching until she found another staircase that spiralled upward. It was unlit, but there was grey light coming down from somewhere above. It was more light than she'd usually had in the Warrens, and Sevora started to climb.

The stair spun, but after a few twists it opened up onto a new floor of the tower, somewhere above the buttressed ceiling of the panopticon. This floor had the same arched windows, but while the ceilings were high they only stretched five yards above her head, not a hundred. The stairway kept going up, but Sevora stepped out, blinking at what she saw.

Unlike the great open chamber below, this floor was divided into a labyrinth of rooms. The walls were made of the same smooth, dark stone, but here they were painted. Not flat colours, but images – murals, pictures, portraits. Even in the dim light their colours were vibrant, almost glowing. Sevora walked slowly, staring at them, wondering at the different styles. Some paintings were incredibly detailed and realistic: landscapes like windows overlooking some vista from far away, or portraits that were like catching a glimpse of someone across a room. But others were stylised, abstract, their colours and shapes hinting at things rather than describing.

As she studied them, Sevora realised that despite the differences, the paintings were all done by the same hand. The difference between them, realism versus abstraction, was determined by their subject. Wild landscapes, animals, people like farmers and merchants and children – all of those were done with exquisite detail. Battle scenes, executions, warbeasts wrapped in armour, cities in flames – those were all done in hints and shadows, vague yet somehow terribly evocative. Was the painter trying to hide those atrocities? Or make them worse by leaving them to the viewer's imagination? Sevora wasn't sure, but it was effective. She turned away from a room that seemed to be mostly pictures of a band of daemons and blood and followed a series of landscapes around the corner into another room with an arched window. The grey light spilling through it gleamed off stark, beautiful landscapes of sand dunes and buttes, mixed with portraits of people dressed in white tunics and colourful headcloths.

She stopped, staring at a portrait of a cloaked woman whose bright green eyes glowed against her dark skin and dark hood. Sevora was so caught by the lost, haunted expression on the woman's face that she didn't notice that someone else was in the room. Until she stood from her crouch in the corner, her great grey wings flaring out as she turned.

'I don't know why she's sad.'

The woman's voice was a mellow alto, quiet despite the fact that she stood so tall over Sevora, her graceful body wrapped in the dark patinated armour of the Ruination Chamber. Her wings of blue-grey flame were tucked away, but their armoured mantle framed her head nonetheless. It was the woman Morgen had called a Prosecutor, and named Jocanan. She had been beautiful when she was flying high above, and this close... She was still beautiful. She had brown skin, lighter than Morgen's but darker than Sevora's, and those same startling green eyes as the woman in the portrait. Her black hair was cropped short, but there was enough of it to show loose curls, and her face was finely made, the smile on it small but sincere. Beautiful, but her size, her armour, and those wing-mantles, they made her terrifying too. Sevora might have ducked back, but for that smile on the Stormcast's face and the paintbrush she held in her hand, its hairs dripping white onto the dark silver armour covering the woman's thigh.

'I'm sorry, I–' Sevora shook her head and took a breath. 'Your paint is dripping.'

'Oh?' Jocanan looked down and laughed. She stooped and picked up a rag, wiping away the spot. 'Thank Sigmar that his metal does not take up paint easily. Otherwise the sombre patina of this would have turned into motley a long time ago.'

Sevora didn't know what to say in response. She didn't know how to respond to anything now, really. 'I didn't know Stormcast Eternals painted,' was what she managed.

'I do not know that many do,' Jocanan said. 'Lord-Veritant Morgen suggested it to me.' She picked up a paint pot stained with white, swirled her brush in it and crouched again, making tiny flowers in the grass that grew beside a spreading tree. 'I could not meditate, could not pray, because of the images in my head. They crowded in and they wouldn't leave me alone.' She added more paint to the brush and slowly, delicately dabbed another flower, somehow creating it out of nothing but a few strokes. 'Morgen suggested I try drawing them out, and gave me some charcoals. That helped, but I wanted colour.' The Prosecutor shrugged, the motion making her great wing-mantle shift.

'They're beautiful,' Sevora said. 'Well. Some are…' She trailed off, not knowing what to say about the frightening pictures, but Jocanan nodded.

'I know. Some are bad.' She looked over her shoulder before Sevora could say anything. 'Not badly done. My hand and eye are very good. But…' She cleaned the brush of the white. The new flowers looked real enough to draw bees. 'Morgen says these are my memories. Echoes of my past that I can't recall, but aren't quite gone. Things that meant something. Things I loved, like flowers or trees or that woman, though I can't tell you who she is or what I loved about her. But others are things that made me angry, or frightened. Ugly things, but I have to paint them or they will block all my thoughts. I try to keep them vague, but I have to give them life. I hate that.'

She hovered over her paints, mantle flexing, like a hawk searching for prey. She scooped up a jar of red and began to carefully apply it to the trunk of the tree, somehow blending the colour in and making the bark look more real.

'Does it help?' Sevora asked.

'Help?' Jocanan shrugged again, wings shifting. 'Have my memories come back? No. I know exactly what these pictures should look like. The images are clear in my head. But what do they mean? I don't know, but it feels good to get them out of my head. It makes me feel lighter.' She stopped her painting, staring at the tree. 'It's better than all that damned meditation at least.'

'Hmmph,' Sevora grunted. Anything seemed like a better tool than the meditation and prayer Morgen had led Corus through the night before. Corus had seemed eager to pray, but the words meant nothing to Sevora.

The Prosecutor's mouth quirked into a smile. 'You don't like it either?' She looked her up and down. 'You are the new Memorian. The one that came in with Corus Stormshield.' The woman waited, patient, until Sevora shrugged. 'I saw him down in the courtyard earlier. Sparring with others. Sparring and drills are another thing which helps some. Why aren't you with him?'

'Because,' Sevora said.

'Hmm,' she said. 'From the way he was looking at you, I would have thought he would have wanted you near. Most members of the Ruination Chamber keep their Memorian close when they are new to the chamber, and learning how to live on the other side of the storm.'

Sevora frowned. The conversation had been good, at last a distraction from what was happening. Now she was once again faced with it, this trap she'd found herself in. The one her brother had tried to warn her about.

'There's no one with you,' she threw back. 'Where is your Memorian?'

'Dead,' Jocanan said. 'I had very little family when I was a mortal. The only person close enough to still be called a relative was already old when he came here with me. He only lasted ten years before his death. I still remember him, though. The pictures in my head… he could help them go away by talking to me, or by singing, or by…' She laughed, suddenly. 'Or by sketching me something on scraps of parchment. Little drawings of silly things. Watching him do it always helped. Maybe that's where this started.' She waved a hand at her paintings. 'I don't know. But I know that I probably would not have made it through those first few years without him. The things in my head, the things I saw, they wouldn't let me go. Without him, they would have never let me go.'

'Never let you go,' Sevora said. 'The way I'm never going to be let go?'

They're coming for you. The ravens...

Anger ripped through her: at Morgen and the Ruination Chamber, at the Whitefire Court, at her mother, at her brother. At herself. Anger enough for her to look up at this giant woman with her stormcloud wings and attack.

'The way your Memorian was held here... Or did you think he gave up a whole life of living out there because he wanted to come and die in this place, drawing funny pictures for a sad immortal?'

She half expected Jocanan to pick her up and toss her out of the window behind her. Her hand was on her knife, ready to fight, and she could feel the air around her moving, like a breeze before a storm. Sevora wanted a fight, and she didn't much care if she lost. But the Prosecutor just gave her another smile.

'We talked about that. About what he had to give up, coming here.' Her smile faded. 'We talked about loss a lot. That helped too. Though I like the pictures better.' Jocanan bent and picked up another pot of paint. 'You are caught here. We all are. No member of the Ruination Chamber chose this fate, just as no Memorian did. But here we are, and so we do what we can.' She dabbed her brush in the pot, and began to mark moss on the tree, deep green overlying the bark. 'We do what we can.'

Hours later, Sevora was standing above the courtyard.

She wasn't sure why. After Jocanan, she'd wandered the upper storeys of the tower. The floors were empty, abandoned, until she finally reached where the tower had been broken and there was only sky above. Here was a ruin of stone and sticks, the rubble from the broken tower mixed with raven nests. Their suspicious eyes and warning caws were enough to make her want to turn back, but there was also a monstrous nest in the middle of the ruin, and curled in it was Korfan. The gryph-stalker could've been sleeping, but Sevora thought she caught a glimpse of one dark eye on her. When she turned back to the stairs and started down the spiral, she heard something mixed with the cawing. A voice, inhuman, harsh – like Peace's voice but deeper.

'Serve,' it muttered, and the word echoed in the narrow stairway. 'Hope is dying.'

Sevora fled that voice, rushing down the spiral until she was back in the panopticon. Not where she wanted to be. Even in the deserted upper layers, she could feel the eyes of the Lord-Veritants on her. Morgen Light and the other Lord-Veritants had not fallen from the Storm's Eye, like Corus and Dreskir and all the others in the Ruination Chamber. Morgen had told Sevora that last night, when she had led her and Corus to their shared cell. The Lord-Veritants were Stormcasts that had proven themselves as healers, not just of body but of mind and soul. So when they were Reforged they were given a gift of sight by Sigmar himself. Sight that let them see into the very souls of their charges – and anyone else they cared to turn their blindfolded eyes upon.

Which is why Sevora didn't feel right in that space, under their gaze as they moved around the central tower, watching their... patients? Prisoners? Neither word felt right. But she wasn't staying here with them, and so she took the stairs down until she found a door that opened onto the top of the wall that formed the fortress' courtyard. It was dizzyingly high, but it had parapets on either side, so she walked it without fear, staring out at the island.

It was all dense forest before the tower, but behind it there was nothing. The arc of the tower's wall ran just inside the edge of a high cliff that plunged down to the clear lake far below. It was as if some vast giant had cut the island in half and gobbled up the other piece. Sevora spent a long while staring out at the view. The clouds were piled up against the mountains, their grey bellies caught on the peaks' shining white teeth. Clouds and crags were reflected in the lake, which stretched away flat as a mirror. At the distant shore, the water lapped against the feet of the mountains. There were broken beaches and craggy cliffs where waterfalls shuddered down, glinting in the grey daylight. She watched them, and wished that their distant thunder was loud enough to cover the cawing of the ravens overhead, or the sounds of fighting below.

They were still sparring in the courtyard. Giant figures in their patinated armour, stalking around each other, then crashing together, the clatter echoing off the walls. Impossible to ignore, no matter how Sevora tried, and eventually she gave up and walked across the wall to stare down at the combatants.

Despite the armour and helms, she could pick Corus out easily. She stared over the parapet at him, trying to figure out how she knew him so easily, and then he looked up at her, picking her out on the wall as easily as she had found him. Luck, or was there some connection between them, some mystical bond between Memorian and Reclusian?

The thought made her nauseous. She turned away, walking until she found a doorway that led to yet another staircase, one that wound down into the dark spaces built inside the wall.

The rooms and halls in the wall were like the high spaces in the tower, dusty and empty, but darker. There were few windows here, and she had to take a lantern from the entrance to light her way as she paced the halls. They were arched, tall and wide and perfectly made, unaffected by age except for the dust and dirt that had accumulated over centuries. She wound through them until she finally heard something that wasn't the distant din of sparring. Voices, and there was light too, coming from somewhere up ahead, so she blew out the lantern and crept closer.

An arched doorway opened into the hallway, spilling out the light and the sound of conversation. It was Morgen and Avarin, the Lord-Veritant and the Lord-Vigilant, two of the people she least wanted to meet, but that didn't stop her from standing outside the door in the shadows to listen.

'–fine for now. But Dreskir has an edge.' Morgen's voice had lost any hint of its easy congeniality. She was formal, her words precise. 'This was only his second Reforging. He barely held himself in the Storm's Eye following the first, and fell through it fast on the second. There is a flaw in him, I think, a fear of death which is robbing him of his gift of immortality.'

'The chronicles of his actions show that all the traumas he has suffered, whether as a mortal or a Stormcast Eternal, were because he sacrificed himself for others.' Avarin's voice was slow, considering. Not challenging Morgen, but seeking an answer.

'Yes,' Morgen said. 'Dreskir is frightened, but he is also brave. When death is close, for him or someone he cares about, his fear of that possible loss can unhinge him. Make him act rashly, without thinking. That is my read of him so far. That he fights his fear of loss with such violence it breaks him.'

'Breaks.' That was Peace, echoing Morgen. His voice was small compared to the gryph-stalker, but Sevora still had to steel herself not to step back from the door.

'Thankfully his Memorian shows a sincere dedication,' Morgen continued. 'Avil Tawn was only too eager to leave his old life behind for one of greater purpose. He will be a good anchor for Dreskir, who I expect will be a challenge, but no more than anything we've dealt with before. Corus and Sevora, though. They are different.'

'The chronicles of Corus are exemplary,' the Lord-Vigilant said. 'An excellent fighter, especially on the defensive, especially in dire circumstances. That ability to fight and hold in the face of overwhelming odds is extremely valuable, but it has also cost him. Nine times Reforged, in less than a century.'

'But each time he came back whole.' Morgen sounded less brisk now. 'Corus was able to hold himself right in the centre of the Storm's Eye, and he emerged from each Reforging with his soul intact, not a memory lost. Until his tenth death, when he came back with no memory of his life after being reborn a Stormcast Eternal.'

'We lose our earliest memories first,' Avarin said. 'The memories of being mortal. What makes Corus different? Why did he not lose any memories, then suddenly lose so many, but so differently to all the rest of us?'

'He was studied in the Shining Cathedral in Hallowheart. They didn't understand either.' Morgen's voice sounded like a shrug. 'Eventually, they felt they had to send him here. He is too caught up in his memories of his mortal life. They drag him down, pull him away from what he is now.'

'He needs an anchor too. But Sevora Cinis is no Avil Tawn.'

'No,' Morgen said. 'She is not. She is smart, independent, and doesn't trust anyone or anything. Especially her family, especially us. Both she and her twin brother were flux-touched. The magic of the Shimmering Abyss got into their blood. She can call the wind, at times, and her brother has – had – visions. Prophetic ones, maybe.'

Not maybe, Sevora thought. *He saw you coming for me.*

'Flux-touched. She attempted to train as a mage, didn't she?'

'She wanted to stand the trials at the Whitefire Court. But they didn't want her. I think they doubted they could handle her.' The contempt in Morgen's voice was clear.

'But you can?' asked the Lord-Vigilant.

She would like to think so, Sevora thought. *But I am no ox.*

'I certainly have a better chance than the mages of the Whitefire Court. They have no patience for anything that does not immediately advance their power. I think Sevora will eventually be a great help with Corus. But her life has been hard, especially recently. We will need patience, and time. On both my part and yours, Memorian.'

Sevora heard Morgen's voice change, pitched to reach the hall, and she began to turn to try to vanish into the shadows. But Peace was already standing in the doorway, his sharp eyes on her. Would he run her down if she tried to go? Sevora doubted that the gryph-crow would hurt her. But hold her, or drag her back? That, she thought he would readily do.

So she walked into the room, keeping as far as she could from the lean, raven-headed beast. Was he how Morgen had known she was out here? The way he looked at her as she passed made her wonder if Peace could see through walls.

The room was plain, its smooth stone walls the same as all the others Sevora had found. But this room was not dusty, or empty. It was immaculate, and at one end sat a round table with heavy chairs, all sized for Stormcast Eternals. At the other end of the room was a shrine to Sigmar, spare but clearly well-tended. In the middle of the room was a ring of more huge chairs, with several mortal-sized ones scattered among them. The Lord-Veritant and Lord-Vigilant sat there, watching as Sevora walked in. Morgen's torch stood beside her, its spark shining, and their helms sat on empty chairs nearby.

Even at their ease they were still intimidating, and Sevora's hand dropped to her belt, fingers touching the knife she'd slipped behind it. It wouldn't do a thing to these two, but it gave her enough strength to speak.

'*You* think,' she said. 'You think a lot about me, Lord-Veritant. But you don't think to ask me what I think.'

'Do I not?' Morgen said. 'At the Shining Citadel. In the wagon. This morning. I tried to reach you and you turned away. You've armoured yourself, Memorian. I understand that, given your life. But if you want to tell me what you think, then you have to actually do it. Honestly.'

'Honesty?' Sevora snapped. She wasn't looking at Morgen, or the man sitting beside her. She couldn't, without feeling that aura of divine intimidation that surrounded them. But if she glared at the wall she could growl out her accusations. 'Is that what you want? I *honestly* think you snatched me from Hallowheart and dragged me out here to this prison of broken immortals, expecting me to play at being some kind of nursemaid to the man who destroyed my family generations ago. How is that?'

'Lacking,' Morgen said.

If Morgen had been mortal, Sevora would have pulled her knife and gone for her. As it was, her hand tightened on the handle of her blade and a wind whipped around her, stirring her hair and scattering orange sparks through the dim room. But attacking would have seen her knocked across the floor, so she spun away, and found herself glaring at the altar of Sigmar.

Then she finally saw the figure of the Lord-Terminos, standing in one shadowed corner, so still she hadn't noticed them before. She noticed them now though, as they tilted their head and studied her through that hauntingly ambiguous mask that covered their face. The mask seemed to twist again, reflecting hers, but the metal features were different, softer. It was her face but younger, childlike, and twisted with anger and petulance. Another wash of anger went through her, and her hand gripped her knife even tighter, but she didn't dare draw it. Not when the Lord-Terminos had their massive axe sitting beside them, its edge glittering.

She took a step back, moving away from them all. But Peace was now sitting on his haunches in the middle of the door, his eyes on her, blocking any escape.

'I told you that I saw you, Sevora Cinis. The day I met you.' Morgen stood, and even in this tall, wide room she loomed over Sevora. 'I told you that the divine light of my torch let me read your soul. Let me tell you what I saw. Honestly. You were told by your mother, a woman who is fundamentally unworthy of your trust, that you could only trust in your family. The last words of your father were that hope was a lie. The only person you ever trusted was your brother, but even that trust faltered when you realised that he was afraid of an outside world that held bright dangers and obligations he could not, would not, understand. So you started to take steps to go out on your own, to reach for power and freedom like you never had, so you could live in that light that your brother feared. For the first time in your life, you started to try to escape the darkness of your home, your family, your history. You took your first faltering steps out of the darkness and into the light. And then the darkness came for you and pulled you back in.'

Sevora didn't look at her. She stared at the smooth stone floor and shook her head. She couldn't flee, couldn't fight, she had nothing but the wind that ruffled her hair and her robes, but it wasn't loud enough in her ears to drown out the Lord-Veritant's words.

'You were getting ready to face the trials of the Whitefire Court. And then your brother was killed.' Morgen's voice was steady, unemotional, a flat recitation that dug into Sevora's head. 'Yevin was murdered, horribly, and that's when your true dream died. Not of gaining power. Of rising to the heights of Hallowheart's elites. But of taking him out of the dark. Of saving Yevin and proving that you were right, that you both could live in the light, could leave the Warrens and your mother and all the filth and dark and despair behind. He died, and your dream, your real dream, crumbled into dust.'

Hope is a lie. Her father's voice echoed through her head as Sevora finally looked up at Morgen.

'He tried to warn me about you,' she said, her voice barely above a whisper. 'Ravens, coming for me. Scavengers, come to tear my life apart.'

'What life?' Morgen asked, and suddenly the fear and frustration in Sevora flared into anger. Anger and wind.

The air moving around Sevora spun into a scream, the orange sparks in it brightening, then lashed out. The wind slammed into Morgen, staggering the Stormcast, and she crouched, face set as stone as she fought to keep her feet despite the gale that was trying to smash her into the back wall of the room. She was slowly losing the battle as the roar of the wind drowned out Sevora's howl of rage. Then something hit Sevora from behind, knocking her to the stone floor.

The wind flagged and fell, the sparks swirling in it fading and dying, and the chairs that had been tumbling across the room came to rest. Morgen straightened, and kicked away the remains of a broken chair that had wrapped itself around her leg. Sevora watched her, breathing hard, feeling the claws on her back that held her down.

'Warn,' Peace croaked, standing over her.

'Release her.' Morgen reached down and picked her helm up from where it had fallen, the chair it had been resting on now shattered against the wall. 'This is precisely the kind of storm the mage at Whitefire Court was concerned about. You almost knocked *me* over, but to others more vulnerable you pose a real threat. Lady Lysiri and others at the Whitefire Court do not take kindly to ungovernable sorcery.'

The gryph-crow stepped off her and Sevora rose, palms and knees stinging from the fall. She could taste blood, had probably bitten her tongue, but she wasn't angry or frightened any more. The wind had taken it all out of her, and she stared blankly at the Stormcasts. The Lord-Vigilant hadn't moved, except to pick up his helm before the chair beneath it had blown away. His face was impassive, and on the other side of the room the Lord-Terminos stood still as ever.

148

'Will you burn me for this?' she asked dully, not really caring.

'Of course not,' Morgen said. 'I told you, we need you.' She pulled an intact chair out of the wreckage, set it near the Lord-Vigilant and sat. 'We need your help, Sevora. Corus Stormshield is a Reclusian. He contains within him a spark of Sigmar's divine might, granted him for his heroic sacrifice in life. A sacrifice that saved your great-grandmother, a noble deed that should not be reduced because of the evil of others. What happened to your family was a crime, but it was not your great-grandfather's crime.'

'I don't care.'

'I know.' Morgen reached out a hand, and Peace walked over to her, letting her pet the black feathers of his neck. 'But you are going to have to care, and that's a terrible thing. Look at Corus. Whatever happened to him, I can tell you one thing that I know is true – it happened because he cared. This world is a terrible place, and caring for anything in it can break anyone. But without caring… well, that is why this world is a terrible place.'

'So you won't kill me because you want me to care,' Sevora said. 'To care for a man I know nothing about, except that he has my dead brother's eyes. I hope you're ready to wait.'

'We are immortal,' Morgen said. 'It grants us some patience. But we don't have all the time in the world. Corus especially. So please, think it through. Think about what I said. Think about what you want, what you've always truly, honestly wanted, and I think you will understand what he needs, and what you need.'

Sevora frowned at the floor, then turned, walking out the now empty door. 'I need you all to go to Nagash's deepest hell,' she whispered, slipping into the dark. Did they hear? She didn't know. Didn't care. But Morgen spoke one last time, her words rolling down the hall.

'Sevora Cinis. Memorian. Do not allow space for the delusion that there is no hope. Believe in something better. For you. For

Corus. For all the realms. Because we all need all the hope we can get.'

Outside in the courtyard the Reclusians were still sparring. Sevora sat watching them without seeing them.

She'd taken the first door she'd found, and of course it spilled her here, right where the clack and clatter of weapons and armour was loudest. Sevora didn't want to go back in, though. Instead she walked down the wall, to put space between her and the Memorians who were standing and watching the Stormcasts spar, and dropped down onto the hard stone, back against the wall. She pulled out her knife and rubbed it between her fingers, the metal worn and familiar. Reassuring. The only reassuring thing within these walls. Still holding it, she leaned her head back and closed her eyes.

It didn't matter; she knew exactly where Corus was. Sevora could have pointed the knife straight at him without lifting her head or opening her eyes. She knew he was coming towards her, even before she heard his boots against the stone, the click of his armour against the wall as he sat down beside her.

Before she smelled him.

'I didn't know you sweated,' she said.

'Why wouldn't we?' Corus said. 'We bleed.'

'But you don't die,' she said. 'You were forged in the heavens, immortal. I don't think of you doing mortal things. You shouldn't sweat.' She turned her knife in her fingers, its metal cool in her hands. 'It's not right. You're not right. Nothing is right.'

'Yes,' he said with perfect conviction. Not mocking her. Agreeing with her.

They sat in silence for a while, then Sevora eventually opened her eyes. She could see him on the edge of her vision, a giant with her brother's eyes, his lips shaping the words of a prayer as he stared at the sky above. She thought about getting up and leaving, but there was nowhere to go in this ruin.

There was nowhere to go in her life.

'That's a work knife. Not a fighting knife.' Corus had finished his silent prayer, and was watching her spin the blade through her fingers. The movement was awkward, even though she'd done it so many times, because the balance was bad. 'But you've fought with it. You have the scars. Is it still touch blades and ten back?'

'Still,' she said. 'You've heard about Warren fighting.'

'Heard?' Corus leaned forward and grabbed his gauntlets, sliding them off. He held out his huge hands – then made a disgusted noise and shook his head. 'I keep forgetting.'

The backs of his hands were thick with muscle, powerful, and smooth. Unlike Sevora's, they were free of scars.

'You don't have scars because you were reborn,' Sevora said. 'Remade.' She finally looked at his face. 'You used to?'

'So many.' He flexed his hands, frowning at them.

'You were from the Warrens?'

'You didn't know that?' he asked.

'No,' she said. 'You were a minister of Sigmar. I thought...' Sevora hadn't really thought anything about where he'd come from. 'I thought you were from up the spire. From in the light.'

'No,' he said. 'I was a Warren brat. Orphaned when I was six. I survived by being a terrible little bastard, thieving and fighting. Until I was around your age and took a knife to the gut. The wound infected, and I prayed to Sigmar that if I survived I would serve him. When I didn't die, I went to his temple and... well, some years passed before I learned to act properly. But eventually I did, and I was made a minister. And I found a wife, and we started a family.' He looked at her, and there was a deep longing in his lightning-marked eyes. 'What was your family like?'

'My family,' she said, stilling the knife in her hands, staring at its blade. 'The only good thing my mother Siki did for me was not strangling me and my brother at birth. A choice she told us often that she regretted. She did leave us to die, but my grandmother saved us and raised us, until she died of tunnel cough. We almost died again, but then our father found us, starving.' She turned the blade slowly in her hands, staring at her warped reflection. Neither she nor her brother resembled their father. 'He'd been in and out of our lives before. He had other women, other children, to keep him busy. But for some reason he decided to care for us. Feed us. Teach us the Warrens, how to steal, how to cheat at cards and dice, how to fight with knives. And then when we were ten, he was murdered, and I took his knife.'

'Sevora. I'm sorry.' He sounded it, sorry to the bone. 'My family, my children. I wanted something so different for them than what I had.'

Sevora gave a bitter laugh. 'Then you should have simply died, Corus. Instead, you martyred yourself and saved your daughter, but the life she had was the same one you grew up with. If not worse.' She looked at him. 'Did you know? Did you know that Aika lived? Did you know that your daughter grew up in darkness? That your grandchildren did? That I did?'

Cursed. Gods, maybe her mother was right. Maybe her family was cursed to live in the Warrens, in the dark, and that trying to fight it led to what had happened to Corus. To her.

'I don't know,' he said. 'I only remember my mortal life, and nothing else. I don't know if I knew about Aika's fate. Or yours.' His great hands, so smooth despite the violence they were clearly capable of, so different to her thin, small ones, marked with a map of scars, balled into fists. 'I don't remember.'

'Of course not,' she said, and then they sat in silence beside each other, until somewhere a bell began to ring, over and over, and all the Reclusians stopped their sparring as the ravens exploded out overhead, wheeling and calling out an alarm that mixed with the deep, tolling sound.

'What is it?' Sevora asked.

'I heard bells like that at the Shining Citadel,' Corus said, standing. 'They are a call to arms.' A shadow passed over Corus' eyes. 'Rookenval is going to war.'

CHAPTER NINE

THE HALT

The darkness seethed around Amon, and there were no stars.

Dead trees surrounded him, clutching at the empty sky with limbs warped by the poison that filled the air, the smoke that ate light and skin and lungs. Things staggered through the trees, ridge wolves and deer, cave bears and elk, all of them twisted and shambling, their flesh sliding off their bones, exposing the claws and teeth of the things slithering behind their ribcages. The Astral Templar pulled his weapons, holding them out as he watched the terrible things move slowly closer – then lowered them.

A dream. A dream, because how else could he be wrapped in darkness, but seeing all of this horror so clear?

Dreams. Nightmares. More and more, every night. When he was a mortal, Amon Solus' sleep had almost never been troubled with dreams. They came even less frequently after he'd been Reforged. Now, after dropping into the smoke, they came every night. Dreams of fighting, dreams of failing. He didn't like them. Dreams were traps, and even when he knew they weren't real, they wouldn't let him go.

Amon hated dreams, and especially nightmares.

Around him, the animals had changed. They were people now, soldiers dressed in the uniforms of the Golden Lions, but they were still hideous, their too-soft skin tearing open to show the monsters writhing within them, nests of rats with no fur, their fleshy bodies wet and gleaming like maggots, their huge eyes sewn shut above puckering mouths full of sharp teeth. The soldiers were moving closer, weeping as they came, tears of water and blood and bile and pus. Tears of anger and sorrow, tears that dribbled down their ruined skin and fell on the weapons they carried in their hands. Weapons they lifted as they shambled forward, the terrible rat-things clawing their way out of their bellies as they moved.

'Nightmare,' he said, waiting for it to be over. 'Not real.'

The rats fell from the soldiers' bodies, slicked with blood. They grew in instants, became skaven with sewn-shut eyes and bloody hides. The ratmen reached out and caught the tattered skins of the soldiers they had grown in and pulled. The mortals stumbled and fell as their skin tore off in long sheets, which the skaven wrapped around themselves in red, red robes. Around their claws looped chain whips made of vertebrae and finger bones.

They stepped forward, their gory weapons spinning around them, and they hissed.

Shhhh.

Amon gritted his teeth. Usually he could force the dream to change, or better yet to dissolve away into nothing, but not this time. This time he had to watch as the skaven cast out their chain whips, not at him but high into the air, and when those bony chains came down they were wrapped around General Kant, her armour smashed, her face a sheet of blood, both eyes gone. Held up like a marionette, her body jerked, head rolling. Her mouth opened, letting out a thick flood of blood clotted around broken teeth.

'They broke us, as they broke the wall.' Her voice was a whisper of pain. 'As they broke the realm. As they broke the heavens!' Her voice rose to a shriek at the end, and the skaven hissed and jerked the handles of their chain whips, ripping the general apart. Blood fell like rain, but every drop exploded when it touched the smoke, and the sky was full of fire and blood, until it was gone. And then there was nothing but an arch of darkness over Amon. A darkness beginning to break. There was light there now, pinpricks of it slowly growing. Emerald light. Poisonous light. Terrible, nauseating light, stars of venom, constellations of infection filling the sky.

'I did that.' The voice was soft beside him, and Amon turned and there he was. Brevin Fortis, Lord-Ordinator of the Hallowed Knights, staring at the ruined sky. 'I broke the Halt for them. I let them through.' The Stormcast shook his head, and Amon could see that he was split, a line running down his face, his body. On one side he was flesh and armour, and on the other simply darkness, a shadow somehow given shape and detail and life. A shadow dotted with motes of green, like the sky stretched over them. 'I let them through, but you let them have me, Amon.'

The shadow side of Brevin was growing, sending out tendrils into his living half. They ate into the polished silver of his sigmarite, into his skin. Black swirled, like blood dropped into water, and overtook the Lord-Ordinator, faster and faster. 'Your hunt was to find me, Amon,' Brevin said, his voice growing harsh, distant, like a whisper of wind across jagged rocks. 'To find me and bring me home. But you haven't, have you?' The last bits of colour vanished from Brevin; he was just a shadow now, marred with green. 'You failed your hunt, you failed Sigmar, and you failed the realms. You failed, Knight-Questor.' Brevin was growing, his shade becoming the size of an ogor, a gargant, towering over Amon, blending with the poison sky. 'Failed. Failed. Failed…'

The word rolled through Amon's head, loud as thunder, filling him, and then beneath it, another voice. Uncertain and mortal.

'Lord Amon. Knight-Questor?'

He opened his eyes, and the ceiling above him was as black and empty as the sky in his dreams, before it had been infected by the green stars. Not a dream, he thought, and then he was up, out of his bed and standing in the middle of his small room. At its door, a soldier flinched back, almost running. But he stayed just long enough to speak.

'The day fails, Lord Amon. You wanted us to wake you.' Then the man was gone, fleeing into the growing shadows of dusk. Amon was awake.

Though it felt like sleep had barely touched him.

The stars were bright overhead, and the fiery moon Thaquia was spilling its ruddy light over the realm, but the light of the heavens couldn't touch the darkness that seethed below Amon. Standing on the top of the Halt, Amon paused his careful examination of the harness that was buckled over his armour and watched as a flicker of green ran through the smoke. Like the shadow in his dream.

'Ready?' General Kant asked, and her voice broke him from his dark reverie.

Amon jerked one last strap tight and nodded. He looked at Kant, and for a moment saw her as she'd been in his nightmare, eyes gone, face a mask of blood. He shook his head, and the leader of the Golden Lions 27th Regiment was back to looking as she always looked, haggard and worn, her mouth a line of bitter determination. She looked better than most of her soldiers. The churning smoke and its accompanying nightmares took a greater toll every day. It was a constant wearing down of the soul, and the mortals were breaking.

'We lost five more last night,' Kant said quietly. 'Two to the skaven. I don't know how they're getting onto the wall – we've put lanterns up everywhere, but it seems they only need the small-est shadow to hide in. The other three ran.' She frowned, and the exhaustion in her eyes was driven away by anger. 'I can't even send anyone to bring them back, because I fear they wouldn't come back either.'

Amon listened without speaking. He had nothing to say, he was just waiting until–

'Shadow mark!' a voice shouted. It was the name given to the green glow, the sign that the Lord-Ordinator's shadow was coming.

'Far end.' Kant pointed to where the guards were waving a torch, but Amon was already running towards it. His long legs carried him quickly across the top of the Halt, but the green glow was already closing in by the time he reached the knot of soldiers around the torch.

They were holding a heavy rope, with a hook secured on its end. Amon slipped the hook through a thick iron ring attached to the back of his harness, then jerked the rope once to make sure it was secure.

'It's coming!' one of the Golden Lions shouted, and Amon raced to the edge of the Halt and threw himself off.

Amon let the rope sizzle through his gauntlets, controlling his fall. There was a hard jerk when he hit the end, just above the smoke, and he felt a strap pop, but the harness held. He drew his weapons, standing with his boots on the Halt's face, rope holding him up, and glared at the poisonous glow of the shadow mark.

It surged in, moving at an angle away from Amon. He started to move along the wall to meet it, the rope slowing him down – until it began to move too.

They had been playing this game with the shadow of Brevin Fortis for five nights. Trying to get Amon close enough so that the light from his mace would drive the shade back, without him falling into the smoke. All while dealing with the chain whips that sometimes struck from the dark. A stupid game with ropes and harnesses and the contraptions that Kant had ordered her engineers to make, when Amon wanted to just destroy the shadow with sword and mace. But crossbow bolts simply sliced through the thing without affecting it, and even the Knight-Questor was hesitant to fight a shadow he might not be able to see or touch in that black poison.

He couldn't risk his hunt. Especially now that they knew help was coming.

The rope attached to him jerked, moving along the wall above, and Amon moved with it. The other end was fixed to a wagon full of stones, heavy enough to counter his weight, and there was a team of mules pulling it along the top of the Halt. It was a cumbersome, ridiculous arrangement, and it made Amon long for the drakes that some of the Stormcasts were allowed to fly into battle. But he didn't have a drake. He had a wagon, and mules, and a rope, and a weapon that burned with the holy light of his god. That would be enough.

The green light had almost reached the wall, and Amon was pulling at the rope, willing the mules to haul faster. He'd grown keenly aware of how close he needed to be for the light of his mace to affect the shadow, and he wasn't there yet. Amon strained against the ropes, and then the first blade flew up out of the dark at him.

The tip of the chain whip arced through the air, and Amon's sword rumbled as it moved to block the razor edge. But the blade was moving past him. A miss, he thought, but then he felt the thrum as the chain whip hit his tether. The blade nicked the rope, freeing a few strands to fray away, but then another blade struck. They were trying to make him fall or flee. Up above, the

Golden Lions fired their crossbows into the smoke, likely striking nothing, but at least it would give the skaven pause.

In the meantime, the shadow mark had surged in, coming for the wall.

Amon pressed forward, pulling the rope tight, trying to drag the wagon faster as he swung his weapons together. An instant too late. The Halt bucked beneath his feet and Amon was spinning on the rope like a toy. But he held his weapons tight and smashed together sword and mace, bringing thunder and fire.

The smoke below rippled out, pushed away in a spinning circle. There was a hint of dark-robed figures, the eyeless skaven with their chain whips, then they were gone, fleeing the noise and the light. But in the middle of the open space, the shadow remained. Brevin's shadow, warpstone pendant hanging around its neck, its green colour shimmering through the shade. The thing looked up at Amon with one eye, pointed its hammer at him and then pulled it back, getting ready to swing at the wall again. Amon moved lower, so he was right above the shadow, and let the light of his torch blaze.

The shade had always fled when he'd come this close before. Amon could see that it was disintegrating under the storm of light, its darkness flaking away like ash and dissolving into smoke. But tonight it wasn't retreating. The shadow pulled back its hammer and struck again, slamming the blow into the same spot it had struck before, making the quartz crack as the wall shuddered. Amon strained to hold the mace closer, but the shadow was resisting. It was dissolving, but not fast enough, and it swung the hammer back to strike again.

Sheathing his sword, Amon ripped at the buckles of his harness, breaking them. Suddenly he was free, and he fell. Fell until his free hand caught hold of a broken strap, letting him hang so low his legs would have been covered by the smoke if it hadn't been driven back. He thrust out his mace, and the fire in its head was only a few scant yards from the shadow.

The light blasted into the thing. The great hammer it swung towards the wall dissolved, along with part of one arm. It turned its face up at him, mouth opening into a wordless howl, and Amon could see its head melting away too. The shade finally turned and ran then, the green stone around its neck glowing through the smoke until it was gone.

'It grows stronger. Fights longer and does more damage each time.' Amon set down his cup, the water gone, and stared at the shadows shifting across the blank stone walls of the empty guardroom. These shadows were normal, the simple blockage of the lantern light by him and General Kant, but in them he could see the Lord-Ordinator's malignant shade.

'The Halt is huge,' Kant answered. 'And still healing, if slowly. That thing, whatever it is, can't bring the entire fortress down with a hammer. Can it?'

There was a kind of exhausted desperation in that question. It was why she had brought him here, after the shadow mark disappeared, so that her soldiers wouldn't see the crack in her certainty. Or the way Amon frowned at the question.

'There is a plan to this,' Amon said. 'I don't know the how of it, except that it hinges somehow on Brevin and his connection to the Halt. But I do know the skaven mean to bring this wall down, with that shade and its hammer.'

'And if they plan that...' The general frowned at the map that was spread out across a table, beneath the one lantern that lit the room. 'That means there's something waiting out there in that smoke. An army, most likely, an army of skaven waiting to flood through the Warrun and pour out into the Great Parch. It's the only thing that makes sense. Else why all this? Why break our spirits, and take Brevin? Bad as that is, there's more that we can't see, hidden behind that smoke. Something terrible is happening out there, beyond the Adamantine Chain, and I can't see it. But I know, I know whatever it is it's going to be turned on us soon. It won't simply be assassins, picking off a guard or two in the night.'

'No,' Amon said. 'When the skaven come at you, they come as a flood. There's only one rule to them. There are always more. I'm sure you're right, there is an army out there, and if this wall does fall it'll race through this valley and out into the plains, and then...'

Then there were so many targets, he had no idea where and how to defend them. This was the choking point. The place to stop whatever was coming. The Halt must hold, and the key to that, he was sure, was Brevin. That was why Sigmar had set him this hunt. That was why he had to finish it. As soon as he could.

'We need the Ruination Chamber.'

'Rookenval's Hallowed Knights.' She looked at him, her face skull-like in the lantern's glow. 'The Stormcast Eternals are our best hope, and I'll be grateful to see them. But I've never heard of the Ruination Chamber. Why do you say that we need them specifically, Knight-Questor? And why were you so hesitant to send for them?'

'Because I fear them,' he said. *Fear the shadow of what you trust! Trust the shadow of what you fear!* Yes, these last nights he had learned to fear the shadow of Brevin, a Hallowed Knight, a Lord-Ordinator. Would he learn to trust the Ruination Chamber so quickly?

'Fear them?' Kant's eyes widened. 'I've watched you throw yourself into that sea of poison to fight that shadow thing. Your bravery seems unbounded. What is it about your own kind that makes you fear? Are they not like you?'

'No, and yes. They are too much like what I could be.' Amon shook his head. It was hard to talk about, but in his brief, terrible time at the Halt he had grown to respect the general. She had a solid pragmatism about her that he could understand, could respect, so he pushed through his reticence and explained. 'The process of being Reforged is not always perfect. Sometimes bits of our souls, bits of ourselves, are lost. We can find ourselves reduced as we are remade.'

Reduced. What was the name of his father? What did his mother look like? He had a brother, but did he have a sister? Amon didn't know. He had died only once after being made an Astral Templar. Only once, and he had lost all that. 'We have a way to fight it, but some of us lost too much before that technique was mastered. Or could not make it work. Every time they are Reforged, they are less and less themselves. This is why I fear them. Because they are what I fear I will someday become. They are the victims of the curse that stalks all the Stormcast Eternals. They are…'

Amon trailed off. Self-control. Self-discipline. These were the qualities he valued most, both as a mortal and a Stormcast Eternal. He didn't understand other people, what they did or why, but he could understand himself. He could control himself. But then he was Reforged, and the brutal truth came out. Despite holding himself in the Storm's Eye, he'd still lost parts of his past. Parts of him. He'd lost control, and every time he died, he'd likely lose more. Until he'd lost everything, and was nothing.

It was something he hated thinking about. Why he hated the idea of asking for help from the Ruination Chamber. But he would wield whatever weapon he must to finish the hunt.

'Those of the Ruination Chamber may be reduced, but they are also strong,' he continued. 'They are some of the oldest and most experienced of us. Fell fighters, they can often match two to three other Stormcasts from a different chamber. And the lessening of their souls makes it hard for magic, especially the corrupt magic of Chaos, to grip them. They can smash their way through spells that would strip flesh and soul from a mortal. They are the strongest of us, even though they are the ones that suffer the most.'

'Then why do they not fight more?' Kant asked.

'Because we hope to draw them back,' Amon answered. 'So that they can live and fight on, instead of falling into dissolution. Every fight risks their loss, forever.'

'Like a mortal, then?' she said, and the exhaustion on her face gave way for a moment to a wry smile. Amon didn't know how to answer that, so he stayed silent, but she shook her head. 'I don't envy you, Stormcast. I didn't before I heard about your curse, and I definitely don't after. I've spent my whole life fighting. I don't want to come back from death just to fight some more. No offence, Astral Templar.'

'None taken.' He could understand that sentiment. Sometimes. But now he wanted nothing more than to fight. To break out of this place and find Brevin. To end this hunt, and bring him home.

Outside there was a peal of the morning bell, the sound that marked the dawn.

'I need to see what losses this night has brought us.' General Kant went to the door, and Amon followed. Light was spilling across the sky, setting the tips of the mountains ablaze. On the ledges around them, soldiers were moving slowly, looking exhausted even as they rose from what should have been their rest. 'Gods help us,' she said, watching them. 'Do you think your cursed hope will come today? Sigmar grant it, because I don't think–'

She cut off when a bird, huge and black, landed on the curved lintel of the arched door and stared down at them.

'A rook,' Kant said, staring up at the bird. 'Omens of battle.'

'And of those who bring it,' Amon said. He pulled his spyglass from his belt and stared down the back of Warrun Vale, out towards the Great Parch. It was empty, but at the very limits of his sight something flickered, dark against the pale. Like black wings against a lightening sky. 'The Ruination Chamber comes.'

CHAPTER TEN

GALLOGAST

Brevin smashed his fist into the skaven's chest, but the guard only lurched back a little, baring its long teeth, and then Brevin was jerked back by the chains.

'Damn you,' he said, and it should have been a shout, but he could barely gasp. Could barely stand as the Sisseris guards forced him to stagger back into the centre of the crumbling corridor. So weak, dying by inches, but not fast enough, damn it. He'd struck out at the creature, hoping to find the handle of a chain whip, a dagger, anything he could have driven into a skaven's throat before slashing it across his own.

But he couldn't even knock one of his guards down. Sigmar, what had Skein done to him?

The first time the Grey Seer and Varus Hish had given his shadow hideous life and sent it to attack the Halt, Brevin hadn't understood. He had thought that Skein was just stripping his connection to the Heart away from him. But when his shadow had come back, when Skein had taken the flawed warpstone pendant from around its neck, that connection and all the pain that came with it had punched back into him.

With it had come a vision of the quartz crystal face of the Halt, cracking beneath the blow of a black hammer. And below the crystal, hidden deep in that great pile of basalt, the Heart. Shuddering as the hammer hit.

In that moment, choking on the pain, trying to withstand the burning acid feeling that filled his chest, Brevin had understood. The Grey Seer had drawn him out so that he could use him to weaken the Halt. To smash the quartz facing open, so the emberstone beneath was bare.

Why? Brevin wasn't sure. But he was sure of one thing. Skein thought that by doing that, he could destroy the Halt.

In that moment, chained and writhing in agony, Brevin had tried to throttle Skein again. And failed. And he'd failed every time after, when they'd dragged him out to rip his own shadow away. And so now he was reduced to this. Not striking at his enemy, but at the tool they were using to break the Halt.

Him.

'Damn me,' he muttered, and the guards jerked his chains around him and whispered 'Shhh,' and the agony bottled in his heart grew and grew.

They chained Brevin to the walls of the candelarium, stretching out the links so that he was forced to stand and project his treacherous shadow across the wall. He'd tried fighting that once, and the Sisseris guards had beat him with his own chains, whirling the links through the air like their chain whips and slamming them across his shoulders, back and hips. They did it until his muscles seized and he could barely move, then dragged him upright and used the chains to hang him in place. Broken and bleeding, still they dragged the shadow from him.

The shadow. Brevin turned his head just enough so that his one eye could see it, a black shape against the stone walls. This was the only place he could see in the dark abyss the skaven had made of this ruin, but he hated that ugly green light. Warpstone was Chaos made solid, its magic malign, corrupt, poisonous. Brevin hated its green glow, but he hated the shadow it made from him more. The shadow Skein and Varus made into a weapon.

Varus was there now. Standing in front of him, his claws clicking across the copper rods that made up the triangle that the skaven always hung between him and the blighted flame. He was moving it back and forth, adjusting it again to whatever position this foul sorcery required.

'Varus Hish,' Brevin said softly, when the skaven drew close. The ratman's ears twitched, and one bulging eye shifted towards the Lord-Ordinator. 'You know I'm going to kill you.'

'Yes-yes,' the skaven whispered, moving the corroded copper triangle a little closer. The creature's breath reeked of carrion, his splotchy fur of caustic fumes. There were burns in the fur, patches charred by fire or eaten away by corrosives, and scars on the hide beneath. But it was the scar that marred Varus' throat which always drew Brevin's eye. Neat and precise, right along the voice box. The same scar the rest of Skein's eyeless clan bore. But Varus was no Sisseris.

'He took your voice, but not your eyes.' Brevin watched as the skaven finally stopped moving the triangle, then let it go. It hung in the air, waiting. 'Is that why you serve him? So he won't take your eyes?'

'Yes,' Varus answered, in the same harsh whisper. It was the only answer, the only word Brevin had ever heard him say. The Lord-Ordinator knew little enough about skaven. Their creations were too dangerous to study, relying on warpstone and other tainted magics to work, and it was better to destroy them. But Brevin knew that some skaven clans were dedicated to the creation of their awful contraptions. He suspected that Varus belonged to one of those.

'Skryre.' The name fell out of Brevin. Days in the dark had gone by as he fought to remember that name, and failed. But suddenly it floated up from his memory. 'The Clans Skryre.'

Varus went still and tilted his head, staring at Brevin. 'Yes,' he said, and there was something to that word this time, something raw and painful. Anger, hatred, shame… It was hard for Brevin to tell, but emotions were woven into the skaven's only word, and he wondered if they were directed at the Clans Skryre, the Grey Seer, Clan Sisseris, Brevin… or maybe all of them. A mad, bitter fury flashed through Varus' eyes, bristled his fur and drew his lips back from yellow teeth. Then it was gone, the skaven turning away from Brevin as Skein slipped silently into the room.

'He has no clan,' the yellow-robed skaven said. The green light gleamed on the threads running through his eyelids, darkening them, but they still shone against Skein's grey fur. Behind him, like the seer's shadow, one of the Sisseris moved. Lisstis, recognisable by the bloody tears still running from the hollows of his eyes. He paced behind Skein as the Grey Seer approached, one clawed hand resting lightly on his chain whip.

'He is slave.' Skein looked from Varus to Brevin. 'Slave like you, storm-cursed. Cursed to serve. Forever.' The Grey Seer walked towards him, stopping just at the limit of Brevin's reach. The Lord-Ordinator's hands twitched, but Skein had played this game before. If Brevin went for him, the pain in his chest would smash him down, leaving him hanging and choking from the chains.

'Still you speak,' Skein whispered, his tail twitching behind him. 'Speak too much.' He pulled his hands out of his robe, and the bladed hooks were on his thumbs, shining green in the warpstone's light. 'Taste of immortal flesh has faded.'

The Grey Seer twitched his weapons and Brevin tensed. What

could he do? Little, but he would do something. If Skein came for his other eye, he might be able to drive one of those hooks into his brain. And then maybe the lightning strike of his soul returning to Sigmar would catch the skaven right between his empty eye sockets. But then a sound went through the chamber, like a tiny bell, and Skein turned to face Varus. The little skaven had pulled a long, thin shard of obsidian from his ragged smock, a knife blade of chipped stone. Its crude hilt was wrapped in tarnished copper wire, and from it dangled a tiny, ringing bell. The Sisseris guards twitched their ears and showed their teeth at the sound, soft as it was. Varus grabbed the bell, silencing it, then looked at Skein. The Grey Seer tapped his thumb claws together, staring at the copper-wrapped obsidian.

'Reekbite demands to speak.' Skein's whisper was a hiss. 'Impatient. Impatient.' The Grey Seer ground the razor edges of his claws together, then drew them apart with a keening hiss. Stepping away from Brevin, he folded his arms into his robe. Beneath his yellow hood, his eyeless head tilted towards Lisstis. 'Bring a smoke childe.'

The smoke childe had patches of feathers in his fur, matted with blood and dirt. His eyes were huge and devoid of anything but hate. He struggled as he was staked to the floor on the other side of the warpstone from Brevin, but his long arms had been broken, the bones jutting from his variegated hide. The Sisseris had to do little to ward off the thing's claws as they fixed it to the floor, and then they pulled away, leaving him to Skein.

The Grey Seer stood beside the childe's head. He breathed deep, then crouched just out of reach of the warped skaven's muzzle, a thing half fur and half beak, a jagged hook replacing the long incisors. 'Ill-made thing,' he breathed. 'Thing twisted out of inferior flesh. Flesh forged from dross of these light-cursed realms. Birthed by apocalypse, childe of smoke. Chaos servant. Servant of Skein.'

The thing looked at him with crazed, unblinking eyes and snapped, trying to reach him with his malformed mouth. When he couldn't, he shrieked, a sound that filled the candelarium and made even Brevin wince. The guards hissed, and Skein flattened his ears.

'Servant. Serve in silence.' Skein's hand flashed out, and the claw on his thumb punched into the thing's throat, cutting off another scream as it began. The childe choked and thrashed, a trickle of blood flowing down feathers and fur, and Skein reached a claw out behind him, palm up, waiting.

Varus moved forward, the knife shard of obsidian gripped in his hand. The black stone glinted, green light fractured by its sharp edges, and Brevin watched the skaven hesitate for just a moment. *Strike,* he thought, but beside the Grey Seer, Lisstis tilted his head and moved his claws on the handle of his chain whip. Varus stopped and slowly turned the blade in his hand, laying the copper-wrapped handle into Skein's palm. Then he backed away, claws raised placatingly.

Coward. There was anger in Brevin, but not enough. Not like there should have been. He was weak, and getting weaker, but he began slowly shifting his balance, pulling at his chains to conceal his purpose, while Skein continued his foul craft.

'Reekbite.' The Grey Seer raised the obsidian shard, its bell silent. 'Clawlord Reekbite, hear!' Skein brought the blade down, driving its point slowly into the edge of one of the smoke childe's round eyes, digging it past the glaring gaze. The thing twisted and choked, trying to make noise as Skein dug the obsidian point deeper. There was an ugly wet crunch as the blade dug through the back of the eye socket, and Skein continued pressing forward until the blade reached the brain. The childe convulsed, blood and yellow fluid leaking out around Skein's hand, slicking the hilt of the crude knife, running down to touch the bell.

The little bell tolled then, at a higher pitch than it had earlier, a note that rose higher and higher until Brevin couldn't hear it any more. The skaven could though, and the Sisseris guards flattened their ears and hunched. Then they relaxed. The note had finally stopped, Brevin suspected. But now the blade began to glow.

It was a dull green light, and at first it could have been a reflection of the warpstone. But the glow intensified as more of the smoke childe's gore spilled over the knife. The noxious fluids began to sizzle, as if the obsidian were hot, though it did not burn Skein. Soon the blade was smoking, black tendrils rising from it. Skein watched them, and carefully twisted the knife so that more gore ran down the blade, ignoring the writhing of the childe.

Dark smoke rose, hitting the curved dome of the ceiling. It rolled over itself, not diffusing, pulling in on itself instead, until it looked almost solid, as dense as the obsidian blade that had birthed it. The cloud stretched and pulled, like clay moulded by invisible hands, until it had taken the shape of a head. A skaven's head, formed in black and outlined in green, hideously like Brevin's shadow when the Grey Seer brought it to life.

The shadow skaven wore a helm with horns, sharp and angled back over his head. The helm curved around his scarred, tattered ears and flared out around his neck, where metal plates hung that were marked with intricate, hideous charms. A scar ran up the right side of his muzzle and across his right eye, which was ablaze with green flame. His teeth were long, the incisors filed into fangs, and the whiskers around that mouth were thick and heavy, more like the barbs of a catfish than the thin hairs of a rat.

'Skein.' The mouth of the skaven moved, and the name came out on a wisp of smoke that curled and frayed apart in green-tinged air. 'We march.' The voice was deep, guttural, a growl roughly shaped into words. 'We march, with teeth and claw and blade. The smoke thins, the time of tearing is done. Now is the time-time to *reap.'* The smoke suddenly swirled, dissolving for a moment into an indistinct mass, except for the green flame of the right eye. Then it snapped back into shape, larger, the head looming over the Grey Seer. *'Have you cleared the path?'*

'The wall weakens, Clawlord,' Skein answered.

'Weakened is not clear-clear.' The head dissolved again, leaving the baleful eye, then re-formed. Larger again, more diffuse but filling the dome of the candelarium. *'Destroy the wall. Clear the path for hordes unending. Or see-see suffering unending, eyeless one.'*

The Clawlord's head frayed apart, and there was just that one flaming eye, shining hideous green. Its light filled the room to blinding as Reekbite roared.

'Clear-clear the path!'

The words rumbled through the room, and the Sisseris covered their ears and hissed.

Then the eye closed and there was nothing but smoke and echoes.

'Other clans threaten death,' Skein whispered, his voice barely heard through the reverberations of the Clawlord's order. 'Death to other clans.' Below him, the smoke childe choked and convulsed, and the Grey Seer shoved the obsidian shard deeper, making the thing quiver, then finally go still. Skein wrenched out the obsidian shard and the childe's eye. Biting into the eye, he turned to Brevin.

'Storm-cursed. Cursed man. Enough. Tonight your dark shatters the light. Light breaks, crystal on wall breaks. Emberstone exposed, and when warpstone touches...' Skein touched the flawed warpstone pendant hanging around his neck. 'Fire. Smoke. Destruction. All paths cleared. For Reekbite, and for Clan Sisseris.' He reached for the corroded green triangle, still hanging in the air, and Varus came forward, reaching too, and at their touch the film of green stretched through it, focusing the light of the green flame on Brevin.

When warpstone touches...

An image filled Brevin's mind, of that night when the smoke came. Of those flashes of red and green. Sigmar save him, the skaven had somehow exposed deposits of emberstone from deep in the realm, and brought them into contact with warpstone. When those two volatile elements had touched... Fire. Smoke. Destruction. Skein's plan fell into place. The Grey Seer was using Brevin's connection to the Heart both to smash at the quartz sheath on the Halt's face and to keep it from healing back. So that the veins of emberstone beneath would be exposed, and Brevin's shadow could touch that warpstone pendant to them. And cause a reaction that would tear the Halt apart.

That understanding swept through the Lord-Ordinator as the unclean heat of the warpstone flowing through the green film of the triangle touched him. With a shout that made the eyeless skaven snarl, Brevin threw himself against the chains with everything he had left. The steel shuddered, but did not break, and with the last of his ebbing strength Brevin dropped, pulling himself down, trying to break his own neck on the iron collar that held him, but all he got was pain as his muscles wrenched and he bit his tongue.

'Your weak god made you strong,' Skein whispered, staring at him through the filthy green film that stretched across the triangle. 'Strength for us to use.'

Brevin snarled and pulled up his feet, hoping he would be strangled on the collar's rough edge, but Skein waved a claw and the Sisseris jammed a rack beneath his arms, a support that kept him from falling and choking, and all he could do was watch as his shadow grew dark on the wall behind him. Hang there, as the pain in his chest grew until it was ripped away and he was left feeling nothing but the empty chill of defeat.

CHAPTER ELEVEN

THE HALT

'Why us?' Sevora asked, staring at the massive wall that rose before them. It was made of the same dark rock as Rookenval's broken tower, and it loomed over the ruined city that spread around them.

'Because we are the last hope.' Morgen wasn't driving a wagon this time. She was walking, as were the rest of the Stormcasts. They were moving at a deceptively easy pace which had eaten up many miles along the foothills of the Adamantine Chain. They'd given Sevora a mare to ride, chosen from the stables hidden beneath the trees of Rookenval's island, a gentle beast that still made her nervous. Even perched upon the horse, Sevora was lost in the Lord-Veritant's shadow.

'I thought you were a refuge. A place where the lost could find themselves again.' Sevora looked ahead to where Corus was marching with the other Reclusians. When she did, his helm turned, his lightning-haunted eyes looking back at her. She looked away. *Hope for something better.* What was better? A life where all her choices weren't taken away?

Hope is a lie.

'We are,' Morgen said. 'When we can be. But we are Stormcast Eternals. Made by Sigmar to defend the Mortal Realms against destruction, death, and daemon. We are weapon and shield, and we will be used.'

'No matter your condition?' Sevora asked.

Morgen frowned. 'Reclusians are not helpless, broken things. You've seen your great-grandfather spar. They are in some ways the strongest of us.'

'Gods, don't,' Sevora said.

'Don't what?'

'Don't make me have this fight.'

Sevora looked at the line of Reclusians that stretched in front of her. Fifty warriors in darkened silver armour, their cloaks marked with symbols like tiny stars. Their Memorians were moving beside them, childlike figures despite their own sombre clothes. Besides Morgen there were two more Lord-Veritants, moving through the Reclusians with their torches and their gryph-crows, searching souls for signs of dissolution. Over them, grey wings beat. Jocanan, free from her roost in the tower and her endless painting, circled by the ravens that had followed them when they had left the broken tower. And at the end of their line, solemn and alone, the Lord-Terminos. So few and so many at the same time, and Morgen was right, they did look deadly. But that was because she couldn't see their eyes.

'You said I didn't want to care. You were right.' Sevora looked at the wall they called the Halt, a pile of black basalt. It was as if the great tower at Rookenval had fallen across this pass, blocking it. 'I don't want to care about any of you. About Corus.'

'But you do care about broken things,' she said. 'Like your brother.'

Sevora gritted her teeth. 'Do you think comparing Corus to

Yevin is going to help? I was getting ready to walk away from my brother. I practically killed him.'

'You didn't kill him. You just didn't save him.' Morgen looked at her, and for the first time Sevora saw something in her eyes like the pain and loss in the Reclusians. 'I know the difference. You need to know it too. Before you lose him.'

'I don't care about losing him!' Sevora snapped. 'I never had him! He was dead long before I was born. When he was reborn, he was out there somewhere fighting while his family was suffering. Dying.' Wind whipped around her, hot on her skin, tiny sparks riding it. 'I don't want to care about someone who never cared about me. If I want to care about something broken, maybe I'll care about myself.'

'Have you ever considered that the best way to do that might be to talk to someone who cares about you?' Morgen asked.

'You, Lord-Veritant? You care about me, the Memorian who won't do as they're told?' The wind gusted out at Morgen and ruffled Peace's feathers. The gryph-crow croaked in annoyance as Morgen shook her head.

'No,' she said, stroking Peace's feathers back into place. 'I want to care about you, the way Sigmar cares about us all. But I am no god. I am still human, flawed in my way, and you are no fool. You can see that. What you refuse to see is that Corus already cares for you. You are all that is left of his family. The only thing he ever really wanted.'

Sevora looked away from her, glaring up the line at where Corus marched. His head turned again, looking back at her, and she closed her eyes. Part of her wanted, desperately, to tell the demigod walking beside her to shut up. Maybe half-hoping that Morgen would kill her for her impertinence. But she gritted her teeth and kept her mouth shut. When she opened her eyes again, she could see Avil Tawn, Dreskir's Memorian, looking back at her with disapproving eyes. She made a rude gesture at him, and felt better when he turned away, frowning. But when she saw Morgen looking at her with those calm, all-seeing eyes, she felt childish and ashamed and had to look away.

Sevora stood atop the Halt and stared down at the smoke pooling against its base. It was like looking down from the back wall in Rookenval, a great plunge of nothing ending in darkness. That view gave her vertigo. This one made her nauseous in a completely different way.

'It's poison,' she muttered to herself. A vast sea of poison, stretching down the pass and covering the lands beyond as far as she could see. A few trees stuck out of the dark cloud, but their tops were dead and no birds perched there. The ravens that had accompanied them sat on the massive wall but did not cross out over the smoke. They stared at it with their dark eyes and grumbled to themselves, like old men watching a storm roll in.

'What in all the hells of Shyish are we supposed to do?' Sevora backed away from the parapet. 'Are the Reclusians supposed to go to battle with that?' She had kept her voice low, but she still saw one of the guards watching her. A Golden Lion, from the city of Hammerhal Aqsha. A long way from home, but apparently they guarded this forgotten frontier. The soldiers should have looked smart in their pretty uniforms, but instead every one of them looked sick, exhausted. The Golden Lions had watched the Stormcasts, and despite what Morgen had said, the mortal soldiers didn't act like they were seeing their last hope arrive.

The looked like they had already seen their hope die.

Sevora turned away from the man and stared down the wall. Morgen, the other Lord-Veritants, and the Lord-Terminos had vanished into one of the arched doorways built into the back side of the Halt, meeting with the leaders of this place, leaving the rest of the Reclusians and their Memorians to roam the top of the massive wall. They stood impassively in little groups, clusters of dark silver armour and robes like giant corvids, waiting. Twenty yards from her, Corus stood beside the parapet, looking down at the smoke. He had held that position since they got to the top of the wall, and she wondered what he saw in that roiling mass of darkness.

Images from his life? From his death?

Whatever he saw, it was enough to keep him from looking back over his shoulder at her for once, so she finally let herself stare at him. Corus was a myth, the central character in the stories she'd heard when she was a child. Siki had only told them when she was intoxicated, and the stories had been dark, bitter things, but even in them, Corus had been a hero. The man who had saved their family from murder and then was betrayed, by the cult and Whitefire Court. So he'd come to stand for the father she'd lost, for the heroes that other people spoke of in reverent tones, for the gods that others prayed to, a distant, perfect thing. Now here he was in the flesh, and he was everything and nothing like she thought. A giant figure, familiar but alien, human but divine, heroic but broken.

He was a man, hungry to speak to her, to build the family with her he had always wanted in his mortal life. He was a man with her brother's eyes, the only person she had ever trusted. He was a man who needed her, according to a woman who had been judged worthy by a god. And what was she?

Angry. Alone. Petulant.

That last thought made her angrier, but it also gnawed at her. Everything in her life had gone wrong, everything had broken, but staring at this smoke, she was beginning to think that all that destruction was larger than her. It wasn't just her life falling into ruins now. It was everything.

The Golden Lions at the top of the stairs came to attention, and Sevora pushed aside those thoughts to watch Morgen and the others step out onto the top of the Halt. When the Lord-Vigilant had stood before the Reclusians in the bleak shadow of Rookenval and told them that they were summoned, he had split them into two groups, for the tower had received two messages. One by messenger-bird from Hallowheart, one by some other means from the Halt. Avarin Day was taking the larger portion of his Reclusians to battle in some god-forsaken part of the Great Parch. The rest, a mere twenty or so, he'd sent here, naming Morgen Light their leader. But he trusted they would soon be joined by more of their Stormcast brethren who had picked up a summons in the Parch.

The Lord-Veritant walked to the edge of the wall with the Golden Lions' leader, General Kant, the two of them staring at the smoke, talking in low voices. Making plans to assault the vapour? Sevora frowned at them, then finally gave up and walked over to the edge of the wall to Corus.

'What's going on?' she asked.

'I can't hear everything. But they're discussing attacks which occur each night. Something involving the Lord-Ordinator who was here. They're planning to put a stop to them.' He looked back at the smoke. 'Which means we won't be going into that until at least tomorrow.'

'That's poison,' she said. A shimmer of green flickered through it, and Sevora's stomach turned.

'It is,' he agreed. He looked to her. 'I talked to the others on the road. I haven't fought with the Ruination Chamber before, and I need to know how they fight. One of the things they told me is that their Memorians join them in battle. They are deemed as necessary then as during meditation and prayer.'

'Deemed necessary,' Sevora said flatly. 'So when the Reclusians wade into that poison to fight whatever lurks in it, they will be bringing with them Avil Tawn.' She pointed towards Dreskir Skyvault's Memorian. The pudgy, middle-aged man was still trying to look serious, pious, purposeful, but instead he looked ridiculous in his black raven-marked robes, like a grocer who'd changed clothes with a sorcerer. 'Because he is necessary.'

'They will,' he answered.

'And that means me too, doesn't it?' Sevora looked down at herself. Did she look any less ridiculous in her robes than Avil? Not really, not when compared to her great-grandfather. All the Memorians, even the ones in arms and armour, were laughable compared to the Reclusians.

'I will protect you,' Corus said.

'You will protect me.' She wanted to rage, wanted to push Corus off this wall into the darkness, walk back to Hallowheart and blow the Whitefire Court off the top of the spire in a surge of flux-touched magic that would shatter the whole Shining Abyss. She wanted to close her eyes and open them and find herself with Yevin in the Warrens, stealing food and laughing as they ran, alive and hungry and free. But she couldn't do any of that, and she couldn't get angry. No wind whipped around her, no bright shining rage filled her. Everything was falling apart, and what was here to check it but the Ruination Chamber, broken immortals and their useless mortal minders.

Hope when hope was dying.

Hope is a lie.

Sevora stared out at the blighted landscape that lay on the other side of the wall, the churning dark and the dying trees, all those words clashing in her head, 'You've died before, Corus. Would it be better to choke to death in that smoke, or get gutted by whatever is hiding beneath it?'

'You won't choke,' Corus said. 'Memorians aren't fodder, to be thrown away. We need you. We will protect you. We won't let you wade into that poison and die, and we won't let the skaven hurt you.'

'Skaven?' She'd heard the name before. Some kind of monster the miners fought in the Shimmering Abyss sometimes. But she couldn't remember what they were, daemon or dead or something else.

'Chaos worshippers.' For once there was something hard in Corus' voice. An edge of anger, but from him it seemed dangerous, the lightning in his eyes growing brighter. 'Things that walk like men but are shaped like rats.'

'Rats,' she said. 'Of course.' Rats and ravens. Yellow teeth. Sevora remembered the thing that had burst out of her brother's body, remembered its teeth and claws and the way it had tried to rise up on its rear legs before she and Siki had cut it down. A shudder went through her before she could hide it.

'Morgen told me about what your brother said.'

'Morgen talks too much,' she said. He didn't answer, just waited in silence until she spoke again. 'She didn't tell you how he died. Something bit him. Infected him, and then something grew inside him, and when my mother Siki slit his throat it came climbing out. A rat, with yellow teeth, and it carved its way out of him and tried to kill me.'

'Your mother slit... Sevora, what happened?' he asked.

There was such concern in his voice, such genuine horror she wanted to draw her father's knife and stab him. But she just shook her head.

'It doesn't matter,' she said. 'I just told you because if you want to protect me, here's how you can do it. If one of those things bites me, and I get infected like that... then Memorian or not, you cut my damn head off before one of those things starts gnawing out my guts.'

* * *

The Halt was quiet when night fell.

The wall was lit by lanterns, and the glow of the quartz on its face. It was light enough for Sevora to see all the way up and down it, to see the guards peering out into the dark with frightened eyes, to see the Stormcast named Amon Solus making himself ready. He wore armour that was the purple of the sky in deep twilight, with a cloak that was as dark as the Reclusians. He was taller than most of the other Stormcasts, but leaner, the sharp bones of his face pronounced beneath his tanned skin. He wore no helm, just a circlet of sigmarite that bound back his long black hair, and his green eyes were hard as he pulled a leather harness over his armour.

'What is a Knight-Questor?' she asked Corus.

'They can be many things,' her great-grandfather said. He'd been careful all that afternoon, speaking only when spoken to, not getting too close. Treating her like a skittish animal he was trying to tame. It was annoyingly close to the truth, when Sevora thought about it. But she'd stayed near him. She didn't know this place, didn't like it, and what else could she do? She might as well stay with him and at least learn a few things before she was dragged off to some ugly death. 'They are servants of Sigmar, as we all are,' he continued. 'But more directly. He sends them on quests, to learn things, to find people or objects, or to slay a certain foe.'

'Assassins.'

'Sometimes,' he said. 'But they are more generally useful than that. But Amon Solus...' He trailed off, his flickering eyes suddenly muddled.

'What?' she asked.

'I was going to say that Amon Solus is a hunter. But I don't know how I know that.'

'You must have met him before,' Sevora said, and he nodded, but he still looked strange. As if he were standing on a precipice, staring at some vast abyss. 'Corus. That's good, isn't it? You're remembering something. Isn't that what you're supposed to be trying to do?'

'It's what the Lord-Veritant said I should do,' he said. 'But I don't know. It doesn't feel good.'

His eyes were wide, and even with the lightning flickering in them they looked so much like her brother's as he struggled with the aftermath of one of his visions. She started to reach out her hand to take his, the way she used to hold Yevin's hand to calm him, but she stopped herself. This wasn't Yevin. This was the dead man who'd saved her family, then abandoned it, long before she was born. So she pulled back and watched him shake his head, confused, alone, and part of her wished she had taken his hand.

Then came the shout.

'Shadow mark!'

A flurry of activity erupted along the wall. Soldiers pointed out into the darkness where a faint green glow could be seen moving through the smoke towards them.

'That's what Morgen described,' Sevora said. The Lord-Veritant had assembled the Reclusians at sundown and briefed them on the attacks, and her plans for them to thwart them. Down the wall, Amon was tying himself off to a long rope. The wagon and mules used to anchor him before were gone, now replaced with five Reclusians. Near him, Morgen and the other two Lord-Veritants were getting ready with their own ropes.

'It's coming in!' a soldier shouted, then cursed as a massive pair of wings swung over his head. Jocanan had taken to the air when the day had gone, disappearing into the night, but she was back now, javelin in her hand, circling over the glowing circle. Waiting, as Morgen had told them all to wait.

'You should pull back,' Corus said, freeing his shield and his axe.

'I want to see this,' she told him, watching as the shadow mark sped up, heading towards the centre of the Halt. But she spared a look for him, a single quick glance that told her he was remembering her anger over the idea that she and the other Memorians would be dragged into the Reclusians' battles. Remembering it, but smart enough not to remind her of it. He just moved closer, his shield ready. Morgen had told him and the other Reclusians that weren't holding ropes to stand ready.

Amon waited where the green light was coming in. With sudden grace, he threw himself from the wall, as if he believed he had Jocanan's wings. He plummeted down, a shadow against the glowing wall, the rope playing out behind him. When the line went taut, the Reclusians holding it swayed but held firm. They fed the rope out, and Amon continued down the wall until he was just above the smoke. There he stopped and pulled his weapons free, a heavy sword and what Sevora had thought was a mace. But its head was a hollow cage with a mote of fire floating within, much like the Lord-Veritants' torches.

He brandished them both, and as the green light approached he slammed the flat of his sword against the haft of the strange mace, and there was a roll of thunder, a wash of flame. Before him the smoke smashed backward, like the tide rebounding from a stone.

Sevora's eyes were dazzled by the light, and when she could see again Amon had dropped to the ground, holding his sword and flaming mace before him. There was a semicircle open in the smoke, showing dead grass and a length of wall that was glowing fitfully, cracks marking the quartz. In front of the Knight-Questor, at the edge of the clear air, was a Stormcast carved out of darkness. A green glow came from the pendant hanging around the shade's neck, and its one black eye was fixed on the Astral Templar as the shadow leaned forward and charged.

Amon held out his mace, the fire directed at the charging figure. Black flecks were flying off the shadow, like ash blowing in the wind, but it rushed forward and swung its hammer at the Knight-Questor. He spun out of the way, the black weapon passing through where he'd been. Amon's sword scythed through the air, hitting the shadow figure, the blade leaving a rippling trail of emerald as it passed through. But otherwise the blow affected the shadow not at all.

The shadow shaped like the Lord-Ordinator turned to face Amon Solus, holding its hammer with one hand while the other reached back to touch the wall. It merely brushed the cracked quartz face with its fingers, but the whole wall shuddered as if struck by a monstrous blow. More cracks ripped through the quartz, rising above where the smoke had been covering it, and chunks of broken crystal flaked and fell away. Before the shade could strike the wall again though, Amon attacked, driving the fiery end of his mace into the shadow's body.

This time Amon's weapon found resistance. The fire in the mace seemed to catch on the shadow, and the darkness wrapped around the flame. The mace stuck halfway in, its light fading as it changed from crimson and gold to green. The shadow was losing more and more pieces, streams of black flecks drifting away, but there were tendrils reaching out from the smoke towards the shadow. Like thin, grasping arms they groped until they touched the shadow and flowed into it, and the dissolution of its darkness began to slow. The shadow of the Lord-Ordinator kept losing pieces as it fought to blot out the holy fire of Amon's mace, but the smoke was rebuilding it, growing back the darkness that made it, keeping the shadow from dissolving away.

Amon was standing before it, his body rigid as he kept driving the fire into the thing. The shadow seemed solid now, as if this fight against the fire had given it weight. It reached out and grabbed Amon by his throat, throttling the Knight-Questor as it fought to drown his flame.

'Now!'

The order snapped out from Morgen, and she and the other two Lord-Veritants threw themselves from the top of the Halt. They were not as graceful as Amon had been, but they dropped fast, their boots sending out ripples of light over the Halt. They hit the ground and let go of their ropes, moving to take position around Amon and the shadow, careful to avoid the twisting black lines that connected the shade to the smoke, then raised their torches.

'By Sigmar, we bring the light!' they shouted in unison, and slammed the ends of the heavy torches into the earth. The caged motes of light at their tops exploded, whirling out into gouts of flame. Even at the top of the wall Sevora could feel the heat, and when that light faded the smoke was smashed back, much farther than before.

In the dazzling light of those torches, the shadow was tearing apart again, pieces flying off faster and faster. The shadow's hammer was almost gone, and the edges of the shade's head and limbs were fraying, falling apart. A hole had formed around Amon's mace, a crater in the dark, and the fire at the end of his weapon burned bright.

But one black tendril still connected the shadow to the smoke, and the shade took a step away from the wall, then another, trying to escape the light, trying to reach the seething mass of smoke. As it moved, the dark tendril connecting it to the poison vapour grew thicker. The dissolution of the shadow began to lessen, its darkness slowly beginning to rebuild.

Then Morgen drew her sword.

Sevora had never seen the Lord-Veritant's weapon unsheathed. It was as dark as her patinated armour, but when she raised it and touched its tip to her torch, flames rolled down the blade. As they did, runes lit up along it, glowing bright against the dark metal. Morgen held the sword out, and great tongues of fire rose from the metal's razor edge. Stepping forward, she swung the flaming weapon down upon the tendril of smoke.

Where sword and smoke met, the force of the impact was that of one powerful, solid object striking another, fire and flakes of darkness spinning through the air. The fire rolled harmlessly off the Lord-Veritant, but the flakes of black flashed to that ugly green when they landed on her armour or skin. Morgen didn't flinch. She raised her sword and swung it again, cutting into the cord of darkness until it shattered at last like smoked glass, flying apart, and the smoke cloud below the wall flickered with green light.

The shadow flickered too. For one moment it tried to close in on the fire that Amon was holding in its chest, trying to smother it, but the light tore through it, and the shadow fell apart.

Like a statue made of ash, it crumpled. The last dark flecks of it wrapped like a cloud around the glowing pendant and blew away, taking the ugly green light back into the smoke where it faded, then was lost.

Sevora stared down at the battle, at the light pushing back at the smoke and the four Stormcast Eternals standing with their blazing torches, and it was beautiful and terrifying. Then all around her, the wall erupted into shouts. Cheers were sweeping down the Halt, shouts of triumph as the Golden Lions saw the darkness finally get pushed back. It was a shout of defiance, and it went on and on, until the first scream.

It came from down the wall, almost lost in the cheers, but Sevora saw Corus snap his head in its direction, heard the cheering falter.

'What–' she began, but then there was another, louder scream from the other side, and she caught sight of a soldier plummeting off the top of the Halt, smashing into the wall halfway down and leaving a smear of blood across the glowing quartz before crashing into the ground. The cheering died, and General Kant was moving down the wall, shouting for the soldiers to move back.

But she was answered with more death, as another Golden Lion was jerked off his feet and over the low parapet, his only sound a strangled gurgling as his hands clutched at something that had grabbed him by the throat.

'Sevora, move.' Corus' words were calm, but they were orders nonetheless, and at that moment Sevora had no interest in disagreeing. She started to step away from the parapet when Corus moved, whipping his shield up beside her with such speed Sevora barely saw it. She was shoved backward, and there was a wall of sigmarite where the world had been.

She blinked up at it, and the shield *clanged* and vibrated, like a struck drum. A hit, she thought, the world going very slow around her, the way it had when she duelled with knives in the Warrens. The thought passed through her head as Corus whipped his axe around to strike over his shield. He pulled the axe back as fast as he had struck, and in the slow crawl of time Sevora could see he'd caught something on the hooked bottom of its blade, a black line like the tendril of smoke that Morgen had cut.

This wasn't smoke, though it was as silent and dark as the vapour below. It was dark links of steel studded with cruel barbs. There was a blade on its end, its tip bent from striking Corus' shield. That piece of reasoning flowed smoothly through Sevora's head as she watched her great-grandfather twist his wrist, looping the chain around his axe. Then he pulled his arm back, giving the chain a mighty jerk.

The shadow the skaven was hiding in was a splotch smaller than Sevora's hand. A real rat would have had a hard time fitting within it, but the thing holding the chain whip was Sevora's size, taller but leaner, with glossy black fur and a bare tail almost as dark. It wore a black robe, whose hood had fallen backwards to reveal the sunken spots where its eyes should have been, hollow lids now stitched shut with yellow thread. The skaven dropped

GARY KLOSTER

the handle of the chain whip that Corus had used to jerk it out
of the tiny shadow, and dipped its clawed hands into its robe to
pull out two curved daggers.

'Chaos vermin,' Corus said, flicking his axe and sending the
chain whip tumbling silently across the stone. He shifted his
shield, stepping smoothly in front of Sevora. 'You made a mistake.'

The thing's head shifted back and forth, nose and ears twitching, as if taking in the other Reclusians that were moving closer.
Then it hissed, a drawn out *Shhhh*, right before it launched itself
at Corus, curved knives aimed at his throat.

Corus didn't move his feet. He stayed between Sevora and the
skaven like a wall, and when the ratman leapt he lifted his shield
and smashed it into the skaven's face. Then he moved, turning
to crush the stunned creature between his shield and the stone
beneath him like a mortal would smash a roach upon the floor.
He straightened, and the skaven lay sprawled, its chest crushed,
blood flowing in jagged pulses from its mouth and nose. Dying
but not quite dead, its breath frothing the blood on its muzzle.

Time had begun to flow normally for Sevora again sometime
after Corus had smashed the skaven, and now she stood behind
him, trying to breathe. She stared at the thing's long yellow teeth,
the thick incisors that tipped its muzzle. The teeth matched the
triangular wound that had marked her brother's shoulder, and
she wanted to get up and kick the skaven in its broken ribs until
she smashed its heart. But instead she simply whispered, 'Monster. Murderer.'

The thing tilted its head towards her, and through its broken
teeth came that horrible sound, a *shhhh* made liquid by the blood
in the skaven's throat. Then its head fell back into the pool of gore
that surrounded it.

'Are you alright?' Corus asked, reaching out to help her up.

'I'm fine,' she said softly. She was, thanks to her great-grandfather and his shield. She shivered, thinking of the way that guard had fallen, thinking that could have been her, and wind gusted around her, stirring her robes. Then it was gone. She reached out her hand and took Corus', and something snapped between their palms like a shock of static, but stronger. Something ripped through her mind, an image of someplace she'd never been, a memory of something she'd never seen.

'It's gorgeous.'

It was, in a way. The Oasis of Tears was a pool of water, clear and blue, surrounded by trees and grass. The green stood out against the desert's browns and greys, a blotch of colour so bright it almost hurt the eyes. But that piece of beauty was so small compared to all the blasted landscape surrounding it.

'You always have a way of finding beauty, Aika,' Corus said, and smiled at her. His wife smiled back, beautiful even with her face half-hidden by the scarf that protected her from the blowing sand.

'And you always find danger,' she said, reaching out and taking his hand. She was right in that too. Corus could see the hard lines that were blurred beneath the oasis' greenery. There had been buildings here once, a town, the start of a city. Ruins now, long deserted. Something had happened here, long ago, to make the people flee this place.

'I can see it in your face,' she said. 'The worry. Have no fears. We have the support of the Cult Unberogen, and the Whitefire Court. Your congregation will flourish here.' She looked back as she spoke, at the lines of people with their packs, the laden wagons, everyone staring with excitement at the oasis ahead.

Corus hoped she was right. These people had been lost when he found them, abandoned by the rest of Hallowheart to rot in the dark of the Warrens. They deserved a better chance, a life in the light. But he couldn't stop thinking of the wastelands they'd crossed *since leaving the Shimmering Abyss, the distance they were from the safety of the city and the Hallowed Knights that guarded it. That distance weighed on him, no matter how many reassurances he had been given by the cult and the mages of the Whitefire Court.*

'*I pray for that,*' *he said.* '*I pray to Sigmar every day that this was the right decision. For them, and for us.*'

'*It was,*' *Aika said, and she moved his hand to her belly.* '*For all of us.*'

Then it was gone, the memory shattered, and Sevora was standing, gasping, at the top of the Halt. The heat and light and dry-dust scent of the desert replaced with darkness and cool air tainted with the smell of blood and smoke. She stared around wildly, letting reality flood out what had taken her over.

A vision, just like when Yevin had forced them into her head. But Yevin was dead.

'Sevora?' Corus was watching her, his huge hand still holding hers, supporting her.

Touching her. This was the first time their hands had touched, and when they had, that vision had smashed through her. But it wasn't a vision. This wasn't from Yevin. This was a memory, Corus' memory. That place had to be the doomed settlement he had been tricked into founding. And that woman. Aika. Her great-grandmother. Seeing the parts of her face not covered by her scarf had been like looking in a dusty mirror.

'I'm fine,' she said again, pulling her hand out of his. His eyes were on her, flickering with lightning, concerned, and she knew he didn't believe her.

'Clear the way.' The voice was sharp, and broke Sevora out of the confusion of her thoughts. Silent Golden Lions stood around them, gawking like the crowd in the Cave of Knives. General Kant was cutting through them, her face hard, but when she saw the corpse lying in its pool of blood she nodded. 'One of them. That shadow, and one of these damned assassins. Finally.'

'Two.' The voice was a deep rumble. Sevora recognised Dreskir. The Reclusian pointed back along the wall. 'The Prosecutor Jocanan knocked one off the cliffside.'

'Knocked off the cliff,' Kant said. She looked less exhausted for once, the clean viciousness in her eyes pushing away her weary despair. 'Good.'

She snapped orders to the soldiers, and in a few minutes the smashed body of the skaven had been hung over the side of the Halt, its black silhouette staining the glow of the front of the wall.

'Golden Lions!' Kant shouted, her voice carrying through the night. 'My Twenty-Seventh! Attend! This is our enemy, who brought smoke, nightmares, and death. This is a skaven, a servant of Chaos, and it is not a thing of shadow and fear, it is flesh and blood and it can be killed!' She paused for a moment, then pointed down, to where Amon and Morgen and the other Lord-Veritants were being pulled back up the wall, their torches still blazing, keeping the smoke back. 'But we have seen tonight that even shadows can be killed! Sigmar has blessed us with the Stormcast Eternals, and with their strength we shall see this smoke lifted, the skaven dead. The Halt holds!'

'The Halt holds!' was shouted back, and in the eyes of the soldiers Sevora finally saw something like hope. It was powerful, and good, but a voice in her head whispered, *Hope is a lie.*

She looked away, and down the wall she saw Morgen pulling herself up over the parapet. When the Lord-Veritant's boots touched the top of the wall, Peace was there to meet her, his eyes flashing in the light of her torch. Sevora watched Morgen stroke the gryph-crow's feathered head, but then her eyes shifted to the rope that sat beside her. Its end was marked with burns, as if it had been dropped into acid.

Tomorrow at sunrise. That's when she would follow Morgen and Corus and all the rest out into that poison.

Tomorrow.

They didn't make them use ropes at least.

When the sky lightened from black to purple, Sevora and the other Memorians followed their Reclusians, winding their way down the stairs on the back side of the wall until they reached the ground. There was an empty square in the ruins of the old city, a great clearing where the gate lay. It was a tangle of gardens and pasture now, the ancient cobblestones torn up and used to repair the buildings that the villagers of Halt's Shadow had claimed. But there was still a clear space before the huge arch that stood in the middle of the Halt.

The gate was formed by two perfectly square pillars jutting from the wall like a bas-relief, crowned by a smoothly curving arch, all of them carved with intricate, curving symbols that flowed over and through each other so that they were all one. But for those carvings, it would have been a simple opening, impressive only for its size. Except that there was no opening. The thin dirt track that led to the gate ended in a wall of basalt, a blank face of stone identical to the rest of the wall, unmarked by seam or hinge. Sevora stared at the blank stone face, wondering what would happen when they reached it. Because Morgen would not have brought them here if the path were blocked.

Sevora knew she was not that lucky.

A sergeant of the Golden Lions waited beside the arch, and Sevora watched her as they approached. Was there some secret mechanism? Or was the stone wall an illusion? But the woman just touched the stone between the pillars and it pulled back on itself, the massive wall of basalt folding in like a curtain until it was gone. Now a tunnel lay open, wide and long and tall, glowing red as if lit by the coals of a banked fire.

They moved into it, the huge figures of the Reclusians lost in the space. It was much like the tunnel through the wall of Rooken-val, except larger. Behind them, dawn's light was suddenly cut off as the gate swept shut again, and for a moment she was certain that the whole tunnel would close, collapsing in and crushing them, and Sevora shuddered.

Beside her, Corus looked at her with concern. She hadn't talked to him after the fight on the wall, of the vision that had swept through her. Corus had shown no sign of knowing what had happened to her, of realising that his memories had spilled into her, and she didn't feel like telling him.

Was this what happened with Memorians? Was this what she was here for, somehow, instead of just being a lackey meant to supply encouraging words? If so, was this worse? She didn't know, and she damn well wasn't going to ask Morgen, or any of the other Lord-Veritants.

At last they reached the end of the tunnel, where another wall of blank basalt waited, and like the entrance this one swept itself out of the way at Morgen's approach. Outside was daylight, dead grass, the churning black bank of smoke, and Amon Solus. The Knight-Questor stood framed in the newly opened arch with his mace held high, the flames of it pressing the smoke back away from the entrance. As Morgen stepped out, she struck the base of her torch against the ground and it lit, its flames further pressing back the smoke. Carefully the Reclusians stepped out of the gate, forming a semicircle of armoured bodies, their Memorians in the middle. The torches of the remaining Lord-Veritants blazed to life, and they were all standing in a clearing. They could breathe – but they were so packed together Sevora was having a hard time keeping herself from pressing into Corus' armour.

'We can't fight like this,' Amon said. 'We can barely move.'

'We must spread out.' Morgen looked out over the ranks of

Reclusians. 'It is time to test the mettle of this poison. Which of you will chance it first, so we may measure its potency against the strength of the Ruination Chamber?'

'I will.' The voice was immediate, and familiar. It came from Dreskir, and Sevora remembered Morgen telling the Lord-Vigilant about the fear of death in him, the fear that made him reckless. The Lord-Veritant's eyes narrowed just a bit, but she nodded.

'Go.'

Dreskir hoisted shield and axe and stepped away from the group and into the smoke. His patinated armour blended in with the swirling dark, and he was gone, vanished in less than three steps.

Sevora looked after him, then swung her eyes to his Memorian. Avil Tawn had raised his hand to the sky, a hammer-shaped sigil of Sigmar gleaming in it. Still trying to look pious, but obviously puffed up and proud that Dreskir was the first.

Shaking her head, Sevora looked away from him and to the sky. It was a deep, clear blue in the morning light, and high above she could see Jocanan circling, her wings gleaming in the sun. Rookenval's mob of corvids still refused to fly over the smoke and instead perched on the Halt, black dots high above, watching them. Waiting with the patience of carrion birds.

'How long is he going to be out there?' Sevora muttered, just as the smoke swirled and the Reclusian reappeared.

'It reeks. Bad enough to taste,' Dreskir said, stepping into the clear. Wisps of smoke followed him, like grasping claws, but they frayed away in the light of the torches. 'But I could breathe.'

'Your eyes?' Amon asked. 'Did they burn?'

'No,' the Reclusian said. 'But I could see no more than a few yards. I walked to the far cliff and back, and had to stay close to the Halt so that I did not lose my way.'

Amon frowned. 'If the Reclusians can stand the smoke, they

can spread out beyond the borders of our torches' effect. But not very far, or we will lose each other.'

'It will be sufficient,' Morgen said, and organised them. The three Lord-Veritants formed a triangle, with the Memorians between them, furthest from the smoke. The Reclusians formed up around them, a wall of sigmarite that faded in and out of the smoke. Amon and his torch stood at the front, cleaving their path forward. It was awkward in the middle, and Sevora was jostled by the other Memorians, but it worked. The smoke rolled back from them, and though she could smell its acrid rancidness she could breathe. Maybe she wasn't going to choke to death out here after all.

When they moved away from the Halt, and the smoke rolled in to surround them, she felt less reassured. If something happened to the Lord-Veritants' torches, that black cloud would roll in and drown them in its noxious dark. Morgen and the others held their torches close in their gauntleted hands, but what if one of those chain whips came sweeping out of the dark? The skaven Corus had smashed would not have been strong enough to wrest a torch from the grasp of a Stormcast Eternal, but how many of them were out there? How many of those eyeless assassins were slipping through the smoke unseen, waiting to strike?

It was an unsettling thought, and a breeze whispered around her, little sparks flickering against her hair. Sevora tried to settle her magic and her anxiety, but she knew this mission couldn't be this easy. There would be an attack, soon.

She still missed it when it came.

There was the sound of coughing and cursing behind her, and she spun to see a thick tendril of smoke, like the ones that had fed the shadow last night, reaching into the cluster of Memorians. It wrapped itself around the face of a young woman in black armour. The smoke wasn't drifting, it was moving with a purpose, driving itself into her mouth and nose, choking her. Black flakes were coming off it, drifting away through the air as the torchlight tore at the smoke's substance, but it wasn't dissolving nearly fast enough.

The Memorian was on her knees, her hands struggling uselessly with the smoke enveloping her face. The Reclusian closest to her was swinging his huge black axe into the tendril, but the keen edge was having as much effect as the dying woman's hands. The Reclusian kept swinging though, growling oaths over and over as he tried to shatter the insubstantial attack.

'Clear, brother!' The shout came from the Knight-Questor. Amon Solus had left his spot at the front and was running down the side of the triangle, his mace raised high. When he reached the tendril he swung his weapon down, and fire smashed out of it as it crashed into the black, twisting line. The mace broke the tendril, and the Memorian fell forward and retched, spewing black vapour out of her mouth as if she were vomiting up night. She was alive. But there were shouts all around Sevora now. More black tendrils were flowing from the smoke, reaching out to catch and choke.

One hit a man just beside Sevora, smoke lashing onto his face like a striking snake. She saw the Memorian's panic as the poison poured up his nose, and she slashed at it with her knife, the worn blade doing nothing at all – then it happened again.

In a rush of light, a memory flooded through her that wasn't her memory at all, and everything else went away.

'They're coming,' Ishvan gasped. His hand was pressed to his side, and blood ran between his fingers, dripping down to pool upon the broken rock that had once been part of a wall around the ruins.

'How big is the band?' Corus asked. Two months they had been at the oasis, rebuilding these ruins, and this would be the eighth time one of the loose bands of Chaos cultists that haunted this desert had attacked. How much longer would this go on? They already had too many dead, too many wounded.

'Not a band.' Ishvan coughed, and blood spattered from his mouth. Corus held him up, until the coughing slowed. 'Army,' the man gasped, his voice barely a whisper. 'Damn army. Come to kill us all.'

He coughed again, and a torrent of blood splashed out against Corus' chest. Then Ishvan sagged, and Corus lowered him to the ground. He could hear the others on the broken wall muttering in fear, asking him questions, demanding answers, but he ignored them. He rose and scrambled up the ruins until he was at the top. Behind him was the oasis, green and full of the people he had brought to this place, working, talking, laughing, singing. Before him was the desert, a wasteland blotched now with warriors. An army of them, carrying standards stained with blood and topped with skulls. An army of the Blood God, the Skull God. An army driving towards the Oasis of Tears. Driving towards Aika.

'No,' he whispered. Then he raised his voice to a shout. 'No!'

'No!'

The word ripped out of Sevora, torn out by the horror of that terrible memory, by the terror of what was happening. She shouted her denial, and with that word came the wind. It whirled down from the sky above, a gale full of glowing orange sparks that whipped around the Memorians like a tornado, tumbling some of them to the ground. But it also whipped away the reaching lines of smoke and drove them back into the cloud with a flurry of sparks. The tornado grew, spreading outward, lashing over the Reclusians who were unmoved by its violence, bracing themselves against its fury. But the cloud was shoved back, driven away so that the circle of clear air was suddenly twice the size. Then Sevora fell to her knees, gasping, exhausted, and the sparks faded as the wind died.

'Sevora!' Corus was there, picking her up before she could pull in enough breath to tell him to get away from her, to get out of her head. 'Did it touch you?'

'No.' It was Amon who answered, the Astral Templar looking at her. 'She drew the wind, and pushed it away.'

'You did well,' Corus said, letting her go when she weakly pushed him away.

'I'm going to pass out,' she muttered, then regretted it because he tried to hold her up. She moved away, like a toddler from a doting parent, wavering on her feet but free.

'Excellent, Memorian,' Morgen said. She was staring out at the smoke, which was slowly beginning to creep back in. 'We will take advantage of this, and move a little faster, at least until it closes in once more.'

'And when it goes for us again?' Sevora asked, her voice weak.

'We will do the same, but faster,' Morgen answered. 'Hold position, Amon will strike what he can, and you will draw your wind to force the smoke back.'

Sevora was still pulling in her breath to protest when Corus spoke.

'She did it once, and saved us, but it cost her. You can't force her to do it again.'

'Trust me, I know I can't force anything from your Memorian,' Morgen said. 'But the Knight-Questor has told us what happened to at least some of the beasts that breathed this poison. They became infected with monsters. So unless she wants to share her twin's fate, she will find the strength.'

Rage ran through Sevora, and she glared at Morgen Light, her hand on her knife. Then from behind her she heard Corus growl.

'You push too far, Lord-Veritant.' The lightning in her great-grandfather's eyes snapped as he spoke.

Peace bristled, his feathers rising, but Morgen simply nodded. 'Look around us. I push as far as is necessary, Reclusian. Always.'

Then she turned away and started walking, driving the wedge of Reclusians forward with her, like a knife thrust into the dark.

CHAPTER TWELVE

WARRUN VALE

The last time Amon had walked through the smoke, he could barely see. Now, in the clearing created by the torches, he could make out more of the land languishing beneath this corrupting dark. It was a place of nightmares.

Warrun Vale beyond had once been a broad line of green cutting through the Adamantine Range, a verdant stretch of grass and pines that stood in stark contrast to the barren, jagged peaks that rose above it and the dry, dusty plains that spread below. That lush beauty was gone now. The long grass they were moving through was dead and white, and it fell apart when touched, dissolving into a stinking liquid ooze like clotted pus. There was no sound of birds, no insects; nothing to be found save one partial skeleton, of what he couldn't say, the bones too gnawed and twisted to be recognisable.

When the track they followed went into the forest, everything got worse.

The trees were as dead as the grass, leaves and needles lying in drifts below them, dissolving into a black sludge that sucked at Amon's boots like mud. The bark had mostly fallen away, leaving the white trunks exposed like fresh bone. Deep channels marked the wood, twisting carvings like beetle tracks but tinged green, that same ugly green of the pendant that had adorned Brevin's shadow. Whenever Amon passed a tree, the channels shifted, twisting to form pictures against the dead wood. Ugly things, like flayed faces, swarms of misshapen rats, or bloated eyes punctured with thorns. He stopped looking at them after the first tree. They were disgusting and distracting, a sick spell meant to draw attention and nauseate, easy enough to ignore.

Unlike the Reclusians.

Amon couldn't ignore those dark figures, no matter how he tried. They were like him, Stormcast Eternals, taken from death to serve Sigmar in the never-ending battle for the preservation of the Mortal Realms. Hallowed Knights instead of Astral Templars, but that was just the difference of siblings. The Reclusians were much the same as Amon, and that was why he couldn't look at them for long. Those dark-armoured warriors had been like him once. And they were what he was fated to be.

No matter how hard he tried, how disciplined he was, the storm of death snatched away the memories that made him who he was. It had already happened once, and that thought gnawed at him. What might have slipped away? There were things he couldn't remember from his mortal life. Many things. That was normal, mortals forgot much of what they did. Not everyone remembered the sound of their grandparents' voices. When their father had gone grey. The length of their first love's hair. Obsessing over every detail of his mortal life wasn't going to tell him if some tiny part of himself had slipped through his fingers. But sometimes, when he wasn't on the hunt, he couldn't help worrying at those thoughts, like a starving dog with a dry, ancient bone. If he was slowly losing pieces of himself while he managed to stay in the Storm's Eye, then he was going to inevitably slip from that precarious balance point and shatter. He would be sent to the Ruination Chamber, a broken glass missing too many pieces, and he would be a Knight-Questor no longer. And the hunt, the never-ending, always changing hunt, would be over, ended, lost. Forever.

And would he even know it?

Probably not. And that thought brought him no comfort, only more despair. So he avoided it as assiduously as possible. What use was it to dwell upon fate? It was distraction, like the terrible runes writ in the dead wood of the forest surrounding him. But those dark thoughts were hard to ignore when the Ruination Chamber was right there with him, walking in his shadow.

'Have we gone beyond the place you were attacked?' Lord-Veritant Morgen's voice was quiet, almost lost in the low sucking noise of the dissolving leaves against their boots. But the question still grated against Amon's ears, even though he knew silence was impossible when moving with this many. Hunts were better done in silence. And alone.

But this hunt wouldn't be happening at all without the Reclusians and their resistance to the noxious smoke. Or the Lord-Veritants, and the flames they wielded.

'We have,' he said. He'd spent long hours back at the Halt going over the maps of Warrun Vale, and had spoken to the Golden Lions who'd served at Gallogast, learning the lay of the pass and the ruins. They'd just passed through the Narrows, a place where the cliffs on either side of the Vale pressed in close, where the pass shrank to only a few hundred feet wide. It would have been a better place for the Halt, except that the cliffs on either side were low and too easy to climb. But it was a clear landmark, even in the smoke. 'We're almost halfway there.'

Then he cut off, raising one hand. Something had moved in

the slurry of rotting leaves and bark, slithering beneath its thick decay. Behind him, the rest came to a stop, waiting, watching. At least they knew enough not to raise their voices, though he could hear the thick breathing of some of the mortals. He ignored it and waited, his mace held high, his broadsword gripped tight. When the dead leaves finally stirred again, he lunged forward and stabbed the blade into them.

There was a low rumble of thunder as he struck, and he felt the impact run up his arm. Whatever he'd hit felt wrong, hideously yielding for a moment, then fibrously tough. The sword jerked in his hands, as whatever lay beneath the slimy leaves thrashed, but Amon drove the point deeper. Then he hoisted the blade up, muscles straining as he heaved the thing into the air.

It looked something like a snake, but it was thick, almost as big around as Amon's thigh. It had legs, but they were vestigial, flailing uselessly from the bloated body. It had no fur, feathers or scales, just wrinkled, baggy skin pale as maggots and covered with oozing boils. The ears and eyes of the monster were tiny, but its mouth was huge, a great circle of churning teeth and flailing tongues that whipped around like a nest of centipedes. Some lashed at the sword, their pointed tips ringing off his blade, while others flew towards his face, cutting through the air in front of him.

'Is that one of the things that came out of the wolf you fought?' Morgen asked.

'Or something like.' Amon swung his sword down, pinning the thing at his feet. Its tongues scraped across the armour of his leg as it tried to pull him to its churning circle of teeth, but he smashed his mace down on its head, pulping it. He left a ruin of ruptured flesh, twitching tongues and broken teeth, steaming and boiling in the muck. The tail flailed, scattering blood and organs across the ground, and it tried to crawl away when Amon pulled his sword free. He crushed it again with his mace, letting the fire burn it too, but as the flames ran down the long body, the boils on the thing's skin burst, spilling out thousands of tiny young. Most died in the fire, but far too many writhed away into the muck, disappearing. To feed and grow, Amon thought.

'Skaven-wrought,' Morgen said. 'Verminous parasites. They would consume the realms, and leave nothing but themselves and beasts like this, twisted, monstrous reflections of themselves.'

Amon straightened up, wiping his sword blade clean on his cloak. 'There will be more. Keep them from your mortals.' He could see them, silent, waiting. Well trained in that way at least, if almost useless in a fight. One of them was staring at him – no, at the gore he was wiping from his sword, rust-red blood and a phlegm-like yellow ooze. The one who had called the wind. Sevora. She was watching him strip his blade clean, eyes seeing but not seeing, lost in a memory that twisted her face with horror and rage. She'd seen something like this once before, and it had left its mark. Too bad. She would see worse, soon enough, and she probably wouldn't survive it.

'Come on. Gallogast is waiting.'

At twilight, Jocanan swung between the rotting trees that now filled Warrun Vale from cliff to cliff, the wide sweep of her wings tilting to avoid the clutch of dead limbs. She landed before Amon, grey-blue wings of flame and dark silver armour blending with the smoke that was pushing closer as the day failed, but the light from his torch caught in her eyes and on the javelin she carried.

'The trees thin half a mile ahead,' she said. 'The smoke does too. I can see Gallogast, shrouded, but it's there.'

'It thins?' Amon asked. The smoke hadn't thinned all the days he'd been here. All the weeks since it had arrived, according to General Kant.

'As I said. Maybe half as thick as it is back at the wall.'

'Does it get thinner beyond the ruins?' Morgen asked. 'Could you see what lay beyond them?'

'Night is coming,' the Prosecutor said. 'It is hard for me to say if it is thinner. But I can see lights out there now, that I could not the night before. Sparks of fire, and green lights like the flickers that sometimes run through the smoke. There is a light like that in Gallogast. Hard to see, but a slip of it shines up through a crack in the foundation of that fallen tower.'

'What else is there?' Amon asked. Half a mile. It would be full dark by the time they reached Gallogast. Whether the smoke had thinned or not, they would have to keep the torches up to protect the Memorians. They would be a blazing target in the night for whatever waited there for them.

'Dead men,' Jocanan answered. 'And skaven.'

Amon stood at the edge of a line of trees, his spyglass held to his eye, staring through the smoke and the dark at the hill that rose before him. It was a low pile of dark stone crowned with a ruined tower, which jutted up from the stony hill like a shattered bone shoved through skin.

The Prosecutor was right. The smoke was thin enough here to see the shape of the ruin against the greater dark of the night, but little more. There were shapes hanging from it, things that might have been corpses, but even with the glass he couldn't be sure. Jocanan had described them though. Human bodies long dead, skin and muscle withered against the bone. They had been tied to crude wooden frames, their arms and legs stretched out to form an X. That was what she had seen around the ruins, and that little flicker of emerald light. That, and shadows.

Shadows with eyes that gleamed in the light of the dying day.

Amon swept the glass back and forth across the hill, searching. Finding nothing. But he trusted the Prosecutor. And he trusted his enemies. He'd seen no sign yet of the dark-robed skaven with their eyes sewn closed, but they would be waiting for him. Now though, with the Ruination Chamber at his back, they would not come for him just four to one. There would be more. There were always more.

Amon snapped the spyglass shut and moved, stepping silently despite the decaying sludge that covered the ground. Soon he could see the light of the Lord-Veritants' torches gleaming through the trees, a beacon in the dark and haze. A clear target. That worried him, but as he grew close he took a deep breath, relieved to breathe air that wasn't full of the poison. The smoke had thinned enough here that he could risk not lighting his mace. Still, his eyes and lungs burned from its polluted touch, and he was glad to be back to where the torchlight forced the smoke away. Even if it meant facing the ones who bore that shining, holy light.

Morgen still stood at the forward point of their formation, her torch gripped in both hands. Behind her the other two Lord-Veritants anchored the remaining corners of the triangle. With the smoke less thick here, they were able to stand farther apart, giving the Memorians room to spread out. Each one of the mortals was fixed on one of the Reclusians that stood like statues on the edges of the smoke, barely visible. Whatever the bond between Memorian and Stormcast was, it was powerful. On the march here, they'd encountered more of the scavenger things burrowing through the muck and the Reclusians had cut them down with brutal, silent efficiency. But then one of the monsters had surged up out of the rotting leaves almost beneath the feet of one of the Memorians. The thing had gone for the mortal, sharp tongues striking like whips, but they were all blocked by the shield of a Reclusian. The massive warrior had attacked with such ferocity the worm-like beast had been reduced to twitching chunks before Amon could take two steps towards the fight.

The Memorians... Amon didn't understand the purpose of these mortals. What benefit did they offer the Reclusians that made up for their liability in the field? Perhaps he was better off not knowing. But watching the Reclusian butcher that monster with complete and utter ruthlessness, he understood that whatever those mortals represented to their protectors, it was a bond that would make the Reclusians ferocious.

'Knight-Quester.' Morgen's eyes touched him, then flicked past his shoulder, staring into the long shadow he cast on the smoke behind him. 'What waits?'

'Gallogast. And whatever defends it.' Amon tapped the hilt of his sword to the handle of his mace, making the fire bloom from the heavy sigmarite cage mounted on its end. 'I can add nothing to the report from your Prosecutor.'

'Then we advance as planned,' she said. Morgen turned, her black cape flaring out, and unsheathed her sword. She touched its dark metal to the fire of her torch, and the flames licked down the sigmarite, making the symbols etched in the holy metal come to life, glowing bright in the darkness.

'Reclusians. The last hope of the light. Make yourselves ready, for the enemy is before us, and we move to meet them. Form up.'

The Reclusians moved, and though the click of their armour and the sound of their boots was loud in Amon's ears, they did so without speaking and with a precise efficiency that would have been enviable on a parade ground, much less in a dead forest drowning in darkness and poison. Their deftness shook Amon. Looking at their faces, at the lost look in so many of their eyes, he would have expected their efforts to be a shambles. But whatever shredding the Reclusians had endured of their souls, it had not touched their skills. That was both reassuring and disturbing, but Amon had neither the inclination nor time to think on it. Instead, he waited until the Reclusians had formed up into a shallow V shape, the Memorians clustered behind. In their midst he could see Sevora, her face grim and a knife in her hand, a tiny thing that was as ill-suited for a battlefield as she and most of the mortals around her.

Well, the Memorians were the Reclusians' responsibility. Amon turned away, taking his spot before Morgen. His responsibility was his hunt, and Brevin was at last at hand. Whatever was left of him.

Amon started forward, mace raised like a beacon, and behind him the boots of half a hundred Stormcast hit the ground in unison, marching to war with axes sharp as honour and fates as dark as the heavens that stretched forever above.

The ground around Gallogast was a barren circle of dead grass. The ruins stood upon a hill of the same black basalt that made up the Halt, boulders pushing out of the ground like knuckles tearing through leprous skin. The ancient tower was barely more than a pile of rough stone. On that pile the skaven had set heavy wooden beams, and the bodies Amon had seen hung from them, ugly scarecrow shapes barely visible in the dark.

Amon halted before the hill. There was a broad path leading to the ruins, and at its end he could see the entrance to the complex built into the tower's foundation. The door that he had been told would cover that opening was gone, and there was just empty shadow, silent and waiting.

The Knight-Questor ran his eyes over the hill, searching for any flicker of movement, anything that could herald the trap he was sure was waiting for them. But there was nothing, and finally he started forward again, walking up towards the broken tower.

This close, the splinters of standing stone were taller than they had seemed. Gallogast must have once been a great tower, rising high over the end of Warrun Vale, before something had shattered it. The beams that the skaven had set here were rough things, crudely hewn from the trunks of pines, spiky with the stumps of branches that had been hacked away. Amon could see the bodies had been arranged as Jocanan described, and now that they were closer he could see that the corpses' eye sockets and mouths had been stuffed with dead grass. Each body's belly was a tattered ruin, the skin hanging in torn strips as if they had been ripped open from the inside, and long braids of dry grass ran between the corpses' outstretched limbs.

Those rough ropes held circles of skin, dried and stretched taut. Drumheads made from the corpses. Strings of braided hair hung in front of them, a tooth hanging at the end of each like a grisly bead. The skaven had been busy here, making these grotesque decorations, but Amon could find no meaning in their hideous art. There probably was none other than obscenity, and he turned his attention back to the shadows that choked the entrance. Nothing.

And then the sound began.

It started quiet, but it snapped Amon's attention back to the corpses and he could see that the teeth hanging from the long braids of hair were stirring, as if moved by a breeze, though there was no wind. As they moved, they rattled against the dried-skin drumheads, making the noise. A strange rattle that sounded unnervingly like a chuckle. These dead had no eyes or mouth, but torn skin and broken teeth came together and they could still laugh, and laugh, and laugh.

It was a hideous display and a perfect diversion. Amon spun, searching behind him, but there was nothing down the hill they had climbed but shadows.

Shadows. Single skaven had hidden in shadows before. But what rule in their twisted magic limited them to one? Even as the thought flicked through his head, he could see some of the darkness between the stones moving, bulging outward like the boils on the skin of the scavenger beast he had slain in the woods.

'Reclusians,' he shouted. 'They come!'

The shadows began to shatter even as he spoke, the darkness rupturing and spilling out horror. Skaven, but they were twisted, haphazard things: ratmen shaped from the pieces of other creatures. There were antlers sprouting from heads and backs, wolves' teeth jammed into rats' muzzles, the thick claws of bears growing from rodent paws. Feathers and scales grew in patches among their fur, and on far too many there were smooth areas of skin, or human eyes or teeth in skaven faces. These were monsters that had been born from those who'd lived in the lands beyond this pass, parasites that had pieced themselves together from the flesh of who they infected. They were things born of the skaven's poisonous, brutal magic, and they were smashing out of the shadows and rushing forward, jaws gaping with hunger, eyes burning with hate.

'Turn!'

The single order snapped out from Morgen, and it reshaped the lines of the Reclusians. The Memorians stayed in place, frozen like prey, but the Stormcasts moved around them, smooth and certain. In moments they had redrawn their lines and formed a wall of sigmarite and shield between the twisted skaven and their mortal kin. A line that did not give an inch when the horde of rat-things slammed into it.

The skaven hit the Reclusians and the night was filled with their shrieks, high-pitched inhuman screams that dug like thorns into Amon's ears. There was a deafening rattle as claws and teeth, clubs and stones broke against the heavens-wrought metal. Then came a different noise, the ugly sound of flesh slitting, of bones snapping. The Reclusians had let slip their axes, and the huge curved blades cut through the skaven, splitting open skulls and lopping off limbs, opening huge wounds in furry bodies, leaving them thrashing and screaming at the feet of the dark-armoured warriors, or silent, twitching piles of gore.

GARY KLOSTER

It was butcher's work, but the Reclusians performed it with simple efficiency. They held their line and worked their weapons, slicing through the horde, each blow flowing into the other, never interfering with the fighter on either side. In the middle of their line, Morgen wielded her burning blade, her torch standing behind her, its bright light making the eyes of the approaching skaven run with bloody tears. She cut through them all, the flames on her sword setting fur alight and making flesh and blood boil and pop. Her gryph-crow, Peace, fought beside her, claws flashing, black beak stabbing like a broad dagger into chests and throats and streaming eyes.

Amon saw this as he picked out his place to move forward to join the fray. But then instinct seized him, and he turned to look back at the dark throat of the entrance to the shattered tower. The shadows there were moving too, as dark-robed skaven slipped silently out into the night. Their eyeless heads were tilted towards the fight, and they were beginning to spin the chain whips that hung from their clawed hands. Amon spun to face the assassins, mace and sword held ready. They spread out before him, skittering over stones and vanishing into shadows, the yellow threads of their eyelids gleaming in the holy light of the torches. Then they struck, the sharp-edged ends of their weapons flying out towards him like daggers.

Amon moved, slapping some of the weapons out of the air, dodging others. He heard the clanging rattle as one struck his armour, but he didn't feel pain or the sudden shock of cold that came when a blade sank deep. Still, the barbs snagged on his armour, his cloak, his weapons. They grabbed and tugged, throwing him off, and Amon felt the slice of a blade above one eye as he was pulled off balance.

'Come close,' he snarled, snagging one of the chains with a looping twist of his sword and jerking on it. But the skaven dropped its

216

weapon, staying back as the others lashed out, making the Astral Templar slip back to parry. The assassin caught up its dropped weapon and Amon felt another blade slice along the side of his neck, a cold kiss of steel that went hot with blood.

There were too many of them, a dozen at least, and they were forcing him back, their flicking weapons driving him closer to the Memorians. What would happen when those barbed chains started falling among the mortals? They would maim and kill, and what would the Reclusians do? If they spun to face the eyeless skaven, they would shatter their line and the horde that was tearing at them would swarm through and pull them down. All would fall beneath darting blade or yellow teeth, Stormcast and mortal alike.

Amon stopped moving, refusing to give more ground. The chain whips fell on him, slashing and snagging, but he ripped his arms free and slammed his sword against his mace. Thunder boomed and fire blazed out, white light flashing across the stones of the hill and making the shadows convulse. The robed skaven hissed, a drawn out *shhhhh* as the thunder rolled, but they were barely slowed by the noise and untouched by the light. They were still moving forward, chain whips swinging in their claws, curving around him and drawing close. Preparing to rush past him for the mortals.

The Memorians were close now, and clearly they had seen the skaven assassins pressing forward because raven feather-fletched arrows were beginning to fly past him as the Memorians with bows made use of their weapons. But the black-furred, dark-robed creatures must have been almost impossible for the mortals to see in the night despite the torchlight. The mortals' shots went wide, and the few that did get near the skaven were slapped down by the assassins' chain whips.

The Memorians' help wasn't backing the skaven away, and the

chain whips were smashing in. Amon knew he must move or fall, but there was nowhere to go and the skaven were driving in. Until one of them jerked back, a silver javelin sprouting from its furry chest. The struck skaven hit the ground, flailing, and storm wings clapped as Jocanan turned in the air overhead.

'Hold, hunter! Help comes!'

The silver javelin disappeared from the chest of the dying skaven, reappearing in her fist, and she cast it down again. It slammed into the stone at the feet of another assassin, the skaven barely twisting out of its way, and the pressure on Amon eased as the ratmen suddenly had to deal with this new threat. The Knight-Questor surged forward, seeking to take advantage of their distraction, but too soon. A chain slashed out and found his throat; the barbed links dug into his skin, the sharp hooks sawing through his flesh, trying to sever the vessels beneath.

Amon flung his sword arm around the chain, wrapping the links around his armour to take the pressure off his neck, then he pulled the chain to drag the skaven closer. But three more ratmen rushed in, grabbing hold of the chain and lending their strength. Jocanan threw her javelin at them, but the silver weapon was smashed out of the air by another skaven's chain whip as the ones on Amon jerked the chain that held him, trying to rip him from his feet. He fought them, muscles straining, blood rolling down his arm from where the barbs had slipped past his armour and found flesh. The skaven jerked on the chain again, bringing Amon to one knee. He fought to stay up, but they were slowly pulling him down.

And then a black shape hurtled past, an armoured giant that rushed the skaven holding the chain. The Lord-Terminos, surging forward like an avalanche of sigmarite, the carved tears of agony and ecstasy clear on their mask, axe swinging at that dark chain. It hit like a thunderclap, cutting through the steel with a shower of sparks, and Amon was free.

He shifted his feet, catching his balance as the chain went loose, then bounded forward. The skaven were scrambling away, the Lord-Terminos in pursuit, but one was not so fast. Amon swung his mace and caught the ratman between its ears. Fire exploded up as his weapon smashed the skaven's skull, and the stench of burning fur filled the air as the assassin fell, claws scrabbling at Amon's boots as it died.

He kicked the skaven away and pulled the bloody chain wrapped around his throat and arm free. Ignoring the pain, Amon flung it away, sharp eyes skimming over the rocks before him. The charge of the Lord-Terminos had broken part of the assassins' advance towards the Memorians, but there were still eyeless ones trying to rush in. They were slowed, though, by Jocanan's silver javelin, and the arrows and bolts coming from the Memorians themselves. The javelin slammed into a skaven's shoulder, shattering it then disappearing, and an arrow took another one in its hollowed-out eye socket, the steel head cutting through yellow thread and eyelids to smash through the thin bone behind. The deadly strikes slowed the other skaven just enough for Amon to get in front of them. Chain whips snapped at him, but he dodged and rushed forward, intent on killing.

The skaven scampered back, trying to stay out of reach, but Amon was on the hunt now. With the help of Jocanan's javelin he backed them up, until he cornered one of the eyeless assassins against a stone with slashing strikes. The rumble of thunder that rolled from his blade seemed to madden the skaven, and the assassin hurled itself forward. The skaven twisted in the air, dodging Amon's mace, and landed on the Knight-Questor's shoulders. The skaven balanced there like a dancer, trying to loop its barbed chain around the Stormcast's neck, but Amon snapped his mace back, cracking ribs and setting the skaven's robes ablaze. The assassin's jaws gaped, as if trying to shriek, and Amon smashed his mailed fist into the skaven's mouth, shattering bone and teeth and sending the ratman tumbling down onto the stones.

He whirled, checking on the Memorians, and as he did there came a shout of warning from the mortals. The Knight-Questor looked back and saw two more skaven falling at him, their weapons spinning in their hands. They must have climbed the stones to set a trap while he fought the other. One cast its chain whip at him, and its blade skimmed the edge of his armour and sank into the flesh just behind his collarbone. The sudden pain numbed his arm, made it hard to raise his sword, and the other skaven was casting its blade straight down at his mouth. It was going to smash out his teeth and drive into his windpipe, and Amon prayed that he'd live long enough to kill the thing before he choked on his own blood.

But then a gust of wind ripped past, making his cloak snap and whirling sparks around him. The wind hit the chain whip and turned it from his face, made it strike his armoured shoulder instead. The Astral Templar slid back, and both skaven hit the ground in front of him, instead of crashing onto him.

They hit hard, thrown off by his movement, and as they scrambled to recover, Amon swept sword and mace past each other, striking the creatures. The blade growled as it sheared through the ribs and spine and flesh of one, while Amon's mace hit the other in its belly, and for a moment the skaven was wrapped around the weapon's burning head like a dark rag. Then it hit the ground, back arching in paroxysm as fire dug deep into its belly.

Amon looked up from the bodies, snapping his weapons automatically as he did to fling away the blood clinging to them. The Lord-Terminos was wiping the blade of their axe on the corpse of a headless skaven, and Jocanan was pursuing the now-fleeing assassins back towards the tower.

The sounds of the other fight were fading too, and when he

looked to the Reclusians he could see the dead mounded before them, the monstrous skaven butchered by the score. The stench of blood and bile and faeces was thick in the air, but it was done. The skaven that hadn't been killed were running, pelting down the hill, disappearing into the dark and smoke, gone.

There was another smell mixed in with the stink of death and corruption, the sharp smell that followed a lightning strike. The victory had cost the Ruination Chamber too. At least one of them had been brought down by the monstrous skaven, killed and sent back to Sigmar as a lightning bolt. To lose another piece of themselves, and come back even less? Or to lose everything, every memory they'd created as a mortal, and come back as something else, something pure but inhuman?

Amon didn't want to think about that.

He went instead to where Morgen knelt in prayer, her flaming sword held out before her, her blindfold on, uncaring of the bloody mud. 'We have to move,' he said. 'The assassins are pulling back beneath the ruins. We still don't know how many are in there, but if we mean to get the Lord-Ordinator out alive, we must go.'

Despite his words, she kept praying, and he could see the other Reclusians had bowed their heads, their lips moving as they silently prayed with her. The only thing that seemed to have heard him was Morgen's gryph-crow, and it fixed him with its eyes and croaked, 'Go.'

He glared at the beast, hating being stuck waiting on someone else for some ridiculous reason. He felt the urge to turn and rush into the ruin without them, but he knew that would be the end of this hunt. A bad end. So he waited until the Lord-Veritant finally stood.

'I know the reason for your impatience,' she said as the Reclusians drew up around her. They were spattered with gore, but it was impossible to tell if any of them were injured. They seemed as impassive and distant as ever. 'But we lost two in this fight, and every loss must be remembered.' She turned her head towards him, her eyes still covered. But he felt she could see him, one hand holding her sword and the other her blazing torch. 'Understand, Knight-Questor, that the Ruination Chamber battles enemies within as well as without. Always. What seems frivolous to you is necessary to us.' She pulled down her blindfold and her eyes settled on him. 'But our purposes are the same.'

Amon kept his face still, hiding the unease that ran through him. The Lord-Veritant might not have passed beyond the Eye of the Storm, but she was as unnerving in her own way as the Reclusians. 'Our purpose lies beneath that ruin. I know the path. Follow, so I may end my hunt,' he said.

'You know the path.' The voice was that of the Lord-Terminos, and it echoed strangely through their mask, but the words were clear. They had come up behind Amon, as unexpected as fate, and their strange mask suddenly bore an eerie resemblance to Amon's own face. 'But my feet shall walk it first, Knight-Questor.'

CHAPTER THIRTEEN

GALLOGAST

The warpstone light turned Brevin's blood black, and it ran like a liquid shadow down the chains fixed around the Lord-Ordinator's neck. He hung in the crude, splintered frame and watched it flow link by link with his eye and wondered if he would ever bleed to death.

It was a grim thing to wish for, but Brevin was being gutted spiritually by the skaven's magic and he couldn't stop it, couldn't fight it. There was nothing but defeat, nothing but this vast emptiness inside him that made his righteous anger a distant thing, one tiny red star in a vast sky of black shot with green...

'No.' Skein's whisper hissed through the chamber. 'No.'

Brevin blinked, yanked from the terrible spiral of his thoughts by the sound. There was something in the Grey Seer's denial. Anger, hate. Fear. Yes, fear. Skein crouched quivering before the warpstone, his claws twitching in the air as if to grab something, to rend and destroy it.

'Light. Light that lies. The dull dark ones have brought more. More cursed light!'

GARY KLOSTER

To one side, Lisstis stirred, the eyeless assassin shifting his head as if he were hunting for the source of his master's anger. On the far side of the chamber, Varus looked up from his pile of rags in one of the niches. His round ears were laid back, flat to his spotted skull, and he hissed a tiny 'Yes?'

'No,' Skein growled. 'Kill. Kill the light and break the wall. Kill!' The Grey Seer's voice rose to almost a shout, and from the shadows the other assassins appeared, moving silently into the room.

Hissing 'shhhh' as Skein ignored them, raging.

'Shadows take, dark devour! Devour the light! Varus!'

The spotted skaven slunk from his filthy pile, creeping towards Skein hesitantly. Skein hissed, and at the sound, Lisstis lunged over and grabbed the smaller skaven, dragging him to his yellow-robed master.

'We must add strength. Strength in shadows.' Skein laid his hands on the variegated copper triangle in the air between the stone and Brevin, and Lisstis shoved Varus forward until he was on the other side. But Varus hesitated, snarling in fear, until Lisstis set the bladed tip of his chain whip against the corner of the spotted skaven's eye. With a sound that was part snarl, part whine, Varus reached up and took the triangle in his claws too.

Brevin could feel their magic in him, curled into his soul the way the smoke had gone into his lungs. But the fear in the Grey Seer's voice had started to rekindle his rage. To give him some tiny portion of hope. Something was happening. Something that Skein feared.

And Brevin wanted to see the skaven afraid. He wanted that very, very much.

The other eyeless skaven leaned in close, lips drawing back from yellow teeth as they tasted the air. Clan Sisseris crouched, sensing some threat to their master that their chain whips couldn't touch. Brevin watched with them, and then he felt something like fire. A thin thread of it, whispering through the hollow in his soul until it touched that spark of anger. And then it exploded.

Light filled him. Heat filled him. Fire. It poured into him and filled the hole that Skein's magic had corroded through his soul. Filled it, and then it flowed away, gone. The hole was still there, but its edges were cauterised, not healed but scarred over, and in the centre of the space floated that spark of anger. It was divine rage, but it was something else too. It was his connection to the Heart, returned. The emberstone heat of that magic, glowing in him again. It hurt. Gods, it hurt, worse than ever. They had harmed the Halt again, but the wall still stood. Something had stopped his shadow, stopped their magic.

He heard Skein's hiss, heard Varus yowl like a kicked animal. The light inside Brevin had faded, but now there was light in front of him, something other than the ugly green glow of the warp-stone. The copper triangle that hung in the air had lost the green sheen that stretched across its middle, and now the copper sides were glowing with heat. Brevin could smell the stench of searing flesh, Varus and Skein's hands burning as they gripped the hot metal, shuddering and hissing but unable to let go. Brevin's lips stretched, and he bared a vicious smile as he watched them suffer.

Then Lisstis pulled Skein away, breaking the Grey Seer's grip and tearing him from the triangle. The skaven leader snapped at his rescuer, ripping open the eyeless assassin's arm, but Lisstis simply let him go and bowed. Skein shuddered, holding his hands in front of him. Then he snarled, and Lisstis turned and slapped Varus away from the glowing triangle with his tail. The smaller skaven rolled across the floor, coming to a stop in a crumpled heap. His claw hands were seared things covered in blisters that wept yellow fluid onto the floor below him, and he curled around them, saying 'yes, yes,' his thin voice a whisper of agony.

Not enough. It wasn't nearly enough, but the pain of his tormentors gave Brevin strength. The triangle's glow brightened until it was incandescent, heat rolling off it, and then the centre of each side melted through. With a series of clangs the corners fell, hitting the basalt floor around a puddle of steaming molten copper that gleamed like blood in the green light.

Brevin tore his eyes from the broken pieces of the hateful instrument to look over his shoulder. His shadow was there, dull and dark, but there was no gleam of poisonous green within it. It was just a shadow. On the floor at its feet, the flawed warpstone pendant lay, the copper necklace it was attached to discoloured from heat.

'Something beat you,' Brevin said, his voice harsh from disuse. 'They beat you. Dissolved your magic and cleansed my shadow.'

Skein was licking his burned hands, his long tongue running over the blisters. But he stopped when Brevin spoke. His hands twitched as if they would scoop his thumb claws from his sleeve, but instead he shuddered in pain.

'Your warlord is coming, and you failed,' Brevin said. 'The Halt still stands, and I hope Reekbite skins your eyeless hide from you before he dies.' It was a goad, deliberate and enjoyable. Brevin still couldn't break the chains that held him, but he dreamed of catching the Grey Seer in the lightning bolt that would fall to claim his body if the skaven killed him. But Skein just hissed and Brevin's guards came for him, each taking a chain and jerking him away into the dark.

They came for him again the next night.

He'd spent the day in his dark cell, listening, waiting. The ruins were always quiet, Clan Sisseris keeping to its silence, but there were rhythms Brevin had grown used to, the distant sounds of things that might have been sparring, feeding, moving. They were different that day. There was more noise, more movement. As if the Sisseris were preparing for something. The arrival of Reek-bite? Or something else?

Stormcast Eternals? They were the only ones with the power, the purpose, to foil Skein's magic. Could they have come here, to smash Skein and his forces? To bring him home?

That hope filled Brevin and troubled him. Despite everything, he had the tattered remnants of his pride. Skein had lured him out here and then used him to attack the very thing he had been trying to defend. It was brutally humiliating, contemplating how thoroughly he'd been beaten. But mixed with that humiliation was a burning anger, which let him push aside his despair, let him embrace his pain instead of being crushed by it.

When the guards came for him that night, he walked easily to the candelarium with them, filled with the strength of that anger, coiled and waiting for its chance to explode.

Skein's clawed hands were wrapped in yellow bandages, but the hooks were back on his thumbs, gleaming in the green light as he stalked in a silent circle around the chunk of warpstone. Around his neck he wore the warpstone pendant, its yellow flaw like a slitted pupil. The puddles of molten copper had solidified on the floor, but the corner pieces of the triangle had moved. They were laid out on the floor on one side of the chamber, where Varus Hish and one of the assassins of Clan Sisseris crouched over them. The eyeless skaven was connecting them together again, using lengths of copper wire and human bones. Varus watched the other skaven with eyes filmed with pain, his ruined hands held out in front of him. They'd not been wrapped, and they seeped an ugly yellow-brown fluid from the burns that covered them. That fluid pattered across the floor when Varus reached out, hissing, correcting the way the Sisseris had been winding the wire. The other skaven hissed back, but changed the way it was joining wire to bone to copper rod, and Varus muttered, 'Yes.'

'Your magic is not mine,' the Lord-Ordinator rasped, his voice barely above a whisper. 'The only thing I know about it is that it is poisonous and corrupt. But whatever you're trying...' His one eye shifted from Varus to Skein, who had stopped his pacing and turned towards Brevin, the yellow threads over his empty eye sockets gleaming like worms burrowing in the Grey Seer's flesh. 'It looks like desperation.'

'Shhh,' the Sisseris hissed, but Skein moved closer, the hooks on his thumbs shining.

'It burns,' the Grey Seer said. 'Burns in you. The Heart.'

'The Heart burns and the Halt stands,' Brevin said. 'You couldn't use me to tear down the Halt's magic. You failed, and now the army that's coming will find itself trapped.' He smiled, not knowing if Skein could sense it and not really caring. 'They'll die there. I don't care how many you have, it's not enough. Your bodies will pile against the base of the Halt in drifts. You failed, Skein. The Stormcasts stopped you.'

'Storm-cursed,' Skein whispered. He stood out of reach, but Brevin could still catch the burnt-flesh stink and the stench of whatever awful medicine soaked the bandages that covered the skaven's hands. 'They brought light. Light lies.'

'Light burns,' Brevin said, and Skein lunged forward, the curved razors on his thumbs rising. Brevin was coiled, waiting, and his anger made him move like a whip cracking. He caught the Grey Seer by the throat and started to clench his fist, even as the curved claws sank into his arm. They tore through skin and muscle, but they were too small to go deep enough to stop him from crushing out the skaven's life.

Then another blade struck him.

The thin dagger-point end of Lisstis' chain whip slammed into his elbow, sinking into the hollow between upper and lower arm. Brevin ignored the pain of it, keeping his grip, straining to crush the Grey Seer's windpipe. But Lisstis snapped the chain, and the blade in his arm tore at him. Brevin's fingers spasmed open, the muscles severed, and–

And pain washed through him, exploding from his chest. Pain that made him stagger and choke on the collar around his neck, made him let go of Skein.

'Light.'

Brevin shook his head, the pain easing, like a beast relaxing its jaws around him. He was on his knees, the guards holding his chains tight. Lisstis clung to his back, and he could feel the point of a blade pressed against the corner of his remaining eye.

'Light,' Skein repeated, his grating whisper harsher now. 'It lies. You think it freed you? Still mine. Mine, storm-cursed. Will use you to fulfil my bargain. Wall will fall.'

Across the room, the assassin working with Varus Hish stood. In his hands he held a new triangle. It was much smaller, made of the three corners of the original joined now by raw red copper wiring and lengths of bone. At each corner of the triangle was a spike of sharp iron. It was crude and ugly, but it glinted ominously in the light of the warpstone. Varus was staring at his burned hands, lips pulled back from his teeth, but when the assassin stood he raised his head and looked to Skein.

'Yes,' the smaller skaven said, voice filled with pain and resentment.

'You want my shadow?' Brevin said, his deep voice a threat as he watched the skaven assassin approach with the spiked triangle. 'Let me stand. I'll–'

A sound echoed through the dark tunnels, a thin whistle that made every Sisseris skaven snap their head around to stare at the empty door.

'Storm-cursed. Cursed men,' hissed Skein. 'Slow them. Stop them. Loose the childe swarm. Bring the darkness. Now!'

The Sisseris poured from the room, dark bodies slipping past each other like a flood of black water out the door into the tunnel beyond. Then there were only the guards holding Brevin's chains, Lisstis, still clinging to his back with the blade of his chain whip pressed against the corner of his eye, Varus, and the Grey Seer.

'They're coming for you,' Brevin said. 'And they're going to hang your hide from the Halt.'

'Coming for you,' Skein hissed. 'You, wall keeper. To bring you back into light.' The assassin that had been holding the crude construct Varus made had gone with the others, leaving the copper and bone thing on the stone floor at Skein's feet, and the Grey Seer picked it up, running his hands over the spikes projecting from its corners. 'Light is coming to save you. Light is a lie.' Skein's ears folded back and he raised his head. He crouched before Brevin, his yellow robes pooling across the stone, like a predator gathering itself to spring, and the flawed green warpstone around his neck gleamed. 'Lies. I will show you.'

Then Lisstis drove the point of his blade behind Brevin's remaining eye.

Another shock of pain, but worse was the world vanishing around him. Brevin thrashed, jerking on the chains that held him. He could feel one of them give, the guards holding it losing their grip and stumbling forward. Brevin kicked, and his foot cracked ribs. Then the pain in his chest grew again, burning through him. Too much for his anger, it left him trapped in agony until it finally receded and he was lying on his back on the floor, furry bodies pinning his arms and legs, a barbed chain wrapped around his neck. Holding him down.

'Storm-cursed. Listen,' Skein hissed somewhere above him. 'Listen to the dark. It holds all the truth. It holds everything.'

'Listen to me, unclean thing,' Brevin snarled. 'The chosen of Sigmar will tear open your eyelids and pour fire into your skull, and that's all the truth you need.'

'Shhh,' Skein said, and the Grey Seer was close, his stinking breath hot on Brevin's skin.

Brevin moved, trying to slam his head up into the skaven, but the barbs on the chain around his neck dug in and held him back. Then he felt two more points against the front of his neck, above the chain and near his voice box.

'Damn you,' he growled, the best last words he could think of, and then the points sank in.

Razor sharp, they went deep, curved hooks sliding around his vocal cords. Then Skein jerked his thumbs back, and the cords slit and popped, flying apart in Brevin's throat. He choked, feeling blood splatter into his windpipe, and wondered if he would die, drowning in his own blood. But Skein had the skill of a surgeon with his blades. He took Brevin's voice, but not his life, and Brevin felt despair clawing through his rage again.

Then a scrap of sound found him in his darkness. A shout thinned by distance and stone, but it made it into his head, and his soul.

'For Sigmar! Forward! Bring hope, when hope is dying!'

Hope, when hope is dying. They'd sent the Ruination Chamber. The last hope. The strongest, and the cursed.

'Death comes. Dark comes. You hear. Hear and feel hope.' Skein had pulled back. There was a sound, a clink and clatter of metal on bone. The Grey Seer had the triangle Varus had made. 'You want light, and lies. Lies, hope. Hope, lies. All the same. I will show you. I will make you know.'

Brevin felt the skaven holding him tighten their grip, and then a trio of blades slammed into his chest. They punched into the flesh around his heart, grating off his ribs. A feeling hit him, the hollow, weak feeling that had swept through him when Skein and Varus had taken his shadow, but it didn't take away the fire in his chest, the pain. It mixed with them instead, became a sickening, spinning sensation. It felt like he was being broken, every bone shattered as he was folded in towards his centre, towards the hole that had replaced his heart, and he was being twisted inside out and pulled through it.

It was all pain and vertigo, and then the darkness before him split open with poisonous green light.

Eyes. Vast eyes staring down at him, filled with hate. And then there was Skein's voice, cutting through it all.

'The dark, storm-cursed. Listen. Listen. It will teach you truth. It will teach you despair.'

CHAPTER FOURTEEN

GALLOGAST

Sevora sat on a stone, gasping, pushing back her sweat-soaked hair.

'Are you all right?'

She didn't need to look up to know that it was Corus. Her sense of him had sharpened after his memories had spilled through her head on the wall. But then it had happened again, during this fight. They had been surrounded, the deformed skaven on one side, the eyeless on the other, and she had stood with her knife, not knowing what to do. Then the memory had taken her in a rush of light.

It had been a battle, and Corus had been fighting cultists, worshippers of the Blood God dressed in the skin and bones of those they had slaughtered. Then she had been back in the night, crowded in with the other Memorians. The whole fight had been like that: battle with the skaven interspersed with flashes of fighting beneath a blazing desert sun, and she had been swept back and forth between past and present with vertigo's ease.

She had flashed back from the desert, staggering against another Memorian, to see Amon standing atop the hill, sword bloody, mace blazing. He was looking at her, and she tried so hard to remember if she was Sevora or Corus, if this was happening now or a century ago. Then someone shouted, another Memorian pointing at something, and she watched Amon turn his back to her and stagger as something flashed through the dark to strike him in the neck.

Her vision flickered, almost popping back to that bright desert, but then it stayed in the night and she could see the skaven falling on Amon, one of them whirling its chain, starting to release it. That snapped her out of her confusion, made her understand that this was real and that one of the Stormcasts standing between her and the skaven was about to die. Her fear roared through her and lashed out as sparks and wind, throwing off the chain whip and driving both skaven back.

Exhaustion swept through her then, and she let it bow her head, snatching her eyes away from the slaughter dealt out by the Knight-Questor's weapons.

She slumped on a rock after that, still vaguely unsure if this was real but fearing that it likely was, until Corus had come with his question. *Was she all right?*

'I'm here,' she answered him. The answer was probably nonsense to him, but it was true. She was in this terrible place, not lost somewhere in his memories, and that was better.

Corus' dark armour was splattered with blood. Scratches marred it, gleaming silver against the patinated black. But he was uninjured, his breathing smooth, his face barely marked with sweat. It was eerie how much he looked like Yevin sometimes, the resemblance ruined only by the lightning that danced across the dark brown irises of his eyes. Looking at her great-grandfather, seeing that face and knowing it wasn't her twin, gave her a different kind of vertigo, and she looked away.

'Is it over?' she asked, even though she knew the answer.

'No,' he said, and hard on his words was a shout from Morgen to form up. 'Now the ruins. You will be in the middle, with the other Memorians. We will keep you safe.'

She snorted, and he laughed, a low rueful sound.

'Safer.' He stood for a moment, strangely awkward. 'Be careful,' he said, and then he was gone, joining the other huge, armoured shapes. He was worried about her. Where had a Warren brat learned to care about someone like that?

The answer wasn't written in any of the memories that had rushed through her tonight. Not buried in the screams and bone cracks, the splash of blood and the reek of opened guts. And she wasn't going to ask him, any more than she was going to ask him about the memories that were spilling out of him and into her head. Did he know about them? She doubted it. But Sevora knew who would.

Morgen stood near the front of the group, with the Lord-Terminos and the Knight-Questor. She was snapping orders, forming up the ranks, and Sevora had to move to join in with the other Memorians as they formed up between two groups of Reclusians. Most of the Stormcasts would walk before them, with five Reclusians and one of the Lord-Veritants with his blazing torch guarding the back.

The Lord-Terminos led the way into the ruins. They followed, and she threw one last look up at the sky. The smoke was thinner, and in the dark overhead she thought she could almost see the gleam of stars. Then they were eclipsed by wings, blue-grey wings of cold flame fanning over the smoke. Jocanan, circling, watching them go in.

'May she watch us come out too,' Sevora whispered to herself, and then there was nothing but stone overhead as they swept down the tunnel into the broken tower's foundation.

The Lord-Veritants' torches were bright, and the smoke ended at the door, kept out of this ruin by the skaven somehow. But the tunnels beyond seemed to eat the light, even worse than the smoke had, and they moved through shadows and gloom.

Sevora walked beside Avil Tawn, and she was oddly grateful for it. She didn't like the man, but she at least knew his name, which was more than she knew about the rest of the Memorians. And he was as Morgen had described him back in Rookenval, dedicated, eager. The gloom didn't affect him. He seemed convinced that the Stormcasts who surrounded them were undefeatable, and that Dreskir himself was untouchable. It was an attitude that was as enviable as it was annoying.

But every once in a while, he would twitch.

Whatever was happening with her and Corus, with the memories, they weren't coming now at least. She'd felt them, the sudden feeling of hot sun on her skin, or a flash of light that wasn't there, and she'd gritted her teeth and clutched at her father's knife, waiting for them to take her, but the feelings passed, leaving her edgy but alert. Alert for the first time to what the other Memorians around her were doing.

There were others besides Avil that would twitch sometimes. She saw tears appear, to be wiped away, saw odd smiles and frowns flash across faces. Heard Memorians sigh or start to laugh, or mutter words disconnected from anything that was happening around them. The woman in front of her kept humming, switching from song to song, and one of the men behind her loosed a stream of curses so vile they would have impressed a Warren-born thug, but he spoke them in a dull, monotone whisper. She watched and listened, focused on the Memorians instead of the dark which was crushing in on them, and the next time Avil Tawn twitched she grabbed his arm.

'Excuse me,' he said, pulling his arm away and brushing at the dark cloth of his sleeve, as if her discontent might be contagious.

'What just happened?' she asked him, and he stared back at her blankly. 'You twitched. You keep twitching. Why?'

'Oh,' he said. 'It's the visions, of course.'

'Visions?' she asked. 'What visions?'

'The sacred visions that Sigmar grants us.' Avil touched the silver sigil hanging around his neck. 'The histories of the Stormcast we serve. You see them, don't deny it. I've seen you fall, overwhelmed by their power. Unlike me. All the Memorians are blessed with them. Which you would have known, if you had listened to the Lord-Veritant instead of trying to argue with her.'

She frowned at him, so smug in his sureness, and started to open her mouth to argue, but then he twitched again. Afterwards he went pale and quiet, staring ahead in the dark.

'There have been many visions tonight. The fighting brings them. That's what Lord-Veritant Morgen told me.'

Morgen hadn't said anything about them to her, Sevora thought. But as Avil had pointed out, she'd been refusing to listen to the woman for most of the time she'd been with her – and that time hadn't been very long. Maybe that had been a mistake.

'These visions–' she started, then stopped. The light of the torch behind her had caught on the walls, walls that were as seamless and smooth despite their age as those in Rookenval. But there was something ahead, a line of shadow that made all Sevora's Warren-born instincts scream. The line marked something different in the wall, and she watched it. And saw when it started to move.

'Stop,' she snapped, grabbing Avil's shoulder, making him stumble to a halt as a section of the wall slid to the side, vanishing. The space behind was seething with shadows, misshapen bodies that surged into the tunnel before them. Skaven, like those the Reclusians had fought outside, with skin and horns and scales mixed in with their fur. They slammed into the pair of Memorians in front of her, and in the torchlight Sevora saw a skaven with the muzzle of a wolf tearing out the throat of the woman who'd been humming. She had her knife in her hand, but that blade was nothing, and fear ripped through her as she watched blood splatter and heard the screams.

Then the wind came.

It roared down the tunnel, whirling sparks around the skaven. Fur whipped back, blood flew up from the pools on the floor and splattered against the wall, and the monstrous ratmen were shoved back, squealing and snarling, into the hole they had burst out of.

Sevora stood in the tunnel, knuckles white as she clutched her father's knife, staring at the skaven with rage and terror, but she could feel her strength fading. It was draining away, no matter how her fear increased. The wind flagged, slowed, the first skaven starting to push forward through the fading sparks. It lunged towards her, with gleaming eyes and yellow teeth–

And the Reclusians behind her slammed past, their armoured forms smashing into the skaven like hammers. Their axes flew, somehow never touching each other or the walls in this narrow space. They moved with implacable precision, reducing the first line of skaven to bloody chunks, which they crushed beneath their boots as they drove the monsters back. Then Sevora was staggering, falling to her knees, unable to stand. The wind was gone, and it felt like she could never pull it back. Fighting the smoke, then saving Amon, now this…

She knelt on the stone, gasping, when an armoured hand touched her. It wasn't Corus, but the Lord-Veritant who marched behind them, his torch pushing back the unnatural dark.

'You did well, Memorian,' he said. 'But you must rise. Help her,' he told Avil, who was still standing nearby, blinking at the carnage around him. He nodded and straightened, grateful for the Stormcast's order, and hoisted Sevora up as if she were a sack of grain. She grunted, but she was on her feet, with Avil's arm supporting her.

'Take her–' the Lord-Veritant started, then cut off as a barbed chain slashed out of the dark and wrapped around his head, catching him across the eyes. Blood poured down his cheeks, like an explosion of red tears, but he swung his sword up, smashing it into the chain. At his feet, his gryph-crow made a harsh noise and rushed away into the dark, tearing after the skaven that held that chain. But there was a screech, and other chains were flying from that direction, one wrapping around the Lord-Veritant's wrist, another catching the great torch he held in his other hand. Then one of the bladed tips slammed into the wall between Sevora and Avil's head.

The chain fell on Sevora's arm and barbs snarled in the cloth of her robe. The sharp steel dug through the fabric, metal teeth biting into her skin as the chain was hauled back. Sevora was jerked down, pain flaring up her arm. The chain was tangled in her sleeve and she was dragged along the tunnel, flailing to find something to grip as she was hauled by shadow hands towards the dark. Until a hand grabbed her ankle and pulled her back the other way. For an agonised second she hung between the two grips, hand and chain – and then the cloth of her robe ripped and the chain whip slithered free, sliding silently away across the stone.

'What do we do?' Avil stood over her, his hand on her leg, his eyes wide. But Sevora's gratitude was washed away by frustrated anger as he pulled her up, cradling her in his arms, and just stood there, staring at the battle between the Lord-Veritant and the hidden skaven assassins. 'I don't see Dreskir! What do we do?'

'We go,' Sevora screamed at him, and that finally made him move. Avil ran down the tunnel, carrying Sevora with him as he went.

It was only when the darkness closed in around them that Sevora realised Avil had gone the wrong way, away from the rest of the Memorians, the Reclusians, and the light, taking them at a panicked sprint into the black labyrinth of the ruins.

'Stop!' Sevora shouted. For a moment Avil ignored her, and she was convinced he was going to run until they cracked their skulls into a wall. But before she could start throwing elbows into his side, Avil pulled up, stopped, and set her down.

'You said go.'

If he'd sounded petulant, she might have swung at him, even though she couldn't see a thing. But he sounded lost instead, confused and frightened, and he'd kept her from being dragged off into that hideous dark. So she knotted her fist around her father's knife and took a breath.

'I did. But we should have stayed near the Stormcasts.'

'Yes,' he said. 'Yes, of course. It is our duty to be with them. They need us.' Woven into the tension in his voice was Avil's desperation to be with the dark-armoured Stormcast. 'Dreskir is that way.'

Sevora blinked in the darkness, then realised he must be pointing. She let herself sigh, but kept it silent, and worked on guessing where they were. Avil hadn't run for long. They shouldn't have gone that far. But in the dark, she couldn't find a speck of light.

She could feel Corus, distant but there, like the warmth of a candle across a cold room. And that was something.

'Here,' she said, and took his hand. Holding it, she started off in the dark, moving carefully, sliding her feet, knife hand extended in front of her. She only went a few steps before she felt the blade click against a stone wall. She turned, and started moving along it, trying to follow it to Corus, using all the old tricks she'd learned moving through the Warrens' dim tunnels. But she would have sworn Avil hadn't taken any turns when he had run. How could there be a turn there now?

Shadows and tricks. Something was wrong here, in this unnatural dark. Moving slowly, silently, she pressed ahead, hoping they would somehow find the others, while in her head a voice whispered.

Hope is a lie.

Hope was a damned lie.

Sevora touched the wall in front of her, smooth and cool and invisible in the dark, the same as every other wall she'd touched in this labyrinth. They hadn't been walking long, she knew that, but it had felt like years. A slow crawl through the dark, feeling things out, being wary of traps, of pits, of ambushes. Trying not to think of the skaven with sewn-shut eyes moving silent and sure through the black towards them, chain whips swinging in their hands.

When her adrenaline finally faded, Sevora began to feel the pain in her arm, and reached up to touch the stinging marks left by the steel barbs. The wounds weren't deep, but they were ragged tears that sent screams of pain through her when her fingers touched them. With that pain had come something else. A flash of memory, bright and hot as the desert sun.

'They're almost on us.' Corus leaned against the wall of the temple, holding himself still as Aika sewed up the deep cut in his arm. 'You have to go now.'

Aika pulled the last stitch tight, tied it off then bit through the bloody cord. 'And you?'

'We'll go to the temple.' He stretched his arm, ignoring the sharp jolt of pain that went through him. Corus could move it, the bleeding had slowed; that was all he needed. 'We can stop them there.' It wasn't a lie. Not exactly. The Khornate madmen that were smashing into the walls of the settlement would stop there, to slaughter all that remained.

Aika looked at him, her eyes clouded with despair. She knew the truth of his words. His hand went to her belly, fingers sweeping across the small curve. Aika wasn't that far along, not yet. It wouldn't slow her.

'You have to go,' he said again, and she nodded.

'I know.' Then she kissed him, kissed him hard, even as the sound of war drums and screams echoed through the oasis, drowning out the mournful sound of the temple's tolling bell, then stepped away.

'Remember, my love. Remember hope,' she whispered, tears in her eyes, and then she was gone.

Then she was back, blinking in the dark, stunned by the heat and the pain and the grief.

'Thanks for that,' she whispered softly, then forced herself to move on, trying to forget the memory that wasn't even hers.

Now Sevora moved, fast as she dared, trying to reach whatever safety there was in being that much closer to the Reclusians, and the source of these memories that stabbed through her head like bright, hot knives.

'You know where you're going?' Avil asked. 'You can get us back to them?'

He was standing behind her as she rested her hand on the wall, and his voice dragged her out of the spiral of her thoughts. Fear was woven through every word, a desperate shakiness that was completely different to the sanctimonious surety that had filled him when he had been close to Dreskir. He was hanging on to her now, counting on her to save him, but she was no Stormcast. And she had so little hope that either of them were going to survive. But when she answered him, she made herself sound certain, because if Avil panicked, what little chance they might have would probably be torn away from them by ragged claws and yellow teeth.

'This way,' she said, turning to the left. Corus felt like he was straight ahead, somewhere on the other side of all this stone, and going left… It felt like it might be getting her closer. Maybe. That had to be good enough.

So they crept carefully through the dark, until Sevora heard the dull click of claws on the stone.

She froze, tightening her hand on Avil's. Thankfully the man understood and stayed silent. She listened intently, trying to block the soft sound of her and Avil's breathing, and there was that click again, slow and quiet. Then, hard after, the skittering of claws across the hard floor. Something was running towards them. Sevora let go of Avil's hand and raised her knife, holding it in front of her. Such a tiny thing, compared to Corus' axe, or the cruel chain whips of the skaven assassins, but it was comfortable in her hand and she was determined that whatever was coming would feel its blade.

Then the claws went silent.

The skaven had stopped, but it was close. Sevora could hear the panting rasp of its breathing, could smell the foul reek of its body, like a diseased animal dying in its own waste. She stood perfectly still, holding her breath, waiting for silent steel to flick out at her, but it never came. It was as if the thing were searching for her too, and with that thought came the realisation: this wasn't one of the eyeless assassins. This was one of the ill-wrought ones, separated from its swarm and running through the dark, blind as they were. Still deadly, but if it couldn't see either, maybe…

The breathing of the thing changed. The skaven was sniffing the air, tasting their scent. Trying to find them with that, and she silently cursed and raised her knife. Then Avil made a noise behind her, a strangled sneeze or cough or gods knew what, a faint little thing hastily covered, but in that silent dark it might as well have been a scream. There was the sound of claws again, running and leaping, and Sevora felt the skaven cutting through the air towards her, and she threw herself to the side as hard as she could, dodging the thing's leap – throwing herself headfirst into the stone wall.

There was a lightning flash followed by a thunderclap of pain, and she almost fell, but something slapped her leg – something hot and fleshy and coiling. The monster's tail, and she fought the pain, desperate to stay conscious. The image of teeth was clear in her mind, yellow and dripping foam-like venom. She stayed on her feet, stayed awake, brought her knife up and turned to face the sound of scrabbling claws, of gnashing teeth, of Avil grunting with pain.

And then a different kind of light filled her head, and she clenched her teeth to keep from howling her denial as it swept away the darkness into painful, blinding light.

The sun was in his eyes, blinding him, and Corus tried to blink against its light but couldn't. He couldn't shut his eyes; the light hurt, the gritty air hurt, his eyes burned with dust and light and blood, and he couldn't close them. Couldn't blot out anything as his head swung around, from sky to stone to sky. Someone was carrying him, carrying him down the aisle of the temple, past the benches his congregation had sat on while he told them of Sigmar and his plan for them.

Sigmar's plan.

Was it Sigmar's plan that those benches be ripped apart, their wood used to fashion the eight-pointed stars that were hanging from the walls, every one of them decorated with the mangled, decapitated bodies of the people who'd trusted Corus? Who had followed him out of the darkness of the Warrens into this wasteland seeking the promise of light and life? Was that what the god's plan had been all along?

Corus wondered that as his eyes throbbed and his head bounced, until he was finally dropped to his knees on the stone floor, facing his altar. Its carved stone had been utterly defiled, lacquered in layers of blood. As he watched, a screaming man was laid across it, pinned in place by men and women dressed in scars and blood and spikes, their lips pulled back from file-sharpened teeth, their eyes gleaming with rage and madness. Standing over the altar was a towering figure, a hideous caricature of a warrior, a man whose grotesquely vast muscles were covered in bronze plates, armoured scales that cut through his skin like blades. Blood ran from them, a never-ending cascade that flowed down his face and chest, arms and legs, puddling on the floor below. He held an axe in his hands, a vast thing whose shaft was shaped like a spine, the curved blades worked to look like split-open ribs. He raised the axe high, as if it weighed nothing, then slashed it down, ending the man's screams with a terrible crunching noise as his head tumbled away to join the pile that was rising up at the end of the temple.

The Chaos-tainted warrior raised his ugly axe again and stared down at Corus with eyes that ran with blood.

'A skull for the Skull Throne, priest.'

He reached down and grabbed the corpse's leg, raised it up and held it over the altar, letting the blood pour from the stump of the neck over the tainted stone. His followers howled, reaching out with their hands to gather palmfuls of gore to smear over their faces and pour into their mouths.

'And blood for the Blood God.'

The warrior threw the body away, and the savage cultists gathered before him ran after it like dogs chasing a bone. The Chaos warrior stepped around the altar, staring down at Corus, filling his vision. There was nothing Corus could do to blot out the sight of the gore-covered warrior, and that was when he realised that he couldn't close his eyes because the lids had been torn away.

'What will you offer him, priest?' the warrior asked. His voice was strangely beautiful, deep and resonant, and it filled the temple. 'Your skull? Your blood?' He crouched down, staring into his eyes.

GARY KLOSTER

'He will have them, of course. But you could offer more. He could have you. He could have your soul. Offer that to the Blood God, and you will be baptised. Born anew in anger so pure that you will forget the pain of this loss. The despair of your impotence. You can forget it all, and be pure in your savagery, your hate.' The bleeding giant reached out one red hand and held it a few inches from Corus' forehead. 'I can paint his mark upon you, and give you a gift of such glorious beauty, priest. I can give you the peace of war, and you will never feel despair again.'

'And what do I have to do to earn this great gift?' The words fell from Corus' mouth like rusted razor blades, every one of them cutting his throat and lips, making him ache. He hurt. By Sigmar, he hurt. What had their axes and teeth left of his body? Nothing but pain, it felt like, nothing but raw, ragged flesh singing with agony.

'Revoke him,' the warrior said, his deep, beautiful voice filling the temple. 'Revoke the name of the weak, petulant thing that you dedicated your soul to. Revoke Sigmar, and give yourself to a true god, a god that will give you exactly what you need. Revoke him, and dedicate yourself to Khorne. Just that, and all this pain will flow from you and become a weapon. Revoke him, priest, and you will no longer be the one who hurts. You will be the one who HURTS.'

'Just that,' Corus whispered. So easy. So quick. So tempting. Forget everything else, merely the idea of having this over instantly tugged at him. A few words and then it would be done, and all this pain, all this loss, would be subsumed in raging madness. And what did eternal damnation matter, when there was nothing left but blood-lust? It was just another kind of oblivion, and wouldn't oblivion be the sweetest gift right now? And so he almost said it. Almost sold his soul for the gift of nothing. But, almost lost in the dull pounding that filled his head, there was a voice, faint as the wind sighing through the temple's shattered windows.

'Remember hope.'

The words he could ignore. Their meaning was lost in the smell of blood and shredded bowel. But the voice... That he couldn't ignore, or the realisation that he would never hear it again if he said those words. And that was an eternity he could not abide. So Corus raised his burning eyes, stared into the bleeding face of the massive warrior, and drew back his lips into a smile.

'Take my head, damned one, and add my skull to Khorne's ugly throne.' The words hurt, but he made sure to speak every one of them clearly. 'Place it so that my teeth are right below him, and I can spend eternity being a pain in your cowardly god's arse.'

With a low snarl that rose to a roar, the Chaos warrior swung his axe in a circle around him, then lashed out, the weapon headed straight at Corus, who couldn't even blink as it smashed into him and everything became blood and pain.

Pain.

It didn't matter that it wasn't her pain, that it happened a century ago. It filled her, and she writhed on the stone floor, kept from screaming only because she was choking on the smell of blood.

Blood.

That smell was real. Reeking of rust and life, it filled the air. A real smell, just like the muffled grunts and squeals that filled the tunnel were real, real as the darkness that covered Sevora's eyes.

Real. This was real, this was happening, and if she didn't do something soon, she was going to die.

She launched herself up from the ground, knife in hand, ignoring the echoes of the pain still ringing through her nerves. The skaven had struck at her, missed, and fallen on Avil. Holding her knife close to her chest, she reached out with her other hand, circling in carefully towards the fight. Something smashed her reaching fingers – a boot, she thought as she snatched her hand back – and then there was fur, coarse and greasy beneath her stinging fingers.

She grabbed a handful and her thumb ran over a stretch of bare skin. It wasn't like the tail, scaly and rough; it was soft and hot like touching a fevered person's cheek. She had a moment of doubt, wondering if this could be Avil or someone else, but it was too late. She was already driving the blade in.

The knife bit and she pulled it back and thrust again, punching the blade forward until the handle hit the thing's flesh, and Sevora could feel the terrible, sticky heat of blood rushing across her hands.

Something squealed as she stabbed, a terrible, inhuman noise, and she felt a moment of relief that she hadn't stabbed Avil to death. But then the thing was twisting in the dark and something hit her in the ribs, tearing at the robes she wore. The skaven's muzzle slammed into her, trying to bite, and she stabbed her knife down. She missed, stumbled, and something struck her legs, knocking her to the ground. Carrion breath washed over her as the skaven tried to drive its teeth into her face.

Cursing, she drove her knife up and felt the blade hit something hard. A tooth, and then she felt a disgusting warmth and wetness over her hand and realised she had shoved her knife into the skaven's mouth. She turned the blade, stabbing it upward, making the skaven open its jaws instead of snapping them shut to bite off her hand. She jerked her knife back as the skaven made a terrible coughing noise, sputtering on its own filthy blood. Then they were separated, standing apart in the absolute darkness, until the skaven lunged for her again.

Sevora could feel herself reaching for the wind, trying to strike, but it was useless. She had no strength left, and the bare breath of a breeze that flowed around her could have hardly fluttered a bird in the sky. All she had now was the sliver of steel in her hand. She drove it forward again and met the skaven's strike, the knife somehow finding the monster's throat.

The blade sank in, driven by her arm and the skaven's lunging advance, and then it was on her, claws scrabbling. But when she kicked the skaven away, it didn't try to come back. The skaven twitched, and then finally fell still. The tunnel was silent again, but for Sevora's ragged breaths and Avil's low groans.

'Bloody Nadir,' she breathed, then spent a moment cataloguing her hurts. Bruises and scratches and nothing more. Then she started towards Avil, moving carefully. 'Avil. It's Sevora. Avil?'

'Sevora?' His voice was distorted, mushy with blood and fear. 'Where is it?'

'It's dead. I killed it.'

'Thank Sigmar.' He sobbed, and when her fingers found his robe he caught her hand and held it, and they stayed like that for a while, holding hands like children in the dark, breathing and bleeding and hoping the other monsters would pass them by.

CHAPTER FIFTEEN

GALLOGAST

The skaven had done something to this place.

Amon stood in the torchlight, staring into the dark. It was too close. The shadows were crowding in, pressing against the light, and the flames of his mace and Morgen's torch could only hold them back so far. Even his heaven-crafted eyes couldn't see through their thick gloom. But it wasn't just the dark.

He'd spent hours with the soldiers back at the Halt, interrogating them about the corridors and vaults below Gallogast. They'd drawn out maps and gone over them so many times their lines were carved deep in his memory. But none of it helped. The spaces they walked through twisted on themselves, curved in strange circles, stretched far too long, and the simple maps in his mind didn't match the labyrinth they now wandered. They were caught in a trap of shadow magic, and illusions of confusion and darkness surrounded them. The skaven were using the shadows to fight for them, and every wasted minute Amon spent turning circles in their treacherous dark made him angrier. Gripping mace and sword tight, he longed to stride forward and smash the shadows aside, to cut his way to the heart of this false maze. But blocking the passage before him, wrapped in their dark patinated armour, was the Lord-Terminos.

And no matter his frustration, he would not shoulder them aside. The dreadful aura that clung to the Ruination Chamber was strongest around the Lord-Terminos, and being this close to the masked Stormcast unnerved Amon. So he held his mace high, the flames fighting the dark, and gritted his teeth. He wished that the gloom would part and the skaven would spill out so that he could kill them all, end their filthy magic, and finish this hunt. Because hidden somewhere in this maze of shadows was Brevin Fortis, Lord-Ordinator.

Or whatever was left of him.

'We must move faster.' He looked over his shoulder at Lord-Veritant Morgen, striding behind him with sword and torch blazing. 'We have to push through the spells they are using to contain us. We have to press the skaven, and their magic, and get to Brevin before they slit his throat.'

'We move as fast as we can,' Morgen said. 'The Memorians must be protected.'

He looked past her, but he couldn't make out the mortals marching behind the Reclusians. The Memorians had slowed them this whole time. Why were these mortal vassals so important? Besides firing a few arrows, and that one with her wind trick, they'd done nothing but hinder this hunt. Amon wanted to tell the Lord-Veritant that the mortals could learn to fend for themselves or fall behind. But the gryph-crow walking beside her raised its eyes to him and croaked 'must,' and he kept silent.

Until the tunnel behind them suddenly filled with screams.

'They've struck the middle of the line,' Morgen said. 'Anchor this end, they may be trying to flank us.' Then she was gone, slipping between the Reclusians. Their close-packed ranks opened and closed around her, moving with perfect synchronisation, and she and her gryph-crow were gone, leaving him standing between the Lord-Terminos and two Reclusians who were staring back at the sounds, their mouths drawn into hard frowns beneath their haunted eyes.

'I would–' one of them started, hefting his axe and taking a step towards the fight.

'No, Dreskir,' the other Reclusian said. He was looking back too, with eyes that snapped with lightning, but he was standing firm. 'We hold, and keep the skaven from breaking our formation.'

'Of course, Corus,' Dreskir said, but his gauntlets creaked as his hand tightened on the handle of his axe.

Breaking their formation. Amon's anger made him want to go after Morgen, to plunge into the fight back there and destroy the treacherous ratmen that were twisting the dark. But he had to leash it, knowing the Lord-Veritant was right. Amon tapped a knuckle against the metal band holding his hair, and stared at the dark waiting beyond the Lord-Terminos, who had stopped in the centre of the passage, axe in hand, motionless as stone.

Amon settled his anger, shifting into the watchful stillness of a hunter in a blind. There was nothing to see, and his ears were filled with the sounds behind him, of shouts and snarls and the snap of bone. But there was a thin trickle of air moving down the corridor, and he breathed in deep, searching for scents. There was only stone and sigmarite, but he kept breathing deeply as he waited. And then there was something else. A sour-sweet stench, like carrion and old sweat.

'They're coming,' he said, and the Lord-Terminos leaned forward. Raising their axe, just as the barbed chains shot out of the dark.

Two of the chain whips went for the Lord-Terminos, one clinking off the blade of the axe as the Stormcast parried, the other making a shower of sparks as it cracked into the Lord-Terminos' helm. Two more lashed out at Amon. They both came high, one ringing off the armour covering his forearm, the other wrapping around the handle of his mace, its bladed end smashing into his fingers. Even with his gauntlet, the blow almost broke his knuckles, and his hand spasmed. When the chain jerked back, the mace tumbled away, its flame dying the moment it was gone.

The darkness rushed forward, wrapping around them. The light from the Lord-Veritants was too far away to stop it, and Amon was almost blind. The only thing he could see was the spark that hung centred in the sigmarite cage at the head of his mace, but the darkness was trying to blot out that bright speck, was making it dim and distant. He threw himself forward, reaching for that wisp of light, but it was moving, being dragged across the floor away from his hand. Scrabbling forward, he felt across the smooth stone, trying to see that faint spark, trying to free his mace of the chain that held it, but then came a sudden searing pain in his head. One of the chain whips had found him in the dark, the sharp point glancing off his sigmarite headband and barely missing his eye. He shook his head, but the chain whip looped around him, the barbs digging into his face and scalp as it began to tighten.

Amon slammed his fist into the blade of his sword and made it boom, a heavy roll of thunder that echoed down the corridor. Almost lost in the roaring echoes was an angry hiss, and the chain whip went loose around his head. Amon grabbed it, freeing himself and ripping the weapon out of the skaven's hand.

Pulling the barbs from his flesh, Amon stood, dropping the cruel weapon at his feet. It landed, steel links not making a sound in the dark, and he started forward again, sword extended in front of him, blinking back blood from his useless eyes.

'Knight-Questor.' The voice was near, one of the Reclusians.

'Here,' he said, and as he spoke he saw a light in the dark, a tiny mote hovering before him.

'Your mace.' The light grew close and Amon reached out, finding the familiar hilt. He took it, and gripping it tightly in his aching hand, bent and rapped its pommel against the stone floor. The spark blossomed into flame and the shadows pulled back reluctantly, as if hesitant to give up their prey. When they finally receded, Amon found himself standing beside Corus. The Reclusian's axe was coated in fresh blood, and Amon almost asked the lightning-eyed man how he had found his weapon in the dark. But the Lord-Terminos was stepping out of the dark, the shadows clinging to their armour before sliding away, like claws clutching. The long curve of their axe was marked with gore, dark fur and red blood showing in the light, and more blood marked their uncanny mask.

'They sought our light,' the Lord-Terminos said.

'They did.' Morgen was moving through the Reclusians, shouldering her shield. Her torch followed her, moving on its own, staying as close to her as her gryph-crow. Her flaming sword sizzled, the gore that clung to it burning away. 'They hit our rear too. Lord-Veritant Gracin has fallen, and his torch with him.'

'All honour to our fallen,' the Lord-Terminos said. 'Are there more?'

'Several Memorians,' Morgen said. 'We would have lost more if not for Sevora, Corus. She stopped the ambush as it began, and gave us time to shield the other mortals.'

'And where is she?' Corus asked. 'I can feel her. Alive, unwounded. But she doesn't feel as close.'

'When Gracin fell, some of the Memorians were taken by the dark,' Morgen said. 'Caught on the other side of these shadows. Lost, for the moment.'

'Lost,' Dreskir said. 'I can feel Avil. I can feel him getting further from me.' The Reclusian looked to Morgen. 'But I can find him.'

'We can find them,' Corus said, staring back into the dark.

'You can find them after,' Amon said, his voice hard. 'The skaven seek to break you apart, to pick you off. It's their only chance. We must deny them, stay together, and find the centre of this maze and the Lord-Ordinator.'

Dreskir turned to him, the worry in his eyes gone, replaced by anger. 'Your quest does not rule us, Astral Templar. We will seek our own.'

Amon wiped the blood from his face, looking silently at the Reclusian. If they took this bait, he would leave them. They had got him through the smoke, got him to Gallogast. He had worked with them enough. But Morgen shook her head.

'Amon is correct. I know you worry for your Memorian, but if we turn now the skaven will keep laying more traps, more ambushes. More Memorians will die, and more Reclusians, and the Lord-Ordinator may be lost. We all may be.'

'We can't leave them.' Dreskir stood before her, glaring into her eyes. 'I will go for him. For them. Take the rest, and I will seek them out.'

'No,' Morgen said. 'We will not be further divided.'

Dreskir looked at her for a long moment, his eyes burning, until the silence was broken by Peace croaking out 'no.'

Dreskir snarled and suddenly surged forward, dropping his armoured shoulder and slamming the Lord-Veritant back. She staggered, almost falling, but she caught her torch and barely kept her feet. Dreskir was stomping past, sweeping Peace out of the way with his shield. Amon watched, willing to let the Reclusian go, but the Lord-Terminos was moving, stepping forward, their heavy axe rising fluidly.

Corus was closer. He stepped in behind Dreskir, grabbing his shoulder with one hand, and swung him around. Dreskir spun, axe coming up in a vicious blow that would have smashed through armour, but Corus moved in and pushed his chest into Dreskir's. That close, the blade of Dreskir's axe struck only air.

They stood there, chest to chest, eyes inches apart, Dreskir's glowing with anger while Corus' flashed with lightning. 'I want to go for Aika–' Corus stopped, and drew a breath. 'Sevora too. I want to. But Lord-Veritant Morgen is right. We go, we weaken this strike, and the skaven come closer to crushing us all. We finish this and then we'll find them.'

Dreskir looked up at the other Reclusian until the anger drained from his eyes, leaving him looking lost again. 'Then we must go fast,' he said.

Corus stepped back, looking to Amon. 'We must,' he said.

'I'll leave you in the front, Amon, and move to the middle,' Morgen said. She was ignoring Dreskir, acting as if he'd never struck her, but Peace was watching the Reclusian with wary intensity. 'Lord-Veritant Innovi can move to the back to take Gracin's place.'

Spreading their light out through the line. Spreading their light out.

'No,' Amon said. 'The skaven are trapping us in darkness, and now we have less light to push it back. They're going to lead us in circles, wear us down. We have to break out of this dark, we have to find the centre of this nest.'

'How?' Morgen asked, and he stared at her, angry, unable to think of any way.

And then Corus spoke. 'Lord-Veritant. You don't always need eyes to see.'

'This is not the reason we were given the sight.' Morgen stood in the tunnel beside Amon, the cracked, stained stone walls crowding in on them like broken teeth, and stared at the seething dark that lay ahead. 'But there's no reason not to try.'

'Then try now,' Amon said. They had rearranged themselves, the Lord-Veritants at the front of the line, their torches blazing. The light was not bright enough, though, to shelter everyone from the dark. The Memorians were pulled in close, the Reclusians and the Lord-Terminos behind them, a wall of sigmarite partially lost in shadow, and the skaven would soon move to take advantage of that.

Morgen nodded, reached down and took hold of the black scarf knotted around her throat. She raised it to cover her eyes, and the other Lord-Veritant, Innovi, did the same. They both placed their torches before them, their flames growing again as they held them out. Their gryph-crows stood at their sides, eyes picking up those flames, staring intently into the dark. They stood like statues, motionless and silent, and Amon's hands tightened on his weapons. They were spending too long here.

'They're coming,' Corus said. Corus and Dreskir had stayed at the front to help Amon guard the Lord-Veritants, but Corus had turned to look back. There was nothing to see there but the crowd of Memorians fading into the dark, but Amon could hear something now too. The squeal of teeth and claws against sigmarite, the sound of axes biting through flesh and crunching into bone. There was a smell too, rolling down the passage, the stink of skaven mixed with something else; a tangle of odours, animalistic, human. More of the smoke-made ones, the things that had ripped their way out of bodies and birthed themselves in murder and pain. Driving through the dark in rabid fury, battling the Reclusians again.

How many? There were always more, and if enough skaven came at once, pouring forward like a flood of filth, they would tangle the Stormcasts in their bodies and bury them in fur and teeth and gore.

How many, how long? He looked at the Lord-Veritants. They stood unmoving, their eyes bound. The gryph-crows stood beside them, narrow black beaks shifting as their heads turned, as if they were hunting. Was this working?

They had no time. No time, then Corus and Dreskir were moving, shields up and axes slicing through the air as chain whips flew in. The eyeless assassins were moving in on them again, trying to back them up, to pin them against the battle in the dark behind them.

It was too late. Amon heard a crack of thunder behind him, saw a flicker of light rush up the dark passage. A Reclusian, flashing into lightning after being torn down by the skaven. This was where the hunt was going to end. Lost in the shadows, in the dark. He snarled, stepping forward, weapons rising. What else was there to do, but face death with death, to fight until there was nothing left and then be ripped back into the heavens, the hunt failed...

'Knight-Questor!' Morgen's voice cut through the sounds of battle, a knife of command. Her hand was raised, pointing down the passage towards the assassins. 'Drive them back! Ten paces!'

Ten paces? He would drive them back to Nagash's deepest hell.

'For Sigmar!'

He hurled himself forward with the Reclusians. They flowed easily, moving almost like dancers. Dreskir swept his shield up, blocking a striking chain whip, and Corus' axe sliced through the air barely a finger's breadth from Amon's ear, catching another chain and knocking it away before it could wrap around his head.

Then he was past them, and the light of his mace was splitting the dark, pushing it back. Chains gleamed in the light, and then there was a claw, a black fur-covered arm, the suggestion of a muzzle, and he lunged for it. The skaven jerked back, but not fast enough. The end of Amon's sword caught the assassin's wrist, rumbling as it cut to the bone and shattered it. The chain whip fell to the floor, silent, and the claws of the severed hand made a terrible sound as they scrabbled against the stone.

But more blades smashed against his armour, barbed chains

wrapping around his arm and leg, jerking at him. Too many, and Amon's momentum was faltering. Until Corus slammed past him, the Reclusian charging forward with his shield raised. In the light of his flaming mace, Amon could see Corus slam into one of the eyeless skaven, smashing it down before it could turn and run, and then the lightning-eyed man scooped up the twitching body of the assassin with his hooked axe and threw it down the tunnel. There was a heavy thud and squeals of pain as the skaven's broken body smashed into the others of its kind that still hid in the dark. Corus stopped, shield still held high, and Amon moved up with him as Morgen called out.

'There!'

There was nothing. Just more corridor, more blank basalt walls. But then Peace was driving forward, slipping past them to throw himself at the wall beside Amon's left shoulder. The dark stone rippled, then popped like a dark bubble of blood in a dying man's mouth. Gone, and there was a wide stair running down into the dark.

'Go!' Corus shouted, forming a wall with Dreskir across the corridor just beyond the opening. The eyeless skaven were fighting hard, trying to drive them back, to protect the stairs, but the two Reclusians were a wall, unmoving as the ends of the chain whips rattled off their shields and armour.

Amon was just about to pound down the stairs, the Lord-Veritants following him easily despite their blindfolds, when he caught a blur of motion coming out of the dark and along the ceiling. A skaven, claws clinging to the stone like a lizard, rushing forward over the Reclusians, heading for the Lord-Veritants. Amon began to turn, but the ratman was already dropping, its chain whip flicking out to snag the torch Morgen carried. The barbs on the chain bit, and the skaven hit the ground, rolling, using every bit of its weight and momentum to try to rip the torch from the Lord-Veritant's hand.

Until a black shape slammed into the assassin.

Peace's beak hit the ratman in the gut, driving in like a spear point. Fur and flesh tore as the gryph-crow drove forward, then Peace pulled his beak free and blood splattered from the wound, a stinking gush that covered the floor. The skaven thrashed, coils of bowel spilling across the stone like eels as the ratman convulsed and hissed, trying to rise. Then Morgen slammed the base of her torch into the skaven's head, crushing its skull as she shook loose the barbed chain.

Satisfied they were following, Amon started down the stair, his mace lighting the way. There was another long corridor at the bottom, and at its end a door that spilled out a sickening green light that made Amon's eyes ache. Warpstone light, Chaos light, and Amon moved towards it, weapons ready, a hunter closing on his quarry at last.

CHAPTER SIXTEEN

GALLOGAST

Sevora moved through the dark, one hand trailing along the wall while the other held Avil's hand, keeping him close. Keeping him alive.

'It hurts,' he muttered behind her. His voice was too loud, and she clenched his hand hard, but it was hot in hers, feverishly hot. Blind in all this black, she hadn't been able to see Avil's wounds, but Sevora knew that the skaven had bitten him.

The way her brother had been bitten.

She could leave him. She should leave him. But he'd saved her from the eyeless assassins and their chain whips, and he'd held onto the skaven in the dark long enough for her to stab it. He was going to die, she knew this, but she didn't want to leave him to suffer and die alone. In her head, a flash of memory: her mother's knife slashing across Yevin's throat.

She didn't want to be her mother.

'Dreskir,' Avil muttered again. 'Where's Dreskir? Need him. Needs me.'

'Shhh,' she said, and pulled him along behind her, trying not to imagine his belly opening up in the dark and spilling out something part rat and part Avil, a monstrous parasite born to kill.

They came around a corner, and beyond it was a narrow opening in the wall. Feeling around with her free hand, Sevora traced it out. A stair, going down. Down seemed dangerous, and she started to move past, but there was a sound. A soft, hissing snarl, a squeal and a growl. Skaven, fighting amongst themselves, moving down the passage towards them.

Not rushing forward. Not silent. More of the smoke-made ones, then. Which meant they hadn't seen them yet. Which was good, because just one of those things had almost killed them, and from the sounds she could hear, this was more than one.

Sevora turned and went for the stairs, dragging Avil with her. He muttered, a low whisper of words, but still too loud, and she almost let him go. They could take him and miss her; he was dead already. But the image of her mother's knife passing across her brother's throat wouldn't leave her, so she kept his hand and pulled him down the steps after her, moving as quickly as she could in the dark.

The stairs were a tight spiral, narrow and steep, and they had barely rounded the first turn when Avil stumbled, starting to fall. Sevora got beneath him, somehow holding him up, bracing herself against the smooth walls. He leaned on her, his skin ragged beneath her hands, slick with blood. He groaned, and she shoved a hand over his mouth, shutting him up as she fought to keep him from dragging her down. From above came the sound of tapping claws, low growls, and deep, snuffling breaths.

Breaths. Sevora felt the terrible urge to laugh. It didn't matter how much noise Avil made. The skaven above would scent them and pour down the stairs after them, a flood of teeth and claws in the dark.

Teeth. The yellow teeth her brother had tried to warn her about. They would come for her, rip the flesh from her bones, and if she was lucky she'd be dead before they started eating her. Either way, she would suffer less than Yevin, who had been torn apart from the inside because he had tried to warn her, tried to save her from the teeth.

And yet here they were, coming for her.

Around her the air moved. Her hair stirred, drifting in the faint breeze. Sevora felt it, felt the deep ache in her as her magic tried to work and she fought to will it, to draw out another hurricane like the one that had flung the skaven back before. But all that came was a breeze, thinner than hope, carrying one dim spark around her. Useless.

Unless... She reached up and caught the raven clasp that held the top of her robe closed and ripped it off. 'Please,' she whispered silently to herself. 'Damn you, please. Listen to me. For once.'

The moving air slowed and died, and she almost screamed a curse. But then it started again. Light and thin, but focused. It wrapped around her hand, touching the clasp. Then the wind snatched it up, spun it away, up the stairs, out somewhere in the hall, going, going – until her magic fell apart again and it dropped, rattling on the stone of the floor somewhere away from them.

There was a moment of silence from above. Then a hiss, and the sound of claws rushing across stone. The skaven were running away from them, searching for what had made that sound. And as they went, Sevora started down the stairs again, holding Avil, praying silently he wouldn't fall until they reached the bottom.

There was another passage there, more smooth walls stretching away from her in either direction. But there was something else, besides silence and stone. There was light. Sevora blinked at it, wondering if it was a hallucination, but the faint glow didn't disappear. She started towards it, making herself slide her feet slowly as she pulled Avil behind her. It wasn't easy. Her eyes were hungry for that light, thin and ugly though it was. It wasn't the torchlight of the Lord-Veritants, it was something else – something green, the same ugly green that she had seen flashing through the clouds of smoke gathered at the Halt.

Not a good light, but it was light, and she was drawn to it like a moth. Whatever was up ahead, however dangerous it was, she would at least be able to see it. But she didn't see the thing that clicked against the toe of her boot. She pulled her foot back, staring down. In the dim she saw something jutting up from the dark floor. It was three pieces of thick iron wire, their ends cut into sharp points. They'd been twisted together, bent so that one point stuck upwards. A spike, a trap, and if she hadn't been slowly sliding her feet, that rusty iron would be in her sole.

Sevora started forward again, sweeping her foot carefully out before her. There were more of the spikes, and she shifted them away, making sure Avil had a clear path. It took time, but she had a vicious feeling of glee at the thought of what would happen to any skaven that came after them.

As if it weren't the skaven that had set up this trap.

Her thoughts were a tangle of anger and fear, and she shoved them aside the way she shoved aside the caltrops, and pressed forward towards the door she could now see, outlined by the slowly swelling light. It opened off this side of the passage, which ended just beyond it in a pile of broken stone and dirt. When she reached the door she stopped, held her breath, and carefully looked around the corner of the opening.

The room beyond was choked with things that made grotesque shadows in the green light, but she saw nothing that looked like a skaven, nothing that moved. Sevora waited until her lungs began to burn, then she slowly let out her breath. The room was far from empty, but there didn't seem to be anything alive in there.

That didn't mean it was safe. She ran her eyes over the doorframe, up and down, searching. There. Just above the floor something caught the light. A thin wire, stretched across the empty doorway. She patiently searched for anything else, but that one thin wire was all she could see.

From the door she traced it over to a table where something was hidden in a clutter of bones and scraps of copper. It looked like a crossbow, but instead of the curved arms of a bow it ended in a fan of stubby metal barrels. There were five of them, splayed out like the fingers of a hand, made of iron but wrapped with copper wire. That wire held slivers of bone, chunks of raw crystal, broken pieces of stone. It was haphazard, ill-made and unwieldy looking, but the wire ran to its trigger, and it was pointed at the door.

'Don't move,' she whispered to Avil, and let go of his hand, setting it on the wall. Not trusting him to listen, she moved as fast as she dared away from him, stepping over the wire and to the table, standing behind the not-crossbow. She carefully slid the wire from the trigger and the weapon – if that was what it was – quivered. But then stilled. Sevora wiped the sweat from her hands, and then jerked her head up as Avil stumbled through the door, lurching towards her, his feet tangling in the wire.

'Dreskir?' he groaned. Sevora held herself still, making sure nothing else was connected to the trap, then caught him. Holding him close, before he stumbled into something and sent it crashing down.

Sevora wanted to snarl at Avil, her terrified anger desperate for a target, but the green light fell across the man and, for the first time, she could see him. The skaven's claws had drawn deep furrows down the side of his head, bloody rents that revealed the dull white of his skull, and ripped off an ear. But his face was worse. The skaven had bitten him deep, its teeth tearing an ugly crater in his flesh. His nose was a shattered ruin, the right eye a gory pit. His cheek below was just gone, and she could see his broken teeth beneath. Avil's face had been ripped half off, and Sevora had to snatch her gaze away before she got sick.

'Stand still,' she whispered to him, not looking at him. Then she searched the room.

It wasn't large, but it was crowded with things. Heaps of junk almost filled it, leaving only narrow paths threading through. There were bones and weapons and armour, cookware and tools, jewellery and trash, but there was a method to each pile's madness. Like was grouped with like, and Sevora stepped around heaps of iron, copper, bones, and hides. In the room's centre was a long table covered with things half-built from junk, tools piled around them. They looked less like machines and more like rusty, sharp-edged toys built by children who had looted a graveyard, midden, and blacksmith's shop. None of them looked complete, but it was hard to tell. None made any sense, and a few were smashed, as if their creator had grown angry and beat them apart with whatever tool was closest.

The light was coming from the far corner of the room, and she moved carefully down one of the paths until she could see it. There was a crack in the wall, a place where the basalt had broken long ago. Through it flooded the green light, so bright now it hurt her eyes. Bright, but sickening. She'd wanted light, but this was nauseating. Still, she needed to see what made it.

She retrieved Avil and led him to a spot that was a little clearer, where two of the narrow paths crossed. She pushed him down, trying not to look at his wounds. 'Stay here,' she whispered, but he shook his head, trying to rise. Blood dripped and splattered as he moved, getting on her, running along the lines of scars that covered the backs of her hands. 'Stay,' she said, pushing him back down. 'I'm going to find Dreskir, all right?'

'Dreskir,' he muttered, and she nodded, holding him in place until he stilled, his one eye staring at nothing, blank and filmed with pain.

Then she turned and crept along the paths, moving as silently as she could. She knelt beside the crack, contorting herself so that she was still hidden by the wall, and stared out into the light.

The light.

It hit her then, and she only had an instant to pray that she wouldn't fall back into the pile of scrap behind her as the memory took hold.

There was light up ahead.

Corus stopped, wiping a hand across his brow. After the battle, he'd taken his helmet off. These slot canyons were treacherous things, narrow and rough, and despite the shade of their walls they were hot. The heat of the desert flowed overhead, an oven wind that dipped down between the stones and baked anything caught in the twisting passages. Sweat was pouring out of him, filling his armour.

Armour.

He looked at his hand, gauntleted in sigmarite, and thought of a desert long ago, his bare hand, covered in blood. It had been so much smaller then. When he was mortal. Before he had been reborn, remade, Reforged into an instrument of his god's will. Of Sigmar's vengeance.

Vengeance.

He thought of the feel of the axe in his hand. The way the handle shook when he slammed the blade home, cleaving away limb or head, shattering ribs, destroying flesh. Killing the murderers who had dedicated themselves to the destruction of his faith, his family, his everything.

Killing.

He walked down the canyon, towards the light, and he heard a voice deep as thunder speak.

'Revoke him.'

* * *

'No,' Sevora gasped, then slapped her hand over her mouth, terrified she'd shouted the denial. But no. She was standing beside the crack, the green light pouring out beside her, blinking from it. Blinking from the memory that had flooded through her. Again.

Corus' memory, filling her head like some kind of waking nightmare, telling her some terrible story she didn't want to hear, that didn't make any sense and she didn't want it to. She just wanted it gone, out of her head. Before it killed her.

She shook her head, and her hand tapped the knife inside her robe. Its touch reassured her, and she took a breath, cleared her mind of the memory that wasn't hers, and bent to look through the crack once more.

Light. Green, poisonous light. She forced herself to stare into it, waiting for her eyes to adjust. But she flinched back when a bellow boomed through the crack.

'Damn you!'

The voice was deep, powerful. It was a Stormcast, shouting his defiance. That realisation hit Sevora, and she was pressing her eye to the break in the stone, blinking against the light, desperate to see. There was a stone – a crystal, green and large as her fist – set on a rod of copper. Shadows flitted around it, the lean and ugly shapes of skaven. Black-furred and dressed in dark robes, eyes sewn shut with yellow thread, there were a dozen arranged around the huge shape of a Stormcast Eternal. They were hauling him up to his knees, using the chains that were connected to the iron collar around his neck, keeping him in place, keeping him captive.

The Stormcast had been stripped of his bright armour, and his body was wrapped only in rags. Filth covered his bruised skin, tracks of blood cutting through the dirt, and his face was a ruin. Both eyes were gone, the sockets empty holes, one crusted with dried gore while the other dripped fresh blood like tears.

More blood marked his throat, running from narrow cuts that ran beside his windpipe.

Lord-Ordinator Brevin Fortis, alive, if barely. But for how long?

A skaven stood before him, wrapped in yellow robes, his fur grey as fog. He was whispering something to the Lord-Ordinator as he crouched down to pick something up from the floor. Brevin's eye, its filmy pupil reflecting the ugly green light. The yellow-robed skaven held it before itself a moment, then popped it into his mouth, gnashing it down with relish. It licked its lips, catching the blood and clear fluid that had spilled out, then bent to pick up a crude, spiked thing made of metal and bone from the floor.

'You want light, and lies.' The ugly device looked like the half-finished contraptions littering the table behind Sevora, and when the yellow-robed skaven held it up, the smaller skaven stared at it with wide, covetous eyes. 'Lies, hope. Hope, lies. All same. I will show you. I will make you know.'

Then he slammed the thing into Brevin's chest, driving the spikes deep, and the Lord-Ordinator contorted, his throat bleeding as he screamed wordlessly. Around the grey skaven's neck a green stone pendant flared to life, glowing the same ugly green as the larger stone on the copper rod, and something began to happen inside the triangle, something like a mote of darkness blooming, a hideous flower beginning to unfurl…

Then there was a noise behind Sevora. A squeal, agonised and ugly, from the hall beyond the room's door. The other skaven had found them.

Sevora rushed back through the narrow paths, hissing 'Stay!' as she pushed past Avil and headed for the door. She could hear pained squealing and the sound of fighting in the corridor beyond. They'd found the spikes with their malformed paws. But by the sound of it, the traps weren't driving them away, they were just maddening them, and she could hear metal crashing into stone.

They were picking up the spikes and throwing them, and the sound was getting closer.

She crouched beside the table, her knife clutched in her hand. How many were there? It didn't matter; there were too many. She wouldn't stop them with her knife, her magic was gone, and if the Ruination Chamber was coming for Brevin, they were still too far away. But on the table beside her, the not-crossbow sat, its splayed barrels still pointing at the door. She didn't know what it was, what it was meant to do, but she had a guess that if she'd tripped that wire across the door, it would have unleashed something awful from those barrels. So she picked it up, held it in her arms, and pointed it at the door, resting her finger on the crude trigger.

And they came. The first was long and lean, and there were scales mixed with its fur, and its mouth held a set of sloping fangs. The skaven crouched at the door and two more appeared, one with curving horns growing from its head, the other with patches of smooth, pale skin and disturbingly human blue eyes. They searched the room from the door, the way she had, and then the snake one saw her. It hissed, and the others snapped their heads towards her. Three of them now, and more coming, shadows and movement creeping up the passage behind them. Sevora aimed the not-crossbow at them and growled.

'Go. We're not your meat.'

'Meat,' the one with the blue eyes whispered, and they started to move. Sevora hit the trigger.

Green fire burst from the weapon's five barrels, streams of destruction that ate through everything they touched. Scrap piles and stone wall were chewed away, and things were falling with a thundering crash as the emerald fire poured out. It had caught the serpent skaven point-blank, dissolving it away in a wash of green flame. All that was left of the horned one was its head and one arm, tongue and fingers twitching. But the blue-eyed one was the worst. It had almost dodged, which meant that the flames only took the right side of its body. The other half fell to the floor, spilling blood and guts across the stone as the half-corpse twisted in its horrifying death spasms.

The noise and the flames made Sevora want to throw the thing away from her, but she held it tight, desperate to keep that hellish green fire pointed away from her. But the weapon was shaking in her hands, pieces of it popping off as the fire went on and on, tearing through the wall, vaporising the skaven that had been standing outside, eating into the wall beyond. Then one of the barrels came off, falling from the thing while still spurting flame.

It spun in the air as it fell, and Sevora dodged a gout of green fire. It sizzled by, eating the corner of her robe, barely missing her. The iron barrel hit the floor and sprang up, flying through the air like a crossbow bolt, propelled by the lance of green death still pouring out of it. Sevora had to throw herself to the side to avoid the fire, and she tossed the weapon away. Thankfully, its own flames washed over it, consuming it before it could tumble and turn on her. The one free barrel cracked off the ceiling, a wall, and then it was gone, flying out the hole in the wall and clanging down the passage outside.

Let it chase whatever skaven survived, if any had, she thought, staring at the charred stump of the weapon's stock. Then there was a noise from the crack in the wall, a shout, deep and loud. The voice of a Stormcast Eternal, and suddenly she realised she could feel Corus close by. She turned towards the sound, about to shout herself, and then the heap of scrap iron beside her shifted, tottered, and fell on her with a crash like a roll of thunder.

CHAPTER SEVENTEEN

GALLOGAST

There was darkness in the heavens. Brevin held onto that thought as the agony rolled through him. There was nothing blacker than the space between the stars, and that was Sigmar's domain too. He may have lost the light, but he hadn't lost his god, or the blessings that had been forged into him. Brevin was still alive. He was still a Hallowed Knight. He would endure, and when he had the chance he would fight with all the strength Sigmar had given him.

That belief filled him, almost. But there was still that agony in his chest, where Skein had stabbed that thing into him. What cursed magic was that? He didn't know, and there was pain in that ignorance too. Skein wanted the Halt to fall, and Brevin was certain that his connection to the Heart was still at the centre of the Grey Seer's scheme.

Despair. Hope. Fighting in him, tearing him apart, as painful as the metal spikes in his chest. But in the distance, he heard another shout – 'Forward! The last hope!' – and that gave him the strength to hold on. They were coming for him. The Ruination

Chamber was coming, and when they reached this place they would tear Skein apart.

Then the sounds of shouting were lost in a booming roar of thunder.

'Shhhh!' the Sisseris hissed, and over them came Skein's voice, as loud as Brevin had ever heard it.

'Is this something of yours, Varus?'

'Yes,' came the answer, nearly lost in the cacophony, then there was a sharp squeal of pain from Varus.

'Enough,' Skein said, his voice a harsh whisper of rage. 'It is time, Sisseris. Go!'

For a moment, Brevin almost toppled, as the chains on his collar were dropped. But he caught himself with his unwounded arm and surged to his feet, chains rattling around him. He wrapped the chains around his arms, ready to swing them like crude imitations of the Sisseris' chain whips. Then something hit him, a blow to his chest like a hammer. Brevin lurched back as the pain flared – and then dulled. The hollow feeling in him grew, and as it spread through him he went numb, losing the agony along with every- thing else. When the next blow hit the pain was less, but so was everything else. It was like the hole in him was growing, hollowing him out. He staggered, swinging his chains in desperation, trying to hit Skein, Lisstis, Varus, any of them, but nothing connected. And then another blow hit him. And another.

Brevin was on his knees again, trying to stay up, but he was losing everything. He was in the dark, and all sensation was leaving him, but he wasn't dying; somehow he knew that, knew there was going to be no easy release at the end of whatever was happening. Hit again, he toppled forward, barely feeling it as the triangle in his chest was slammed deeper into him by the fall.

No pain, no fire, no nothing, just ghosts of sensation, and was he being turned over? Maybe. And then the hits began again, each one tearing out his insides, leaving him an empty husk. And then, finally, one more. One more strike, and suddenly, horribly, he could see the eyes again. Those green eyes, filling the dark that surrounded him, and then they were filling him, filling him with their foetid, terrible light, and he opened his mouth to scream but there was no sound, nothing, nothing but the light of that carrion god's eyes.

Green light.

Amon moved towards it, eyes narrowed against its glare. He could hear the Reclusians behind him, moving down the stairs and spilling into the passage, an avalanche of weapons and armour.

He didn't know what awful thing that baleful light would illuminate. But he was sure this was where his quarry lay, and he walked towards the light cautiously, but with purpose. Then a roaring noise poured down the corridor, a roll of thunder that went on and on, and the stone tunnel shook like the ruins were about to collapse.

With the noise came light, more of that terrible green light, and Amon cursed and started to run. Was the room collapsing? Was the whole purpose of his hunt about to be buried beneath tons of broken stone? He flung himself through the door, weapons ready.

The room was a circle, alcoves built into the walls. A duplicate of the place they called the candelarium, except half ruined, and empty but for a rod of copper sticking up out of the floor, a crude setting on its end empty. The light and noise were coming from a crack in the far wall, the brilliant green glow lighting the dust that filled the air. Then it flickered and disappeared. There was only a low rumble of settling stone and the light from his torch, casting strange shadows across the dusty floor. And sprawled in the middle of it, half-cloaked in shadow, was a body. Huge, dressed in rags, covered in blood.

'Lord-Ordinator Brevin Fortis.'

Amon moved away from the door, eyes still sweeping the room. There was nothing: no skaven, no sign of what had made that noise and light. He stepped carefully towards the body. Brevin hadn't reacted to his name, but he wasn't dead. He moved, his body shifting as if he were caught in a dream. Amon looked down at him, taking in his wounds. No eyes, cuts to his throat and arm, and deep stab wounds in his chest, in the shape of a triangle around his heart. Not a dream. A nightmare.

'Is he alive?' Morgen walked into the room, torch in one hand, her sword burning in the other. She had lowered her blindfold, and her eyes flashed in the light of her torch as she swept them across the room. Peace paced beside her, head turning constantly.

'Yes. But badly hurt.' Amon crouched and shook the man, carefully. Brevin twitched again, but made no response. 'Unconscious.' Stormcasts could be knocked out, but not for long. Their god-wrought bodies recovered quickly. 'They did something to him.'

The Lord-Veritant walked to the Lord-Ordinator and crouched down beside him. She frowned at his maimed face, but her eyes fixed on the wounds in his chest. 'This wasn't a weapon. This was... I don't know what this was.'

More Stormcasts were moving into the chamber, a dozen Reclusians, and she looked up at them. 'Search this place. I want the things that would dare do this to one of Sigmar's chosen.'

'You won't find them,' Amon said. 'Skaven know how to run, how to hide. When we broke their magic, they fled.'

'Skaven are cowards, but not ghosts.' She rose, looking around. 'Where did they go?'

'There's something there,' Amon said, pointing to the alcove. Now that it wasn't spilling out light any more, the crack was almost impossible to see. She nodded, and gestured to Corus and Dreskir, sending them over to investigate while Amon turned away. He didn't care about the missing skaven. He would have killed them if they were here, but they weren't his hunt. His hunt was to find Brevin, and to bring him home.

He pulled off his cloak and spread it on the floor beside the Hallowed Knight, then started manoeuvring the man onto it. 'We should be gone too. We have what we came for.'

'We–'

There was a crashing noise across the room, making Peace crouch and both of them hold up their torches. Corus and Dreskir were smashing the ends of their axe handles into the stone around the crack, widening it.

'What are you doing?' Morgen snapped.

Dreskir kept going, smashing into the wall like a miner gone berserk, but Corus stopped and spoke.

'Sevora. Avil. When we got this close, we could feel them. They're in there, but they're hurt.'

Morgen started towards them, but as she moved she pointed to two other Reclusians. 'Take the Lord-Ordinator to the Memorians. Carry him with them, and guard him.'

They nodded and came over, gathering the corners of the cloak and lifting the senseless Stormcast. Amon started to follow, but Morgen pointed to him.

'Knight-Questor. We need your mace.'

He hesitated, but the faster this was done, the faster he could move the Ruination Chamber out. So he went and waited for Morgen to clear the two Reclusians out of his way. Corus went easily, but she had to grab Dreskir's arm.

'He's hurt,' Dreskir said, his voice tight. 'I thought I could feel it, and now, this close, I know it. Avil's hurt.'

'Then let us get to him,' Morgen said calmly, pulling him back. He resisted for a moment, but the Lord-Veritant held his gaze, and he finally got out of the way. Amon sheathed his sword as

Dreskir moved, took his mace in both hands, and then swung the fiery head at the wall.

Stone crumbled and fell. Two blows, three, and a great chunk of the back wall gave way, crashing into the room beyond. Amon ducked through, leading with his flaming mace. The room was heaped with junk, which he ignored. There was no sign of skaven, but something had happened here. The far wall was gone, dissolved as if something had eaten through it, and it stank of ashes and corruption. Amon moved through the debris carefully, his light making a thousand strange shadows, and found Avil. The Memorian's breathing was harsh through the shredded ruins of his face, and Amon could see his fate clearly. He was dying, but not mercifully. He'd be something else to slow them down. Dreskir frowned at the maimed mortal, but then he picked him up gently. Avil groaned, and that painful sound was answered by a noise from beneath one of the collapsed mounds of scrap.

'Shhhh.'

The mace in Amon's hand flew up, its flame brightening, but as he stepped towards the sound, a hand caught the weapon's haft. Amon spun, but it was Corus standing beside him, his lightning-marked eyes fixed on where the sound had come from.

'It's her,' he said, letting go of Amon's mace. He picked his way through the debris, bent, and carefully shifted the pile to reveal Sevora. Battered, but nothing like Avil.

Corus whispered a soft prayer, then reached out and picked her up. As he lifted her, she opened her eyes and looked at him, and whispered, 'Again?'

Then her eyes rolled back in her head and she shook, convulsing in his arms.

The maps in Amon's head were perfect now.

He brought the Reclusians out of the ruins, moving fast even though in some places they had to wade through piles of skaven dead. The last smoke-made ones had broken off their attack and fled around the time Amon had found Brevin.

They've done something to him. His words were true, but they didn't help. What had the skaven done? They'd torn out Brevin's eyes, wounded his throat, his arm, his chest, beaten him. Was that part of whatever ritual they used to wrench his shadow away to make it attack the Halt? Or was there more?

The one rule of skaven was that there were always more.

Amon shoved the circling thoughts from his mind. He could see light ahead, the door to the ruins, and he led them out into a world grotesquely changed.

Day had dawned while they battled beneath Gallogast, and with the light the smoke had thinned even more. It still filled the mouth of Warrun Vale, stretching away in all directions, but now Amon could see almost fifty yards before the haze grew too thick. Not so far, but the smoke was clearly finally going. He could see the broken tower above, and the frayed cords the mutilated bodies had hung from, empty now. But looking away from Gallogast he could see something else. He could see a world that had been broken.

The rolling land around Gallogast had once been thick with grass and shrubs and patches of forest. That was gone, dissolved into sludgy patches of white and black and dark brown, the decaying, foetid corpses of the plants slowly dissolving. Through that muck there were new things growing, plants that twisted out of the ground like grasping claws. They spread leaves of dull brownish green, thin and leathery, like the membranes of bat wings, and their roots were gnarled, grasping things. There were hideous blossoms on some of them, ugly flowers whose petals burned that same awful green as the warpstone. Things buzzed around them, pulpy, bloated bees furred in brown and black. They swelled as they danced around the burning flowers, growing too big for their wings and falling to the ground with ugly plops, or catching fire and flying in circles, flaming and smoking until they burst. On other stems the fiery flowers had burned down into dark seed pods shaped like bells. They tinkled and rang with tittering music, scattering thin, needle-shaped seeds that drifted through the air along with their awful noise.

Creatures burrowed through the rotting remnants of the dead trees and plants, things like the ugly worm-like beasts they'd found in the forest, and worse. Some were legless, others had far too many legs; some were coated in fur that was glossy and wet from the vile liquids that dripped from the new plants, while others were bare and scaly. All of them were horribly reminiscent of the skaven in some way, though.

This was Aqshy dying away, rotting and being replaced by the monsters that had killed it. This was a world remade. This was the realms as the skaven would have them, corrupted and changed, with every living thing a reminder of them and their dominion.

The smoke was pulling back, and everything it revealed was grotesque, but Amon didn't have time for it. He had to bring the Lord-Ordinator home.

The dark-armoured forms of the Reclusians were moving out of the darkness of Gallogast behind him, forming up with smooth, silent efficiency. The Ruination Chamber had an uncanny ability to move as one, to anticipate each other as they rearranged their formation into a protective block around Brevin and the Memorians. They had shown the same skill in battle, even in the dark. The Reclusians never blocked each other, never struck one of their own by mistake, even when they could not see. And they were stronger, tougher, faster than most other Stormcasts Amon had seen. They were peerless fighters, but-

'Ruination Chamber. Gather to me.' Lord-Veritant Morgen was

facing away from her forces as she spoke, staring out at the wastelands that had been revealed when the toxic smoke had frayed
away. Her torch burned bright in the day, and her sword even
brighter as her eyes studied what the skaven had wrought. 'We
will pray.'

Pray. Amon had to bite back an angry shout. Victory was the
greatest form of prayer; let them raise their voices to Sigmar from
the top of the Halt after they had returned the Lord-Ordinator
home. But the Reclusians were already bowing their heads as
Morgen raised her torch, and he turned away in frustration, the
side of his fist tapping against his temple.

'Lord Sigmar.' Morgen's voice rose behind him, clear and resolute. 'You gave us life, strength, arms, and the will to use them all
with courage and conviction. And in exchange we offer you ourselves. Our lives. Our souls.'

Broken, ravaged souls. The words ran through Amon's head,
and he barely checked a shudder.

'We have spilled our blood today. Some have given their lives,
and their souls now fly back to the heavens, to your hands. We
pray now for their next battle, as they brave the fury of your
Reforging and hope they can find the strength to hold themselves in the Storm's Eye, so that they may return to us, as whole
as they can be.'

'To Sigmar we pray,' the Reclusians intoned, the higher, softer
voices of their Memorians mixed in.

Amon looked back, to see if that was the end of it, but Morgen
held her torch aloft while the Reclusians bowed their heads, still
as sombre statues of sigmarite as they offered their silent codas to
that prayer. The only noise came from the Memorians, low moans
and choked sobs escaping from the ones who had lifted their
heads enough to see the hideous, blasted landscape around them.

Brevin was with them, carried in the midst of the mortals by

Corus and Dreskir on the improvised litter of Amon's dark cloak. Neither the prayer nor the thin sunlight piercing the smoke overhead had revived him from whatever the skaven had done to him. But he still lived.

Sevora did too. She had recovered from whatever fit had taken her in Gallogast and was moving on her own feet, staying near Corus. The mortal Avil was on a litter of his own, made from Dreskir's folded cloak, carried by four other Memorians. His wounds had been dressed and covered, but he was fading, his blood and his life ebbing out of him. Not quickly enough, though. Amon didn't know Avil, but he was sure the man didn't deserve this slow, painful death. And the Knight-Questor was sure that he didn't want to see what might be trying to grow in Avil's flesh as he breathed out his last. He would have suggested a mercy kill, a clean death with fire to follow, but he knew better than to mention it, looking at Dreskir's eyes, shining far too bright in his pale, haggard face.

'For his purpose,' Morgen finally called out, breaking the heavy silence, 'we persevere.'

'We persevere,' the rest of the Ruination Chamber responded. 'For we are hope when hope is dying.'

'We go,' Amon snapped, finally giving his frustration vent. 'Now.'

'Of course,' Morgen said. She snapped her wrist, and the fire wrapped around her sword winked out, except for one tiny flame that danced along the edge of the blade. 'Lead us, Knight-Questor.'

He nodded, already starting towards Warrun Vale, and then another voice rose.

'There.' It was the Lord-Terminos, their strange, sombre mask turned up to the sky. 'Jocanan is come.'

Amon stopped yet again, silently growling something that could have been a prayer or a curse. But he wanted to know what the Prosecutor had seen from on high too.

Jocanan was coming down fast, her grey wings folded as she dove through the smoke. A flicker of green passed through it as she dropped, like a sheet of lightning cutting across the sky, and she had to jerk one wing in and tumble to avoid being struck. The sudden move ruined the elegance of her dive, but she snapped both wings out at the last moment to land in a crouch beside Morgen.

'Lord-Veritant.' Jocanan snapped her wings, folding them. 'You were long beneath the ruin, and I have seen much, none of it good. But what is necessary for you to know is this. An army approaches, a force of skaven that blackens the land. Their movement is haphazard, their formations chaotic, yet somehow they advance with great speed. Do you have any water?'

Morgen pulled a skin from her belt and handed it to the Prosecutor. She drank deep, then handed it back.

'The forward edge of that army will be here in hours. They'll pour up the Warrun Vale and be at the Halt in a day. They will be right behind you if you go now. They will catch you if you delay.'

'Then we go,' Morgen said.

Amon whispered a prayer of thanks. 'We go,' he echoed, moving again, so eager to see this hunt done. 'Let us get Brevin to the Halt, and then the skaven can break their teeth on that pile of stone for a thousand years.'

CHAPTER EIGHTEEN

WARRUN VALE

An army approaches. Jocanan's words ran through Sevora's mind as she stared out at the corrupt, apocalyptic landscape. She had been eager to leave the darkness of the ruined tunnels below Gallogast, but when she had stepped into the light and seen the horror that had been revealed when the smoke faded, she'd almost wanted to go back in. Darkness seemed a mercy compared to seeing what the skaven had wrought. And now this. An army. Of course this wasn't over yet.

'Hope when hope is dying.' She didn't realise she'd said the bitter words aloud until Corus spoke softly to her. They were standing together, in the middle of the other Memorians, Corus holding one end of the cloak that supported the Lord-Ordinator.

'It's not over,' he said. 'I will get you through this.'

Sevora looked up at him, and for a moment his face changed in her mind, became mortal, ravaged, covered with bruises and blood, the face he'd worn right before he'd chosen to join the immortals. And with that image came her remembrance of his memory, the one that had surged through her when he had picked her out of the pile of broken metal in that rat's nest of a room below Gallogast.

'Revoke him!'

The shout rang down the slot canyon, filling Corus' ears. The stone passage twisted, water-worn walls rising over him, then opened into a larger space where multiple slot canyons came together. It was deep and shaded, despite the day overhead, except for its very centre, where the light above poured down in a single thick column and fell on a rocky outcrop that jutted from the sandy floor. The outcrop was shaped like a massive egg, its dull brown top shattered to expose the crystals that had formed on the hollow inside. They were white as snow, and the light hit them and splashed away, forming bright reflections that slowly crawled across the dark canyon walls.

Standing before that stone was Lavin, commander of this sortie, a harsh man who had been a member of the Hammerhal Aqsha Inquisition when he was a mortal. Being reborn as a Stormcast only increased his righteous anger, and now he stood like an avatar of justice, his silver armour rippling with the reflected crystal light. Arrayed around him stood a dozen other Hallowed Knights, helms hiding all but their eyes, which were focused on the huge figure hunched on the bloody sand at Lavin's feet.

A Chaos warrior. A giant of a man, armoured in plates of bronze that ripped through his vast muscles and lay across his skin like sharp-edged scales. Blood ran from where those armour plates cut through him, a thick, clotted torrent that never stopped dripping down his body. An axe lay beside him, its vertebrae-shaped haft broken, and there were wounds in his chest and belly, on his legs and arms. Places where his bronze scale armour had been ripped out, leaving craters in his skin that wept more blood. A cut ran across his face, a deep ravine of torn flesh that had destroyed one eye, smashed his nose into ruin, and split open his lips and cheeks. But when he raised his head, the warrior's deep voice was still strong, still defiant.

'Revoke my master?' He laughed, and it was a strange thing to hear such a beautiful sound coming from that pile of ugly flesh and bronze. 'The Lord of Blood is not denied. He is not revoked.'

'He is a lord of slaughter. A lord of cannibals. And like all Chaos gods, he is a lord of lies.' Lavin reached down and grasped one of the bronze plates that sprouted from the Chaos warrior's skin. 'Revoke him, and see the truth.'

Khorne's Chosen smiled, showing sharpened teeth. 'The only truth is blood.'

Lavin looked at him, his eyes glittering with hate, and then ripped the armoured scale from the man's chest and threw it away.

It flew through the air, gleaming in the spangled light, a great shower of blood arcing after it, and landed at Corus' feet. He stared down, and in that bloody bronze he saw his own face reflected: smaller, battered, the eyes raw red, lids ripped away. He stared at that reflection of his mortal self, and he heard Lavin shout 'Revoke him!' again, and those words echoed through the canyon and in his head and joined with the memory of that deep, terrible voice saying the same thing, over and over again...

Sevora shuddered, her memory of his dying face raw in her head, and almost stumbled. They were walking now, following Amon back into Warrun Vale, the rotting grass smearing beneath their boots.

I'll get you through this. How could Corus hold such determination, such hope, in the middle of this wasteland of horror, after all he had been through?

'I'm not Aika,' she said. 'This isn't the Oasis of Tears.' *Hope is a lie.* She looked up at him, meeting those eerie eyes, so familiar in their shape and colour, so foreign with their flickering sparks. 'But maybe it's your temple, after. With the bloody man, and everyone dead.'

'How do you know that?' Corus asked, his voice tight with pain. Hurting because of the memory. Hurting because she'd seen it, been exposed to that terrible day.

Hope is a lie.

'I don't know,' she said. She looked ahead, picking out Morgen at the head of the formation. 'Last chance to find out.'

She started walking faster, moving through the Memorians, and she could feel his eyes watching her, but she didn't look back. She wound her way through the Reclusians, who gave her space without even looking at her, until she reached the Lord-Veritant. Peace watched her, eyes bright, black tail twitching.

'You're late for your lessons, Memorian,' Morgen said. 'But better late than never.'

'Never is coming, isn't it?' Sevora said, choosing to walk on the side away from Peace.

'For some. But not for all, I pray.' She turned her head and looked down at Sevora. 'Whatever else, we have little time. What do you need?'

'I need Corus out of my head,' she said. 'I need to stop having his memories take me over, make me useless and helpless.'

'No,' Morgen said. 'That's the last thing you need. You have to take those memories. You are his Memorian. This is why he needs you.'

'Why I'm necessary.' It was almost there in Sevora's head, the truth of it, finally. 'You said we were here to help them remember. But we're not just reminders. We're something else.'

'You're a Memorian,' Morgen said, and for a moment the anger that had died in Sevora flickered to life again, but then the Lord-Veritant went on. 'The Reclusians must remember. They must hold onto their past life, or be lost. But there is a hazard to that.

Stormcasts live lives of violence, of battle, and our memories can be terrible things sometimes. Those awful memories are as necessary as any others, but they can be dangerous. Overwhelming. They can take a Reclusian out of the moment, wrap them in the past and render them useless. Helpless.'

'Overwhelming,' Peace muttered beside her.

'This is the true work of the Memorians,' Morgen continued, her voice soft. 'This is why you are so necessary, why you must be with them as they fight. Those memories can come back at any time, but they are more prone to do so during battle. And if they do, they can render a Reclusian helpless in the thick of a fight, when their strength is needed most.' She shook her head and sighed. 'Memory, for those who have passed through the Storm's Eye, is a difficult thing. It can heal, and it can kill. But you Memorians are armour for their souls. You stop the dangerous memories, keep them from coming back at the worst moments, and let the Reclusians fight on. You are your great-grandfather's shield.'

'And so I absorb the blow,' Sevora said. 'I almost died because of those memories.'

'Then you understand how necessary you are.'

'I… begin to.' Sevora could feel her familiar anger at being caught up in this madness rising, wanting to lash out at Morgen once again, but she leashed it. It was getting in the way. 'Everything is breaking. The skaven… They're doing it, trying to destroy everything like they've destroyed this place. Like they destroyed my brother.' That was an anger that was good, the rage at these monsters that bit, that infected, that corrupted. 'I'm starting to see why the Ruination Chamber must fight, even though they're broken. And maybe I understand why I have to fight too.'

Maybe. Even if I'm broken too.

Gods, she couldn't say that. Couldn't even think that. She was fine. It was her brother, her mother, her dead father, her whole family – everything and everyone and not her. Not her. She shook her head.

'It doesn't matter. It is what it is, now, and I'm trapped in it with Corus. With you. I just wish... I wish I'd had a choice.'

'We all do,' Morgen said, her voice soft. 'But none of us do.' The Lord-Veritant saw Sevora's frown, and her lips sketched out a smile. 'Do you think I had a choice, being brought back as a Storm-cast?' she asked. 'Do you think Corus did? Any of us?' She shook her head. 'We were chosen, but we had no choice. We were chosen to defend the realms from nightmares and daemons, without even death to free us, until our very souls begin to wear away. But we do it, because we know what would happen if we did not. We know the realms would be lost, and replaced by this.' She gestured at the wastelands that surrounded them. 'The real reason we didn't have a choice isn't because Sigmar forced us into this role. The real reason is because he looked into our souls and knew we would take this burden, knew that we would fight for him, forever if need be. Because we were the kind of people that would never, could never, let the realms fall into a hell like this.'

She looked down at Sevora. 'It is the same for you. I looked into your soul back in Hallowheart, and I saw your grief, your anger, your bitterness. I saw that, but I also saw your truth, Sevora. I saw that when you were chosen, you would rage. You would fight. But in the end, I knew you would be with us.'

Sevora stared ahead for a long time, silent. Then she looked back at the Lord-Veritant again. 'I kind of hate that.'

'So do I,' Morgen said. 'Sometimes. But don't let that distract you from the real enemy, the monsters that pursue us now. The skaven would destroy everyone and everything, and Corus is one of the weapons that our god has put here to stop them. Remember that, and help him.'

'Remember,' Peace croaked, and they walked on as Sevora stood still and watched them go, until Corus caught up with her, still holding the silent, twitching Lord-Ordinator. Then she started walking again.

'What did you ask her?' he asked. 'What did she say?'

Sevora ignored the first question, flipping her father's knife in her hands. But she answered the second.

'She said you were playing touch blades and ten back with Shyish's deepest hell.' She caught the knife and held it, its little blade gleaming in the smoke-tainted light. 'And I'm the one watching your back.'

At the Narrows, where the stone cliffs of the Warrun pressed in closest, Jocanan spiralled down from the sky with blood on her armour.

'What is she fighting in the air?' Sevora asked.

'Something with claws,' Corus said, watching as the Prosecutor spread her wings and landed beside Morgen. 'The cuts on her face are too ragged for blades.'

Sevora couldn't see the Prosecutor's cuts, but she trusted her great-grandfather's eyes. Claws. Did that mean the skaven had something that could fly? Why not. Why not rat-things with wings. The thought should have horrified her, but the grotesque landscape they moved through had shown her worse. The ugly plants growing through the festering muck were bad enough, but the creatures that moved through it…

She couldn't stop thinking of the thing that had lunged squealing at the Reclusians ahead of her an hour ago. It looked like a nest of baby rats, pink hairless things whose dark, bulging eyes were still covered with a translucent membrane. But these were the size of dogs, and they moved hideously, unnaturally, a squirming mass of pale, wrinkled flesh and grasping mouths with needle teeth. It was only when the Reclusians began to smash into it with their axes that Sevora realised it was not a nest of giant rat pups, but a single creature, a roiling mass of flesh that was constantly pushing out those bare, hideous forms in snapping waves.

The grotesque thing had almost rolled over two of the Reclusians, but they caught its pulpy mass in their arms and threw it off, its teeth and claws scraping ineffectually at their armour. The other Reclusians had fallen on the thing, blades tearing it apart. They had left it in pieces, a quivering mound of ruptured, shredded flesh. Sevora watched it as they walked away, and the pieces had been moving back together, forming more of the rat-pup shapes to savage and feed on each other.

No, rat-things with wings were well within her comprehension now, and she shrugged off that fear. It could come back as nightmares later. If she lived long enough to sleep again.

They came to a stop, and she sagged, exhausted, as Morgen conferred with Jocanan. They had left the Halt the morning before, walked through the poison smoke to Gallogast, then spent all night fighting through the ruins. Now they were walking back up the Vale. The Memorians around her were sagging too, but some were reaching into their packs, pulling out food and waterskins and passing them around. Sevora took a half-empty skin and drank, but she stared dully at the handful of nuts and dried fruit she'd been given.

'Eat,' Corus said. He and Dreskir were setting Brevin down. Her great-grandfather showed no sign of fatigue, despite carrying that weight halfway up the Vale. None of the Reclusians looked tired, and none of them were eating, they merely passed waterskins between them. Of course. They were immortals. What was a day of marching, a night of fighting, no food and hardly any drink, for them?

But she was mortal, so she forced herself to eat the handful of rations. The moment the food passed her lips she became ravenous, and wolfed it down instantly. She washed it down with more water, then brought the skin over to where Dreskir crouched over Avil and knelt down beside the injured man. He was breathing, soft, ragged breaths, but he was unconscious.

'Should I?' she asked Dreskir, holding up the skin, and the Reclusian nodded. His face was stern, but Dreskir's eyes were unsettled. It made Sevora wary, but Corus was there too, standing right behind them. So she made herself focus on the injured man.

'Avil. Water, Avil. You need it.' He made no sign of hearing her, his only movement a weak twitching of his hands beneath the cloak folded over him, but she pressed the skin against his lips and carefully dribbled a bit of water in his mouth. For a moment she was back in the dim hole of her childhood home, trying to get Yevin to sip watered wine to recover from a vision. But this memory wasn't like the ones from Corus; it flashed through her head and was gone when Avil choked weakly and sputtered as the tiny trickle of water touched his dry tongue, then leaked out through his shredded cheeks, adding more red to the blood-soaked bandages that had been placed over the side of his face.

'It's no use,' she said, but cut herself off before she said he was dying. She didn't want to look at Dreskir. Her eyes went instead to Avil's hands, clutching at the cloak.

The sight troubled her, then she remembered the motion *under* the cloak, what she had previously thought was his hands moving. Cursing silently to herself, she took hold of a corner of the cloak and pulled it off Avil.

Beneath the torn remnants of his robes, Avil's torso was moving, his skin shifting and bulging as something squirmed beneath.

Her knife was in her hands before she even thought of it, blade out and ready. But as fast as she was, Dreskir was faster. His huge hand closed on her arm, his gauntlet a cage around her bicep.

'What are you doing?' His voice was hard, with an intensity that made her want to back away. Except he was holding her.

'She's stepping back, Dreskir,' Corus said. He was there, right beside them, both hands up but empty. His deep voice was level, perfectly calm. 'She's not going to hurt him. Let her go and she moves away.'

'She moves away?' Dreskir asked.

'Soon as you let me go,' Sevora breathed. She dropped her knife into her sleeve, and showed her empty hands. For a long moment he stared at her, his grip so tight her arm felt close to breaking. Then Avil groaned. A thin sound, a whisper of air through clenched teeth, but it made the Reclusian forget her. Dreskir opened his hand and Sevora shot backwards like a cat from a trap, dropping her knife again from out her sleeve and catching it. Then Corus was there, putting his armoured body between her and Dreskir.

'Are you hurt?'

'No,' she lied, shifting her knife to her other hand. Her arm throbbed, but her attention was focused on Avil. 'Those things are in him.' She watched his stomach ripple, remembering her brother. Yellow teeth. Yellow teeth in Avil's belly. She didn't know him, didn't know anything about him except that he had saved her once, so she had tried to save him, and now he was going to die in pain and horror. Like her brother had died, trying to save her. 'Kill him,' she said. 'Kill him and burn the body before they tear their way out.'

There was a rasp as Dreskir drew his axe. He held the weapon in one hand and gathered Avil into him with the other. 'Avil will not die,' he said, his voice low and flat. Certain.

'No. Fine.' Sevora held the knife down by her leg. Corus had his hand on his axe, but he hadn't drawn it, not yet, and she didn't want him to. There would be dying enough soon, it didn't need to start like this. 'Take him, Dreskir. Take him, be with him, protect him, just go. Away from us, away from here. Take him.'

The Stormcast stared back at her in silence, his eyes too bright.

Others had gathered, a silent ring of Reclusians, walling away the rest of the Memorians from what was happening. But no Morgen, the one time Sevora desperately wanted her.

'He cannot.' Corus' voice was heavy but final. 'Dreskir is one of us. A Reclusian. He can't just walk away. He is with us until the end.'

'Our end is chasing us!' Sevora snapped. 'Tell him to take Avil and walk down the Vale! He can fight the skaven about this, and get vengeance!'

'That is not–' Corus started, but then it was decided for them. Avil, who'd been lying limp in Dreskir's arms, convulsed, his body twitching, and then vomited. Bloody yellow foam poured out of his mouth, a flood that gushed over his chin and through the wounds in his cheek, turning his bandages into masses of gore. Foam and blood cascaded down Dreskir's armour, coating it, and the Reclusian stared down at the dying man, shouting.

'No, Avil! No!'

But it was already done. Avil stopped arching, and the flood of noxious fluids from his mouth became a dribble as he went limp. But not still. Avil began to jerk, flopping as the things in his belly and chest fought to free themselves. Sevora heard her own voice shouting, 'Throw him down, throw him down!' Willing the Reclusian to drop the body so that Corus could stomp the horrible things before they could tear their way out, but Dreskir wasn't listening. He clutched Avil close, his axe out, and when Corus took a step towards him he swung the huge weapon in warning.

And then Avil fell apart in his arms.

The monstrous young growing inside the man tore free all at once, breaking bone and shredding muscle and skin. They shattered Avil's body and wriggled free, three rat things slimed with blood and yellow foam, their teeth gnashing, their eyes blinking in the light. Fur covered them in patches, white fur tainted red and yellow by their butcher's birth, while the rest of them was bare skin, pale as Avil's had been. They pulled themselves out of his body, squealing and snapping at each other and at the armoured arms that held them. Held them, and kept them from escaping, even as Avil's broken remains slipped down to the ground and landed in a heap of torn meat and shattered bone.

'There,' Dreskir said, his voice low but triumphant. He had to struggle to hold the things as they thrashed in his arms, claws scrabbling against his armour. 'He's not dead.'

'Light above, end this,' Sevora said, sickened. Avil's death, followed by Dreskir's fall into whatever madness this was, ripped the scabs from her soul and left her raw, exposed, teetering on the edge of her own madness.

That's when the air stirred. A sluggish wind rose from nowhere and spun a slow circle around her, pulling at her hair, her robes. 'Not now,' she whispered to her magic, but as ever the chaotic power in her was uncontrollable. One of the rat-things in Dreskir's arms turned its head towards her and hissed, blood dripping still from its yellow teeth, and the wind suddenly sharpened, flew out with a trail of sparks and struck, slamming the hideous little thing back into Dreskir's chest, breaking its thin neck.

It squealed once, its body thrashing before it went limp. The other parasites hissed, then sank their teeth into it, ripping at its flesh as Dreskir watched, his eyes far too bright. Then he looked up, staring at Sevora. His grip tight on the horrible things fighting and feeding in his arms, Dreskir started towards her, and Sevora tried to turn the wind on him, to form it into a gale to force him back. But her power was either too exhausted or too fickle. The wind fell apart, and the Reclusian was charging her, his axe swinging down far faster than she could dodge.

Until another blade smashed into it, crashing it away from her. Dreskir staggered, thrown off by the blow, but he recovered, turning to face Corus. Sevora's great-grandfather had stepped in front of her, blocking her, his shield and axe ready. In the polished blade of his weapon, Sevora caught sight of Corus' eyes: focused, furious, the lightning snapping like an approaching storm.

'You won't hurt her, Dreskir,' he said, and for once Sevora believed him.

'Not dead,' Dreskir said, his voice harsh. 'Not death. Never death!' Then he launched an attack at Corus, his axe flying in vicious arcs.

Dreskir was hampered by the monsters he held in one arm, but he was a Reclusian, fast, incredibly strong, trained for decades by battle. He hit like a hammer, and even though his eyes were glowing with madness, he didn't overextend, didn't expose himself.

But Corus was a Reclusian too, and he met every strike with his shield, blocking and turning Dreskir's blows, keeping himself always in front of Sevora. But he was checking his own blows, unwilling to kill or maim. 'Dreskir! Remember yourself! Remember the face of the god that forged you!'

As he shouted, Corus swung his axe, cracking its blunt haft into Dreskir's arms and side, trying to slow him. But when one of the skaven young snapped at his arm, Corus had no hesitation. He twisted his axe and caught the thing behind the head, yanking it out of Dreskir's arms. It landed on the ground between them, squealing and snarling, and Corus swiped his axe across it, opening its body up from chin to crotch with one strike. The skaven squealed and twisted on the ground, biting at the gory mess of its own innards.

Dreskir screamed and charged Corus, his axe spinning through the air so fast it was a blur of bright metal. Bright. So bright.

The memory hit Sevora before she could even shout her denial, and everything was lost in the light.

* * *

*'Revoke him!' Lavin's voice filled the canyon and filled Corus' head.
The smell of blood was thick in the air, and suddenly he was on
his knees.*

*'Revoke him!' The Chaos warrior was standing over him as the
light burned in his eyes, flashing off the bronze armour embedded
in his skin.*

*'Revoke him!' And he was standing, watching as Lavin grasped
another armour plate and pulled, tearing it slowly from the Khorne
worshipper's skin, like tearing away a toenail. The warrior snarled
and snapped his filed teeth, and the blood stink filled the canyon.
Corus could smell the blood, smell it on the Chaos warrior's hand
as he held it out, inches from his face.*

'I could paint his mark upon you...'

*The words echoed through Corus' head, and he staggered forward,
staggered back, and in the canyon, in the temple, the words echoed
around him in two voices that were one: 'Revoke him!'*

'No,' Sevora breathed, blinking against the light. The muddled,
dull light that fell through the haze of smoke, she realised, and
blinked, trying to pull herself back from the confusion of shouting voices, the smell of blood.

But there was the smell of blood here too, and a sound like
thunder.

Corus was in front of her, catching blows that would have
shattered the skull of an ox. It was a brutal dance of blades and
armour, the strikes so fast Sevora could barely follow them, but
she saw her great-grandfather block a slicing cut at his head and
then kick out with his boot, hitting Dreskir in his armoured
stomach and sending him staggering back. The Reclusian stopped,
breathing hard, his eyes bright and blank as stars. One of the last
skaven clung to his arm, its head buried in the crook of Dreskir's
elbow, digging through the space between armour plates to tear

at the flesh beneath. The Reclusian took no notice of the teeth tearing at him, of the blood and bubbling yellow foam that rolled down his arm. He was raising his axe again, getting ready to charge once more, when another shape stepped towards him.

The Lord-Terminos moved silently, precisely. The mask over their face was turned to Dreskir, smiling as it cried, and the metal features had become Dreskir's face, composed and peaceful.

'Lay down your burdens, brother.' The Lord-Terminos' voice was smooth, peaceful, perfect. 'Lay them all down.'

Dreskir stared at the masked Stormcast in silence, not blinking, and the brightness in his eyes faded, became muddled with grief and horror. His arm shifted, as if he was about to cast down the ugly things that squirmed in his grip. 'Lay them down. Lay everything down. Just... end it. I...' He stood still, silent, a pause that lasted a moment but seemed to stretch forever before he finally spoke again. 'I cannot,' he whispered, and his arms tightened again on the monsters he held as the grief in his eyes was swallowed by rage and hate. Then he was rushing forward, for Sevora once more.

Corus raised his shield, catching the massive blow that would have split Sevora in half. Then he slammed the side of his axe into Dreskir's knee. There was an ugly crunch, and the Reclusian staggered back, dropping his axe, barely standing as his leg buckled. His eyes danced between madness and confusion, and he turned to look at Avil's ruined body one more time as he still held tight to the last of the monsters that had killed the man.

'I am undone,' he said softly. 'Avil. Sigmar. I am done.'

And then the Lord-Terminos stepped close. They moved with stunning speed, and when they swept their massive axe around, the strike was so smooth and fast it looked like liquid light. The blade caught Dreskir in the neck, slicing through sigmarite armour, skin and muscle, nerve and bone, and for a bare instant Dreskir's head was flying away from his shoulders, brilliant red blood boiling out.

Then something ran up the Lord-Terminos' axe, a brilliant ball of lightning, white and crackling, and when it touched Dreskir the ball exploded.

Sevora had seen other Stormcasts die, fallen beneath the skaven's dirty teeth and claws and knives. She'd seen them dissolve into lightning and crack back up into the heavens, a bolt of destruction carrying them back to their god. But this was different. When the ball of lightning struck Dreskir, it flashed through him and he flared up with it, his whole body growing incandescent, too bright to look at. Then it dimmed, and Sevora's dazzled eyes caught his form one more time, dark as char. Crackling lines of white ran through that black, and it was like watching paper burn, the page's edge glowing red before falling apart into ash. The jagged white lines ran over Dreskir and he dissolved, falling apart into a thousand motes of white that drifted through the air. The motes swirled, like leaves caught in a whirlwind, over the shattered wreckage of Avil's body, and one more mote rose from that broken form and joined them as they floated into the air, spinning into the uncorrupted heavens to vanish, like stars fading into the day.

Standing below them, watching them go, the Lord-Terminos bowed their head, their mask once more ambiguous, the face of no one and everyone. 'In your final death, may you finally find peace, my brother.' Then they raised their boot and brought it down on the head of the last new-born skaven, which lay writhing in the muck where Dreskir had stood. The thing's skull cracked and it whimpered once as its body jerked and spasmed beneath the Lord-Terminos' boot.

'May he find peace.' Morgen had appeared, finally, her face as calm and smooth as ever. 'Let us pray for Dreskir, our fallen brother.'

The Lord-Veritant bowed her head, and all the Reclusians and Memorians did the same, leaving Sevora standing and blinking.

She tore her eyes away from the skaven's twitching corpse, from the place where Dreskir had been, and she found herself staring at Amon. Like her, the Knight-Questor had not bowed his head, and was instead staring up at the sky where all those white motes had drifted and vanished. There was no reverence in his eyes, instead an all-too-mortal queasiness.

And then, with eerie precision, Morgen raised her head, followed by every Reclusian.

'And now we must attend to other endings. Our enemy has out-manoeuvred us. Jocanan has seen skaven crossing the mountains and moving into the forest before the Halt. They are between us and the wall, in numbers great enough to stop us, until the army behind can catch us. And so we are caught, by our enemy and our fate.'

Caught. Of course. Coming on the heels of Avil and Dreskir's end, coming after everything that had happened, Sevora had to fight not to laugh. Because if she started, she wouldn't stop until she was weeping.

Hope is a lie.

She barely heard Morgen continue.

'We are not helpless, though. We are Stormcast, we are the Ruination Chamber, and we are hope when hope is dying. We shall prepare for both our enemy and our fate, and make this place our final stand.'

'Corus. Sevora. Attend.' Morgen was standing in the middle of the Narrows, at the space where the rough cliffs pressed in closest. It would take less than a dozen Reclusians to block it, standing shoulder to shoulder. How long would they be able to hold out against an army of skaven here?

Despite their bravery and preternatural skill, not that long, Sevora thought. She watched as the Reclusians and their Memorians prepared, felling dead trees, shifting huge stones, making make-shift barricades to slow and blunt an attack, but she had stayed still, toying with her father's knife, wondering what the use of any of it was. This was apparently Morgen Light's plan, forged the moment the Lord-Veritant had heard they were trapped. To make one last stand against the skaven, and slow them a little more.

Useless. Useless as this whole quest, apparently, which had done nothing but got them all killed.

But she got up when Morgen called, and walked with her great-grandfather to join the Lord-Veritant. She was bent over, stroking her fingers through Peace's feathers as the gryph-crow rubbed its long beak against her armoured side. Lord-Veritant Innovi was there too, her gryph-crow crouching beside her, along with Knight-Questor Amon, the Lord-Terminos, Prosecutor Jocanan, and the still-unconscious body of the Lord-Ordinator. Sevora stared at his maimed face and shook her head. All this, just so they could drag his almost-corpse a few miles up the Vale to die. Along with all of them.

'Jocanan has had one more look at the foe for us,' Morgen said, not looking up from Peace.

'For as long as I could before those ratwings came for me again,' Jocanan said. She was crouched on a stone, wings folded behind her, a stick in her hand. The Prosecutor was scratching a picture onto the stone, a few thin lines cutting through lichen and muck that somehow evoked a face. The face of that woman she had painted on the wall in Rookenval.

Morgen continued as if the Prosecutor hadn't spoken. 'The army has entered the Vale. Many thousands of skaven, and with them fell beasts. Their forward elements will be here within an hour. Two at most. On the other side, in the forests between us and the Halt, their infiltrators have taken position. They seem content to stay where they are for now, and I think that they won't move as long as we stay caught in their trap. So we shall, and focus the skaven's attention on us. While you move on.'

'Move on?' Corus asked, before Sevora could.

'The entire purpose of this mission was to free the Lord-Ordinator from the skaven and return him to the Halt,' Morgen said. 'The approaching army has only made that more important.' She gave Peace one last pat, then stood. 'It seems we cannot bring him back in force, so we will do it in stealth. You will take Brevin Fortis up the cliffs on the other side of the Vale and move with him through the heights until you reach the Halt. Knight-Questor Amon Solus will lead you. Prosecutor Jocanan will guide you. The Lord-Terminos will fight with you. And I will send Peace too. His eyes are keen, and he will help you find any skaven scouts that might be hidden up there.'

And you don't want him to die, Sevora thought, and a tiny flicker of hope went through her. But…

Hope is a lie.

'Why us?' *Why me* is what she meant, but Corus was standing beside her, close as a second shadow.

'The Lord-Terminos will need a hand carrying Brevin,' Morgen said. But then her brown eyes fell on Sevora. 'And you, Sevora. I keep telling you, I have seen you. Seen you through and through.' She reached out and took Sevora's hand in her gauntlet, turned it so the scars showed in the dull daylight. 'You will never give up. You will keep fighting, on and on, no matter the odds, and Corus will too, to protect you. I need a Reclusian to help the Lord-Terminos, and that means sending a Memorian, and while you might not be the strongest, or the most loyal, or the most cooperative, you are the one I would bet on to survive anything.' She let go of Sevora's hand and shrugged. 'And who knows, that flux-touched magic of yours might come in handy again.'

'When do we go?' Corus asked. He seemed suddenly eager, and

Sevora understood. He'd been promising to save her, despite all the odds against them, and this… well, it wasn't salvation, but it was a better chance than a last stand.

'Now,' Amon said. The Knight-Questor rose, obviously impatient to be gone.

'Yes,' Morgen said. 'We will hold them here, and give you time. Get the Lord-Ordinator back, as Sigmar bade you. Hold the Halt. Serve our god.' She raised her torch, its light falling on them like a blessing. 'You are the Ruination Chamber. Hope when hope is dying. Go, and hold our memory in your heart.'

Hold our memory in your heart.

Sevora already felt overcrowded with memories, but this last wish of Morgen's… Sevora looked up at the massive warrior in dark armour and nodded.

'I won't say thank you. Or I'm sorry,' Sevora said. 'But I want to say that I think I understand you, now. A little.'

Morgen tilted her head, and a faint smile played across her lips. 'I do what I must, whether I am understood or not. But I am still human enough to appreciate it.' She stared at Sevora, and for a moment her brown eyes flickered to silver. 'I think you have gained a more valuable understanding too, Memorian. An understanding of your own self.' Her voice went low, pitched for Sevora alone. 'There is something I have learned, from seeing into so many souls, Sevora Cinis. We are all broken.'

Sevora flinched at the word, but she nodded, saying nothing. Morgen touched her shoulder, her huge, gauntleted hand light.

'You will do well, Memorian. You will be his shield, and he will be yours, and you shall both be our hope when hope is dying.'

Somewhere down the Vale, something shrieked, monstrous and terrible and distant, but getting closer. Sevora shook her head. 'I wish I could have your faith.'

'Faith is hard to find on your own. Like hope.' Her eyes shifted to Corus, then back. 'Sometimes it is easier to borrow it from another.'

Then she turned, and with one last touch to the top of Peace's head she was gone, walking away from them, and they were going too, falling in behind Amon as he led them up a goat track that climbed through the rough cliffs. When Sevora thought to look back again she couldn't see them – Morgen or any of the Reclusians they'd left behind. To face death again, and another Reforging that might finally wear away what was left of their souls, leaving them shadows fading into the darkness of a never-ending night.

CHAPTER NINETEEN

WARRUN VALE

Amon was in the lead, picking out the path as they climbed the rough cliffs that rose from the Narrows. It was slow going, especially carrying the Lord-Ordinator, but the Knight-Questor felt light with elation. A strange feeling, knowing what faced the Stormcasts they'd left behind. But he couldn't help it. They were moving, bringing Brevin with them, and his hunt wasn't over. The chance of it succeeding was thin, but it existed, and that hope blazed in him like the fire burning at the end of his mace. He could do it. He might even live, and not have to dance with the Storm's Eye. But most importantly, he could end this hunt.

And so they climbed, and he couldn't help but be ecstatic. A feeling he hid from the others, all except for Peace. The gryph-crow's attention seemed mainly split between looking around them for threats and looking back towards where he'd left his Lord-Veritant, but Peace still found the time to give him an ugly look and croak, 'Serve.'

But I am serving, Amon thought. Better now, with fewer allies around to deal with.

They scrabbled over a rough boulder and he stopped, crouching to hide his silhouette. He reached back to pluck Sevora off the stone and set her beside him. The mortal looked ragged with exhaustion, her robes shredded and marked with blood, but her eyes were fierce over the dark circles that ran beneath them. Morgen had made a good choice with her, he thought. If they had to bring a mortal along with them, this one might be useful.

Behind her, Corus and the Lord-Terminos were picking their way up the rock, and he moved to help them manhandle Brevin to the top. When they finally got him up and laid him out, he groaned and hissed something, then fell silent again, but his hands were twitching.

'Give me some water,' Sevora said, and Corus handed her a skin. She tore the least bloody piece from the hem of her robe, wet it and placed it against Brevin's lips. The Lord-Ordinator's mouth moved, sucking the water from the cloth, and then with sudden speed Brevin leapt to his feet.

Corus caught Sevora as she was tumbled away, turned with her so that the kick Brevin lashed out struck his side and not her. Brevin stumbled back, almost reaching the edge of the stone but the Lord-Terminos caught him, wrapping armoured arms around him and holding him tight.

'You are with your own, brother,' the masked Stormcast said. 'Sigmar protects.'

Somewhat, Amon thought, looking at the bandages wrapped over the Lord-Ordinator's empty eye sockets. 'We came for you,' he said. 'Saved you from Gallogast, and the skaven.'

Brevin stopped moving, and when the Lord-Terminos let him go he made a noise, a harsh whispering sound that had no meaning, and raised his hand to the cuts that marked his throat.

'The skaven did that? Torturing you?' Sevora asked, and the Hallowed Knight nodded. *Yes* and *no* he could do, and Amon could see the woman and Corus leaning in, ready to ask him more.

'There's no time,' he said, cutting them off before they could begin their interrogation. 'We're in the cliffs over the Warrun, Brevin. Just a few of us, escorting you back. The skaven are bringing an army to lay siege to the Halt.'

The Lord-Ordinator nodded, understanding. Good. They would move much faster with him up, even blind and injured.

'We are taking you there, to repair the wall and–' And he didn't know what else. Even the repair was an assumption. All he knew was that the Halt was where Sigmar wanted the Lord-Ordinator, so there he must go. 'And protect the realm,' he finished.

Brevin turned to his voice, frowning. One hand was raised to his heart, half-covering the wounds driven into his chest as if they hurt him. Then he shook his head.

'No?' Sevora asked. 'You don't want to go?'

And now Brevin was nodding.

'No,' Amon said, curt. 'That's where you must go.'

'But–' Sevora started, and he cut her off.

'Sigmar gave me this quest with his own voice,' Amon said. 'To find the Lord-Ordinator Brevin Fortis and to bring him home. Whatever doubts you have, let them go. This is the will of our god.'

Sevora didn't say anything more, but she looked to her great-grandfather. 'He is a Knight-Questor,' Corus said. 'He is Sigmar's hunting hawk.'

Sevora frowned, still unconvinced, it seemed, but Amon ignored her. He knew his hunt.

Brevin grated out a whisper, words mangled to meaninglessness by his injuries, but Amon recognised the cadences of prayer. He resisted saying anything and cast his eyes upward. The haze of smoke made the sky murky, but he saw a gleam through it.

Jocanan's javelin, catching the light. Still watching, but not diving down in warning. Brevin finished, his hand still at his chest, but he finally nodded.

'Sevora, Corus, lead him,' Amon said. 'We go.' He started moving down the trail, Peace trotting silently in front of him, heading through the slowly dying day towards the Halt.

When Brevin first woke, it was to the sweet taste of water on his tongue, the feel of light on his skin, and for a moment he had peace. Then he felt the pain in his chest, the raw, sickening feeling of those iron blades punched into his flesh, and he had lurched up, ready to fight–

Until he felt the smooth touch of sigmarite, and heard a voice, a Stormcast's voice, calling him brother.

Rescued. Going back to the Halt.

He couldn't feel it. Couldn't feel the heat of the Heart in his chest. There was pain, but it was different now. Not the burn of the Heart's pain, not the hollow feeling from Skein's magic. No, now he felt full. Full of poisoned mud, of rusted iron thorns, of carrion, and bile. It was the thing they'd stabbed into him, the shoddy piece of cursed patchwork magic that Varus had wired together from the broken pieces of the triangle that had taken his shadow.

The thing that felt like it was still stabbed into his chest.

He ran his fingers up yet again, feeling his bare skin and the cloth bandages wrapped around him. But no construct of copper wire and bone interrupted his hand. It wasn't there. Of course it wasn't, the Reclusians would have pulled it out before wrapping him in bandages. But when he took his hand away, he could feel the blades digging into his flesh, its weight pressing into him. It was gone, it was there, and he had no idea what the thing had been meant to do.

What was Skein's plan? What had he made Varus create? What

curse had he put on Brevin? He didn't know, and he couldn't ask what the Reclusians had seen when they had freed him. His voice was gone, and he had no parchment or etching-plate. Skein had taken his eyes and his voice, made him helpless when he most needed to fight, and he whispered curses at the Grey Seer as he went down the trail, one hand on the shoulder of the mortal Sevora. Reekbite's army was on the move, coming up the Warrun. The Halt may have been weakened, but not enough. Had it?

He didn't know. He couldn't know. He couldn't know anything, and it tore at him like the wounds in his chest. *To find the Lord-Ordinator Brevin Fortis and to bring him home.* The words of the Knight-Questor. That's all the hope he had, so he repeated those words over and over in his head. The words of Sigmar. Somehow this was meant to work out. Somehow his pain would end. Somehow he would redeem himself.

Somehow.

Before him, Sevora came to a stop. 'Look,' she said softly. 'You can see most of the Vale from here.'

'Not the Halt,' Amon answered. 'Not where we are going. Come.'

'No,' Corus said. 'Wait. The haze over the bottom of the valley is breaking. You can see them.'

Brevin could see nothing but Skein's promised truth, the dark all around him. He squeezed Sevora's shoulder and felt her flinch. Then she shifted, moving closer to him.

'The smoke you came through has thinned to a haze,' she said. 'It's almost gone up here, but it's been covering the Vale below. We haven't been able to see anything. But now… do you feel it? There's a breeze.'

She laughed, a strange, quiet laugh, which he didn't understand. But she was right. He could feel the air moving. With it came a smell, of rot and waste, and a sound. A low, distant roll, like far-off thunder.

'The breeze has shifted the haze. We can see. All the trees below are dead, they've lost their leaves and needles, half of them have fallen. We can see the skaven. Gods, we can see them.'

He could hear the horror in her voice. She was speaking barely above a whisper, her voice even, but it was there, threading through the words, giving them weight.

'I thought an army would be like a crowd, except moving together, like the Reclusians. But this – it's like a flood. Just bodies, thousands of them, moving together, climbing over each other, just one terrible mass, and it goes on and on and on. There are things in it. Wagons and war machines, being pushed and pulled by lines of skaven. And there are giant beasts, wading through the swarm. Monsters – but skaven too. They must be killing the ones that can't get out of the way, crushing them, but they don't care. It's like insects. Carrion bugs the size of people, carrying banners and weapons and… gods. What is that?'

'An effigy of the Horned Rat,' Amon answered. 'The hide of the head is made from the flayed skins of their enemies, the horns and teeth from their bones. The eyes are cauldrons of blood, fresh every day. From their enemies, or sacrifices from the swarm.'

'It's the size of a house,' Sevora breathed. 'Why is it moving like that?'

'I don't know,' Amon said. 'But we've seen enough. Watching them come only gets them closer to us.'

'They've stopped before the Reclusians.' The Lord-Terminos wasn't loud, but their voice cut through the others.

'They'll attack soon,' Sevora said. 'And–'

'And we know what will happen.' Amon's voice was hard. 'So let's make it worth something. Come on.'

Worth something. Was he worth that? Mute in his darkness, Brevin couldn't answer that. But he could try. He rested one hand on Sevora's shoulder as she started to lead him away, but with his other he reached beneath his bandages, feeling for his wounds. He ripped open thin scabs, until he could feel his blood warm on his fingertips. Carefully, he pulled his hand out, and traced the blood over the top of his bandage.

And as he worked, he tried not to be distracted by the flickers that moved across the black, the thin yellow lines that twitched across the dark, like echoes of the stitches that had closed Skein's eyes.

The edge of the skaven army arrived like carrion birds, and perched in the dead trees before the Narrows, staring at Morgen with hungry black eyes. Just a few at first, then more, a slow saturation of the blasted landscape of the Vale.

'There's ten times our number already.' Innovi stood beside her, torch blazing, staring out at the gathering skaven with weary annoyance. 'And their army has not even reached us.'

'More than ten.' Morgen could see the shadows moving between the rotting trees. For every skaven they could see, there were at least two more hiding, and she wasn't counting the huge rats that moved through the dead forest with them, or the crow-sized ones that flapped from branch to branch on bat-like wings.

This was just the ragged forward edge. Morgen could feel the faint vibration in the ground. The tramp of feet, the grind of great wheels. They were coming. A storm of skaven that would try to sweep them aside in a torrent of rusty blades and teeth.

'Take your place.'

Innovi nodded and moved away. Her gryph-crow went with her and Morgen felt a pang. Sending Peace off with the Knight-Questor had felt like cutting off her hand and giving it away. She still kept feeling for his feathered head, wanting to touch him and draw comfort from his quiet presence. But he was gone.

Maybe that meant he'd live.

She tried to draw comfort from that thought. That he might be here, waiting for her after her Reforging. If she survived it.

She'd never been beyond the Storm's Eye. She had walked right up to that line but not stepped across, had held herself above that void and stared into her own destruction. Then pulled back. That was why Sigmar chose her for this service, why she'd been given some fraction of Sigmar's vision. But that also meant she knew how fragile her own grasp on herself was. Her memories were slippery things, and she knew in her bones how hard it was to hold them. To keep herself, and stand again in the Storm's Eye.

Distraction. It tore at her. But she forced it down, kept her surface of focused calm. This wasn't the time for fear. This was the time for faith and destruction.

In the Vale below, the skaven army was appearing out of the haze. A wind came with it, warm air that stank like a carrion eater's breath. Despite the stink it brought, the wind also shredded the last of the smoke and made clear what hell was coming. A tide of bodies poured up the slope towards them, washing away rock and muck and dead forest, leaving only fur and eyes and teeth and rusted weapons. Banners waved over them, ugly things marked with a horned rat skull with one glowing green eye, and through them moved machines with rusted arms holding crystals that glowed that same ugly green, and monsters vast and awful.

Morgen smiled. They were outnumbered a thousand to one. Maybe ten thousand, and the absurd odds released her from fear. Striding forward, she mounted a stone, part of the rough barricade they had set before their lines, turned her back on the approaching army, and faced her own vastly outnumbered force.

'Stormcast Eternals,' Morgen called out, her voice rich, calm, precise. 'Reclusians. An army stands before us, an army of Chaos, of corruption. Around us lie the fruits of that army's ambition.' Her sword swung out, gesturing at the disfigured landscape that surrounded them. 'This is what they would do to all of Aqshy. To all the realms. This is their nightmare hope. This is the paradise of corrupted souls. This is an abomination. This is what we were forged to fight against.'

Fire flickered around Morgen's sword, tiny candle flames dancing on the edge of her blade, running up and down the runes traced in the dark sigmarite, growing as she spoke. 'Stormcast Eternals. Ruination Chamber. Reclusians. These are names we hang upon ourselves. What we are, what we will always be, below those names, below everything else, is the chosen of Sigmar. We are his shield to protect the world. We are his wrath at the loss of what should be. We are his weapons to strike down that which would corrupt, which would break, which would end. We are Sigmar's chosen, Reforged in his crucible, remade into vessels of his divine will. And we are not bowed. We are not broken. We are the wrath of a god.'

Morgen Light raised her sword, and the flames running along it flowed together, became a blazing storm of fire that roared up and cast its shining light across the dark-armoured figures that stood before her.

'We are the Ruination Chamber! We are hope when hope is dying!'

There was thunder as every Reclusian raised their axe, the blades shining in the fiery light of Morgen's sword. 'Hope when hope is dying!'

Lord-Veritant Morgen looked at them all, her eyes still calm. 'Hope,' she said one more time. Then she turned and levelled her burning blade at the army that was still assembling before them. 'Take your places,' she called, her voice certain. 'And we shall stand at the gates of hell, with the name of our god on our lips and his fury in our hearts.'

And they did. A line of them across the Narrows, Reclusians

with their tarnished armour, shields and axes at the ready. In the middle, they raised their standard, a silver hammer with two lightning bolts descending from it – sigil of the Hallowed Knights – but atop the hammer's head perched a rook. The banner snapped in the foul wind, and they stood silent, ready. There were so few of them they should have looked foolish, but Morgen didn't feel foolish. They were a blade of denial thrust into the teeth of this monstrosity, and they would draw a torrent of blood before they were broken.

Before them, the skaven army shifted, its front line constantly in flux. Skaven squabbled and fought, units breaking and re-forming, a scramble of motion, never still, but all their dark eyes were focused on the foe standing before them. The Reclusians stared back, impassive, still. All of them had died before. All of them knew they would die again. All of them waited for it, and spoke their prayers in silence.

Waiting for the rats to start their run.

But what came for them was something else. Through the swirling lines came a skull, a massive rat skull crowned with horns. It was made of human skins stitched together over a framework of bones, and more bones made up the horns and teeth. Great cauldrons of blood were set in its eye sockets, though one of them was covered with a pane of green stained glass. It was huge and hideous and unholy, and the whole thing rippled as if infested. It stopped at the edge of the skaven army's line, and there were shouts and screams and squeals as the army shifted around it. Lines of skaven armed with huge shields appeared on either side of the skull, forming a funnel away from it, aimed towards the Reclusians. When their lines were set, six skaven wrapped in green robes moved out in front of the giant skull. They carried with them a cauldron, which they set before the skull and crouched, waiting.

Waiting for a group of heavily armoured rat ogors carrying

a litter. On it stood a skaven, tall and lean and encased in dark armour. He wore a horned helm that wrapped around a scarred muzzle and ears. His whiskers were heavy and drooped, and one of his eyes was gone, replaced by a burning coal of poisonous green. Banners snapped behind him, all hideous and meaningless to Morgen. But this was their leader, she was sure of it.

She hadn't thought to see him. Skaven were cowards, and their leaders were usually well hidden. But she was glad, because whatever drama he was acting out for his army was wasting time. Glad, too, to meet their enemy eye to eye.

Morgen reached down and found her black scarf and raised it, covering her eyes. There was only darkness first, then her other sight flashed to life. Mountains and sky and trees faded, mere faint sketches against the world. What she saw instead was the brightness of souls flowing around her.

Hers and Innovi's were like their torches, bright patterns of brilliant orange and yellow. The Reclusians were different. They were like fires banked, mounds of coals with sparks dancing over them, bright, beautiful, but fragmented. On the edge of burning out. But she was used to those. The skaven's souls were something else.

They glowed, but not like fire. They were like molten glass, liquid in their brightness, and they mixed together, browns and bronzes and dull ugly greens, colours like old bruises. Their soul light flowed through them, around them, bunching and spreading, rushing back and forth. It was as though the skaven shared one massive soul between them, but every one of them wanted it all. Every skaven was fighting for more, constantly drawing in light and colour from those around them and having it stolen back, a never-ending battle to grasp the essence they all shared and hoard it in themselves. The skaven in some ways were all one, but it was a one at war with itself; predatory, hungry, consuming. And the Clawlord that stood on that litter was the hungriest of all, his essence a vast mass far larger than his body, a barbed tangle of thorns limned in that toxic green fire that ripped at the souls of the skaven surrounding him and pulled their pieces into himself.

Reekbite. The name came to her from out of the seething mass. This was the Clawlord Reekbite, and he was an abomination to the world and to his own kind, and when Morgen pulled the blindfold away she could still see his evil aura. It flared around him as he drew his sword, a saw-toothed blade that burned with green fire, and raised it. Below him, the green-robed skaven pulled the cover from the iron cauldron. Something glowed within, green like the Clawlord's eye. One of the skaven pulled a glass vial from his robes, containing something red and bright. Like a glass full of coals burning. He threw the vial into the cauldron, turning to run even as he did. The others were running too, green robes flapping behind them, but fire was already spewing out of the cauldron. Green and red flames caught them, wrapping around the fleeing skaven and burning them into mounds of smouldering meat and rags.

The flames died back, but smoke began to pour out of the cauldron, thick black smoke that shimmered red, then green. The smoke swirled over the cauldron, then moved, heading straight for the skull, as if the ugly construct were somehow breathing it in. The smoke poured into it and the rippling beneath the skins slowed. Stopped. Then it began again: began and increased, until the whole thing was shaking like a banner in a hurricane.

Reekbite pointed his sword at the Reclusians, and the mouth of the huge skull creaked open. Bone teeth spread, and the construct began to vomit out skaven. Hundreds of them, and Morgen couldn't understand how so many had fit inside it. They kept pouring out, a massive stream of furry bodies that clanked and rattled as they came. There was metal sticking out of the skaven, iron thorns jutting from their bodies like quills. Blood and pus flowed down them, but the pierced skaven seemed oblivious to whatever pain they might be feeling. Their eyes were burning, red slashed with green, and the dark smoke curled from their muzzles as they raced forward.

Some tried to turn on their own, but they slammed into the skaven shield wall and were stopped. The vast majority hurled themselves forward towards the Ruination Chamber.

'Reclusians!' Morgen shouted, leaning forward. 'Know your god! Know yourselves!'

'Hope when hope is dying!' they shouted back.

And then the skaven were upon them.

Morgen smashed the first away with her sword, the flaming blade cutting through its gaping jaws and ripping its head in half. She smashed into the second with her torch, and the frothing skaven hit the ground, back broken. Then there was another, and another, and another, jaws and claws snapping around her, yellow foam splashing across her helm, rusty spikes screeching as they dragged across her armour. It wasn't a fight. It was a great wave of bodies hammering into her, sharp iron, teeth and claws all snagging at her, trying to strip her flesh from her bones. There was a snap of lightning as a Reclusian fell and was called home. Then another, and another, then one right beside her, the crackle of electricity racing through her as it blasted skaven apart. The Stormcasts were killing so many skaven the ground had gone to bloody mud beneath Morgen's feet, but there were so many more.

So many that she couldn't draw breath to pray; so many they were dragging her down, and Morgen was falling backwards beneath a surge of stinking, heaving bodies, the crack of their iron blades against her armour like hail. But she kept moving, driving her sword up, trying to carve out room to breathe in the avalanche of bodies.

And then it was over.

The bodies above her still thrashed weakly, but there were no more piling on. Desperate to not drown in blood and stinking yellow slime, she shoved the corpses away until she was free.

Morgen rose to her feet, balancing on the bodies of the dead. Skaven surrounded her, mounds of shredded flesh and rusted blades, smoke trailing up from their muzzles. So many dead, all of the smoke-frenzied skaven, but the Ruination Chamber had suffered too. Morgen looked around, counting. Innovi was gone, buried somewhere, her torch jutting from a mound of corpses with its flame extinguished. Of the Reclusians, there were a bare dozen left, their armour scarred and smeared with pus and blood and foam. Of the Memorians, there was no sign but a few splashes of black mostly hidden by skaven bodies. She whispered a prayer for them all, then turned to look again at the army arrayed before them.

Across the churned ground, Reekbite stared back, snarling. Behind the Clawlord, currents of movement rippled through the army as two of the war machines were dragged forward. Reekbite was done spending blood on them, it seemed, and was going to smash them from a distance.

Morgen saw their banner, lying among the bodies, and picked it up. Blood dripped from its black and silver threads, but it snapped in the charnel wind as she gripped it beside her torch, the flames rolling over the cloth but not burning it.

'Reclusians!' She went forward, careful not to stumble over the dead, and the others gathered in until they stood as a group just before the Narrows. Reekbite might think he was done spending blood, but there was a cost to attacking the Ruination Chamber, and Morgen Light meant him to pay. 'Advance.'

It took a moment for the Clawlord to notice them, to turn and level his flaming blade, snarling. In that moment, Morgen lifted torch and banner and shouted, 'For Sigmar! For hope!'

'For hope when hope is dying!' they shouted back, and she began to run. Charging forward, making for that litter, her sword and torch blazing like bonfires. She could hear the others behind her, their boots like thunder. Before them, the skaven army swirled, ratmen flinging themselves out of the way, and for a glorious moment Morgen could see a path to the litter open before them. Reekbite was pointing his sword at them, his lips drawn back to reveal sharpened teeth, and she aimed for him, pulling her sword back to strike, as the rat ogors that bore the litter stepped forward, massive blade-limbs raised.

Morgen and the Reclusians met them, their weapons flashing, and the sound of thunder filled the day.

When the first roll of thunder echoed through the Vale, they all stopped moving.

Amon looked back, past frowning Corus and wide-eyed Sevora, who were both leading the blinded Brevin, past the silent Lord-Terminos and down the narrow path of the valley. There was nothing to see but the dying trees, but somewhere below their twisting branches the Reclusians had stopped that monstrous swarm of skaven. Had stopped that vast army, and now they were bleeding it, making the skaven pay for every step closer to the Halt. But they were dying as they did it. The thunder rolled again, and again, and Amon could see the lightning snapping up into the clear azure vault of the heavens.

'There were so few of them,' Sevora said, her voice almost lost in another peal of thunder.

So few, and now fewer and fewer. The thought spiralled through Amon's head, and he tapped his knuckle against his temple to get it out.

'We have no time to stop. We have to–'

He cut off as the thunder suddenly peaked, a massive roaring crescendo that filled the Vale. The sound blotted out everything, shaking the ground beneath them, and the lightning was rising together into one monstrous bolt so bright Amon had to look away.

Then it was gone, leaving nothing but afterimages flaring across Amon's sight, and the low boom of echoes drifting back from the mountain peaks that surrounded them. As the echoes faded, Amon could hear Corus murmuring a quiet prayer. Almost hidden beneath his voice, just a scrap of noise, Amon could hear Sevora echoing her great-grandfather's words with a near-silent whisper.

They didn't have time, but Amon waited until Corus was done, until the final echoes of that terrible thunder were lost, to start them moving again.

The goat path they were on twisted, turned away from the pass and wandered into the mountains. Ahead was a stone face, sheer and high. Amon stopped and pulled his spyglass from his belt. Through it he tried to trace out another path, but there was nothing. The cliffs curved out here, a wall of impassable rock. But in the Vale below, at the edge of his vision, was a gleaming sheet of quartz veined with red.

'We go down here. The Halt is just ahead.'

'Wait,' Sevora said. She was looking at Brevin, whose hand was at his chest again. Tapping this time, fingers pointing to bloody lines drawn across the cloth of his bandages. 'What are these?'

'Alchemical symbols,' he said, though it was hard to be sure. They were roughly made, but Brevin nodded. Amon frowned, wanting to move, but this was something the Lord-Ordinator thought important, so he tried to remember the lore he'd learned for a hunt long ago. 'Warpstone. Emberstone. I don't know this one. Air?'

Brevin shook his head.

'Smoke?'

The Stormcast nodded.

'This last is destruction.'

'What does it mean?' Sevora asked.

It means we are playing pantomime games I didn't want to start, Amon thought. 'We don't have–'

He stopped, suddenly thinking of that first time he went into the smoke, when he'd sent the tiny piece of emberstone at the skaven. It had hit the smoke and exploded. The smoke that rippled with the ugly green light of warpstone.

'Warpstone and emberstone.' He looked at Brevin. 'When they touch, there is smoke, and destruction.'

The Lord-Ordinator nodded again.

He thought of that tiny grain of red, and the huge flash of fire after. Of the Halt, with its web of emberstone beneath the quartz face, and the cracks the shade had been hammering into that crystal. If that thing had smashed through it, exposed the emberstone, how big would the explosion have been?

'So–' Sevora started, but Peace cut her off. The gryph-crow made a soft noise, its eyes pointed to the sky. Amon looked up and saw the storm wings there. Jocanan heading towards them, fast, and a flock of shapes pursuing her, bat-like wings clawing through the sky.

The Knight-Questor grunted, unsheathed his sword and felt it rumble in his hand. Corus and the Lord-Terminos moved up beside him, while Sevora held the Lord-Ordinator out of the way. The Prosecutor was diving in, twisting through the air to avoid the attacks of the ratwings swarming her, her javelin flashing. When she landed she rolled, wings snapping in so that they wouldn't catch Amon or any of the others. The ratwings followed, teeth gnashing and talons slashing. Amon struck and ripped the wing from one of them; swung his mace and caught another, smashing it from the air and leaving its corpse smouldering.

Corus hit one with his shield, then split another in half with his axe, while the Lord-Terminos cut more of the things from the air with smooth, sweeping strikes. They fell in pieces, twitching and shrieking, and then the flock spiralled away, fleeing into the twilight sky.

'Vicious things.' Jocanan was sitting on the stone, breathing deeply. The ratwings had gone for her face and eyes, and she swiped a hand across her brow, wiping the blood away from the cuts that marked it. 'More and more of them come, and their numbers give them bravery.' She made a sketch on the stone with her blood, a quick thing that was all wings and teeth. Crude but horribly evocative, and she frowned at her art then stepped on it as she rose. 'The army advances again. Now's your best chance to make for the wall.'

'Our only chance,' Amon said. Close. So close. 'Let's go.'

CHAPTER TWENTY

WARRUN VALE

They slid down the cliffs that made up the side of the Vale, leading Brevin through the rough stone and gangrenous scrub. When they reached the ground, their boots squelching into the rotting corpse-carpet of grass that covered the bottom of the pass, they started to run. Sevora made it two paces before Corus snatched her up. His armour was uncomfortable but reassuring as he cradled her in one arm like a child, and she was too tired to protest. Sagging into him, she watched as the corrupted Vale flashed by as the Stormcast Eternals raced for the Halt.

The Halt holds!

The battle cry rang through her head as the massive wall appeared before them. The day was almost done, and the Warrun was filled with shadows, but the Halt glowed in the twilight. So close, but Sevora could hear the low thunder of the army behind them.

'We'll make it,' Corus said, as if he could hear her doubt.

They crossed the clearing, Jocanan flying in the lead, wings beating hard as she skimmed up the face of the Halt. Corus was right behind her until he reached the base of the wall, with Amon and the Lord-Terminos following, Brevin between them.

This close, Sevora could see the damage. Most of the massive wall seemed pristine, untouched and untouchable, but where the smoke had been it was different. Layers of soot coated the quartz, dulling its glow, and cracks radiated away from the circular impact marks that marred the crystal. The places Brevin's shadow had struck the wall, trying to break open the quartz and expose the emberstone beneath. In far too many places, the shadow had come very close.

'No gate,' she said, looking down the smooth, unbroken expanse. The shadows beneath the dead trees were seething. They were at the wall, but they were still on the wrong side.

'They won't open it,' Corus said. 'Too much chance a rat will get in.'

'They'll drop a rope.' Amon was standing with his back to the wall, looking back. A flurry of arrows had swept out of the trees. They fell well short of them, but each arrow seemed to pull at the gathering night, and where they landed a clot of darkness formed. Skaven ran forward into it and disappeared. 'Brevin goes first. Corus, follow and defend.'

Corus nodded to Amon, but spoke to Sevora. 'I'll carry you too.'

'With what hand?' she said, staring out at that clot of darkness. 'Set me down.'

'Sevora—'

'Don't argue with me,' she snapped. 'I'm not staying here and dying, I'm going to tie myself to your bloody back.' He set her down, and with her belt and his he made a loop that fit under her arms. It was awkward and uncomfortable, but it worked. She was settling into it when Corus stepped back and the end of a heavy rope hit the ground near them. Then another fell next to it.

Amon pressed the first rope into the Lord-Ordinator's hands.

'Climb,' he said, and Brevin nodded. His body was mottled with bruises and cuts, but his massive muscles bunched beneath his skin and he began to pull himself up, climbing quickly hand over hand. 'Corus, go!'

The Reclusian caught the other rope, climbing fast, Sevora's weight not slowing him at all. Below, Amon took hold of Brevin's rope and started up while the Lord-Terminos climbed behind Corus and Sevora. They were leaving their pursuers behind.

Then something smashed into the wall beside Corus with a screaming hiss, flying apart in green flames and chunks of iron, sharpened twists of scrap that rattled off Corus' shield. But one found its way to Sevora, and she gasped as the hot metal punched into her calf.

'I'm all right,' she gasped as Corus twisted his head to look at her. The shrapnel hadn't gone deep, and she reached down and jerked the burning metal out of her skin like a thorn. 'Keep going!'

But that hissing noise grew around them as more of the things smashed into the wall. Corus swung his shield, stopping the shrapnel, but he couldn't climb with one hand. They were stuck, an unmoving target, and Sevora could see the hissing missiles rising from that patch of darkness the skaven had made. Crossbow bolts were raining down from the Halt, but the shadows made the skaven impossible targets.

'Protect Brevin!' Amon shouted. 'Keep going!' The Knight-Questor loosened his grip, the rope sizzling through his gauntlets as he dropped back to the ground, with the Lord-Terminos right behind. The two raced away from the wall, heading towards that patch of darkness. Then they were gone, lost in the black.

Corus started to climb again, and the missiles smashed into the wall around them. They were badly aimed but their explosions spread out their damage, and another piece of shrapnel drew a burning cut across Sevora's arm. She gritted her teeth and kept silent, looking up to check on Brevin, who was climbing with silent determination. Then she was grabbing onto Corus, holding tight as he kicked out from the wall, shield extended to block a missile that was heading straight towards the Lord-Ordinator. The shield knocked it away, to explode somewhere beneath them, and Sevora hung grimly on until Corus started climbing again. Then there was the sound of thunder and inhuman screams, and she looked down. The black patch was gone, shredded by a blaze of green flame. Skaven were running from it, wrapped in that emerald fire, but she couldn't see Amon or the Lord-Terminos.

Sevora was so intent on searching for them, she didn't see the flying things until they were swirling around them, shrieking and biting.

Talons raked her shoulder, and something tried to bite her neck. She slammed an elbow back, knocking the ratwing away, but there was another, snapping and tearing. Corus swung his shield, deflecting wings, but there were more, always more, diving in to attack, sensing their prey was helpless.

'Get off,' Sevora shouted as she swung her knife, cutting wings and slashing muzzles as the ratwings dove at her, but she was bleeding from half a dozen cuts already. Corus was smashing the things away even as he struggled to climb up to the same height as Brevin, who was catching the horrors out of the air and crushing them.

They were so close, why couldn't these things just leave them alone? The thought was irrational, childish, but it filled Sevora's head as one of the ratwings landed on her arm, snapping at her face. But then a flick of silver caught it, skewering it and flinging it away.

Jocanan's grey-blue wings burned bright as she slammed through the flock, her javelin stabbing. And surrounding her were black-feathered pinions. Bleak ravens, the ones who'd followed them from Rookenval, diving through the ratwings, their black bills stabbing like daggers. The Prosecutor and the Morrda-sent birds worked together, stabbing and cutting, and the ugly flapping things spiralled away, shrieking.

'Climb!' Jocanan called. 'There are more! There are greater!'

Greater? Sevora thought, as Corus swarmed up the rope. The Reclusian was moving fast now, catching up with Brevin. The Lord-Ordinator was bleeding, but moving with steady speed, and Corus matched him. Close, so close, and she could hear the shouts of the Golden Lions, the snap of crossbows. But there was a clap of wings larger than Jocanan's, and talons like daggers slammed into the Halt beside them as Corus pushed off the wall, dodging away.

Sevora couldn't stop it now. The shout was pouring out of her: 'Leave me alone!' And with it the wind whipped around her. She felt magic moving in her again, and for once she caught it, focused it. Made it into a weapon, a blade of wind that she would use to cut this thing apart.

And then there was light, and the night and her magic were all gone, and she was lost in the memory of her great-grandfather.

'Brother.'

Corus stood in the centre of the canyon, blinking in the light. He wasn't sure how he'd got there. He thought he was in his temple, surrounded by the dead and the damned. He thought he was dying.

'Brother,' Lavin said, standing beside him, his face perfect except for a thin line of blood that marked one cheek. 'Why do you stand here?'

Here. Why here… Corus stared at the monster, the bronze-scaled Chaos-tainted man that knelt before him. 'This one,' he said slowly. 'This one killed me, long ago. He led the Chaos band that destroyed my settlement. He captured me, tortured me. Trying to make me renounce Sigmar, to revoke him.'

'Sigmar blesses you,' Lavin said with vicious satisfaction. 'Your mortal life was stolen by the cruelty of Chaos. Now you have a chance to face the author of that pain.' Lavin looked down at the Chaos warrior, whose blood was flowing down the chains that held him. 'Face him, and show him the truth. Make him repent for the sins he visited against this world and against you.' Lavin took Corus' hand and laid it on one of the bronze scales that grew from the warrior's chest. 'Show him the strength Sigmar gave you in your new life, and make him revoke the daemon god he worships.'

Corus held the scale in one hand. He could feel it was solid, rooted deep. It would hurt, tearing it free. He pulled a little, and the warrior stared at him, his bleeding eyes burning. It would hurt a lot.

'Do it,' the monster said, smiling with his filed teeth. 'I dare you.'

And Corus pulled.

Amon let the rope fly through his gauntlets, clamping down only when he was almost at the bottom of the massive wall, slowing just enough to turn his fall into a run.

He knew the Lord-Terminos was there right behind him, racing with him through the rotting-corpse grass towards the darkness the skaven had made, sword and mace ready. Determined not to see his hunt thwarted right at its end.

The clot of darkness lay halfway across the clearing that stretched before the wall, a darker piece of night that hid the skaven and whatever weapon they were using to fling those explosions at Brevin and the Halt. When Amon hit that circle of shadow, he slammed his sword against his torch, making thunder and light. Pained squeals followed the roll of thunder, but the light didn't flash like lightning – in the darkness it only made a dim, hazy glow. But it was enough to see a skaven just before him, holding something that looked like a blunt spear. The ratman snarled and threw the thing at him, but Amon slapped it out of the air.

It landed at his feet, the length of cord sticking out of it sputtering and sparking. Like the fuse of a cannon.

Amon dug his boot under the sputtering thing and kicked it away. It arced through the air, and when it landed the sparks coming from it flared up, showing the pile of other blunt spears it had rolled into and the blinking skaven that huddled over them.

Amon saw that and turned. The Lord-Terminos was at his shoulder, and Amon caught them and knocked them back and down, sending them both sliding across the slimy ground and out of the darkness just as an explosion ripped through it, green fire and iron splinters flying through the air. Amon felt some of the shrapnel tick off his armour, but there was no pain other than a ringing in his ears and spots in his eyes from the flames.

Thunder and light. It was what he wanted, and what he had got.

The Lord-Terminos rolled to their feet, their axe taking the head off a smoking skaven running past. Amon came up too, spinning back to face the wall, looking for Brevin and finding the Lord-Ordinator almost at the top, surrounded by a wheeling, screaming flock of ratwings.

'Damn,' he sighed, and started running back, making for the ropes.

'Knight-Questor! Stop!'

Amon almost ignored the Lord-Terminos, focused on getting to Brevin and finishing this, finally, but there was an urgency to the shout that made him slow. Made him see.

Rats. A massive swarm of them, like a dark pool around the end of the ropes. They were climbing, tiny claws digging into the thick ropes and carrying them upwards. The ones closest to Amon were starting to move in his direction, too, a swarm of teeth, and he backed away, looking up at the fight far overhead.

Jocanan was there now, her silver javelin flashing as she cut the skaven-made things out of the air, and there were other feathered wings spinning around her, the black wings of the ravens. They were driving the ratwings back, and now Brevin was close, so close. He was going to make it, the climbing rats far too late to catch him, the ratwings too small to bring him down.

Then there was a crack of wings, and something slammed into the wall near Corus, a ratwing bigger than Jocanan. It snapped at them, Corus smashing his shield into its teeth. Then it was shoved back, as if by a gust of wind. The beast screeched and lashed forward again, this time at Brevin. Amon raised a hand, waiting, watching, helpless.

The huge ratwing lunged forward, jaws gaping, and Amon heard Corus shout. He couldn't make out the words, but he started as he saw Brevin suddenly let go of the rope.

The beast's mouth snapped shut, barely missing Brevin as he fell. Corus was swinging out, clinging to the rope with his shield hand, his other arm reaching for the Lord-Ordinator. Brevin slammed into the Reclusian's arm, then started to slip away, falling. Until Corus wrapped his legs around Brevin's waist, catching him. They hung there, spinning, as the huge ratwing turned in the air towards them.

Just in time for Jocanan to meet it.

The Prosecutor buried her javelin in the thing's belly, and it squealed. Then the ratwing's talons caught her, holding the Prosecutor as the creature fell, the ravens shrieking around them. But Amon was focused on Brevin. Corus still held him with his legs as he pulled himself to the top of the Halt. And then there were hands reaching for him, taking Sevora, helping him with Brevin, and they were over the top.

Amon let out a great breath, the tension in him running out, gone.

He barely noticed the soldiers cutting the ropes, letting them fall with their great weight of rats to the ground.

'Done, Stormlord. Done.'

'You have a strange sense of completion, Knight-Questor.' The Lord-Terminos stood beside him on the empty no-man's-land before the wall. In the air and in the ground was the low rumble of the skaven army drawing close. They'd be overrun soon. Very soon.

'Quests end. Everything else is chaos.' Amon looked to the cliffs at the edge of the Halt, where the beast had fallen. 'There was no lightning. Let's find Jocanan.'

The Lord-Terminos nodded their head, and the two of them started moving, striding away as the dead trees in the forest began to fall, crashing down before the river of death that was pouring up Warrun Vale.

CHAPTER TWENTY-ONE

THE HALT

Something grabbed at Sevora and she swung her hands, trying to knock it away. But then other hands grabbed hers and she opened her eyes. A woman leaned over her, wearing armour of red and gold. A Golden Lion.

She was on top of the Halt. Exhausted, hurting, but alive. Corus was standing over her, his armour scratched, blood on his face, with Brevin leaning against the stone behind him, his skin mottled with wounds.

'What happened?'

'We made it to the top. Jocanan and the others did not.'

Did not. She started to push up, but the Golden Lion stopped her. The woman wiped at something on Sevora's neck, cold water laced with herbs that felt like fire against whatever wound she touched. 'This needs stitches,' she said.

'Do it while we speak.' General Kant strode up, her lined face looking ten years older. 'What happened?'

Sevora stared at the woman, wondering if she was supposed

to speak, but then the Golden Lions war surgeon started attacking her wound with a hooked needle and thread. She gritted her teeth, trying to ignore the pain. Corus watched for a moment, eyes snapping with lightning, and then he turned to Kant, drawing his breath to speak. But he was interrupted by Brevin, who was snapping his fingers with one hand while miming something with another.

Writing. Of course. He wouldn't have to use blood and bandages here.

'Fetch an etching-plate and stylus for the Lord-Ordinator,' the general said, and Brevin nodded. Kant looked back to Corus, waiting, and the Reclusian began to talk.

Corus briefly recalled what had happened since the Ruination Chamber left the wall, Sevora helping him occasionally when she could, through the pain. By the time the story was done, Sevora's stitches were finished and she was breathing through clenched teeth, waiting for the pain to fade.

'All of them. Lost.' Kant shook her head. 'I knew it when you last few came running. But it's still hard to hear.' From beyond the wall, something bellowed, a noise that shook the air. The general turned and walked towards the wall, her shape a black silhouette against a night dully lit not by the stars or moons, but by something beyond the wall. 'All of them lost, to that.'

Sevora pushed herself up, careful of her stitches, and moved towards the edge of the Halt, Corus right behind her. She stared down, remembering how she had first seen this view, with Warrun Vale lost beneath a tide of smoke. Now it glowed with light.

There were fires, so many fires, the corpses of the trees they'd passed in the smoke torn down and arranged into great pyres dotting the Vale's floor. There were thousands of tinier flames between, bright yellow dots, but mixed in with them were green poisonous lights that pressed into Sevora's eyes like needles. It was a galaxy of ugly stars, large and small, floating in a shifting, seething black firmament.

Shadows: thousands, tens of thousands, maybe more. Shadows small and vast, and in every one black eyes caught the light of the fires and reflected it back, pinpricks of malevolence and rage.

'There's so many,' Sevora said. 'But every time I see them there's more.'

'There are always more,' said Kant. 'That's what the Knight-Questor said.'

'I wish he wasn't right,' Sevora said.

'I wish he wasn't dead.' The general spat over the wall. 'I need him. I need all the Stormcasts, a whole Stormhost, and all one hundred regiments of the Golden Lions. What I have is one regiment, and one–' She looked at Brevin, bent over his parchment. 'And two Stormcasts.'

'And one Halt,' Corus said.

'Yes, and one giant wall, which is why we're not already dead.' General Kant looked again at Brevin, and lowered her voice. 'You brought him back, but… Can he heal the Halt like that? After what they did to him?'

'I don't know,' said Corus. 'But Amon told us that Sigmar had sent him to bring Brevin back. So we did, no matter the cost. He will do something here, something we need. Else why send Amon? Why us?'

Sevora could think of a thousand cynical answers to that, but she knew Corus believed. That he trusted. That he had hope.

Hope is a lie.

Sevora looked at her great-grandfather, and tried to understand. Hope. He always had it. Why? Hope wasn't something you learned in the Warrens. You learned how to fight, how to steal, how to sneak, how to lie; you learned things that let you survive. Corus could fight, he'd been born to fight, and the Warrens had honed that skill, but hope – he hadn't learned that there, in the dark where she had been born and raised. The Warrens didn't give you space for hope. Believing in the future was worse than being pretty; it was an opening in your guard that would let in every blade. So where had his hope come from?

Unbidden, an image of Aika, her great-grandmother, came to her; a memory of a memory that wasn't hers. *Remember hope.* She had taught it to him. That's why he loved her so much, even now, a century after her death.

'General Kant.' A sergeant appeared, his scarred face twisted into an ugly frown. 'We've got deserters on the far side.'

'Damn them,' Kant said, and strode off after the man, leaving Corus and Sevora staring down at the sea of fire and shadow below.

'Do you think I was wrong about Brevin?' Corus asked.

Sevora blinked at him. 'What?'

'You were staring at me, after I told the general that Brevin must be here for a reason. Because of Amon. And Sigmar.'

'Oh,' she said. 'No, I was–' She shook her head. 'I don't know. I'm tired.'

'Tired.' He frowned. 'On the wall, you fainted again. What–'

'I didn't faint,' she said, annoyed, and that annoyance was enough to push her to speak. 'It's you. It's your memories. It's being a Memorian.' She looked into his lightning-flecked eyes. 'That's why I knew about your temple, about how you died. We're not here just to help you remember, Corus, we help *defend* you from remembering. Some of your memories are bad.' She shuddered. 'A lot of them are. They can hurt you, come back when you're fighting, pull you in and get you killed. Unless there's someone to stop them. Someone like me.'

'Stop them,' he said.

'Block them,' she said. 'I'm a shield, Corus, like the one on your arm. But I block memories instead of blades. And I don't bloody faint.'

'A shield.' He shook his head. 'I didn't ask for this. Didn't want this. I wanted–'

'To save and protect and be the martyr and the hero. Like you were for Aika.' He sounded like her, arguing with Morgen. 'Well, you can't be. You don't have that choice, any more than I had the choice to be your Memorian.' And she sounded like Morgen, and she was definitely too tired for that. 'It's just the way it is, and it doesn't really matter, does it? We're going to die as soon as the rats find a way to knock down this wall.'

'You won't die, Sevora.'

'You keep saying that,' she said.

'And you keep hearing it,' he answered. 'With your still-living ears.'

Before she could argue that, Brevin stood, holding out his parchment.

Corus read it, storm-eyes intent. 'He says we have to take him to something called the Heart. He's written down the way.' There was another bellow from below the wall, and soldiers were rushing forward, and somewhere Kant was shouting orders. 'They're attacking,' Corus said, hand dropping to his axe.

'And you won't be able to do anything that matters,' Sevora replied, then pointed to Brevin. 'Except maybe this.'

Corus looked to the wall, to the soldiers gathering there, to where another bellow sounded. Then he nodded in agreement.

The ravens led them to her.

The black birds were silent, but they perched on the stones at the edge of the Halt, and when Amon and the Lord-Terminos approached they flew a little way up the cliff, leading them to a hollow where Jocanan sat with her back against the stone, the monstrous ratwing dead at her feet.

'You're supposed to be on top of the wall,' she said. Her hands were wet with the dark red-black blood of the beast, and she was painting the stone with it. A woman's face, done in blood, the few rough lines somehow sketching features full of deep longing and sorrow.

'The rats had other ideas,' Amon said. 'How badly are you hurt?'

She finished one last line and slowly stood. Her armour was battered, the silvery patina marred with scratches, and her skin was marked with wounds. Most were small, already healing, but her right wing was shattered. Bone jutted out from the grey pinions, and it dragged behind her, trailing blood. 'I have fallen, and will not rise again today. Except to my god, and perhaps my dissolution.'

The Lord-Terminos stepped forward and clasped hands with her, a simple salute, and they both bowed heads, praying. Amon looked away, staring back at the army which was pouring into the Vale below. Skaven. There were always more. But numbers like this were numbing. This wasn't an army, it was an unnatural dis-aster – a swarm of hunger and malevolence. Where had they all come from? The lands beyond the Adamantine Chain had been home to Darkoath reavers and daemons, gargants and savage orruks. Not skaven, not like this. It was as if the lands between the mountains and the sea had ruptured like the rotting belly of a dead thing and spilled these carrion eaters out like maggots.

Maggots that were going to eat them alive.

A shadow slid around a rock, moving on four legs, and Amon pulled back his sword, ready to stick whatever it was through the chest. But he checked the blow, realising the thing wasn't some huge rat but Morgen's gryph-crow.

'Peace. I thought we lost you.' To be honest, he hadn't thought of the beast at all, had forgotten him during the dash to the Halt and the fighting. The gryph-crow cocked his head at him, and Amon was sure he caught a gleam of resentment there.

'Thought,' Peace croaked, and then stepped silently around him and went to Jocanan.

She was standing still as the Lord-Terminos tore strips from his cloak and used them to bind the mantle of her damaged wing. Her eyes were closed, hands moving as though drawing in the air while the Lord-Terminos worked, but she opened them when Peace leaned against her.

'Foolish beast,' she said, stroking his feathered head. 'You should have run for the cliffs.' Peace cawed softly, but he shifted his head to look out of the narrow opening in the stone towards the assembling army and clicked his sharp beak. 'I know what they did,' the Prosecutor said. 'I'm sorry you lost her. We will help you avenge them.' She looked up from Peace to Amon. 'What is our plan, Knight-Questor?'

'Plan?' He frowned at her. 'Why do you look to me for a plan?'

'Because the Lord-Veritant set you as our leader.'

'I had a hunt then,' Amon said. 'A quest from Sigmar. It is done. I have no more idea what to do now than you do. Other than kill as many skaven as we can before we die.'

'I don't want to just kill them,' Jocanan said. 'I want to thwart them. Even for a moment. Like Lord-Veritant Morgen did, and all the others.'

'Yes.' Amon wanted that too. He didn't want to die buried beneath a mass of skaven, no matter how many he killed as he went. It wouldn't be enough. He tapped his temple with his fist. There were always more. Always. But what could they do? 'I want my blood to cost them. But there is no hunt here! This will be a massacre that none of us will survive.'

From somewhere far outside came a deep roar like thunder, and they all stared out of the narrow opening into the empty waste before the Halt. There, in the centre of the field, something was moving. For a moment, Amon thought that the smoke was coming back. There was a dark cloud in the night, eclipsing the torches and bonfires as it rolled forward through the army. A path formed in front of it, panicked skaven skittering out of the way. Then the wind blowing up the Vale tore at the cloud, and through it could be seen the thing beneath.

A skaven. But a skaven vast as a gargant, its body a great twisted mass of muscle half-covered with rolls of fat. There was metal running through that mountain of flesh, struts and cables of brass, a framework to support the beast's bulk. Its right forearm had been stripped of flesh, the bones coated in brass plates and chains that formed a massive flail. Its left arm was almost completely gone, replaced by a tangle of tubes and tanks wrapped in cables and studded with glowing chunks of warpstone. That knotted mass of metal and corruption ended in a huge brass barrel that dripped green drops of a liquid that sizzled into flames when it struck the ground. More brass erupted from the thing's back – heavy pipes that belched out the black smoke that wreathed it. The behemoth stopped at the edge of the army, swung its head back and bellowed again, showing a mouth full of gigantic teeth capped in brass. The terrible sound echoed down the Vale, underlain by a faint counterpoint, a screaming gibber that came from the thing's neck. The giant had another head there, tiny compared to the rest of its form: a skaven head that foamed and gnashed its teeth, dark eyes filmed with madness.

'No hunt, Knight-Questor?' the Lord-Terminos said. 'Sigmar's hunter and Astral Templar, whose Stormhost is also called the Beast Slayers? No hunt?'

Peace stepped forward on silent feet, the feathers on the ruff of his neck rising, while the ravens who crouched on the stones leaned forward, eyes flashing. Then, as one, corvids and gryph-crow looked to Amon. They did not speak, but they did not have to. He could feel the presence inside them, staring at him. Could

hear the echo of his god's laughter in his head. Amon tried to
ignore it as he pulled his spyglass from his belt and stared out at
the thing, and at what was moving up beside it.

It was a platform borne by a gang of rat ogors wrapped in spiked
armour. A skaven armoured in black plate stood on it, one of his
eyes glowing green beneath a horned helm. Banners shifted over
him in the wind, the largest bearing a huge horned skull with one
green eye. The skaven raised a sword over his head, a curved blade
with jagged teeth, and green fire licked up and down the blade.

The vast army of skaven howled then with one voice. 'Reekbite! Reekbite!' The chant went on and on until the Clawlord cut
the air with his sword, slashing a glowing triangle in the air that
slowly faded. In the silence that followed he spoke, his voice mag-
ically amplified to fill the Vale.

'Failure!' Reekbite snarled, his voice filled with anger and hate.
'Clan Sisseris promised destruction and a path to the heart of
this realm. Clan Sisseris failed-failed. Treacherous and useless,
Sisseris will die.' The great sea of skaven hissed at this, a painful
sound that kept going until Reekbite cut another triangle in the
air. 'Death to all who fail us. Death-death to all who stand in our
way. Death to all things that oppose Verminus. Death!'

The hiss echoed out again, mixed now with the crash of weapons and the gnashing of teeth. Reekbite let it go on, before he
finally roared over it:

'This realm, all realms, are ours! For the Horned Rat, we claim
them. Now we smash-smash that wall, and make this a place of
smoke and blood and Verminus, forever!'

'You are right,' Amon said, watching as the behemoth behind the
Clawlord shook its head and howled, spilling more black smoke
into the night. 'I do have a hunt here. We all do. To kill that thing,
and teach that Clawlord pain.'

* * *

Green eyes.

'We're nearly there.' Sevora was leading Brevin down the stairs across the back of the Halt, her hand so small in his. 'Here's the last step.' Her voice was almost lost in the sounds coming from over the wall, despite the weight of stone between them. Shouts and screams and the roar of something angry and monstrous.

Green eyes. Vast and hungry. Mad, but cunning.

Yellow threads.

'What is it?' Sevora asked as he stopped. He couldn't tell her why, couldn't tell her that he saw her. Saw something, a rippling thing that was like the crude sketch of a person, done in thousands of threads of yellow, bending and changing, shaping themselves into what could have been the face of a young woman, or a skull, or just a haze of lines twisting around each other like straw in a whirlwind. Then it was gone, except for a knot of yellow threads drifting where her heart would be. Then that was gone too.

He shook his head and started moving again, not looking up at the sky. At the eyes that were watching him.

I will show you. I will make you know.

Skein's words. Was this Skein's magic? Had the Grey Seer done this to him, when he'd stabbed the thing Varus had made into his chest? Had the skaven taken his eyes and given him this sight, whatever it was?

Madness. That's what it was.

He wanted to shove the thought away, but how could he, with those eyes watching him? They were the eyes of a mad god, and he was under their gaze. He'd been under them ever since the Reclusians had died, died to get him here. They had watched him run, watched him climb the wall and bleed, watched him scrawl out his mad hopes onto a thin slab of metal.

'Here's the door,' Corus said.

'Can you open this, Lord-Ordinator?' When Sevora spoke, the

yellow knot of lines flickered to life again, burst out into the shape of a woman, then dissolved into a whirlwind. Vanished.

Could he? After he'd linked to the Heart, this stone had simply brushed itself aside whenever he approached. What would it do now? Was that connection still there, the one Skein had tried to use to break the Halt? Or had the Grey Seer's magic broken it?

A hand took his shoulder, Corus' hand. The Reclusian moved him, brought him close to the door, and inside his chest there was a flicker. A spark of light in all that darkness, and gods, it burned. Like a drop of molten iron in his heart, boiling his blood and searing his veins. It hurt, but Brevin grabbed hold of that pain and pulled it to him. Embraced it. Because that burning made the eyes fade.

'It's open!' Sevora said. Beyond the wall, something bellowed and the Halt shook, as if kicked by a god. 'Quickly!'

Hands grabbed Brevin's arm and pulled, and then he was moving with them, running, and the distant, horrible noise of monstrous rage faded, a storm on the edge of the horizon.

They were in the Halt, heading for the Heart, and that spark of light and flare of pain was giving Brevin hope again. Skein hadn't cut away his connection to the Heart, the way he'd cut out his voice, his eyes. Just clotted it, blocked it somehow, and a block could be ripped away.

Burned out.

Hope. Hope that he could heal the Halt, restore its magic, and leave the army outside gnawing on stone until they starved. Hope for revenge on Skein, thwarting him and leaving the Grey Seer to the mercy of Reekbite.

'Sigmar,' Corus said, his voice low and full of awe, and Brevin knew they had reached the chamber of the Heart. And yes, suddenly he could see... something.

Yellow lines flexed around him, twisting into shapes. He saw

GARY KLOSTER

Sevora, her face and body flexing around that brighter knot in her chest. A larger form, the form of a man, hideous and jagged. Corus. And beyond them both, a giant ball of lines all twisting together, forming something that looked like flames drifting in the air. The Heart, and far above the green eyes shifted their focus from Brevin to that great chunk of emberstone, hungry and hateful.

'Careful,' Sevora said as he stepped forward. 'The floor is dangerous.'

Brevin nodded, well aware of the swirling patterns of the wrought-iron bars that split the spherical chamber into upper and lower halves. But he pointed, trying to tell her that he wanted to get closer, and she led him out. As they moved, the yellow lines frayed and fell apart, fading again into darkness. Except the ones that formed the Heart: thinner, dimmer but still there. Was this some lesser version of how the Sisseris saw? Possibly. It was ugly, a nasty echo of the world, but it did let him know where the Heart was, and he stared at the twisting patterns of yellow lines as Sevora led him forward.

Finally they were standing just before it, and he felt again that tiny, searing spark in his chest. Dangerous but pure, and in the twisting yellow lines he could see something else, like an echo of colour. A tiny bit of red, thin lines of it like afterimages drifting with the yellow. So faint but there, and he raised his hand, starting to reach for them.

'Lord-Ordinator!' Sevora grabbed his wrist, and he could have broken her grip without thinking. But he paused, because when she touched him he saw something else. The lines of yellow that formed her had flared to life again, and in her chest he could see that knot of yellow, and this time there were echoes of that same red that was in the Heart.

Sorcery, he realised. Sevora was close to that which belonged to the realm, a raw and elemental power, like that of the Heart.

'What are you doing?' Corus asked.

'Stopping him from touching it,' Sevora answered. 'It's emberstone.'

348

'He is a Lord-Ordinator. He knows what he does.'

I wish that were true, Brevin thought, but he nodded and pulled his hand from Sevora's. Years ago, he'd taken a chance and laid his hand upon the Heart and blazed open the connection between them. Now... He stretched his hand out, reaching. Another chance, and he prayed to Sigmar that the Heart's fire would once again burn through him and sear a path to his soul.

Brevin laid his hand on the emberstone, and for one moment he was sure it was working. The pain in his chest increased, went from a dull ache to a spike of suffering, and he could imagine the heat of the magic burning its way through whatever cursed blockage Skein had left in him. But he was wrong. It wasn't fire, it wasn't heat; it was that choking torment, that swelling agony, and he knew then that something was wrong, that he had been tricked again. Laying his hand on the Heart had brought the poison that the Grey Seer had left in his chest to terrible life. It was growing in him, feeding on him, and he threw back his head, trying to scream in agony and warning. And in his head, vicious and cruel, he could hear one sound.

Shhhh.

CHAPTER TWENTY-TWO

WARRUN VALE

Amon crouched in the hollow in the cliff, a hunter in a blind, and watched the churning, shifting skaven lines through his spyglass.

There was a space around the behemoth, a moat of emptiness that grew and shrank as the swarm shifted, the ratmen keeping out of reach of the giant's hooked flails. A small procession appeared, a band of skaven in green robes, their black eyes glazed as if drugged. They were carrying two skaven that had been bound to poles. The prisoners were struggling, jerking against their bindings hard enough to tear their skin, but they couldn't get free. Round cages of brass had been stuffed into their mouths and wired into place so they couldn't spit them out. One cage held a chunk of warpstone, glowing ugly green. The other held a piece of ember-stone, glowing red as a coal.

The green-robed skaven walked in front of the behemoth, and the beast stared down at them, eyes fixed on the bound victims. Its jaws spread, brass-capped teeth gleaming, and foul saliva dribbled down onto the smaller head that jutted from its neck, making it grimace and gibber. The green-robed skaven tried to drive the poles that held their sacrifices into the ground, to set them up before the monster, but they were too slow. The behemoth plunged its jaws down and snatched up the first sacrifice, the one with the emberstone between its teeth, catching two of the robed ones as it did. They disappeared into its maw along with the sacrifice, shrieking as the teeth snapped shut, and the other green-robed skaven simply dropped their victim and ran. The behemoth swept its jaws over, snapping up the second sacrifice with the warpstone in its mouth. It reared up, swallowing, then looked at the army of skaven hungrily, but the smaller head on its neck shrieked and snapped and the behemoth turned back to the Halt and lurched forward.

Then it stopped.

The behemoth shook its head, swiping at its jaws with the brass chains of its flail. It grunted, and then vomited fire. Sheets of red and green flame spilled from its mouth, flashing bright and consuming each other into black, poisonous smoke. The spume ended and the behemoth snarled, boiling spit dripping from its mouth, and the muzzle of the cannon that was its left arm suddenly spewed out a gout of green fire splotched with sparks of crimson. The fire washed across the ground, burning a swathe of dead grass before smashing into the front edge of the skaven army. Shrieks echoed across the field as dozens of skaven were charred instantly to ash, and dozens more were left howling on the ground, toxic smoke boiling off their burnt bodies.

The brass pipes projecting from the giant's back roared as smoke poured out. The black vapour wreathed the behemoth in darkness broken only by the glint of mad eyes and brass hooks, and the rest of the skaven pulled back, putting distance between themselves and the horror they'd unleashed. Amon watched them move, then slapped his spyglass shut and tucked it away. The symbols Brevin had scrawled out in his own blood ran through Amon's head. Warpstone. Emberstone. Smoke. Destruction. The Clawlord was sending the behemoth to smash its hooks into the damaged part of the Halt to expose the emberstone veins beneath. Then it would bathe them in green flame.

What would happen then? Amon didn't know, but he knew that the Lord-Ordinator was desperate to stop it from happening. And so was Sigmar.

'Now,' Amon said. 'We hunt.'

Beside him, Jocanan smiled, and the Lord-Terminos lifted their axe and bowed their mask, praying aloud.

'Sigmar save us, not from death but failure. Let us work your will upon the realms, and when your lightning takes us let us walk the storm and find our way back to this world, whole enough to be your weapons once more.'

Whole enough. The words almost broke Amon out of his focus, but he pulled his weapons free and stepped away from the cliff into open ground.

'For Sigmar!' he shouted, and started to run.

He was the fastest of them, except for Peace. The gryph-crow kept pace with him as he raced towards the behemoth while the others fell behind. It didn't matter. There was no clever plot here to give them hope for victory. There was only the knowledge that this was the hunt that had been set before them, and that was all Amon needed.

A hunt was better than hope.

The behemoth had reached the Halt, and despite the thing's size the massive wall still dwarfed it. Far overhead, soldiers were raining down stones and crossbow bolts, but the feeble onslaught was doing nothing to the monster, the projectiles bouncing off its thick hide. Then the soldiers were screaming and choking, falling back, driven away as the poisonous black smoke boiling up from the giant swept over the top of the wall.

The behemoth watched them flee and roared, lashing out with its flail, but the mortals were beyond the reach of those filthy hooks. It raised its other arm, and green fire roared. The emerald flames caught a few fleeing soldiers and they fell, bodies trailing green flames. Brass-toothed jaws snapped one falling soldier out of the air and crunched bones and armour. Then the behemoth ducked its head to snap up another corpse that had hit the ground at its feet.

Amon had thought he was sprinting as fast as he could, but the sight of that massive head dipping low made him go faster. Peace fell behind as he drove forward, and Amon was alone when he reached the behemoth. The monster wasn't looking at him as it scooped up the corpse, and he charged in with his mace blazing.

The fiery weapon caught it in the side of the head. The behemoth made a noise like metal tearing, and jerked its head around, jaws snapping for Amon. He ducked beneath them and swung his sword, the sigmarite blade thundering as it clashed off the behemoth's metal-capped teeth. It shook its head and reared up, the side of its muzzle catching him and sending him sprawling.

The behemoth slammed its foot down, missing Amon as he rolled away. It stomped again, one claw cracking off Amon's armour, and it roared. Then Peace was there, driving his long beak into the monster's foot. The behemoth kicked out, but Peace hung on, clawing and stabbing, giving Amon time to roll to his feet again. And as he rose, the others raced past.

The Lord-Terminos and the broken-winged Prosecutor split around Amon, one to each side, barrelling into the behemoth. The Lord-Terminos slammed their axe into its leg, the huge blade tearing through thick hide and gristle to find the muscle beneath. The monster stumbled, shrieking, and swung its flail. A hook caught the Lord-Terminos and slammed them backward, but as the behemoth went to swing again, Jocanan threw her javelin and caught it in the belly. The silver shaft sank deep, then it flashed like lightning, disappearing from the wound and reappearing in the Prosecutor's hand.

The behemoth grunted and its cannon gouted fire, the emerald flames ripping across the ground. Jocanan jumped back, the fire barely singeing her.

She'd created an opening, and Amon slammed his weapons together, pulled thunder and fire from their connection and cast it at the behemoth. It roared, and its tail struck the Halt a shattering blow that ripped a sheet of quartz away from the base of the wall, exactly what Amon didn't want. The Knight-Questor skipped back, trying to bait the behemoth away, and the others moved with him.

They danced on the field below the scarred wall, axe and mace, beak and javelin, sword and talon. Tearing into the behemoth, spilling blood and noxious fluids from its hide, clanging off the brass flail and the pipes that ran like veins through its flesh. The skaven army watched, content to let this fight play out without their blood, confident in the inevitability of the behemoth's fury. Because all of their efforts weren't enough. The Stormcasts were faster, nimbler, hitting the thing from all sides, but the wounds they inflicted were minor. The behemoth was huge, its hide layers of iron-hard gristle, and one solid strike from either warpfire or flail would see them dead.

And death was coming. A gout of smoke poured down from the brass pipes on the giant's back and rolled over Peace, catching the gryph-crow as he was lunging in to strike. Peace stumbled back, blinded by the black poison, and in that instant the giant brass flail caught him. The gryph-crow gave one coughing cry as he was flung into the air, then he smashed into the earth, rolling to a stop, still. The watching army screeched as Peace fell. The skaven might not have been willing to join this fight, but they were eager for blood.

Blood they'll have, Amon vowed, ducking beneath a gout of flame. Reekbite wasn't going to break the Halt this easily. He slashed with his sword, and then one of the chains of the flail caught him. The brass links wrapped around his chest and he could feel the hook hit his back, the point slamming through his armour and sinking into his shoulder blade. He barely kept hold of his mace; he was trying to swing his sword, but the behemoth was lifting him from the ground, swinging him through the air, crouching to twist the cannon of its left arm towards him.

Amon hung from the chain, helpless, and watched as the barrel filled with bright green light, a ruin of flame rushing out to sear his flesh away and end his hunt in pain, failure, and death.

CHAPTER TWENTY-THREE

THE HALT

They were so close.

Sevora had led Brevin across the strange, circular chamber to that glowing, terrifying heart, and she had watched him raise his hands to it, and for a moment she thought this might be it. That they might be finally done. And then she had seen his ruined face, and one thought had whispered through her mind.

Hope is a lie.

Brevin's mouth was stretching open, wider and wider, into a silent shriek. He couldn't give voice to whatever agony filled him as his wounded throat spilled fresh blood, but Sevora could see his pain, pain so vast it must have been tearing the Hallowed Knight apart.

And then she could see the blood on his chest.

It pushed through the bandages, swallowing his runes, a triangle of blood. Then something pushed through the stained cloth, cutting the bandages away, a thing of metal and bone, a blood-coated instrument tearing out of the Stormcast's flesh. It began to grow. The ugly thing stretched, and there was a terrible crunching noise of ribs shattering, the ugly squelch of organs being ripped apart, the awful shredding noise of muscle and skin ripping as the triangular thing expanded, opening Brevin up like a butchered animal.

It was terribly like when the skaven things had torn Avil apart, but also hideously worse. This wasn't monsters tearing their way out, this was like a door being forced open in the Lord-Ordinator's flesh – a door through which something was pushing its way out of his blood, starting to step through from the other side, and Sevora fell back, trying to get away from whatever was coming.

But Brevin, still horribly alive, still horribly aware, jerked his hand down from the Heart and caught hers, holding her so she couldn't escape. She pulled at his iron grip, staring at the bulging blood that slicked over the triangular door, the thin skin of red going tight over the muzzle of a skaven shoving its way out of his ruined chest. They were coming: the skaven were coming, murder-birthing themselves into the world, and she couldn't get away because Brevin was holding her. She could feel Corus behind her, his fingers catching her shoulder to pull her back, but it was too late. The Lord-Ordinator dragged her hand up and slammed her palm against the Heart.

The world exploded then, into pain, and heat, and red, red light.

The hiss of the skaven echoed through Brevin's head and into his soul. Hearing it hurt him, worse than whatever terrible thing was happening in his heart. He'd been tricked again, manipulated into doing Skein's bidding, and there was nothing he could do, no way he could fight, no hope–

Hope when hope is dying.

The phrase rang through his head, and with it came an idea. A desperate gamble, but what else did he have? He forced his hand away from the Heart, and reached through the darkness for the knot of yellow that marked Sevora's magic. His hand found her arm, and he grabbed her, pulling her forward, whispering a prayer as he slammed her hand against the Heart.

'–and so I call upon you, Master of the Heavens, guide my hand and guide my heart, and let me serve you now, in my last moments in the Mortal Realms, until you see fit to bring me forth again.'

The light was fading around Sevora, dying back until she could see, but still it surrounded her. Red light, everywhere, and she floated in it like a piece of ash drifting through a fire. And beside her was a man, a Stormcast, wrapped in silver armour, a massive hammer leaning over one shoulder.

'Lord-Ordinator,' she said. It had to be him, though she barely recognised him. His skin was smooth and whole, and brown eyes gleamed in his face, reflecting the red light as the Hallowed Knight finished his prayer.

'Sevora. Thank Sigmar I didn't kill you.' His voice was deep, flowing from his unwounded throat.

'What did you do?' Sevora had thought this was another of Corus' memories tearing through her head, but no, apparently this was yet another kind of vision sent to plague her.

'I acted on impulse,' he said. 'Something I am prone to do, despite all it has cost me. My eyes, my voice, and my life, very soon. I made you touch the Heart. I saw your connection to magic, and...' Brevin shook his head. 'I don't have time. This moment is without time, without place, but it won't last. We'll be back in the Halt all too soon, and I will be rejoining Sigmar. If Skein's corruption hasn't taken that from me too.'

'Skein,' Sevora said. 'Who is that? What is this?'

'Skein. The Grey Seer. Skaven sorcerer. He's the one who was taking my shadow and attacking the Halt with it. The one who is

trying to destroy the wall and its Heart with warpstone.' Brevin shuddered, and his body blurred, changed. For a second his armour was gone, his eyes were gone, he was battered and bloody – and then he was back, whole. 'He used me to reach the Heart by hiding inside me. But now he's tearing his way out, and I can see.'

Brevin crouched and wrapped his hands around her shoulders. His hammer was gone, the way things flickered in and out in dreams. No, this wasn't a memory, but not quite a dream either.

'What is this?' she asked again. Heat was creeping through her, up her arm and into her body. Concentrating in her chest. In her heart.

'I can see,' he said, ignoring her question. 'He was in me, using me, but now that he is coming out I am in him too. Skein came for the Heart. He has always wanted the Heart. The wall destroyed – Reekbite wanted that, but Skein always wanted the Heart, and that is why he wanted me.'

The heat was in all of her now, and in her heart it was beginning to burn. Like a ball of flame. 'What–' she gasped, but that was all she could choke out.

'Skein wants to destroy it,' Brevin said. 'I see it now. He wants to destroy the Heart with warpstone. But not to break the Halt. He thinks he can capture it, all the destruction, all the poison smoke that would come from touching warpstone to the Heart. He thinks he can make it into a weapon, to be released where he wants, when he wants. He wants to be able to turn a city like Hammerhal Aqsha into a wasteland like the Vale.'

Brevin looked at her with eyes he didn't have any more. 'It's in you. The Heart. I made you touch it, to see if it would forge a link to you the way it did to me. You can channel magic, you can reach it, and you have to do something. You have to stop him. Use the Heart, and stop Skein.'

The fire in her was growing, growing with her every heartbeat, and the pain with it, overwhelming Sevora. It was too much, it was *going to kill her, and she fought for some way to contain it, to keep it from burning her up from the inside.*

'I am untrained,' she gasped. 'Uncontrolled. Flux-touched. I can't–'

'Flux-touched,' he whispered, finally hearing her. 'I don't know. Maybe that's better. Maybe that's what the Heart needs. Wild magic for wild magic. Or maybe I've killed you, killed us all. But this was all the hope I had. To strip the Heart from me, and give it to you.'

'Hope.' Sevora's voice was a whisper of pain. 'Hope is a lie.'

'No,' Brevin said. 'No!'

His eyes grew wide, wider, and then they were gone, caving into hollows of blood and pain as his last word stretched into a howl of denial.

'No!'

Then there was silence, their surroundings corroding to nothing as Brevin's face grew dirty and bloody; as his armour fell away; as his chest opened and out spilled darkness, darkness that swallowed everything.

There was darkness. Darkness tinted with the red of flames, flames that felt like they were licking beneath the surface of Sevora's skin.

Then there was confusion.

Sevora was on the wrought-iron floor, gasping, burning up from the inside. Something hit the bars beside her, splashing her with blood. She jerked up and saw teeth – yellow teeth spattered with red.

Yellow teeth. Yevin's warning went through her head, but it was far too late for warnings.

Skaven teeth, the eyes set in the face over them gone, sockets covered by eyelids stitched shut with yellow thread. Sevora twitched back, and only then realised that the head was also missing a body, the stump of its neck dripping blood.

Sevora scrambled to her feet, pulling her knife even as the world swung around her. Heat filled her like a fever, but she fought through it to try to understand what was happening. She was still in the centre of that great circular chamber, that Heart beside her, pulsing with light. Brevin–

Brevin's body was sprawled a little way away on the wrought-iron bars of this treacherous floor. The triangle in his chest had ripped open wide enough for her to fall into, the crude metal and bone marking the edges of a massive wound. By everything holy, the Lord-Ordinator should have been dead. But one arm still reached up, fingers clawing for the Heart. Still alive, somehow, even as something moved in the dark triangle that had ripped him open. A skaven, its fur brown and red and white, its eyes blinking.

'Yes,' it muttered as it dragged itself out of the Lord-Ordinator, trembling and silently snarling as the darkness in Brevin's chest stirred once again. But Sevora's attention went to the shower of sparks bursting out beside her.

Corus was there, shield and axe raised. A blade was smashing into his helm, a blade connected to a long barbed chain. The strike was eerily silent, but the tip of the chain whip tore sparks from her great-grandfather's helm as it came away. Then there was another hit, crashing off his shield, and she saw them: more of the eyeless skaven in their black robes, whipping those barbed and bladed chains around them, sending them out like striking snakes at Corus.

And being stopped.

With shield and axe and armour, Corus moved, blocking and dodging, yet holding his position between the ratmen and Sevora. He was protecting her, battling the eyeless skaven and keeping their weapons away. Three of the assassins lay dead around him, and another was writhing across the bars of the floor, biting at the bloody stump of its leg. There were more, throwing their weapons out as they tried to catch Corus. But he leaned and shifted, raised his shield and swung his axe, and stayed in his spot, unmoving, indomitable, the lightning flashing furiously in his eyes. He was a force of nature, the sparks showering off him like a stone struck by lightning, but by the gods he couldn't do this alone.

'Corus!' she shouted. 'What should I do?'

'Sevora!' One of the chain whips snapped at his face and he ducked the blow, but as he did another wrapped around his arm, and another his leg. They jerked at him, trying to pull him down, but he raised his shield and blocked two more strikes as he spun his arm in a quick, snapping circle that shed the chain that was snagged to it. Axe free, he slammed it down on the chain that was hooked to his leg. The sigmarite blade cut through the chain as though it were links of dry grass, and then bit into the wrought-iron bars of the floor in another shower of sparks. The skaven holding the chain snarled as it stumbled back with its broken weapon.

'Are you all right?' he asked as he turned sideways, avoiding one strike while he punched another away with his shield.

All right. She wavered on her feet, fire roaring through her. The Heart was in her, its heat unrelenting. She felt like she was going to dissolve into ash and smoke and failure. What had Brevin meant to do? What was *she* supposed to do? She couldn't control her own sorcery, what was she supposed to do with this elemental force burning through her? She would have cursed the Hallowed Knight, but whatever was happening to him was worse than anything she could imagine.

'I'm all right,' she said. 'What–'

She cut off as another light, garish green, bloomed to life in the chamber.

Another skaven had pulled itself out of Brevin, this one robed in yellow, the same colour as the thread that stitched its eyes shut. Its fur was grey, and on its thumbs silver hooks gleamed. Around its neck it wore a sphere of warpstone, a yellow flaw marking it like the pupil of an eye, and in its hand it held another piece of warpstone as big as a fist. The stone's radiance pushed back the crimson glow of the Heart, somehow making shadows gather around the grey rat.

Grey Seer. The one Brevin had called Skein. The skaven lifted his eyeless head to the Heart and licked his lips, whiskers quivering. Then he pulled the smaller warpstone from around his neck and pushed it into the hands of the spotted skaven, the only one that still had eyes.

'Varus, take!' he hissed. 'Take to Heart!'

'Yes,' the smaller skaven answered, but he was cowering away from the warpstone and from Skein, terrified, it seemed, of both.

Take to the heart. Emberstone, warpstone, smoke, destruction.

'No,' Sevora shouted, raising her blade, and the one called Varus looked to her, while Skein hissed.

That sibilant threat may have once given her pause, but she'd seen too much, and the heat in her made her uncaring, half-crazed. She tried to call the wind that lay in her, but she found only fire, fire that burned her inside and made her gasp and stumble forward. She caught herself, but it was already too late.

She'd moved away from the shelter of Corus' shield. He tried to move with her, but a barbed chain caught the top of his shield, slowing him. One of the skaven spun its chain whip in a hard loop and smashed the weapon's blade across the front of Corus' helm, sending out blood and sparks. Sevora had stopped and was trying to turn back when another chain whip lashed out and caught her around the waist.

Metal barbs drove through her robes and caught in her skin. Sevora fell, her father's knife skittering across the floor, snagging between the wrought-iron rods. Sevora grabbed onto the symbols woven into the floor, trying to keep from being pulled closer to the skaven. The chain whip tightened, barbs digging in, and the pain of its grip grew to match the fire burning in her. Still she hung on, wrapped in steel and agony, and tried not to howl as Skein finally forced Varus to take the warpstone pendant and shoved him towards the Heart.

The skaven were going to kill them all, and Sevora couldn't do anything about it because some eyeless monster was dragging her across the floor like an animal to slaughter. Frustrated anger swept through her and there, *there* it was, natural as breathing.

Fear had been the key before, the emotion that had made her able to grasp at magic, to make her wind. But she could never control it then. The few times she'd been close to taming it, there had been anger mixed with that fear. The rage had given her an imperfect fraction of control. Sometimes.

Now, the fire that filled her grew with her anger. It hurt, but it made her stronger too. Sevora could use that fire to grasp at the power in her, all around her; to clench it in a fist of heated rage, and then make it flow.

Her control was far from perfect. She raised her hand to lash out at Varus, to knock the warpstone charm from his hand and pin the ragged skaven to the wall. But as the air spun up around her, sparks rose from the wounds the chain whip had gouged into her belly, and with a roar the air raced down the steel links wrapped around her and slammed into the dark-robed skaven that held the weapon. The sparks carried by the wind exploded as they hit, and when the eyeless assassin hit the wall of the chamber it was a bundle of ash and charred bones.

The chain whip went slack, and Sevora came up on one knee, pointing again at Varus. The fire didn't surprise her. She was filled with fire now, and she aimed that heat at the skaven. But if she had some control, her strength was still something that peaked and waned without warning. The wind that roared away from her hand fell to a breeze, and the sparks that rode it flared briefly and went out, barely singeing the skaven's fur and little else.

Varus yelped 'yes', as the sparks hit him, but when they faded away he turned towards the Heart again, rushing forward. He was almost there, the glowing charm hanging from his outstretched hand, when he slammed to the floor.

Brevin, blood seeping from the gaping triangle in his chest, had reached out and caught Varus' tail with his hand as the skaven rushed by, and now he held it and yanked the ratman down. Varus looked at him, eyes wide, and hissed, 'Yes-yes!'

Brevin shook his head no, and spat a mouthful of blood.

'Go,' Skein screamed, but Varus couldn't move. Trapped, the ragged skaven pulled back his claw and hurled the warpstone at the Heart. The green pendant arced up, an ugly star streaking towards that great red sun – and missed. It flew just below it and clattered onto the wrought iron, rolling to a gap in one of the symbols, then dropping beneath. The copper chain attached to it rattled through the wrought-iron bars as the pendant fell, until it stopped, the chain snagging on something.

The worn hilt of Sevora's father's knife.

Skein watched the pendant fall, and the Grey Seer hissed, pointing a claw at Varus, who had twisted around to bite at Brevin's hand. But the Lord-Ordinator had already let him go, and the spotted skaven shot away, vanishing through the chamber's door, gone.

And in the mayhem of Sevora's attack and Varus' failure, Corus struck.

He'd never stopped fighting, had barely slowed when the chain whip struck him. When her wind and flames lashed out, the roar of them had made the skaven flinch back, and he surged forward. He snagged one chain whip on his axe, jerking its wielder forward to land on its belly. When the skaven tried to rise, Corus' shield caught it in the face, snapping its neck with a pop. The Reclusian didn't stop, didn't slow. He charged forward and took another of the eyeless ones out with a sweep of his axe, his blade carving through shoulder and chest, leaving a wound that spilled viscera across the wrought-iron tracery of the floor.

'Kill them both, both dead!' Skein snapped. The Grey Seer was moving around them, staying far from Corus. Heading for where the pendant hung, tangled with the knife Sevora had dropped.

Sevora pulled herself up, the heat still burning in her. Using it to control her wind hadn't dulled the pain, it had made it worse. She could barely breathe, but it made her rage, and maybe that would make her power grow. She pointed her hand at Skein, and tried to burn him the way she had burned the assassin. Corus was shouting, calling on Sigmar, calling on the storm, and she wanted a storm too. The wind whipped around her, sparks pouring off her body into it, and she could see Skein making a warding gesture, but she didn't care: she would burn him to bones too.

And then light crashed in all around her, and everything was gone, and there was only her rage melting into the memory that consumed her.

The scale came out of the warrior's skin with a wet ripping sound.

It wasn't easy. Corus had to put his boot to the man's belly, to brace so he could tear the piece of brass away. When it finally came, Khorne's Champion snarled, baring his filed teeth in defiance as blood gushed from the wound. But something flashed through his mad eyes for a moment when Corus pulled the scale free. Pain, yes, but something more. Despair.

Despair. Yes. Corus threw the bloody scale aside and grabbed another. He braced and pulled, muscles bulging, and stared into the warrior's eyes. The man still snarled, angry, defiant, but again there was that flash when the deep-rooted scale finally ripped free. That instant of despair, and it was a drug that went straight to Corus' soul.

It had been over a century since he'd been killed. He'd spent a hundred years and more as a Stormcast Eternal, fighting for his lord Sigmar. And in all that time he'd never forgotten his mortal life. His mortal death. He'd never forgotten that pain.

That despair.

He threw the scale away, and reached for another. He was dimly aware of Lavin screaming at the warrior, 'Revoke him! Revoke him!' Of the other Hallowed Knights standing silent and reverent, as if in prayer. Of the stink of blood in the heat of the day. He tore the scale away, threw it behind him, and reached for another. For another chance to be the one to inflict pain. To give despair. To take away hope.

Hope.

Remember hope.

Aika's last words to him. And he had. For a hundred years he had. He'd been reborn, and remembered hope. If he could be Reforged, he could believe that she'd survived. That somewhere in the world she'd lived out her life, caring for their child, giving them the life Corus longed for. He could hope for that, had hoped for that for a century of fighting, of deaths, of rebirths. But...

Corus stopped. He was standing before the warrior, holding a bloody brass scale in his hand. Staring into the man's mad eyes, hungry to hurt him, and what would Aika say to this? What hope would she see in a mad demigod wallowing in sadism and despair?

'Another, Stormcast?' the warrior asked. His body was a mess of wounds, blood pouring out of him, so much blood. More than even his grotesquely swollen body could ever hold, it coated the bottom of the canyon. 'Another?' Still vicious as he died, but that despair was there, not as well hidden now, jerked closer to the surface by every wound Corus had inflicted.

What was he doing? What was he becoming? Corus let the scale fall and raised a bloody gauntlet to his face. Remember hope. How could he do that, in a world that was nothing but blood and filth?

'What are you doing, brother?' Lavin asked. 'He has not revoked the Dark Powers. Keep at your good work until he does, or until he dies.'

'Shut up,' Corus said, and he didn't even notice the rage sweeping across Lavin's face. Or the confusion when a warning shout came up from one of the other Hallowed Knights. Lavin was suddenly moving from him, drawing his warhammer and shouting, arranging his men as howls sounded through the narrow slot canyons that led to this place, howls filled with otherworldly rage.

'You drew my blood, Stormcast,' the Champion said. 'And the scent drew the Flesh Hounds. They come, and they will feast upon you.'

The Hallowed Knights spread out, pairs of them taking each narrow entrance to this wider canyon, and there was a shout, the sounds of growls and claws screeching across sigmarite as they fell on first one pair of Stormcasts, then another, and another, until they were all around them, the Flesh Hounds hitting from every side, maddened by the smell of so much blood.

The warrior smiled, his filed teeth limned in crimson. 'I hope you had your fill, Stormcast. Now you die.'

'Hope,' Corus said. He reached out and grabbed one of the scales that grew from the warrior's scalp, gripped it tight in one hand. 'This is what I think about hope.'

He jerked on the scale, fast and hard. Not trying to rip it out, instead using it like a handle to twist the warrior's head around until his neck snapped and the rabid ferocity in his eyes gave way to nothing, not despair but simply emptiness.

'I think it's a lie,' he said to the corpse. He let the warrior drop face down in the bloody pool.

Corus turned, pulling his weapon, and walked to the fight, to death, to resurrection, with nothing in his heart.

* * *

I think it's a lie.

Corus' words went through Sevora's head, and following them, her father's.

Hope is a lie.

Almost the same. Why did that hurt so much?

She shook her head, dragging herself out of that hangover of light, leaving the memory and coming back to reality. To pain.

She opened her eyes, and there was darkness below, and crimson above, and her arm was screaming agony.

When Corus' memory had come, she'd been near the circular opening in the wrought-iron floor where the Heart floated. When she'd gone to that bloody valley, she must have collapsed at the edge of the opening and started to fall through. But Corus had thrown himself across the chamber and caught her wrist. And in doing so, pulled her arm from its socket.

Over her, the chain whips were whirling as they snapped at her great-grandfather. They smashed into his shield, his armour, their blows still weirdly silent. But holding her, Corus couldn't dodge. The blades on the ends of those chains were drawing blood and adding cuts to the ones that already marked him.

'Corus!' she gasped. 'Pull me up!'

At the sound of her voice, Corus surged to his feet, yanking her up with him, and Sevora had to fight not to pass out as her arm shrieked in agony. But the fire in her, painful or not, helped her cling to consciousness and she watched as Corus slid his shield down his arm and threw it. The heavy sigmarite spun through the air without any grace, but Corus' strength had given it momentum. It headed straight for the three remaining skaven assassins, and they dove out of the way, save one. The shield smashed into its side, and the skaven's bones broke with a sound like kindling smashing. The assassin hit the floor, vomiting blood, and went still.

'I'm sorry,' Corus said, setting her down. 'My fault. My memory. I'm sorry!'

Memory. Sevora fought for her balance as the room swung around her. Memory. Memorian. 'Don't worry about me,' she gasped. 'Kill them.'

And as she spoke, an inhuman voice cut across the chamber. 'Kill! Kill him, Lisstis! Now!'

Skein was creeping close, moving to where the pendant still hung from her father's knife. Sevora raised her working arm and pointed at him, trying to use the fire in her to reach her magic, but the attempt made the pain in her rise so much she fell to her knees, nauseous.

'Sevora!' Corus shouted, and she shook her head.

'Fight, Reclusian! Fight!' It was their only hope, and that thought almost pulled a mad peal of laughter from her. But Corus somehow seemed to understand.

'Hope when hope is dying!' he shouted, and stepped forward, stamping his boot down on the handle of his axe. He must have dropped it there when he snagged Sevora's arm, and it flipped up in the air, where he grabbed it and charged forward. The skaven assassins scattered, snapping their chain whips at him. One flung its blade at Corus' face, but Corus spun away. He didn't have his shield to block with, but without its weight Corus was agile as a cat, and he turned his dodge into a lunge at the other skaven. His fist smashed that skaven's head back in a gout of blood and teeth, then his axe sliced across the ratman's belly. Black robes went darker with blood, and the skaven pressed its chain whip to its belly, as if the barbed coils of the weapon could help to hold the spilled guts in.

Skein was moving around the battle, staying carefully away from Corus but moving closer to the pendant. To her father's knife. The thought of the skaven closing his claws around that cheap blade made the anger burn in Sevora, and she was moving, ignoring her pain, dashing forward to pick up the knife. The pendant came with it, heavier than it should have been, a weight in her hand as she pushed herself back, away from Skein and towards Corus.

'Lisstis,' Skein hissed. The grey skaven clutched the larger warpstone in his claw, holding it before him like a weapon. 'Lisstis, kill.' His eyeless head was facing Sevora. 'Kill, and bring me what they have stolen.'

The skaven assassin began to move, angling towards Sevora, but Corus was moving too. He had no shield, and bled from a dozen wounds, but the lightning in his eyes was a storm as he stepped between Lisstis and his great-granddaughter. 'Not another step,' he said, his voice deep as thunder.

Lisstis hissed at him, but he stopped moving, except for the slow circle of the chain whip spinning in his claws, and Skein snarled in frustration.

'Fool. Useless.' The Grey Seer raised the warpstone he held, and a burst of light flashed from its ugly facets.

Sevora had to look away from the explosion of poisonous light, and her eyes caught on the corpse of the skaven Corus had just killed. The warpstone's flash made the body's shadow enormous on the curved wall of the chamber, and then the shadow came apart. The darkness split, falling into a swarm of black shadow-rats careening off the wall and rushing towards her great-grandfather.

'Corus!' she shouted, but the shadow-rats were on him. They swarmed up his leg, black teeth biting. He smashed down with his boots, his fist, his axe, shattering the shadows, cutting them apart, but there were too many. Before he could break them all, they found a gap in his armour behind his knee and bit, their teeth slicing through the tendons that hinged thigh to calf. Corus' leg folded beneath him, but he kept smashing the last rats with his fists and the haft of his axe, breaking them all into darkness.

But the damage was done. Corus couldn't rise, and Lisstis was moving around him, claws skittering fast across the wrought-iron floor. Sevora was starting to turn to try to run, but the skaven was already casting his chain whip at her, flinging it out to catch her and yank her back.

In that moment though, focused on his attack, the assassin had forgotten Corus.

The Reclusian threw himself forward with his one good leg. It was an awkward, lurching leap from the ground, but the power behind it was enough to send him after Lisstis. He swung as he dove forward, and his axe caught the assassin in the leg – not hard enough to smash through bone, but it cut flesh and made the skaven stumble. The smooth arc of Lisstis' chain whip broke, and the steel barbs smashed into the floor at Sevora's feet, showering her with sparks.

Lisstis flipped himself through the air, landing on Corus' back. The skaven jerked his chain whip around the Reclusian's throat, so that the barbs sank into his skin and throttled Corus with the metal links. Corus grabbed for the assassin, rolling, but Lisstis ducked and pulled the chain tighter.

Sevora backed away from the fight, knife and pendant still clutched in her hand, until she heard Skein.

'You.' His voice was a low hiss, sharp, grating. 'You, human. Listen.' Skein was moving towards her, one claw clutching the larger piece of warpstone, the other extended towards her. 'Listen, or suffer.'

Skein stopped beside Brevin, who lay on the floor, gutted by that triangle but still somehow alive.

'Suffer like this one. Suffer, like all who fight will suffer.' The Grey Seer bent down, and with the hook on his thumb he drew a line across the Lord-Ordinator's throat, from ear to ear. Blood flowed, a sluggish trickle, and Brevin collapsed. It wasn't lightning taking him. The Lord-Ordinator pulled in, contracting, as if the hole in his chest were sucking him in, and then he was gone, nothing left but the bone and copper triangle, which rattled hollowly against the wrought iron.

'Listen, human,' Skein told her, straightening. 'That stone. Stone is mine.' He held out his empty hand, the hook on his thumb dark with blood.

'Don't.' It was Corus' voice, and Sevora looked back to him. While she had been watching Skein, he had finally got his hands on Lisstis. Corus held the skaven in one hand, his thumb and one finger digging into the assassin's empty eye sockets, tearing the yellow thread that held the lids closed. Lisstis was still alive, his clawed hand scraping uselessly against Corus' armour, but he was trapped, helpless.

'Leave her alone or I'll crush his skull.'

Skein didn't turn his eyeless face towards him. He just raised the larger warpstone, and it flashed again, the terrible light driving into Sevora's eyes like a migraine. When she could see again, Corus was slamming Lisstis down, smashing the skaven's skull against the floor, breaking it like an egg. But Lisstis' shadow was already stepping away from the wall, a shade assassin wrought by Skein's magic. Fast as fear, it scooped up a chain whip and wrapped the steel around Corus' throat before he could roll away.

The Reclusian reached back, fighting to grab the thing's wrists, but his hands passed through the shadow thing. Lisstis' shade was finishing what the skaven hadn't, and Corus couldn't stop it.

'Listen, human,' Skein said again. 'Give what you have taken. Or this storm-cursed, their soul I will destroy. Destroy like other, no resurrection, no eternal. Eternal darkness only, human, for him and you. Dark, forever, and that is truth.'

CHAPTER TWENTY-FOUR

WARRUN VALE

Amon hung from the brass chain, watching the green fire sweep down the barrel of the cannon towards him.

And then the Lord-Terminos struck.

The masked Stormcast charged up the tail of the behemoth, then launched themselves off. They flew through the air, a dark star of falling sigmarite, and their axe lashed out. Its edge caught the chain wrapped around Amon and the metal parted like a string. Amon tumbled down, still wrapped in the severed chain, and slammed into the dirt. A wash of green fire gouted above him, making the air shimmer with heat.

The Lord-Terminos hit the ground in a crouch, the back of their armour warped and red from having caught the edge of that poison flame. The superheated metal must have been hot enough to sear flesh, but the Lord-Terminos didn't slow. They rolled to the side, avoiding another gout of fire, then came to their feet and raced forward, leaping high as the monster raised its cannon again. The great axe sliced through the air, and the blade sank deep into the warpfire-spewing weapon.

The sigmarite axe bit through brass and warped flesh, rupturing hoses and tanks, and suddenly green fire was ripping up and down the behemoth's arm. It gave its great metal-tearing shriek again, and turned and bit at the fire, burning its mouth. Its clawed feet tore at the ground, and Amon, still ripping the brass chain off himself, had to throw himself to the side to avoid being crushed. He fell into a furrow sloughed through the earth, snapped the final link of chain and came up, weapons raised, in time to see the Lord-Terminos, wreathed in green flame, smashing their axe into the giant's chest.

The monstrous skaven twisted, dark blood and yellow bile pouring from the wound, and its flail caught the Stormcast and smashed them down into the earth. Before the Lord-Terminos could rise the behemoth stomped down, crushing them into the ground.

Amon charged forward as the giant lifted its foot again. He could see the Lord-Terminos, their crumpled armour smoking, pulling themselves up and raising their axe to point it at the behemoth. Their mask was fractured, its cracked pieces twisting into an unending stream of different faces, but they were all defiant as the Lord-Terminos faced the beast.

'No!' Amon shouted. 'Me!' He was roaring as he ran, trying to attract the behemoth's gaze, and Jocanan was shouting too, but the monster's attention was firmly fixed on the Stormcast before it, and it swung the fiery wreck of its cannon down and crushed the Lord-Terminos beneath.

There was a moment, just enough for hope. Then the lightning struck.

The bolt launched itself up from where the Lord-Terminos had died, and the white fire of the returning soul blazed through the massive skaven. The behemoth lurched back, its cannon falling to the ground beside it, smoking and burning. But it still lived, and Amon slammed into it, smashing whatever he could reach with sword and mace, hitting the monster with fire and thunder.

The behemoth hissed and lunged for him. He dodged the flail once, but the chains caught him the second time, a hook ripping into the armour on his leg and tumbling him. Amon had just come back up, smashing at the monster's snapping teeth, when he heard Jocanan shout from behind him.

'The other head!'

Amon didn't question it. He'd been given a task, and he executed. He dove beneath the jaws of the behemoth, and smashed his mace into the smaller head jutting from the thing's neck. It made a hideous screech as he crushed its skull, a piercing sound that went on until he drove his sword through its neck. It finally fell silent, and the behemoth spread its jaws, roaring. And as it did, Jocanan dove forward, driving her javelin into the roof of its mouth.

It almost worked. If her fiery wings had still been whole, the Prosecutor could have driven home the javelin and flown back and away. Instead, the behemoth snapped its jaws shut, catching her, crushing her. And when it did, the lightning struck again.

The bolt smashed between the giant's teeth, melting brass and boiling flesh, and the thing gave a terrible wounded noise as the lightning crackled and arced before soaring up into the sky, gone. The behemoth stumbled, shaking its head as Amon pulled his sword free and struck at it. It was wounded, burned and bleeding, but its pain maddened it, made it keep fighting, until suddenly it screamed again.

The ravens had come.

The black birds, which had been circling the fight far above, avoiding the poison smoke, now came diving in. Jocanan's sacrifice had called them, and though many of them dropped as they touched the black vapour, enough survived to fall, stabbing and clawing, on the giant's eyes.

The monstrous skaven lurched and bellowed, swinging at the birds, the hooks of its flail digging into its own flesh. Amon drove forward, sinking his sword into the exposed underbelly. The behemoth howled and snapped at him, but its wounded legs gave out and it fell. Amon went for the neck again, his sword roaring like thunder as it ripped open hide and muscle and finally exposed the veins. Blood gouted, stinking and corrupt, and the monster shuddered. It swung its flail at him once more, but Amon stepped back, avoiding the broken chains, and when the links hit the ground they didn't move again.

Amon stared at the behemoth for a long moment. Black smoke drifted from it, and green fire burned beneath its skin. Dead.

Dead like the Lord-Terminos. Dead like Jocanan. Dead like Peace. He looked over his shoulder. The army of skaven was watching him, eyes bright, and he could see the Clawlord on his platform, his toothed blade flaming in his hand. Dead like him, soon enough.

But the wall still stood, and from somewhere far above he heard a cry echo through the night.

'The Halt holds!'

Amon raised his weapons, staring at the army before him. He watched as the Clawlord snarled orders, and out of the swarm flowed skaven armoured in chain and leather. Stormvermin, the skaven's fighting elite. They spread out before him, and Amon could see nets dangling from their claws, bone clubs in their hands. The Clawlord meant to capture him alive. Amon looked over the Stormvermin's heads, and from his platform Reekbite stared back, one eye black and one eye glowing green, both full of hate.

'Come, then,' he said, and pointed his sword at the Clawlord. 'Fight me.' A challenge that couldn't be heard over the clamour of the army, but still clear. Reekbite only stared at him, waiting as his forces readied themselves.

'Skaven coward,' Amon said. Calling out the Clawlord was too much to hope for. But he was giving Brevin time.

Amon risked a look over his shoulder, at the jagged cracks that scarred the Halt, the shattered section where the quartz had been broken away by the giant's tail. He could see the red running over the basalt, thin lines of emberstone. Uncovered, exposed.

'Heal,' he whispered, an order, a prayer. 'Damn you, I finished the hunt. I brought back the Lord-Ordinator. Why are you still broken?'

He didn't expect an answer, of course. So when he heard the night whisper 'broken,' Amon raised his mace, making the fire burning on top of it brighter to push back the shadows. In its light, in one of the ruts ripped into the mud by the giant, something gleamed. An eye, half-lidded, staring at him.

'Peace?' Amon looked back to the Stormvermin still gathering. There had to be two hundred now. Reekbite wanted him badly. Still watching them, Amon walked to the rut. It was Peace, feathers torn from his head and fur ragged. One of his forelegs was badly broken, but Peace lifted his head when Amon came close and made a deep clucking noise.

He reached down carefully, still watching the Stormvermin, waiting for their charge, and put out his hand. Animals were better than people, but he'd still spent little time with them. He wasn't sure what Peace wanted. But the gryph-crow pressed his head against Amon's hand and closed his eyes. Probably just wanted company while he died. Amon had heard that was the way with animals and people. Looking up at the skaven before him, he didn't understand the impulse. He was going to die soon, and he'd have much rather have been alone. This company was going to make every last moment hurt.

There was a horn from the front lines, low and ugly, and then the Stormvermin were moving, stepping forward with their nets and clubs.

'Sorry, Peace. I have something I have to do.' He gave the wounded gryph-crow one last pat, then walked forward. He would fight as long as he could. Every moment they spent toying with him was more time the skaven weren't rushing the Halt. More time for Brevin to do whatever he was meant to do.

More time for him to suffer.

But if his last hunt was for pain, at least that was easy quarry to find.

Amon crouched, facing the Stormvermin as they swirled closer, his sword and mace raised. Ready to crash them together one last time.

But when the thunder came, and the fire, it came from above.

Lightning crashed down into the ranks of the Stormvermin, jagged bolts that ripped through the skaven. White-hot arcs of energy snapped from armour to weapon blades, burning fur and searing flesh. Bodies fell, smoking, and others twitched and danced, their muscles locked in torturous rigor. The uninjured Stormvermin were pulling back, looking up, and there was the sound of vast wings beating in the dark above.

Amon stared up into the night, and saw them. Their deep-blue scales were spotted with white, and they blended in with the heavens, but he could see their long outlines, the gleam of their golden eyes, and the shining white of their teeth as they opened their jaws to breathe streams of white fire at the skaven below.

Draconiths, three of them, each carrying a silver-armoured Hallowed Knight. They were shouting Sigmar's name as one of the great beasts folded its wings and dove through the dark towards him. Amon watched it come, a reprieve he never expected, then turned, racing away.

He sheathed his sword as he ran, ignoring the screams of the dying skaven and Reekbite's furious bellows. Not far, and he was back with Peace. Amon gathered the gryph-crow up in his free arm and whirled around. The draconith was still diving towards him, but his pelting run back to get Peace had drawn a pack of Stormvermin after him. They had the speed of rabid wolves, and the skaven warriors would likely be on Amon before the draconith and its rider could reach him. He shouldered the gryph-crow, feeling the beast's warm blood splash his face, and held up his mace, the fire gathered in it shining bright, a challenge to the ratmen poised to tear him down.

Then another kind of lightning fell from the heavens, sweeping through the ranks of the racing skaven.

Bolts of silver pounded down from the sky, arrows long and tipped with pure motes of white like stars. They fell like a storm, and the ones that struck the Stormvermin exploded into flames of white and gold, so thick and hot the skaven flashed apart into blood-coloured steam and ash. The few that weren't hit skidded to a halt, clawed feet slipping in the corrupted corpse-grass, and then they were running back the other way, pursued still by the shining arrows that were arcing out from the top of the Halt.

Amon barely had time to rise from the fighting stance he'd dropped into when the draconith slammed into the earth beside him, the Hallowed Knight on the massive beast's back shouting at him.

'Mount up! Now!'

Amon swung his mace across his back and threw himself onto the draconith's armoured spine, grabbing around the waist of the other Stormcast while still holding Peace.

'Okaris! Fly!' the Hallowed Knight called, and the draconith roared and leapt into the air. But the skaven had their own marksmen, and their jezzail bullets were thick now, rattling off Okaris' scales like hail, and at least one found purchase. The draconith snarled and faltered, powerful wings missing a beat. Amon could feel the lurch as they fell back towards the ground, towards the swarming army below. But the other great-winged beasts had swung in around it, and they were breathing down flamestreams at the jezzail teams, disrupting their fire, until Okaris had clawed his way up, too high in the air to be hit. A few wingbeats more and they were at the top of the wall, the draconith's claws settling on the stone. Shouting mortals surrounded them, jubilant, gaping at the draconiths and their riders.

'That beast better be worth the bullet Okaris took.' The Hallowed Knight who had picked him up pulled off her helm, revealing a woman with short-cropped hair, a neatly stitched wound carved into the side of her scalp. There were scratches and scars across his rescuer's armour, and half-healed wounds marred Okaris' hide.

'Beast,' Peace croaked, and she looked at the gryph-crow, frowning. But Amon was sliding off, onto the top of the Halt, cradling the gryph-crow as he looked down the wall.

The Golden Lions were there, holding their swords and crossbows and staring down at the seething sea of skaven far below. But on the edge of the wall, dressed in armour of white and gold and shimmering blue, carrying long, intricate bows, was a line of aelves. Draconith and aelves – so Hammerhal Aqsha must have finally sent reinforcements. But so few, and far below, like some vast colony of insects, the skaven were swarming around the platform where Reekbite's sword waved like an emerald torch. How would the Clawlord react to this, his behemoth slain, his chosen prey rescued?

The answer came fast. Lines of troops were forming up, a strange kind of order established, and the skaven were moving. Advancing towards the Halt, rank after rank of skaven.

'They're coming!' he shouted, then again, louder, breaking through the mortals' cheers. 'They're coming!'

'Let them come!' General Kant was beside him, staring down at the sea of torches. 'Let them gnaw the Halt and break their teeth!'

'The Halt is broken down there,' Amon snapped. 'The ember-stone exposed! The skaven can smash a chunk of warpstone into it with nothing but their claws!' She stared at him blankly and he tapped his temple in frustration. 'Didn't Brevin explain it to you?'

'Brevin couldn't speak!' Kant said. 'Explain what?'

Amon shook his head. They didn't have time for this. The skaven were getting closer, the first ranks almost at the behemoth's corpse, and the mortals here were just jeering down at them as if the ratmen could do nothing.

'Aelves,' he snapped.

The leader of the archers, an aelf man bearing an ornate lantern, turned. A great silver hawk perched on his shoulder, and its eyes were just as fierce as the aelf's as he frowned at him. Amon barely noticed.

'Keep them back, away from the Halt, as long as you can!' Then he spun back to Kant. 'Where's Brevin! Where's the Reclusian?'

They had to heal the Halt. They had to heal it *now*. The aelven archers, even with the Golden Lions' crossbows helping them, wouldn't be able to hold the swarming mass of skaven at bay for long. This was all going to end in ruin soon, and he had no hunt, no quest, no guidance of what to do.

'Where are they?'

Kant looked at him, her face pale. 'I have no idea.'

CHAPTER TWENTY-FIVE

THE HALT

No resurrection, no eternal life.

Sevora stared at Skein, the warpstone pendant hanging heavy in her hand. 'You want this?'

'Don't,' Corus gasped. The shadow on his back was holding the chain around his neck taut, the barbs digging deep into her great-grandfather's skin. 'Let me die.'

'Shhh,' Skein hissed, and the shadow assassin pulled the chain around Corus' neck a little tighter. 'Silence. Your fate is this one's choice.'

Corus' fate, hers. What would Morgen think? The Lord-Veritant had made her a servant of the Stormcast, hoping to change the ugly trajectory of his fate. What would she say if Sevora let him be destroyed as completely as Brevin?

The same thing she'd say if Sevora took the pendant, destroyed the Heart, and let the skaven ravage the Great Parch. Nothing. Because she was dead, and now it was just Sevora, her great-grandfather, and this eyeless monster.

'Brevin told me you wanted the Heart.' The pendant was so heavy in her hand, and she could barely stand. 'That you wanted to destroy it with this.' She looked down at the ugly pendant, its flaw making it look like a baleful eye. 'So you could capture all the power of its destruction somehow, and the poison smoke it would make. So you could use it later. When you wanted to destroy something else. Like a city.' She frowned at the Grey Seer. 'Were you even going to break the Halt?'

'Some,' Skein said. 'Some, human. Reekbite is not to be denied. Not yet.'

Some. Just a crack through the wall, where the Heart used to be? Rats didn't need any more than a crack.

'Human.' Skein took a step closer, his paws silent on the metal floor. 'Human, listen. Give what you have stolen. Give, and I let you go. Go, and you run, and you live, and this storm-cursed keeps his soul. Not his life. Too dangerous. Shade will kill. Kill, and he goes back to weak thing you call a god.' One more step. 'You are connected. Connected by fate and divine power. I see it. Listen. I destroy his soul, your soul will suffer. Suffer and burn.'

It's already burning, she thought.

'Give what you stole, human.' Another step, and she could see the blood running down the steel claw on the skaven's thumb, onto his hand. 'Human give, and you live to run, far from here. No give? I take. Take pendant, take storm-cursed's soul, then I take your eyes, human, and leave you in the dark with Reekbite's army coming.'

Go. Run. Live. It was so little. But it was more than what Morgen and the Ruination Chamber had given her. Their only gift had been chains, and she remembered Yevin's vision, the golden chains wrapping around her, chains clutched by a fist so high in the sky. Gods, it was so little and it was so tempting. She would be free.

I know you think you are giving up, but you never will. Morgen Light, before she sent her off. The Lord-Veritant had such strange trust in her. Such hope.

Hope is a lie.

'I want to talk to him,' Sevora said, looking at her great-grandfather. 'I want to hear what he says.'

Skein hissed to himself, 'Too loud, too much,' but the shadow eased its grip.

'He lies, Sevora.' Corus pulled in a long, ragged breath. 'They always lie. It's never just serve them or die. There's always another choice. There's always hope.'

'Hope,' she said, and she was acutely aware of her father's knife in her hand. Of Corus' own last words, before he had turned to face the Flesh Hounds and their teeth. 'Hope is a lie.'

'No,' Corus said, and though his voice was rough from the chain, she could hear the conviction in it. She looked at him, at those eyes that flickered with storm-light. Her brother's eyes, except they weren't haunted by fear. Corus' eyes blazed with belief. 'There is always hope, Sevora. Always.'

'So you say,' she said softly. 'Now.'

'Enough,' Skein hissed. 'Enough, enough, enough.' Another silent step, just out of reach. 'Choose, human. Choose.'

She looked at Corus, watching her with her brother's eyes.

Always hope.

I think it's a lie.

Which Corus was right? Sevora felt the pain in her shoulder, in her abdomen, the pain of injury, the agony of fatigue. She felt the pain of the fire burning in her soul, potent, uncontrolled. She embraced all those aches, gathered them in, and with them all her anger. At her mother, at her brother, at her father. At the Whitefire Court and the Ruination Chamber. At the skaven, at their monstrous offspring, at Skein. And most of all, her rage at

Corus – at the man whose memories made her want to kill him, and worse, made her want to care. Which was right?

Always hope. Hope is a lie.

'Only one way to know,' she whispered. And taking all that rage, she grabbed at the wind, raising the knife in her good hand, pulling in a tempest of fire to burn the Grey Seer to ash.

But before she could even cast it out, the skaven twisted his empty hand and snarled, ripping away the magic that her flux-touched power was pulling into her and sending it crashing to the floor around her as a hundred tiny whirlwinds of sparks.

'Magic, human? Human magic is weak. You reach for Chaos and shy away. Even ones like you.' Skein took one more step, reaching out for the pendant, and the pain Sevora had been using to fuel her anger roared up, vast and consuming. She barely noticed the skaven jerking the stone out of her hand, or her father's knife falling from her grip as the pendant's chain pulled on it. Barely heard the little click as the blade fell through the metal floor, and was lost in the dark.

'I see Chaos' gift,' Skein hissed. 'Gift of magic, but weak, uncontrolled. I see link Brevin made. Made between your heart and this Heart. Like him. Can you control it? No?' Skein's lips pulled back, showing his yellow teeth. 'No. Did he tell you how I hurt? Hurt him with his grip on the Heart. No? Fool.'

The pain in Sevora eased. Just enough so that she could understand what was happening to her. She was kneeling on the woven wrought-iron floor, Skein leaning over her, his carrion breath hot on her face. The hand that held the pendant was hovering over her, the silver thumb claw pressed against the corner of her eye.

'Your eyes. Told you I would take,' he growled, spittle falling from his teeth onto her face. 'That is truth. Truth, human, is darkness. I will show that to you before I take everything away. I will make you see.'

'Let her go,' Corus choked out, but his rage was clear.

'Shhhh,' the Grey Seer whispered, and there was a strangling noise as dead Lisstis' shadow tightened the chain. 'Give you darkness too, Stormcast. Give you to the darkness. After. After.'

And then he drove his hook in. Sliding it behind her eye and twisting, and half the world went dark, a moment before this new pain jagged through her head.

Sevora thrashed, ripping herself away from Skein, leaving him clutching her eye along with the pendant. He raised it up to his mouth.

There was a choked roar from across the room. Corus was reaching up, tearing at the shadow assassin's hands, but he couldn't touch the darkness that held the choking chain. Skein bared his teeth at him, mocking him, then popped Sevora's eye into his mouth. And as he did, Corus' hands found the links of the chain wrapped around his throat, tangled in them and pulled.

The steel links stretched, then broke, showering across the chamber. They made noise as they fell, clanging against the metal floor, their silent enchantment broken. Corus lurched forward on his wounded leg, throat streaming blood, a length of chain whip gripped in one hand. The blade on its tip gleamed red in the Heart's light as Corus whirled the piece of broken weapon in a circle, then cast it straight at Skein.

The Grey Seer threw himself to the floor, the blade tip ripping through his yellow robe. The barbed chain tore across his ribs, drawing blood and a hiss of pain. The sound of that hiss didn't cover the clatter of the larger piece of warpstone falling from his hand and rattling across the metal floor. Skein lunged for it, his pain forgotten, but Corus fell on him like a hawk.

The Reclusian wrapped his fingers around Skein's neck, ignoring the silver hooks scrabbling against his armour. Skein was thrashing, his head being forced back, neck close to breaking.

'Kill him,' Sevora rasped, her hand pressed hard to where her eye had been. She could feel the blood hot against her palm, and the feel of the empty socket made her sick, but all she hoped for in the world was to see her great-grandfather rip the Grey Seer's head from his shoulders.

And then a shadow flitted across the floor, lean and long, and with its dark hands it plucked another chain whip up and raced towards Corus.

'No!' Sevora shouted, but she was too late, the darkness too fast. The shadow of the dead skaven slammed into Corus and passed right through him, streaking on across the room to dissolve into the darkness on the other side, gone. But it left behind the weapon it had taken, the blade tip of the chain whip driven like a nail through the back of Corus' armour and into his body.

The force of the blow slammed him off Skein, and he hit the floor, rolling, then came to a stop.

'Corus?' Sevora took a step towards him and he pushed himself up to his hands and knees, raising his face to see her. Blood was flowing from his mouth and nose, down his chin, but his eyes were on her.

'Sevora. Are you all right?'

'Me?' she said, and the word was almost a scream. On the ground between them, Skein jerked and rose, like a horrible puppet.

'Shhh!' he said again, and the pain was back in Sevora, the fire of the Heart magnified a thousandfold. She fell, writhing, as Skein shook out the warpstone pendant from his sleeve, bent and plucked up the broken chain whip that Corus had thrown at him. 'Darkness!' he snapped, and went to Corus, stopping just out of reach, the blade tip like a dagger in his hand. 'Darkness all! Make you see!' He spun the broken weapon, then brought it down like an executioner's axe, straight at Corus' head.

But Corus reached up and caught it, the blade spitting sparks and blood as it drove through his gauntlet and into his hand. The Reclusian held the blade and turned storm-marked eyes to his great-granddaughter.

'Hope, Sevora. Hope when hope is dying.'

In her agony, she heard him. Her lips moved, whispering. *Hope is a lie. Remember hope.*

Hope, when hope is dying.

She reached down. Down into the pain. Into the fire. Skein had made the pain of her connection to the Heart grow into a bonfire. She was burning from the inside. So much pain, she could barely feel her magic. But she pushed her hand against the floor and the wrought-iron bars shifted, parting like grass. The Heart, helping her, and she clenched her teeth and fought through the pain, just enough to send a whisper of wind down into the dark. And then it came back.

Came back and slapped the worn hilt of her father's knife into her palm.

She held the knife. In its pitted, dirty blade she could see a dim, warped reflection of her face, one eye shining with pain, the other a vacant black socket streaming blood. Sevora saw herself, and for the first time ever, in that terrible reflection, she saw not just the lines of her great-grandmother Aika's face. She saw the echo of Corus there too.

'Great-grandfather,' she said, pulling herself up as much as she could. 'I remember.'

Then she threw her father's knife to him.

The worn blade spun through the air, glinting in the bloody light, and Corus caught it. The little knife looked like nothing in his huge hand, but the lightning grew bright in his eyes. With a shout he jerked back the hand that Skein had impaled with the broken chain whip. Skein, feeling the chain in his hand shift, let it go. But the cruel barbs on the weapon caught on the bandages wrapped around the Grey Seer's hand and pulled him forward. Just close enough for Corus to drive the dull point of the little knife into the skaven's throat.

Skein staggered back, ripping the barbs of the chain out of his bandaged hand as he clutched at his throat. The knife was stuck there, blood dripping down the handle. A trickle, not a flood – Corus' strike hadn't cut the great vessels of the Grey Seer's neck, but from the choking, wheezing noises he was making it had lodged in his windpipe, and now Skein was choking on blood and blade. Dying slow, and he was raising his claw as he did, the flawed warpstone pendant shining in it. To make one more lunge for the Heart? Or to lash out with one more cruel spell?

It didn't matter. When Corus had slammed the blade home, Skein's power had slipped, and the pain that filled Sevora had ebbed. Pulled back enough so that she could reach out and feel the power in the Heart. Feel it, grasp it, and use it.

'Skein,' she said, and the wind was wrapping around her arm, a gale full of sparks. 'I see. I see you.' And then she threw her wind at him, and with it, all the fire that the Heart could hold.

The Grey Seer raised the pendant, and its green glow flashed. Sevora could feel him trying to rip apart her sorcery again, but this time the Heart's power was wrapped around it and his denial was swept away by the awful heat of all that emberstone.

Sevora's wind roared out, and the Heart's fire followed. Skein was picked up and flung across the chamber, slammed into the curving wall on the far side. The dying skaven's claws scrabbled still at the knife in his throat, and then the flames hit him. They blasted into Skein, burning away fur and robes, skin and flesh, burning his bones until they turned to ash, burning until the stone behind where the Grey Seer had been began to glow red, began to crack, and the whole Halt groaned.

'Sevora!'

She barely heard Corus. The fire was in her. All the power of the Heart, all the magic crystallised in that great stone and in the web of emberstone that ran through the wall was in her. She had tapped it to break through Skein's defences, all of it all at once, and if she stopped using it, it would rip her apart, then rip itself apart, demolish the Halt just like Reekbite wanted.

'Sevora! Stop!'

No. No, she couldn't stop. Couldn't stop. She was emberstone, she was wind, she was flame. Couldn't stop, and the fire was pouring out of her, the Halt rumbling, shaking, and in the centre of all that flame the knife still glowed. Her father's knife. And her mind opened, and the memory came, almost as intense as when Corus' had flowed through her.

'Daddy, no!'

The fight had been short, vicious. Someone had cheated, she didn't understand who, but there had been shoving, shouting, and then suddenly blades. There was the flash of knives, and Sevora felt a thrill of excitement. Blades were deadly dangerous, but Daddy was the best, he always told them that.

And then Daddy was on the ground, a knife sticking out of his chest. A little thing, a worn work knife, but it was in his chest and thrumming, vibrating as if something twitched beneath it.

'It's in his heart,' Yevin said, his face pale beside hers, staring at the trembling knife.

'Pull it out,' Daddy hissed. 'Pull it out and give it to me!'

Sevora reached out, but Yevin grabbed her hands. 'No! Pull it out and he dies! We can get a healer, he's alive and there's hope—'

Daddy shoved him away, and looked to Sevora. 'Pull it out and give it to me.'

'But—'

He shook his head. 'Hope is a lie, love. Hope is a lie.'

She reached down, wrapped her small hands around the handle, and pulled. It resisted, his heart clenching it, but then it came free with a great gush of blood. She gasped, but she handed the knife to her father and he leapt up, roaring, lunging for the man who had planted the knife in him and slamming the blade into his back.

They both fell, and there was screaming, and blood, and Daddy wasn't moving, and Yevin was grabbing at her, but she darted forward. The bloody knife was lying on the ground, and she picked it up.

'What are you doing?' Yevin shouted. 'We have to run!'

'Daddy's knife,' she said, even though she knew it wasn't. But now it was, and she would carry it with her, always.

'Sevora!' Corus' voice echoed through her head, cutting through the memory, the pain, the flames.

Flames. She was still pouring them into the wall, the knife still glowing in its centre. Hope is a lie, he'd told her. Her father never believed in good things like hope. No.

But he'd believed in vengeance.

The Heart. It understood that too.

Sevora clenched down on the magic in her, on the roar of power that was coming from the Heart. She narrowed that heat down into something tiny, something the size of a knife, and the fire flowing out of her became a bright red lance that bored its way out through the basalt, until it reached the face of the Halt.

There was an instant. It was as if the quartz crystal that sheathed the whole front of that gigantic wall had replaced the eye that Skein had taken. Sevora saw the chamber she was in, the glowing Heart, the bodies, Corus, the fire roaring from her hand. But she also saw the army, the great swarm of skaven filling Warrun Vale, thousands and thousands, all rushing forward.

Banners and weapons in hand, the skaven were charging, a

black mass of death that rolled over the dead body of some vile thing and headed for the Halt, and in their front ranks Sevora could see skaven wrapped in robes of green, carrying chunks of warpstone shaped into spikes. Weapons they meant to jam into the wounded places of the wall, like knives into a heart.

They were being cut down as they ran. Arrows were falling like a great sheet of rippling silver rain, smashing into the swarm of skaven. They came from the bows of strange creatures that stood upon the wall, things that looked human but were not, their handsome features too sharp, their beautiful eyes too keen. They were firing shot after shot, the movements of their hands from quiver to bow to string a kind of graceful, deadly poetry.

Mixed in with the storm of silver shafts was a hail of bolts – crude, heavy things fired almost straight down from the crossbows of the Golden Lions, the soldiers howling their rage at an enemy they could finally see, finally kill. Standing above them, on the parapet of the great wall, General Kant stood with her sword raised, her lined face a mask of furious vengeance as she shouted to her troops to rain hell down upon the horde.

But still the onrush came. Through the storm of silver arrows and heavy bolts, the skaven ran, and every time one dropped, there was another to take its place, to snatch up rusted weapons or warpstone spike and sprint forward, yellow teeth bared. A seemingly unstoppable wave – and then the rain of bolts and arrows from the wall was joined by the flash of lightning.

In that long instant of perfect sight, Sevora could see them. Great-winged beasts the colour of night, noble and terrifying, each bearing a warrior wrapped in silver armour. They swept along the wall, and from their great jaws lightning fell, pure white bolts of death that swept across the charging horde. More skaven dropped, tumbling to the ground in smoke and flames, falling short, leaving the Halt untouched.

But there were always more. That was the skaven's one rule, and the vision the Heart gave Sevora tightened onto one figure standing in the middle of the wall. Amon, the Knight-Questor, stood silent and intent, his hands tight on mace and sword. Staring down at the thin line of skaven that had somehow survived the barrage of silver arrows and heavy bolts, the crackling storm of lightning.

Still caught in that never-ending moment, Sevora watched Amon's body tense, his legs bend. His eyes were on the skaven in the lead, the ratman's yellow-toothed mouth open wide in a scream as it charged forward, green robes burning around it, a shining emerald shard glowing in its upraised claws to stab into an unprotected vein of emberstone in the Halt's battered face. Amon was going to jump, she knew it. Throw himself off the top of the wall, a sure suicide, just so that he could land on that shrieking, burning skaven and smash it into the ground beneath his armoured weight.

What could he hope to do, in giving his life to buy the wall one more second? So that Brevin would heal it? Brevin was dead, worse than dead, and Corus was dying, and all that was left was her, and all her impotent rage. But now, in this one moment, her rage, her fear, her power were joined with that of the Heart. And that great piece of emberstone was nothing but rage and potency, waiting to be unleashed.

So she let it go, let it all go, all that fire and fury, and just before Amon could jump, all the power of the Heart poured into the veins of emberstone and the sheet of quartz that covered them, and vaporised it all.

Tons of crystal suddenly turned to molten shrapnel and flew out on a hurricane of wind. It smashed into the skaven that were charging forward, ripping them apart, leaving nothing left but smoking chunks of bone and burning bits of grease. The shockwave roared on, tearing through the ranks, killing before the skaven had a chance to turn and try to run. They fell, and fell – fell until the fire finally began to fade, the wind to flag. It burned, it bowled over, but it didn't incinerate, and now there were survivors among the smoking dead, squealing out their pain. Then the storm stuttered. Became a hot wind that ripped away banners, tumbled torches. And then even that was gone, and there was nothing but a breeze. A thin breeze blowing away from the plain, dark face of the Halt; a breeze that bore a little cloud of orange sparks that winked out one by one, until there was only darkness and screaming and a slowly fading storm of smoke.

In the chamber of the Heart, Sevora fell to her knees.

She hurt. Gods, she hurt. Eye and arm and waist and… and everything. But the fire had stopped burning in her. That pain was gone.

'Sevora. Are you all right?'

All right. She was sweltering. The stone across the chamber still glowed dully, the spot where she'd pinned Skein a crater in the wall. Smoke wafted around her, and ash, and when she tried to answer Corus she choked on it. Choked until she felt his hand on her, gently patting her back.

'Stop,' she muttered. 'I'm not a baby.'

'No,' he said, pulling his hand back. But he stayed close, and for once that was all right. She leaned against him, and it was all right.

'The Heart?' she asked. The chamber was dim, the only glow coming from the stone. The bright, ruddy light of the Heart was gone.

'Ash,' he said.

Ash. She turned her head slowly and looked behind her. The circle where the huge piece of carved emberstone had floated was empty, except for a few flakes of grey drifting in the air. After thousands of years, it was gone, destroyed by her ignorance and her need.

'What did you do with that fire?' Corus asked.

'I burned them. The skaven front lines,' she said, and coughed again. 'It drove them back.'

'Burned them.' Corus said it softly, but when he turned his lightning eyes on her, they were filled with pride. 'Drove them back.'

'It was chance,' she said. 'But it destroyed the Heart–'

'And it halted Skein, and the invasion.' He smiled at her. 'You did that, Memorian. You brought hope, when hope was dying.'

She wanted to shake her head, wanted to argue, but she was too hurt, too tired. So she watched the red glow of the hot stone slowly fade, until Corus collapsed.

'Damn!' The shadow, the blade, the blood on his face. He'd wiped that off before he'd come to her. But there was blood gathering on his lips again as he rolled onto his back. 'Damn it, Corus! What are you doing, asking about me? We have to get you help! We have to–'

'It's too late.' Corus looked up at her, and the lightning in his eyes was slowing, fading. 'I've died before. I can feel it coming. I just wanted to hold on long enough to make sure you were all right.'

'I'm not,' she said. 'I'm not all right, I've never been all right, but I'm alive. Thanks to you. I wouldn't have been able to do anything but die here, without you.' She wiped the blood from his lips, and she felt the grief in her and forced it back. 'What can I do?'

'Just stay,' he said. 'The lightning will be soft.' His voice was fading, like his eyes. But he frowned. 'The Storm's Eye. Again. You saw my memories. Did they show you anything? About why I can only remember being a mortal? Why I can't remember anything beyond that?'

Sevora went silent, thinking of the Chaos warrior. The brass scales. The blood. Thinking of Corus and his ugly realisation. Thinking of his words, at the end.

I think it's a lie.

Did she know why he couldn't remember? Yes. He had lost his hope in the end. Lost the one thing he'd pledged to Aika to keep. Lost what kept him going, through every other resurrection, kept him centred in the Storm's Eye. Lost his hope, and to get it back he'd forgotten everything that led him to that terrible day.

Hope is a lie.

But what was the truth? Darkness and despair, like Skein promised? Lies were better than that, and maybe sometimes they were the only thing you had left.

'I don't know,' she lied softly. 'They were a jumble, mostly. Fighting. The only clear ones…' She took a breath, and made herself look into the dying lightning of his eyes. 'Except for Aika. You remember her. You remember her so well.'

'Aika,' he whispered. 'I remember. What she told me. Remember hope. Remember…'

The last flicker of lightning died in his eyes, and then they were just eyes, brown eyes. Her brother's eyes. And then they began to come apart into a crackling, glowing mass of white arcs that danced across the metal before her, raising her hair as they came together, and then they flashed off, a single bolt of white crackling through the stone ceiling, and when it faded she was sitting alone in the dark.

CHAPTER TWENTY-SIX

THE HALT

When Amon left the top of the Halt, the stench of incinerated flesh stayed with him, all the way down the back of the great wall, through the tunnel that burrowed into the dark stone, and into the great circular chamber that lay at its heart. There, the smell was replaced with the soft smell of the ash that drifted through the chamber like dead stars.

In the light of the torches the Golden Lions had brought he could see Sevora sitting alone on a floor of woven wrought iron, the bars bent and rippled as if they had been warped by heat. There was nothing else around her – no corpses, no broken weapons, no spilled blood. The only clue to what might have happened here was a great mark on the curve of one wall, a rippled circle of blackened rock that looked like it had begun to run like molten wax before it had cooled again into solid stone. That, and the drifting ash that covered the mortal's black robes and clung to her dark hair and the blood marking her maimed face.

Amon walked out to her and crouched down, staring at her. For a long time she seemed not to notice him, but finally her remaining eye shifted, finding him.

'Knight-Questor,' she said, her voice a harsh whisper, as if she'd ruined her throat with screams.

'Memorian,' he said. 'What happened here?'

She blinked, the eyelashes over her missing eye clotted with blood. 'I – we–' Sevora stopped, going silent for a long time before she found her voice again. 'Everyone's dead. Gone. Brevin and Corus, and Skein, and the skaven he brought with him. All gone. But they did it. Your hunt did it. Skein tried to stop us, but Corus killed him, and Brevin touched the Heart and brought the fire.'

'And you?' he asked quietly.

'Me?' she said. 'I...' A shudder went through her, and her eye shut. 'What could I do? I just hid.'

Now it was Amon's turn to stare in silence back at her. There was a lie buried in those terse, whispered words, along with a story long and terrible. It had been a wind that had rushed out from the wall, furious and fiery and dreadful, laden with molten quartz. He had felt its power, its heat, as he stood on the edge of the Halt, getting ready to leap. It had been a wind like the one she had summoned to save him.

But whatever the true story was, it was Sevora's to keep. Whatever had happened in this strange spherical room was her memory to keep, forever if she wished. Amon was certain this last Memorian had earned that.

'Come on,' he said, reaching out a hand to her. 'I will carry you to the top of the Halt, and you can see what their sacrifice has bought us.'

Sevora wanted to walk, but in the end the stairs were too much, and Amon had folded her onto one arm, carrying her like a child up to the top of the Halt.

He set her down when they reached the top, though, and walked beside her as she limped her way to the edge of the wall, carefully holding her dislocated arm. She could see General Kant talking to one of those tall, inhuman beings with the bows, and one of the silver-armoured Stormcast Eternals she had seen in her vision mounted on the back of the great beasts. The three of them crouched on the wall some distance from them, their scales glinting in the growing light of the coming dawn. They were huge, terrifying, but nothing like the creatures of the skaven. They had a terrible beauty to them, and Sevora felt a surge of exhilaration mix with her fear of them. Looking at them was like watching a great storm approach, wild and beautiful.

'Draconith,' Amon said, catching the direction of her gaze. 'Fell and noble creatures of Azyr. Hammerhal Aqsha answered, if not in full force, and sent what few of them remain, along with the Auralan Sentinels.' When she frowned at the name, he pointed to the creature talking with Kant. 'Aelves. A reconnaissance in force, apparently. The children of the Horned Rat have risen from every hole and crevice across the realms to assault us. That is why they did not respond sooner, and why they sent so few. It is good they sent what they could, but in the end it would not have been enough.'

'If not for Corus. And Brevin,' she breathed. It wasn't a lie. Not really. Brevin had forged her connection to the Heart, something she would have never been able to do. And Corus…

She had to stop for a moment to swipe away a tear on one of her ash-coated sleeves, wondering why they hadn't stopped falling. She had wailed alone in the dark for what felt like forever, until her voice had broken, and when the Golden Lions and Amon had found her she thought she might finally be done, her tears all used up. But still they came, spilling from both the eye that was left to her and the empty socket beside it.

When she pulled back her hand, she could see that Kant had stopped talking to the aelf and was staring at her, her lined face weary but determined. The general nodded to her, a kind of salute between survivors, and Sevora had to turn away before she started weeping again.

At the parapet she stared out at Warrun Vale and the destruction she and the Heart had wrought.

The ground out to where the forest had once stood was scoured to nothing but blackened dirt. No bodies, no bones, nothing: just a wasteland of ash and pale eddies of smoke. Beyond that, there was a line of charred madness and death.

The corrupted trees had been broken and tumbled and lay in great blackened piles. Mixed with them were the bodies, mostly just blackened bones, though scraps of half-melted armour and weapons were scattered with them. There had to be thousands of them, twisted in with the blasted forest, and the stench of burned flesh and fur drifted on the morning breeze. There was another smell too, a sharp smell that came from the lumps of quartz that still glowed among the dead, the last chunks of the Halt's facing that were slowly cooling.

Gone. Sevora looked down the wall below her, and it was nothing but dark basalt, a great sweeping face of harsh stone. An imposing bastion, a wall so high and thick it looked like a piece of the peaks that surrounded it. But it was different now, changed. The Heart of the Halt was gone, burned away by Sevora's anger and fear and ignorance, and now this was just a pile of stone, doomed to slowly crumble away into sand and ruins, like the ancient city that had once stood behind it.

'Dead,' she said, her whisper harsh. 'The Halt. I–' Killed it, she was about to say, but she cut that off. 'It's dead. Its power is lost.'

'But the Halt still holds,' Amon said. He considered her, then looked away, towards what lay beyond the tumbled ruins of the downed trees and dead skaven. 'What was done had to be done, or the skaven would have overwhelmed us. And then Clawlord Reekbite would have marched his army right into the Great Parch.'

Sevora looked with him, out at what was left of the skaven army. So many had died in the night, so many had been incinerated at her hand. Enough to pay for her brother, for Morgen and grey-winged Jocanan, and all the other broken but powerful Reclusians and their mortal Memorians? No. There was no amount of blood and ash that could settle that cost. But she had killed enough to make her sick. So many thousand dead, but as the dawn spread up the Warrun Vale she could see them gathered there still, a great swarm like a sea of filth converging between the high cliffs of the pass.

'Reekbite was dealt a heavy blow last night,' Amon said. He had his glass out, and was sweeping it over the still-massive army. 'But that firestorm didn't catch him. He survived, and he somehow kept his forces from turning and running. He's organising them for a siege now. We won the first battle, but the war for the Halt is just beginning.'

'Why?' Sevora said, staring past the ash and the dead at the great swarm of skaven massing in the Vale. More. Always more. 'What's so important about this place?'

In answer, Amon handed her his spyglass. Sized for a Stormcast, the instrument was huge and heavy in her hands, but he helped her hold it up to her eye, to stare out at the land past the Vale, the realm that lay beyond the Adamantine Chain.

It was a wasteland.

The land was flat plains of white, like a vast desert of bone dust. Rivers cut through those pale plains, veins of something black that looked more like oil than water, feeding patches of hideous growth. They were thickets and forests of plants – twisted, horrible things like she had seen beginning to grow around Gallogast.

Things stirred beneath their branches, monstrous shapes that she moved the glass away from before they could be fully revealed.

The glass swept across that awful, ugly apocalypse until Sevora's view was cut off by a storm, a wall of black rain falling from greasy grey clouds that were split by bolts of emerald-green lightning. It was like the smoke but worse, a perversion of the heavens, pouring down upon a perversion of the earth. And just before it swept across her view, blotting it out, Sevora caught sight of something else. Something awful, that Amon's glass brought far too close, far too clearly, despite it being so far away.

It was the outlines of a never-ending urban wasteland, towers that curved like claws or ended in jagged stumps like broken fangs, vast lumpy pyramids and bulbous domes like blisters, endless blocks of half-ruined buildings webbed together by broken buttress, rope and chain. And all across it, the tiny moving specks of skaven, the whole vast sprawl seething with them.

When the storm swept in and blocked it, the ugly black blot of that hideous rain was almost a mercy. Sevora pulled her eye away, and let Amon take his glass back.

'I have crossed these mountains before,' Amon said, folding the instrument up and tucking it away. 'The lands beyond were a wild, dangerous place, but they were nothing like that hellscape. And that city, the one you can just catch the edge of, that did not exist. The skaven... they did something. I had heard tell once that they had a realm of their own, hidden somewhere in the dark spaces between the stars. It seems they found a way to bring it here, to Aqshy. That poison smoke was born from its arrival, but that wasteland, that city, is not going to go away like the smoke did.' He frowned at the skaven army pulling itself together down the Warrun Vale. 'As I said, our reinforcements brought word of fighting everywhere. But it is thickest all along the Adamantine Chain. I think these mountains now form a wall between those blighted skaven lands and the Great Parch. And the widest road across these mountains is here, blocked only by the Halt. The skaven never meant to stay trapped over there. They want to run riot across all the realms, and Clawlord Reekbite seeks to be the first to shatter our civilisations, to slaughter and enslave us, and to claim all that he can for himself and the Great Horned Rat.'

'And so this fight will never end,' Sevora said. 'No matter what we sacrifice.' As she spoke, her eyes were drawn to a dark shadow limping slowly down the wall towards them. It was Peace, one foreleg stiff with splints and bandages, his once piercing eyes dull with a pain that Sevora guessed had little to do with his injured leg. She reached out a hand, and the gryph-crow came close, letting her touch the shimmering black feathers of his head. 'Was it worth it then?' she whispered. 'Brevin. The Ruination Chamber. The Heart. Corus. My–' She cut off, pain sweeping through her.

'Your eye?' Amon asked, and she shook her head.

'No. My magic.' She could feel that searing scar in her, as if her soul had been cauterised. 'When the Heart burned itself out, it took my power with it. I feel broken inside. Dead. And it's not just my eye, not just my grief. I am broken, more than ever, and I will never be the same. Such a little thing, really, compared to everything else, but was even that worth it, if all that we bought was a little time?'

'A little time,' Amon said. 'And a great deal of hope.'

'Hope when hope is dying,' she whispered, and beside her Peace whispered back, his strange voice as cracked as hers.

'Hope.'

'The fight is far from over, here,' Amon said. From the Vale far below, something bellowed, a monstrous scream of rage that split the air even at this distance. He shook his head, dark hair brushing the battered, blood-splashed shoulders of his violet armour. 'And its outcome is far from certain. But your part here may be done.

You will return to Rookenval to await Corus' return. You should know that it might be some time before he does, and... there is always the chance he will not survive his Reforging. This time.'

Sevora looked down at the death and destruction, and the army of monsters beyond that would wreak that much and more on the whole world.

'I know. And even if he does, he may be so broken by it that he might not recognise me. If he even comes back in my life-time.' She hesitated, tears building again in her eye. 'But I made a choice when he was dying, and I lied to him at the last, and I don't know if that was right. If I saved him with that lie, or if I damned him even more.'

Amon looked away from her, at the dark stone beneath their feet. 'Sometimes hope is a lie,' he said.

'Sometimes it is,' Sevora said softly, her words tangled with the wind that ran over the Halt and down into the ruins of Warrun Vale. 'And sometimes it's a lie spoken with the fervency of a prayer.'

ABOUT THE AUTHOR

Gary Kloster is a writer, a stay-at-home father, a librarian and a martial artist – sometimes all in the same day, seldom all at the same time. His work for Black Library includes the Warhammer 40,000 novel *Lazarus: Enmity's Edge*, the Age of Sigmar novel *The Last Volari*, the Necromunda novella *Spark of Revolution*, and a number of short stories. He lives among the corn in the American Midwest.

An extract from
The Gates of Azyr
by Chris Wraight

Vandus, they called him.

It was a name of omen, one that carried the favour of the Golden City. He would be the first, they said. None would set foot in the Mortal Realms ahead of him, though the bringers of vengeance would be close behind. For a long time he had not understood what they meant, for they had had to school him as a child, teaching him to remember what he had once known by instinct.

Now, with the passing of aeons, he understood. The empty years were coming to a close, and the designs of the God-King were at last reaching ripeness. He was the instrument, just one of the limitless host, but the brightest star amid the constellations of salvaged glory.

For so long now, it had just been Azyr, and all else was lost in the fog of time.

But there had been other worlds. Now, very soon, there would be so again.

* * *

They were gazing up at him – ten thousand, arrayed in gold and cobalt and ranked in the shining orders of battle. The walls around them soared like cliffs, each one gilt, reflective and marked with the sigils of the Reforged.

Vandus stood under a dome of sapphire. A long flight of marble stairs led down to the hall's crystal floor. Above them all, engraved in purest sigmarite, was the sign of the Twin-Tailed Comet, radiant amid its coronet of silver.

This thing had never been done. In a thousand years of toil and counsel, in all the ancient wars that the God-King had conducted across realms now lost, it had never been done. Even the wisdom of gods was not infinite, and so all the long ages of labour might yet come to naught.

He lifted his hand, turning the sigmarite gauntlet before him, marvelling at the manner in which the armour encased his flesh. Every piece of it was perfect, pored over by the artificers before being released for the service of the Eternals. He clenched the golden fingers into a fist and held it high above him.

Below him, far below, his Stormhost, the Hammers of Sigmar, raised a massed roar. As one, they clenched their own right hands.

Hammerhand!

Vandus revelled in the gesture of fealty. The vaults shook from their voices, each one greater and deeper than that of a mortal man. They looked magnificent. They looked *invincible*.

'This night!' Vandus cried, and his words swelled and filled the gulf before him. 'This night, we open gates long closed.'

The host fell silent, rapt, knowing these would be the last words they heard before the void took them.

'This night, we smite the savage,' Vandus said. 'This night, we smite the daemon. We cross the infinite. We dare to return to the realms of our birthright.'

Ten thousand golden helms looked up at him. Ten thousand fists gripped the shafts of warhammers. The Liberators, the greater part of the mighty host, stood proudly, arrayed in glistening phalanxes of gold. All of them had once been mortal, just as he had been, though now they bore the aspect of fiery angels, their mortality transmuted into majesty.

'The design of eternity brought you here,' Vandus said, sweeping his gaze across the sea of expectant faces. 'Fate gave you your gifts, and the Forge has augmented them a hundredfold. You are the foremost servants of the God-King now. You are his blades, you are his shields, you are his vengeance.'

Amid the Liberators stood the Retributors, even more imposing than their comrades, carrying huge two-handed lightning hammers across their immense breastplates. They were the solid heart of the army, the champions about which the Legion was ordered. Slivers of pale lightning sparked from their heavy plate, residue of a fearsome, overspilling power within.

'You are the finest, the strongest, the purest,' Vandus told them. 'In pain were you made, but in glory will you live. No purpose have you now but to bring terror to the enemy, to lay waste to his lands and to shatter his fortresses.'

On either flank stood the Prosecutors, the most severely elegant of all the warriors there assembled. Their armour was sheathed in a sheer carapace of swan-white wings, each blade of which dazzled in its purity. Their spirits were the most extreme, the wildest and the proudest. If they were a little less steadfast than their brothers, they compensated with the exuberance of flight, and in their gauntlets they kindled the raw essence of the comet itself.

'We are sent now into the heart of nightmares,' said Vandus. 'For ages uncounted this canker has festered across the face of the universe, extinguishing hope from lands that were once claimed by our people. The war will be long. There will be suffering and there will be anguish, for we are set against the very legions of hell.'

Besides Vandus stood the great celestial dracoth, Calanax, his armoured hide glinting from the golden light of the hall. Wisps of hot smoke curled from his nostrils and his long talons raked across the crystal floor. Vandus had been the first to tame such a beast, though now others of his breed were in the service of the Stormhost. The dracoth was the descendant of far older mythic creatures, and retained a shard of their immortal power.

'But they know us not. They believe all contests to be over, and that nothing remains but plunder and petty cruelties. In secrecy have we been created, and our coming shall be to them as the ending of worlds. With our victory, the torment will cease. The slaughter will cease. We will cleanse these worlds with fire, and consign the usurpers back to the pits that spewed them forth.'

As he spoke, Vandus felt the gaze of his fellow captains on him. Anactos Skyhelm was there, lean and proud, master of the winged host. Lord-Relictor Ionus, the one they called the Crypt-born, remained in the margins, though his dry presence could be sensed, watching, deliberating. If the lightning-bridge was secured, those two would be at the forefront, marshalling the vanguard to take the great prize – the Gate of Azyr, locked for near-eternity and only unbarred by the release of magics from both sides of the barrier.

And yet, for all their authority, only one soul had the honour of leading the charge. The God-King himself had bestowed the title on him – Lord-Celestant, First of the Stormhost.

Now Vandus raised both hands, one holding Heldensen aloft, the other still clenched tight. His weapon's shaft caught the light of crystal lamps and blazed as if doused in captured moonlight.

'Let the years of shame be forgotten!' he declared. 'The fallen shall be avenged and the Dark Gods themselves shall feel our fury!'

The glittering host below clashed their hammers against their heavy shields before raising the weapons in salute and acclamation. The entire vault filled with the fervour of voices raised in anticipation.

'Reconquest begins, my brothers!' Vandus roared, feeding on their raw potency. 'This night, we bring them war!'

A great rumble ran across the floor of the hall, as if the earth were moving. Arcs of lightning began to snap and writhe across the golden walls of the vault. The sigil of the comet blazed diamond-clear, throwing beams of coruscation across the hall's immense length. Something was building to a crescendo, something *massive*.

'This night,' Vandus cried, glorying in the full release of the divine magic, *'we ride the storm!'*

A huge *boom* shook the chamber, running up from the foundations to the high roof. The howl of thunder-born wind raced through the hall, igniting into white flame as it reached the full pitch of extremity. The golden ambient light exploded, bursting out from every part of the walls, the arched roof and the glistening floors, and lightning came with it in beams as thick as a man's arm.

There was a second rolling *boom* and the space between the walls was lost in a maelstrom of argent fire. The world reeled, as if thrown from its foundations, and the sharp tang of ozone flared, bitter and pungent.

Then, as suddenly as it had come, the lightning snapped out, the brilliance faded and the winds guttered away. The hall remained, suffused with a glimmering haze of gold, still lit bright by the light of the comet-sigil.

Only now the marble floor was empty. No voices remained, no warriors stood in ranks – nothing but the receding echoes of the colossal detonation lingered, curled like smoke across the walls of gold.